The DEBUTANTES

A NOVEL BY
JUNE FLAUM SINGER

AN AUTHORS GUILD BACKINPRINT.COM EDITION

The Debutantes

All Rights Reserved © 1982, 2000 by June Flaum Singer

AN AUTHORS GUILD BACKINPRINT.COM EDITION

Published by iUniverse.com, Inc.

For information address:
iUniverse.com, Inc.
620 North 48th Street, Suite 201
Lincoln, NE 68504-3467
www.iuniverse.com

Originally published by Avon Books

ISBN: 0-595-09064-8

Printed in the United States of America

FOR JOE

Prologue

NEW YORK 1976

Lunch today at the Waldorf. Our annual reunion, our thirty-first. Every year we have a special luncheon to commemorate our debut, and we always have champagne and we always toast any member of our group of four who is unable to make it. But this year all of us will be present: Maeve, at last, home from Mexico for good. Sara, my cousin, in from Hollywood where she makes her home, and staying at the Plaza, as she usually does when she makes the trek in from the Coast. Chrissy, inveterate New Yorker, will taxi the few blocks from her Park Avenue duplex. And me, Marlena, in for the day from Saddle River, New Jersey.

I put on mascara in honor of the day's event. I no longer normally wear it in the daytime. I've always had difficulty applying it and there's so little time these days. Despite the supposedly easy Magic Wand, I have trouble with the black gooey stuff. I think it was easier when we used to spit into the little cake of solid black and work it in with the bristled brush.

I glance at the silver-framed picture on my dressing table. It is of my . . . our . . . debut at the Waldorf. Mine, Sara Leeds Gold's, Maeve O'Connor's, and the inimitable Chrissy Marlowe's. Reading from left to right: Sara, silver gold hair swept up into a bevy of curls, movie-star makeup of the day, doll-like—tiny, fragile, pink-cheeked, violet blue eyes, fuchsia mouth; Maeve, a midsummer's night dream—hair a wild red cloud, eyes green as the Irish sea, fringed with long lashes; Chrissy, eyes kohl-ringed, mouth a dark, dark red, probably Revlon's Raven Red. And there I am, on the right—the only one of the four with a sweetheart neckline. I can still remember the agony of wearing that neckline while the others wore strapless dresses. There we are, the foursome from Miss Chalmer's School for Girls, all wearing long white kid gloves, making our bow into Society.

They played "Stardust" that night, I remember. And there was the promenade of white-gowned debs, the stag line of eligible grinning young men, some still in uniform although the war was over. I can still feel my palms moist with perspiration, my nervous excitement. I remember searching the stag line for a pair of simpatico smiling eyes; Sara smiling archly at me as I whirled dreamily past in a certain uniformed young man's arms. "Your eyes were closed," she told me delightedly the next day. I remember Maeve not smiling at all, and Chrissy disappearing before the midnight supper of black-bean soup and cracked crab was served.

I go through my closet slowly today, hoping that by some miracle a light will shine to reveal a marvelously smart and striking ensemble so that for once in my life I'll look more like my three friends—the unstudied chic, the carefree allure, the distinctive, timeless style that is their hallmark.

I choose a stick-plain black suit, much like the sort of thing I've seen Chrissy wear on occasion. In my mind's eye, I can even see her in the suit. Tall, slim beyond belief, the fall of glossy hair, Indian-straight and Indian-black, swinging like a bell, the marvelous smile, the incredible élan. Maybe the suit will work for me today. I need a blouse to wear with it. I find one hiding in the corner of the closet, white, pristine. Its purchase was a mistake. Soft and dreamy chiffon, flowing, voluminous sleeves. Why did I buy it, then hide it away? So that I would not be reminded of my folly? Sara, ultrafeminine Sara, wore flowing chiffon and looked romantically elegant in it in a world that had all but forgotten that quality. Maeve, in her salad days, could go either way—high-gloss style or romantic sylph and, like Chrissy and Sara, always managed to look so right that anyone else looked wrong in comparison.

Still, I put the blouse on, covering it with the black jacket so that only the collar and jabot show. I try to look at myself in the mirror objectively. Not bad. Not great but not bad. I am not as slim as Chrissy, nor as tall as Maeve, and no one would call me romantically elegant— not even my husband who is the kindest of men. I am a medium sort of person. Medium tall, medium slim, and medium blond. Even my eyes are a medium brown. My style, if it can be called that, is trim and neat. Everyone says I have a nice smile.

I give last-minute instructions for dinner to Jalna, my reticent maid-of-all-housely-trades. She has been with us for years now, but it is only rarely that she unbends a little from her rigid, unyielding self. Today is one of those rare occasions. She fingers the pearl and gold pin I have fastened to my lapel and says, "You'll look better without that gimcrack. That blouse is fancy enough."

I sigh heavily. Even Jalna knows that I am only a pretender when it comes to style. I unfasten the pin and hand it to her. "Put it away for me when you go upstairs, Jalna, please. I'm late."

Still, I pause passing through the front hall to take a look at one of the framed photographs lined up on the console like so many silver-clad soldiers. The picture is of our first reunion. It was the Stork Club then and we are all dressed in black. Little elegant black dresses with strings of pearls. We are all smiling widely and look very Upper East Side New Yorkish. Sherman Billingsley stands behind us. After all, Chrissy, Sara and Maeve *were* café society royalty then—they rated the personal attention of the host. The Stork Club is gone now. Extinct. Victim of less glamorous times? Maybe the New York debutante—glamorous, glossy, is extinct too.

I examine the picture more closely, trying to discern if an objective outsider could tell that, while I was the fourth member of the quartet, I was never *really* one of them. They were the Holy Triumvirate, the Terrible Three, the notoriously glamorous princesses, first of New York café society, then of the jet set, and finally of the Beautiful People. And me? I was the fourth wheel, possibly there to provide stability, and only through the kindness of Cousin Sara. Not terribly needed, always pleasantly wanted. I was simply *me* and *they* were the beauties, the ones with the names, the lineage, the money. The world was their oyster, as they say, and they did what they wanted and went where their fancy took them. They were both kissed and damned by fate; they were the darlings of adversity but, always, they rose like the phoenix to laugh and love and smell the flowers again.

Traffic is heavy as usual, and I arrive late. The three are already seated when I walk in and everybody seems to be talking at once and bubbling over, just as they once did at Miss Chalmer's.

Chrissy tells us that she has just signed her famous Marlowe name to a contract to design swimsuits. Mostly, she says, she will be spending her time promoting the line: personal appearances, television commercials—that sort of thing. But unfortunately, unlike Gloria Vanderbilt she will not be putting her signature on her bathing suits.

"I'm sort of sorry about that," Chrissy laughs, showing her dazzling teeth. "Just think what Aunt Gwen would have to say about my pasting the Marlowe name across the backside of the American woman—not to mention my own—right on TV in everybody's living room."

Sara, hair and skin still glowing golden, claps her hands delightedly in admiration of Chrissy's triumph and spirit. "It would still be the classiest ass in town," she says in her soft, syrupy voice. It has been thirty-five years since I first heard that Southern Comfort drawl, and I still haven't decided whether Sara deliberately adopted her mother's dulcet accent or just assimilated it through osmosis. Perhaps it simply came with the territory, like her daddy's money.

Maeve, looking as fragile as delicate glass, reaches across the table and squeezes Chrissy's hand. "If anyone can make a success of a bathing suit, it's you, Chrissy dear. You always could do anything. You could turn a sow's ear into a silk purse."

Is she referring to herself? Chrissy obviously thinks so. She focuses her bright, dark eyes on Maeve. "Nonsense, you silly. If anyone was born true blue silk, it was you. Always. *You* were gold and I was only silver."

Maeve protests and we all look at her. We can see the physical changes that the years have wrought more in Maeve than in ourselves because we have seen each other more frequently in the last few years than we have seen Maeve. Her hair, once as bright as a fiery sunset, is not quite so bright now. Her eyes are still emerald green, but there are fine lines at the outside corners, as if she had looked up at the sun too often. She is thinner too, whereas once she had been wasp-waisted, round-hipped, and full-bosomed, her figure the envy of all our schoolmates. The long legs are still shapely, the back straight, and the head held high, the long neck lifted up from the shoulders as we were taught at Chalmer's.

"Let's not order lunch yet," Sara says. "Let's just hoist a few first. Shall we have champagne with lunch and a couple of rounds of martinis now?" Without waiting for an answer, Sara beckons to the waiter and orders vodka martinis straight up with an olive all around. "Now we have to hear everybody's news. Who'll go first? We've already heard a little bit from Chrissy, so someone else go now. How about you, Marlena? I *know* you've been keeping a deep, dark secret to yourself lately, so let's hear all about it. Then I'll tell my latest news. And then Maeve will have to reveal all."

I take a quick sip from my glass to prepare myself to divulge that deep, dark secret and everyone starts to talk and laugh again all at once.

Resilient, I suppose, is the word for them because, God knows, it hasn't always been easy for them. Fairy-tale princesses, yes, but only if you didn't read between the covers. They had those pasts to deal with—the secrets, the pain, and the scars. And always, hovering overhead like some black cloud, there was Padraic. Like the other bonds they shared, Padraic touched all three lives and with a cataclysmic force.

When I see Sara, Chrissy, and Maeve together, I cannot help but recall Fitzgerald's line: "—So we beat on, boats against the current, borne back ceaselessly into the past."

Part One

THE GIRLS

Charleston, South Carolina

JUNE 1941

It was the year of my fourteenth summer. It was hot and humid, unseasonably so, even for Charleston in the month of June. School was out and I did the things I had always done during the long, hot days of summer. I went to the Free Public Library almost every day, and almost every day I read and finished one book, sometimes two. I took long walks; I wandered through the Battery, entranced by the pastel-colored houses with their delicate ironwork; I looked out at Fort Sumter, which stood sentry over the harbor as it had in 1861 when the first shot of the War Between the States was fired. I meandered through the Middleton Gardens—its statuary and formal gardens compared with those of Versailles, proud Charlestonians boasted, so I took a special pride in them. My girl friends and I took paddleboat rides through the Cypress Gardens, and while they flirted with the boys in companion boats, I gazed at the moss-hung trees and palmettos. And I visited the Manigault Mansion since it was a landmark of an era long gone and I liked to daydream about the antebellum belles who laughed and danced there against the background of balustraded steps, pillared porticos, and spacious verandas.

I particularly loved to go down to the Ashley waterfront where I ate she-crab soup for lunch and watched the boats on the water. Each time I saw the big ships leaving, I dreamed, as I suppose all children do, of sailing off for ports unknown. I didn't know then that I would be leaving beautiful Charleston sooner than I ever imagined—that I would be leaving by train and not by ship—and that the course of my life would thus be changed forever.

So, I went down to the ice-cream parlor with my girl friends to sip dopes, and while they made eyes at the cute sodajerk, Bus Jenkins, behind the marble fountain, I kept my own eyes cast down. I was almost never forward as they sometimes were. I was naturally shy, and my mother, Martha Leeds Williams, had impressed upon me that I was not to act "trashy," as some other girls did, those girls who could not trace

15

their families back to the time when South Carolina was only a colony. And I worked in the garden with my mother who won prizes for her roses and camellias, and listened avidly to her stories of when she and her sister, Bettina, were young—before they grew up and Bettina eloped with the rich Northerner and my mother turned against her. I rocked on the front veranda and sometimes yelled a greeting to passersby, even though Mother had told me repeatedly that a lady, especially a Leeds, didn't ever raise her voice, whatever the provocation. That is what I was doing on the day Mr. Watkins, our mailman, brought the fateful letter from up north, the letter that would take me away from Charleston and from the uneventful life I led, into a new and strange world—the world of Sara, Chrissy, and Maeve.

SARA

1.

Sara ran up the stairs. She had been waiting with bored impatience since morning, checking the clocks in each classroom at the Tree Day School, period after period.

Her mother's door was closed, but Sara went in without knocking. It was four o'clock of a bright, sunshiny May day but it was dark in the bedroom. The shades were down, the curtains drawn, the heavy, yellow velvet draperies closed. Sara could barely make out the woman in the bed.

"Mama?"

"Sara. Are you home already, darling?"

Sara leaned over and kissed her mother's cheek gently. The skin was soft but very dry.

"How are you feeling, Mama?"

"Well. Tired but well, Sara. How was your day?"

"Okay. May I open the draperies, Mama? It's a lovely day outside."

"No, don't, Sara dear. The light will hurt my eyes. Maybe tomorrow."

"All right. But remember—tomorrow we're definitely going to open the draperies, and the day after that you're coming downstairs. And the day after that, we're going for a ride. It's spring, Mama. It's a beautiful spring day outside."

"Even with the New York traffic and all?" Bettina Gold laughed delicately. "I just bet it's *really* beautiful in Charleston, Sara. You've never been to Charleston in the springtime, have you? Spring in Charleston is . . ." Her voice trailed off.

Sara had never been to Charleston at all, but she said, "Oh, I'm sure. I can see Charleston in my mind right this minute. I'm down by the river and it *is* beautiful. . . ."

"Yes, it's especially lovely down by the river, Sara. I remember one day in June when I . . ." She stopped, as if remembering too vividly, and then realized that she was in the bedroom of the house in New York City. "Mrs. Manero left today, Sara. We're without a housekeeper again. Your father will be so angry! He hates when things don't go smoothly in the house. He thinks it's my fault we can't keep—"

"Don't worry, Mama. We won't hire another housekeeper. I'll take care of everything."

"No, Sara, it's too much of a burden. At your age, you have to have good times. Things to remember when you're all grown up. Parties. I don't want you to . . ."

"We don't need a housekeeper," Sara insisted. She knew how incapable her mother was of dealing with the species. "I know what to do. I can give orders to the cook and the others. I can order the food. I've been learning, Mama. That's why I stayed home this past year instead of going away to school. So I could help you and we'd be together. Remember?"

"Yes, of course I remember."

But it hadn't worked out that way at all. Sara had wanted to spend the time with her mother, her poor mother who was so alone, but in the end her mother had had to go away for weeks at a time to the different institutions that existed for the alcoholic rich. Sara had wanted to keep her mother home, out of those institutions. And she had thought that she would be able to get her father to stay home more, too. But that hadn't worked out either. Now she was going away to school again in the fall. The boarding school trek. Her father insisted.

"Look, Mama, we'll only be here a couple of more months. Then we'll be going to Southampton for the summer. I can easily manage the house and the staff until then. It will be much easier in Southampton. You'll see."

"Will *you* tell your father, Sara? That you don't want the housekeeper. If I say it . . ."

"Yes, I'll tell him."

Bettina Gold relaxed somewhat against her pillows. Her hand agitating about her throat dropped to her side, a graceful white thing in repose. "Thank you, Sara."

"There's another thing I wanted to talk to you about, Mama. I've been thinking. About Cousin Marlena."

"Marlena?" Bettina asked vaguely.

"Yes, Mama. Your sister Martha's child." It came out "chile." "We're the same age, she and I."

"No, Sara, I don't think so. Martha's little girl must be younger, seems to me. Martha married after I did."

"No, Mama. You told me Marlena was born in 1928, just like me. She's just a couple of months younger. My birthday's in January. And hers is in March. Anyhow, Mama, I'd like to get to know her. I don't have anybody else besides you. And Father. . . . I was thinking—why

18

don't we ask her up to visit with us? Or even better, why couldn't we offer to pay Marlena's way through Miss Chalmer's? You said Aunt Martha and Uncle Howard don't have any money to speak of. Then Marlena and I could be roommates there. I would so like to have my own cousin with me, Mama. Sometimes it gets lonely having nobody of my own. No sister or brother. No real friends."

"I know, honey. And I haven't been with you a terrible lot of the time, either. My poor Sara. I haven't been a good mother. And I so wanted to be. I yearned for you so and you were such a darling baby, as good and sweet as a baby could be. And you're still a darling, but I haven't been a good mother. No, I haven't. . . ." Tears welled up in Bettina's eyes.

"You have, Mama, you have!" Sara put her head next to Bettina's on the pillow and whispered in her ear. "You've been the best mother. I love you so, Mama!"

"And I love you desperately, Sara. I think it's a wonderful idea, a really fine idea about Martha's daughter—what's her name again?"

"Marlena, Mama."

"Why don't you speak to your father about it, honey? He'd agree if *you* asked him."

"I will, Mama. Thank you." She kissed her mother's cheek again. This time it felt hot. "I have another idea. . . ."

Bettina laughed, a low laugh set more in her throat than on her lips. "You're always full of notions, Sara."

"We could offer to sponsor Marlena's debut in New York, too. After graduation. That way, I'd have her with me for a long time."

"Maybe we could do that too, Sara. But don't get your hopes up too high. I don't know how Martha will cotton to that idea. She was always a stickler for tradition, for Southern tradition, Martha Leeds was. Martha and I both made our bow into Society in Charleston. All the Leeds girls did. And a debut in Charleston meant something. A Charleston debutante could go anywhere and . . . Why, do you know what they used to say? 'A Boston debutante may be the most proper, but a Charleston debutante is the most cultivated.' And a lot prettier too," she added, with a toss of her head.

"I'm sure you're right, Mama, but a New York debut will probably be more fun. Can we at least make the offer?"

"All right, honey. But just don't get too set on the idea. First you have to get your daddy to agree and then your Aunt Martha." She shook her head, her eyelids drooped. "I just don't know about Martha. . . ."

"Don't you worry your little old head about it, Mama. I'll see to everything. How about coming down to dinner tonight, Mama? Won't you just try? For me?"

"Not tonight, Sara dear. I just don't feel up to it. I think I'll just nap off for a little bit." She smiled apologetically and closed her eyes.

19

Sara tiptoed out of the room. She would have no problem with her father. He was always trying to make up to her. And well he might. He had a lot to make up for.

2.

Maurice Gold had been born Moshe Goldberg in a village near Kovno, Lithuania, which, to all intents and purposes, was part of Russia. At least, it was under Russian control most of the time. When Moshe was ten, his mother's brother, Sam Warner, né Warnovsky, made arrangements for Sarah and her family to come to the New World. Sam himself had gone to America fifteen years earlier, had applied himself diligently, and had acquired a wife, a son, a daughter, and a large shirt factory on the Lower East Side.

As the time of leavetaking grew near, it was discovered that Moshe had the scurf. His scalp under the mass of wiry black curls was an unsavory mess of red sores and yellow pus. The neighbors assured Sarah that the boy would never be admitted to America with such a condition. Drastic measures were called for. There was a cure, harsh but certain. Sarah cut up white cloth into three-inch squares while the tar pot was heated up. The hot tar was poured over Moshe's luxuriant mop of hair, then the squares of cloth were applied to the tar. The next day, after the pieces of cloth were well hardened into the hair, Sarah, a tiny but strong-minded woman, grabbed each piece of cloth and proceeded to rip out, clump after clump, every single hair from Moshe's bleeding scalp. Even as Moshe shrieked in pain, Sarah kept pulling, the tears running down her own cheeks. She had heard of what happened at Ellis Island—medically unfit children being returned to the old country alone while the other members of the family—mother, father, sisters, brothers—were forced by circumstance and finance to stay in the new country, abandoning the rejected member, perhaps forever.

"You want to be sent back to Kovno by yourself, Moshe? Or do you want to be an American? Tell me which?" Sarah scolded as she tore and yanked, throwing the clumps of tarred black hair into the waste bucket and wiping up the blood.

Finally, the ordeal was over. Moshe's scalp was washed with a foul-smelling laundry soap, then smeared with ointment. With luck and God's help, the scalp would dry clean and smooth and the hair would grow back by the time they reached Ellis Island.

With grim determination, Sarah and her family, with as many belongings as they could carry, set out for Germany, the first leg of their journey. When they finally reached the German border, manned by Russian soldiers on one side and German on the other, they, along with the other Jewish emigrants crossing the bridge at the same time, were jeered first by the Russians and then by the Germans. Moshe's father, David, bearded and in his broad-brimmed black hat, took no notice. He had God walking beside him—what did he care that the *goyish* scum pranced and grinned like jackasses? To him, they did not exist. But Moshe was deeply ashamed to be the object of ridicule. He would not forget.

On September 17, the family boarded the ocean steamer toting the collection of pillows and *perinas,* the overstuffed down comforters, the brass *menorah* and candlesticks, and the pillowcase containing what was left of the supplies Sarah had brought from their village—the dried-out salami, bread hard as stone, and a few onions sprouting new growth. They were due to land in America on October 5. This date proved wrong by ten days.

They were escorted to their steerage quarters: wooden bunks tiered to the rafters. They shared these quarters with other Russian-Polish Jews, German Jews, and impoverished German, Polish, and Russian non-Jews. They would all sleep there side-by-side and eat together three times a day at the long wooden tables set up deep in the bowels of the ship.

Each day the steerage passengers ate the same, unvarying menu—porridge, tea, potatoes boiled in their skins, onions, cucumbers, heavily salted herring and, for those fortunate enough to be able to partake of it, sausage and different parts of the pig. For the first few days, Moshe Goldberg was one of the many stricken by seasickness, and each time he passed the galley he was seized with a fresh attack. But after a few days, the condition passed and the sea air sharpened Moshe's appetite to a ravenous state. Sarah's small store of food, practically depleted by the trip overland, was completely gone after two days at sea, and the family had to subsist only on the ship's porridge, potatoes, and onions. God forbid they should partake of the *tref*—the steaming sausage, the odoriferous pork! David Goldberg kept a watchful eye lest his children be tempted.

Envy bored a deep hole in Moshe's stomach as he watched the gentile emigrants dig into the forbidden fare. And shock shook him as he watched the German Jews eat the prohibited meat. It was Moshe's introduction to Enlightenment. He realized for the first time that the German Jews were clean-shaven as well, which was deeply puzzling. Before, Moshe separated the male Jew from the male gentile by his head covering and his beard. *Here, at this table, Jews, beardless and heads bared, ate pork*. His head reeled. He watched them closely. To him they appeared cleaner, superior to the other Jews. They looked more like the gentile peasants.

As the trip stretched on, strange things happened. Some of the other Jews, *Russian-Polish Jews,* started shaving their beards. Outraged, David Goldberg berated them, stamped them infidels, blockheads, *goyim,* destroyers of Israel. A few he sent sprawling across the filthy floorboards. But they simply called him "crazy man" and proceeded to their next step, the eating of the impure meat. His father *was* crazy, Moshe reflected. He had his beard while they, the new converts to Enlightenment, got to eat the succulent, spicy-smelling sausages. Moshe looked at his father with a new contempt, disgusted by the crumbs of stale bread that fell and disappeared within his beard.

One evening, after his father had left the table, Moshe made sure that none of his brothers was looking and made a quick grab at a sausage, which he pocketed. Later, hiding in a corner, he wolfed down the meat. It was good, delicious, but he waited to see if he would be struck down by an angry God. Still standing, he grinned, then suddenly retched all of the heavily seasoned brown meat onto the dirty flooring.

By the time they reached the New Land, Moshe's hair had grown back, more luxuriant than ever. All through the trip Sarah had washed his head daily with the laundry soap until the hair shone like silk. Still, there was some dried-up scarring on his scalp. Sarah worried that this scarring might cause problems at the medical inspection at Ellis Island. She instructed her son to try to get through the head inspection quickly, but to do so in a manner that would not raise suspicion.

As the doctor was about to dip his wooden paddle into Moshe's curls, Moshe took a skip and a jump just out of the doctor's reach, laughed mischievously as he dashed between people's legs and around them. The doctor looked after the skittish boy, muttered, "Ach! Animals!" and went back to his line of aspiring Americans. Sarah nodded approvingly. Moshe was a good boy, both handsome and smart. He would get along in the New World.

Sam Warner moved the Goldberg family into a three-room apartment on Hester Street. It was a tenement, but the Goldbergs did not know it. There was nothing green here as there was back home, but the kitchen floor was linoleum and there was something called an icebox, a truly wonderful invention. For a penny, one could get a block of ice that, once placed in the box, would keep even the milk fresh for at least a day.

Sam Warner told them, "A palace it's not, but soon you'll have better." Sam himself had a house that seemed like a palace to the Goldberg family. It had eight rooms and was in a place called Brooklyn.

Within two days, Moshe's three brothers, Gershon, Herschel, and Simha, were put to work in Uncle Sam's factory. David went to work for Herman the butcher, a job that Sam had arranged beforehand. Moshe and his sister, Rivka, were enrolled in school. They were the youngest and Sarah considered them the smartest. Within one week, Moshe started to speak English and renamed himself Morris. Within three weeks, Sarah, not content to spend her days scouring and cooking in the three-room apartment, had a pushcart and was selling an array of Sam's shirts to the throngs that filled the streets of the Lower East Side seeking bargains.

In a year's time, Sarah managed to save enough for a down payment on a house big enough for her family in Brooklyn. She persuaded her brother to back David in his own kosher butcher shop near the new house, while she herself sold other necessities of the table in a little store next to the butcher shop. Thus, she was able to take over at the butcher shop too when David went off to the synagogue, which was more often than not.

A practical woman, Sarah gave up her dream of her son Morris becoming a rabbi when he barely managed to be *bar mitzvah*. The Hebrew School teacher told her that his inclination was to throw the boy out of the class altogether for being a smart alec, rather than prepare him for his confirmation. But she talked the teacher into keeping Morris long enough to confirm him, then boxed her son's ears, pulled his hair and pinched his cheeks. "All right, you fool, so you won't be a rabbi. Now you'll have to be a doctor."

The last thing Morris wanted to be was a rabbi, the second last thing —a doctor. That would take too long and he was in a hurry to get the things he wanted. He planned to go into his uncle's business and use that as a stepping stone to, perhaps, his own factory.

Morris' oldest brother, George (formerly Gershon), married and was the first of the sons to take off his beard. "The moment he leaves the house he becomes a *goy*," David complained to Sarah.

"This is America," Sarah chided him. "And where does it say in the Law a man must have a beard? As long as he used the powder and not the razor it is permissible, after all."

Herschel and Simha, encouraged by their brother's action, followed suit, acting in concert to fend off their father's wrath. He did not speak to them for seven weeks. "I don't speak to gentiles," he said, "when I am not forced to."

Morris laughed to himself. For months he had been secretly swiping with a razor at each new whisker as it appeared on his pubescent chin hoping that his father would think only that his youngest son was slow in maturing. Sometimes, though, he would find his mother glaring at him. Did she know, he wondered. Probably. His mother knew everything. She also knew when it was better not to speak.

Morris was not yet sixteen when Sam Warner told Sarah that her son had spoken to him about going into business.

"Is it true?" Sarah confronted Morris. "Don't give me any of your fancy words. I want a straight answer."

"Yes, Ma, it's true. I don't want to be a doctor. I can't go to school all those years, Ma. I have to get going. I want to be somebody, Ma. I want to start making money. Now. Not ten years from now."

"Anybody can go into business, Moshe. Anybody, almost, God willing, can make a living. Not everybody has your brains, Moshe. Not everybody can learn the way you can."

"Why do you think Uncle Sam wants me in the business? Because I'm the best one in mathematics in the whole school. Everybody says so. Miss Berkowitz says I'm practically a genius in mathematics. Really, Ma."

"That's why you should go to college, Moshe, not make shirts. A rabbi you won't be, but a doctor you can still be. You can be an educated man. The whole family will be proud."

"You'll be proud of me, Ma. You'll see."

The day Morris graduated from high school, he started work at the factory. But it soon appeared that while he was adept at keeping Sam Warner's books, he was not an "inside man." His uncle agreed that, besides doing the books, Morris would make a good outside salesman, making the rounds of the jobbers who sold to retail outlets. At the same time, he would act as the collector of errant accounts.

Morris moved out of his parents' house and into an apartment near the factory and enrolled in night school. David Goldberg said, "A Jewish boy moves out of the house when he marries. A gentile bum moves out to be a bigger bum." But Sarah was pleased that Morris was going to college. She defended him. "The boy has to be near the factory and the college, no? If a boy is working and going to college too, he has to save time traveling. That makes sense."

Sarah still had hopes that Morris would decide to enter a profession. Not a rabbi and not a doctor, maybe, but a lawyer he could still be. Sarah believed that when God made her Moshe so smart, so tall, and so handsome, He had a good reason. It was not for him to deal in shirts.

Morris was not studying law, however. Like Sarah, he did not think he had been born to spend his life hawking shirts on the Lower East Side. He studied literature, languages, and philosophy so that he would be a cultured man; and finance, so that he could emulate the rich men whose careers he followed.

He still returned each Friday to the house in Bensonhurst to attend synagogue with his father and eat the Sabbath meal with the family. On one such evening, David Goldberg sent his son sprawling to the floor from his chair at the dining table. Morris looked up at his father silently, not protesting.

"What did he do?" Sarah demanded of David.

24

"Yonkel Pipke saw your *goy* son eating in a *tref* restaurant on Canal Street. Without a hat or a *yarmulke*."

Morris's brothers kept their eyes averted. It was not news to them that Morris ate at these kinds of restaurants and that he no longer kept his head covered. Even Sam Warner knew that Morris went about his salesman's rounds with a bared head, although he had never mentioned it to Sarah.

Sarah turned on Morris. "Is this true? None of your stories now."

Morris did not answer.

Sarah sighed. So this was America. Along with the good living and the nice clothes, the stores and the house, came the changes, the break with the old ways.

After that, Morris stopped coming to Brooklyn on Friday nights and never went to the synagogue again. And he changed his name from Morris to Maurice. It had a nice British ring to it.

Maurice Goldberg prospered. He doubled the factory's business by selling in large volume to the jobbers at a reduced cost to them. Only the jobbers had to kick back half their savings from the lower price to Maurice. Still, they profited, as did Maurice. And Sam Warner, unaware that he was being swindled, was happy about the larger volume of business he was doing.

Maurice was also earning commissions as a rental broker. Getting around the city as he did, he often heard about available business space in a burgeoning New York. He married up lessors with lessees. When, on his bill collection rounds, he discovered that one of Sam Warner's jobbers was declaring bankruptcy and that the building he owned was going to go cheaply, Maurice bought the building.

After this first purchase of a business property, Maurice realized, at the age of nineteen, that a young man could buy many business properties by simply placing a small amount of cash down on each property and securing the financing for the rest. One then used the subsequent rentals to pay off the mortgage. By spreading around his available cash, Maurice ended up the owner of several pieces of property. It was a simple enough axiom of business—the remarkable part was that Maurice Goldberg learned it so early in life. Before he was twenty, he was already a man of means.

When Maurice was twenty-one, Sarah died of a growth in her stomach. Only seven days passed from the time she first fell sick and went into the hospital to the day she was buried. The speed of her demise left the family in a state of shock. It had had no time in which to prepare itself for her passing.

When Maurice came to the hospital, and even after, at the funeral and during the *shiva,* the week of mourning, David Goldberg spoke not a word to the son who had gone astray from the path of the righteous. Maurice wept for his mother whom he had loved as much as he would

25

ever love anyone, and retaliated against his father by dropping the *berg* from his name, to become Maurice Gold.

Just before Maurice went into the army in 1917 to fight the Hun, he chanced to acquire some stock in oil and copper. He came upon this stock by an odd stroke of luck. While trying to collect the money due his uncle from one Harry Weiner who was on the verge of going out of business, tall and burly Maurice attempted to strong-arm the jobber into paying.

"What are you, some kind of *goy?*" Weiner asked in horror. "Come to think about it, you look like a *goy*, too. Look, *goy*, you can't get blood out of a turnip. Here." He threw open his safe. "Here, look!" He flung papers around. "Bills! Bills, not money! You see any money here?"

Maurice rummaged around in the safe, found the stock certificates. "What are these?"

Harry Weiner laughed bitterly. "That's what *I* got from a retailer who owed me eight thousand dollars and left me high and dry. You want them? You got them. A bargain. I only owe your uncle five thousand."

"Probably not worth the paper they're printed on," Maurice said, "but I'll take them just to help you out. Here, just to be on the up-and-up, you sign over the certificates."

Weiner was reluctant to put his name to paper, but when Maurice offered to give him in return a receipt marked "paid in full" for the merchandise for which he was indebted, he complied. Maurice immediately checked out the companies he had bought into. They were not prospering, but they *were* in existence.

Maurice had a hunch. He gave his uncle five hundred dollars of his own money. "Weiner's broke," he reported. "He's filing bankruptcy, but I managed to squeeze ten cents on the dollar out of him before the assets are divided up among all the creditors."

Sam Warner groaned. "I suppose ten cents on the dollar is better than goose egg. Maybe next time you shouldn't sell those *shleppers* more merchandise than they can handle."

But there was no next time. Maurice left for the army with his uncle's promise that, upon his return, he would be given his uncle's remaining share of the business. Sam had already given one-third of the business to his own son, Solomon, who had married Maurice's sister, Rivka, and one-third of the business to Maurice's brother George, who had stayed in the factory.

In the army, Maurice passed for a gentile of German extraction. His appearance didn't reflect his heritage, he had a college education, spoke better than most, and as a commissioned officer, enjoyed all the advantages of the upper strata, a position he could never attain as a Jew from Eastern Europe.

Assigned to the procurement branch, Maurice never set foot on foreign soil, but spent his time playing golf, drinking, and whoring with other officers, but only those of social or financial prominence in civilian life. By the time he was discharged in 1918, Maurice decided it was better to feign allegiance to the cross than to the Star of David.

He found postwar New York real estate booming. His own prewar holdings made him a millionaire twice over. Sam Warner kept his promise, retired, and gave Maurice the one-third share in his business, unaware that Maurice had no intention of going back to the shirt factory. What Maurice did was turn around and offer his share back to the remaining owners, George and Solomon, at an inflated price. They had no choice but to buy back Maurice's share if they wanted to keep the business in the family.

Like New York, all postwar America was building, growing, industrializing. Not really surprised, Maurice found that the companies in which he held the stock acquired from Weiner the jobber had not only survived but were starting to blossom. He bought more shares in these companies, thereby becoming a majority stockholder. By the time he was thirty, Maurice Gold had accumulated a major fortune. Not quite as large as the fortune of the Guggenheims, a German-Jewish family he admired, which was almost but not quite as large as the Rockefeller fortune, but certainly as large as other Anglo-Saxon fortunes that had been made in the country in the nineteenth century. And Maurice knew about such things; he was a keen student of American dynasties.

Now he was ready to take his place in a society that would never accept him properly as a Jew. In the army it had been permissible to simply *go* as a gentile. But in the circles that he wanted to enter, they would know that he had not been *born* a gentile. He considered being a Reform Jew, as many German Jews were, and he respected the German Jews as did the New York financial circles. Their fortunes and the swath they had cut were not to be ignored—the Lehmans, the Seligmans, the Loebs, and his particular heroes, the Guggenheims. And they were certainly in the foreground when it came to philanthropy. But the German Jews, having carved their own niche in society, had no wish to mix with New York's upper crust. They were content to stick together, to live comfortable but unostentatious lives. They eschewed publicity and intermarried, restricted their snobbery to their own crowd. This was not what Maurice Gold wanted for himself. What he wanted to be was an Anglo-Saxon Protestant and to mix socially with other Anglo-Saxon Protestants with important fortunes—the Astors, the Vanderbilts, the Marlowes, or even the Belmonts, who had once, years before, been Jews themselves.

Maurice Gold became an Episcopalian. All he needed was a suitable wife and a major residence in the city and another in one of the better resorts. It would be good if the wife he acquired had money too, but it was not a necessity. The important qualities were beauty and impeccable lineage.

Word quickly got back to David Goldberg that his son Moshe had converted, had finally become a *goy*. David Goldberg thanked God that Sarah had been spared the tragedy of a "death" of a son, and he sat down to sit *shiva* for Maurice, as good as dead. Maurice, hearing that his father had sat official mourning for him, was not at all perturbed. It was what he wanted. There was no place in his new life for any part of the old.

On a business trip to Charleston, Maurice Gold found Bettina Leeds. Her family tree could be traced back to the early Carolina settlements. Her ancestors had fought in the Revolution, and more recently in the Civil War, no matter the losing side. Her beauty left him breathless. He had lusted for such violet blue eyes and pale gold hair ever since his loins had come full fruit. Her mode of speech enchanted him, her Southern manners excited in him a passion that other men might have felt at the sight of a full breast or a shapely leg. He carried her away to New York with him and they were married in his Episcopalian church. It was for Bettina that Maurice Gold built his mansion on Fifth Avenue and filled it with treasures.

For a while everything went well, until it became clear that Bettina Leeds Gold could never be the social leader Maurice wanted, needed, demanded. Only at first were Bettina's beauty and Southern fine name enough. New York Society was competitive—to be a leader one needed to be strong and fearless, single-minded and innovative. One needed to be sophisticated, cynical, able to cut out contenders and rule like a queen.

Maurice grew impatient with Bettina's ineptitude. The more impatient he became, the angrier he grew. The angrier he was, the more impotent Bettina became. She retreated within herself; she wept, drank, made mistakes. She bought the wrong dress, hired the wrong caterer, chose the wrong friends. As Maurice became ever more disappointed, he tired of her wan beauty, as he had come to perceive it; he saw her genteelness as weakness; her ladylike manner a cover for ineptitude. Disenchanted, he found her lovemaking inadequate—he hungered for a more passionate, more responsive body. The only thing Bettina did that satisfied her husband was give birth to Sara, named for his mother but like Bettina in appearance. Much as Maurice came to despise Bettina's fragile beauty, he loved the same fragility in Sara, who coupled fine features with joyous, passionate emotions that brought the delicate features to life. Maurice Gold adored Sara, as he had worshipped the other Sarah. If Sara had her mother's looks, she had her grandmother's character. One balanced the other.

Bettina Leeds was the only mistake Maurice Gold had made in his successful career. He realized he had overestimated the importance of the Leeds name. An impoverished Southern family name meant nothing in success-oriented New York. He had likewise miscalculated the effect of the Southern charm. That charm was as nothing without the vitality that New York demanded. What a fool he had been. There were numerous families he could have married into—with names that meant something, women with fortunes, passion and backbone.

He thought of divorce, naturally. But Bettina would not divorce him; he would have to initiate it. This, however, would mean more scandal than he could manage. Those born to name and money were not afraid for their reputations—they had a total disregard for anyone's opinion but their own. Maurice Gold had not yet attained that plateau. And Sara. What of Sara? He had to get rid of Bettina but hold on to Sara. He had to manipulate Bettina into letting go on her own by one means or another.

3.

"What does she think?" Martha Leeds Williams, my mother, demanded of my father as she brandished her sister Bettina's letter in his face, almost as if she blamed him for its infuriating contents. "That she can go away for fifteen years with never so much as a Christmas card, then make up for everything—all these years—with this patronizing offer 'to educate my daughter properly. To present her to Society'?" She finished the sentence with what she imagined was her sister's British accent.

How silly, I thought. Why would my aunt have acquired a British accent just by going to New York to live? After all, Aunt Bettina came from the same neck of the woods as we all did. Unless she had lost all traces of her Charleston speech through her years with the Yankees.

"That doesn't matter," Daddy told Mother. "What does matter is that she's trying to patch things up. And she's made a very nice and generous offer, I think. Giving Marlena a chance at a private-school education is a fine thing. Then Marlena will be able to go to one of those good colleges up north—Vassar, Smith. Maybe Radcliffe."

"Oh? And who'll pay for *that*, Howard Williams?" Mother jeered.

Daddy flushed. "We'll cross that bridge when we come to it."

"Well, I'm against it. I don't want to accept any favors from Bettina. Nor from that Jew, either."

"What does it matter if he's a Jew or a Hindu, for heaven's sake? Your sister has to sleep with him, not you."

"I suppose he's just going along with what Bettina wants. And what

29

Bettina wants is to act the grand lady dispensing favors. What would the money mean to him, anyway? A drop of piss in a pee pond."

I realized then exactly how upset Mother was; otherwise, she would never have used that expression. My mother abhorred vulgarity.

"First, you object to their generosity. Now you're questioning its value. And it's all beside the point, the point being—"

"I don't want them condescending to us. *They're* going to arrange for her debut! I'm a Leeds, I'll remind you. I don't need a *Gold* to assure my daughter's place in Society."

I saw a funny expression cross my father's face. Perhaps he wanted to tell Mother that being a Leeds didn't mean so much anymore, not even in Charleston. But he only said softly, "Your sister is a Leeds too."

"Really, Howard. I don't need you to tell me that. Maybe you had better remind Bettina. Why do you think that Jew married her in the first place? Because he needed a Leeds to forget who *he* was."

I stood there listening, all but forgotten by my bickering parents. Aunt Bettina and Uncle Maurice, the Golds, had apparently offered to finance my education at Miss Chalmer's School, then, after graduation, to sponsor my coming-out in New York. And Daddy seemed grateful—he seemed eager to accept the offer. But Mother was angry, bitter. She couldn't seem to forgive Aunt Bettina for marrying "up" to mounds of money from the distinguished, genteel poverty they had shared. Nor for the fact that her sister had also married *down*—to a "Hebrew," thereby disgracing all the Leedses. What seemed most unforgivable of all was that her sister had left that genteel poverty behind without so much as a glance over her lovely, soft, aristocratic shoulder.

I had heard it all, many, many times ever since I was a little girl. But what I didn't know until only a year or so ago was that Mother had been known in her youth as the *plain* Leeds girl. And that *she* had been forced to marry down too, to a man with a deep, dark secret: Howard Williams had come up from white trash—dirt farmers, sharecroppers, rednecks—a disgrace only slightly nullified by his associate professorship at the College of Charleston. Unfortunately, an associate professor was not highly compensated. Poor Daddy!

I had learned all this by eavesdropping on a bit of neighborly gossip, and when I had first repeated this to my mother she had only straightened her collar and denied its veracity. But then, later, she had explained. *At least my father was a Southerner and in a respectable profession. Even if they didn't have a lot of money, he wasn't a Jew, a Christ-killer.*

At that time I had been confused. I didn't know which was the worst crime—to be like Bettina and forget who you were and where you had come from and marry a Jew and have great wealth and live in New York amidst other famous, wealthy people, or to be plain and be named Martha while your sister was a great beauty and had a beautiful name, too. At least I understood then why I had been named Marlena. Martha Leeds Williams thought that having a beautiful name would help her daughter grow up to be a great beauty.

"And they expect her to go to that school with their daughter Sara. That means, most likely, that Marlena and that girl would share a room. Don't you even care if your daughter shares a room with a Jewess?"

Howard Williams smiled. "I don't think it's catching, Martha."

She glowered at him.

He was contrite. She never considered anything to do with her sister Bettina as amusing. And even in the best of times, Martha did not possess much of a sense of humor. "Bettina's daughter is only a half-Jew, Martha. And she is Marlena's first cousin. Kin."

"More shame on us. But what can I expect of you? You with your—" She broke off mid-sentence. "Besides, I want Marlena to come out here in Charleston. All the Leeds girls have come out in Charleston."

"Let's face facts, Martha. If Marlena comes out in New York she'll have a better chance of marrying well. She'll meet boys from Harvard, Princeton. . . . The odds are better up north, the opportunities more plentiful—"

Mother looked at Daddy oddly, as if his words struck home, as if they pained her. "Opportunities more plentiful for what? For marrying a Jew?"

But I knew from my mother's tone that the argument was settled, this one time, in Daddy's favor. I would be going North. My father's reference to the odds had been a telling one. My mother knew that I was a *plain* Leeds girl too and needed all the advantages and odds I could get.

The summer passed slowly. Now that it was all set for me to enter Miss Chalmer's School, I was eager to get on with it. I shopped with Mother for clothes. Sweaters in ten different colors. Blouses. Pleated skirts. Saddle shoes and loafers, and even a pair of spectator pumps with an inch heel. Knee socks. A velvet dress for dress-ups. A warm, camel-colored polo coat. And three pairs of gloves. If I was going up north, Martha Williams was going to make sure that her daughter was dressed every bit as well as her classmates would be. She used a check list in *Mademoiselle* for the college-bound girl as her guide.

"I don't care how Sara Gold behaves herself," she told me. "I want you to remember that *you* were raised to be a lady and that *you* have good manners. You wear a hat on Sundays and when you go downtown. And your gloves. Especially in New York City. The place is full of all kinds of germs, I'm sure."

31

I was both excited and apprehensive about going up north. I sensed that I was doing more than going off to school with Cousin Sara. I felt that I was saying good-bye to the Charleston that I had known. Old, gracious, romantic Charleston. How could Aunt Bettina have left it never to return? Uncle Maurice must have been so handsome, so dashing, a Lochinvar out of the north, to make her turn her back on her family, on Charleston, on her past. I made a promise to myself. *I* would return. After New York. After Miss Chalmer's. After the debut. After college. Then I wondered if I ever really would.

I wasn't sure that I really wanted to be a New York debutante. The idea was scary. And meeting all those Society girls, those junior debs, at Miss Chalmer's was scary, too! And I was frightened by the thought of the Golds. The Jewish uncle. Did he really have a nose that reached down to his chin? Would he really want some of my blood for his ritual bread? And Aunt Bettina. So lovely that she could make you faint, with a heart so cold that it gave one a chill. Sara, my own age, was the scariest of all. She must be very haughty. I just knew she would mock me as the dumb country cousin, would laugh at my small-town clothes and small-town manners and make fun of my Southern drawl. Yes, most of all, I was deathly afraid of Sara.

4.

My biggest fear concerning my New York kin was confirmed. Sara, not yet fourteen, a gawky in-between stage for most adolescents, was already a raving beauty. And I quickly realized that Sara and I were caught in the same situation our mothers had already acted out. There had been the two Leeds sisters, one beautiful, one plain. Now, there were two Leeds cousins to perpetuate the tradition.

My second-largest fear proved to be groundless. Sara wasn't the slightest bit snooty. Quite the contrary. Sara, accompanied only by the family chauffeur, met me at Pennsylvania Station and literally threw herself at me, hugging me to her breast, covering my face with a machine-gun fire of kisses, murmuring over and over in rhapsody, "Cousin! Cousin! Sweet cousin!"

That I didn't respond in kind was due only to my shyness. I was even too timid to inquire after Aunt Bettina and Uncle Maurice, although I was a little surprised they had not come to welcome me, too. If Sara noticed any reticence in my greeting, she didn't mention it. She quickly stripped me of my baggage claims, handed them over to the chauffeur and hustled me out of the station. "Do you think you'd like some tea? Or a drink, perhaps?"

"A drink?" I repeated dumbly. Did Sara mean a bottle of pop or did she mean *a drink?* Did not-quite-fourteen-year-olds in New York drink?

"We *could* skip over to the Café Rouge at the Hotel Pennsylvania. It's just next door. Or we could go straight home and get you settled in—you must be utterly exhausted after your trip. Aren't you exhausted?"

Sara led me to the waiting limousine, helped me in, then fell back against the luxuriously aromatic leather seat, declaring, "Exhaustion! Utter exhaustion!"

I followed suit. I too threw myself back and agreed. "Yes. Heavens! Me too! I'm utterly frazzled!"

At the same time, I marveled at Sara's accent. Instead of the harsh New York voice I anticipated, I heard the dulcet, syrupy tones of Charleston, even thicker, more syrupy than my own. "You sound just like home," I said to Sara in a slightly accusatory tone.

Sara laughed delightedly. "Do I?" she asked in all innocence. "I must have caught it from Mother. Do you think it *is* catching?"

"Does your mother still talk like that?"

Sara considered. "I *think* she does." Then added, "Mother doesn't say too much, you know," which left me to make of that what I might. Then Sara put her two hands on my shoulders, holding me away from her. "Let me take a good look at you, cousin. A real, good look." She poised her head first to one side and then the other. "You're lovely," she finally proclaimed.

Then I knew that Sara was kind, if not exactly truthful. I tried to protest her evaluation of my looks, but Sara kept on talking. "We have the same color hair, don't we?"

I shook my head. "No. Your hair is golden—pale gold," I said, looking at the curly halo framing Sara's piquant face. "Back home, they call mine dirty blond."

For answer, Sara kissed me again. "I'm so thrilled we're going to school together! That way, neither one of us is ever going to be lonely. We're kissin' kin, that's what we are, and that means no matter what happens, we'll have each other. You're the only cousin I have, the only one I *know* anyway. And it's going to be so good to have family with me at Miss Chalmer's. I just hate getting used to all those nasty strangers, don't you?"

Fresh terror struck in my heart. If Sara, this golden, self-assured, verbal girl, was afraid of the nasty strangers at the Chalmer's School, how would *I* fare?

"We're going to be roommates—it's all arranged," Sara said, looking out the window for the chauffeur. "Where *is* he? . . . And we're going to be best friends, too. Always. No matter what happens. Promise me we'll be best friends forever, no matter. Promise!"

"I promise. . . ." But what did Sara mean? *No matter what happens?* What could possibly happen that would test our relationship to an extreme? It sounded almost ominous.

"I hated Tree's," Sara confided happily. "That's the school I've been going to. The girls there are a bunch of doodies, you can't imagine."

I giggled. "The girls I went to school with in Charleston were a bunch of doodies too," I found myself saying, even though I had never thought of my schoolmates that way before. I smiled widely at Sara for the first time. Sara took my hand and smiled back. She put her head to one side, gazed into my eyes with her violet blue ones and said, oh so sweetly, "Cousin darling, you're going to be the sister I never had."

For the first time in my life, I felt special.

Though I was not unfamiliar with great houses—in fact, I lived in one—the old, formerly very elegant, Leeds house, which dated back to 1830—I was unprepared for the Gold town house on Fifth Avenue. I *expected* it to be grand, but my visions of grandeur had been limited. I had never seen a black and white marble floor, so many rich-hued Oriental rugs, such magnificent chandeliers, such huge paintings, so exquisite pastel velvet and satin-covered French furniture and tapestries. I had thought such furnishings were reserved for estates in France or castles in Spain. And although servants were certainly not uncommon in Charleston and even we had our old Bess, I was not prepared for the army of servants. Butlers in black suits, maids in silk uniforms with ruffled white aprons, all busy, all quiet, slipping in and out of doorways and corners. And all of them, amazingly, were white.

Sara hustled me through the rooms, showing me everything quickly, completely oblivious to my awe. Most surprising was that Sara, who spoke in soft, pleasant confusion and didn't seem to have a brain in her head, managed everything in swift, competent fashion. She issued orders to servants, had my bags brought in, assigned me my bedroom, had my clothes unpacked, the dresses sent off for pressing. She even pulled back the bedspread, inspected the sheets, checking to see that everything was done properly.

I looked around slowly. The bed was canopied and draped in blue satin matching the window draperies. There was a long dressing table festooned with fringe and ribbons, and bouquets of flowers everywhere. It was probably the most luxurious bedroom I had ever seen. "It's beautiful," I breathed.

"It's okay," Sara grudgingly admitted. "I just had the seamstress run up new undercurtains. But it really doesn't matter that much; we are leaving for school next week and then you'll only be here for occasional

34

weekends and holidays. In the summer, we'll be going to the Island. *Nobody* stays in New York for the summer, you know."

I was sure that my parents expected me to come home for the holidays and certainly for the summer, but I said nothing. I was under Sara's spell and already my parents and Charleston seemed far away.

I followed Sara down the stairs to the kitchen, which was at sublevel. "Hilda," Sara addressed the cook, "this is my cousin from down home."

I looked curiously at Sara. *Down home.* What a strange thing for her to say. I was sure Sara had never been south of Washington, D.C., unless her family had gone down to Palm Beach for a winter's sojourn.

"How do you do, Miss?" Hilda said politely. "Can I get you something to eat? Miss Sara?"

"No, we'll wait for dinner. We'll just have some ice cream. My cousin loves ice cream. Everybody down home loves ice cream. But I'll get it myself, Hilda. Thank you. I've told Robert we'll be having dinner at seven tonight. And let's have strawberry shortcake for dessert, please, Hilda." She confided to Marlena, "Strawberry shortcake is my most absolute favorite."

The cook turned back to her work at a marble counter rolling out pastry dough, and Sara led the way into a large pantry. I thought it strange that Sara had instructed the cook as to the time dinner would be served and had specified the dessert, but Hilda did not appear to think it at all strange. And who had ordered the rest of the dinner? Where was my aunt? Shouldn't she have been the one to supervise the help?

Sara opened a huge, white double-doored freezer, pulled out gallon container after gallon container of ice cream. "What flavor would you like? Strawberry? Chocolate? Pistachio? Maybe walnut? I adore maple walnut. Don't you adore maple walnut? Would you rather have butter almond?"

After much discussion, we decided on a combination of chocolate, maple walnut, and pistachio, and sat at the kitchen table spooning the ice cream lovingly into our mouths. "Where's your mother?" I suddenly blurted out. "I was looking forward to seeing her."

Back home, if a cousin we had never met had appeared, my parents would have been dancing in attendance. Mother would have had the dining-room table spread with a multitude of delectable edibles on her best heirloom tablecloth and Daddy would have had on tap all topics of conversation and little jokes he thought would entertain a teenager.

Sara cast covert eyes at the cook and at the maid who had appeared to help her and said in a low voice: "Mother is resting. You'll see her later. Most probably at dinner."

I could feel my face flush. "Oh, good. I'm looking forward to that," I mumbled. I realized I had committed a gaffe by bringing up a personal matter in front of the cook and the maid. Apparently, in New York one did not speak in front of servants as one did back home.

35

"Do you have a boyfriend?" Sara asked.

"No." I blushed.

"Nobody at all? Somebody you left behind with a broken heart crying his little old eyes out?"

"No," I repeated earnestly. "Do you?"

"No. Absolutely not." Sara shook her head decisively, her voice at normal volume. Obviously it was only discussion of her mother that required hushed tones. "I don't have a single one. Not that I wouldn't mind a real boyfriend. I need the experience. But I've always gone to girls' schools and that hardly gives one the best opportunity to meet boys. The only boys I know are the ones I've gone to dancing school with, and they are not even tolerable. Little boys. What I really long for"—she leaned over to confide—"is a real man! Don't you?"

"Oh, yes. I surely do. A real man. I've had it up to here"—I shelved my chin—"with little boys."

Dinner was served at seven in the white and gold dining room. Just before I sat down at one end of the long table opposite Sara, I touched a wall with a fingertip. Yes, it really *was* watered silk, not paper. But where were Aunt Bettina and Uncle Maurice? I wanted to ask Sara, but two butlers hovered and I decided it would be better to wait until we were alone.

The first course appeared. A fruit compote.

I wondered if perhaps I was in the middle of a mystery, like a heroine in one of my teenage novels. Maybe there was no Aunt Bettina, no Uncle Maurice anymore. Perhaps they had died? And Cousin Sara, not wishing to go to an orphanage to live—and who could blame her for that?—was carrying on as if they were alive, pretending to everyone, including the servants, that her father was away on an interminable business trip and that her mother was interminably ill, and therefore always hidden away in her room. And only Sara was able to take her meals on a tray. And then Sara had to eat another meal or wait until everyone was asleep and then throw the food away in the trash.

Maybe it was Sara who had written the letter to my parents in her mother's name? She had tired of living alone with only servants for company. That's exactly what the heroine would have done in the novel. And then when she and I left for school, Sara would announce that during the night, while everyone was asleep, her mother's condition had worsened and she had been taken away to a sanitarium. T.B., or something like that.

The second course appeared. A filet of some sort of fish. I did not know what kind it was, but I ate it anyway while Sara prattled away, laying out for me a program of events for the week. *She wasn't eating much. Was she preparing to eat her mother's tray of food, after all?*

"Tonight we'll stay home and get further acquainted. Tomorrow night, we *could* go to a party. Ginny Furbush is having a fourteenth-birthday party, but it will probably most certainly be a horror. Ginny Furbush is a first-class jerk." Sara didn't stop for a breath. She assured me that the invited boys would most certainly be jerks. There probably would be kissing games, if one could believe it. There probably would also be a three-piece band that would play slow dances, swing, as well as music to jitterbug. She, Sara, preferred the lindy hop but the other girls liked the slow dances so they could rub against the boys and feel them getting a hard-on.

I didn't know what a hard-on was but I guessed that it was something dirty, having to do with *sex,* and since I did not want to appear ignorant or unsophisticated, I didn't ask. "I know what you mean," I said. "That's how it is at home, too."

I still wanted to ask where Aunt Bettina and Uncle Maurice were. I had promised to phone home and I dreaded telling my mother, who would demand to hear all about everything, that I had not yet seen either Bettina or Bettina's husband. My mother would think it was odd; she would grow alarmed and probably order me to come straight home.

After the one butler served the beef Wellington and the other the asparagus hollandaise, and both left the dining room, I gathered up my courage and interrupted Sara, who was now listing the stores we would visit on our shopping expedition the following day. "Aren't your mother and father going to eat with us?" The question was academic by this time since we were already into the main course.

"Oh, Father is out of town. Didn't I mention that? On business, you know," Sara said breezily. "He's a terribly busy man. But he'll be back on Friday. You'll see him then. We're having a dinner in your honor on Friday, you know. But it's all grown-ups. Bores." She giggled, rolling her eyes in graphic dismay. "And Saturday night we're supposed to be having another party in your honor with *kids.* Which I'm thinking of calling off. It would be the same stupes that will be at Ginny's dumb party." She giggled again. It didn't seem to matter what Sara said or how horrendous her words—*everything* amused her.

"But your mother?" I persisted. "This afternoon you said I would see her at dinner."

Sara again cast covert eyes at the closed dining-room doors, to see if the butlers were about to enter. "Oh, I did, didn't I? But Mother still isn't feeling up to par, Marlena. You'll see her tomorrow. Maybe she'll even go shopping with us. Probably, she will."

"Tell me everything," Mother said, her voice sounding very distant. "Did any strangers talk to you on the train?"

"No, Mother. I just read my book and didn't talk to anyone. Just like you said."

"Good. And who met you at the station?"

"Everybody. I mean Sara did and Aunt Bettina and Uncle Maurice."

"Well, go on, Marlena. Tell me everything. How were they? Were they nice to you? Did they make you feel welcome? How does your aunt look?"

"Everyone's been just swell."

"Don't use the word 'swell,' Marlena. You know you're not supposed to use slang."

"Well, they were darling to me. Sara's really as sweet as can be."

"And your aunt and uncle?"

"Really lovely. As sweet as can be."

"How does Bettina . . . your aunt look?"

I sensed this was a very important question. "Mmm . . . nice . . . not terribly young, you know. You look younger, Mother, really. She's . . . uh . . . more wrinkled."

Mother grunted with satisfaction. "And what's their house like? Tell me about it."

"I can't now . . . Sara just came in." I lowered my voice significantly and said quickly, "I'll talk to you some more next time . . . when I'm alone. . . ." I whispered.

"All right," she conceded unhappily. "Your father wants to say hello."

"Hello, baby? Everything okay? You having a good time?"

"Yes, Daddy, a wonderful time. Sara is wonderful, truly. We're having a great time together."

"Good, baby, good. We'll speak to you again next week. After you're at school a couple of days. And remember—even if everything seems a little strange to you in the beginning, it will all get better once you get used to it up there. You hear?"

"Yes, Daddy. I know. Kiss Mother for me. 'Bye."

I hung up and felt guilty about lying to Mother, pretending that Sara was in the room so I wouldn't have to answer any more questions about Aunt Bettina and Uncle Maurice.

Sara came in clad in pink satin pajamas, the kind I had seen worn only by movie stars. "Why did you tell a lie?" Sara asked me.

At first I didn't understand. How could Sara know I had lied to my mother? Then I realized how and I was shocked. "You listened in?"

"Yes, of course," Sara laughed. "On the extension in my room. Do you mind?" Without waiting for an answer, she said: "I knew you wouldn't mind. I just wanted to hear how your mother sounded. Aunt Martha," she said as if tasting the sound of the words on her lips. "But you said we all met you at the train. Mother, Father, me. Why did you lie about that? Not that I care. I lie a lot myself."

"Because Mother would worry if she knew that I still haven't seen your mother. And your father. She would think it's strange."

"Really?" Sara asked very seriously, thinking it over. She came to a decision, it seemed. Not looking at me, she said: "It's really not strange when you think about it. Mama's a drunk and she wasn't in any condition to see you." Sara stared at a place somewhere over my head. "She goes away . . . a lot. To dry out, you know. And this time she came back before she was really ready, because you were coming. In your honor." Sara laughed without gaiety. "So she's not really pulled together yet. And she doesn't like people to see her until she's all together. Mama's very beautiful, you know, and it's hard on her to face people if she's not just right, you understand. Things like this are harder on people that are very beautiful. I know you understand. . . ."

"Oh, of course. Of course I understand," I said quickly, feeling my face grow red as a beet.

"Does *your* mother drink? Aunt Martha? All Southerners are supposed to drink. Heavily, that is. That's what my father says. He says he married into a fine, old Southern family of drunks." Sara smoothed at the bedspread with fluttering fingers. "Personally, I think that's a terrible thing to say. Mama is so beautiful. And very sweet. My father is mean to say that, don't you think?"

I didn't know what to say. Fortunately, I didn't have to answer for Sara went on talking. "Is Aunt Martha a drunk? Is your daddy? My father does take a drink, sometimes a few, but he's not a drunk. He says Jews are never drunks. But you know"—she dropped her voice to a whisper even though no one could possibly hear her—"Father isn't a Jew anymore. He's a Protestant now, but still he's not a drunk. I guess things like drinking or not drinking don't change just because people change their religion. I guess those things are just in the blood. And your blood wouldn't change just from walking up the stairs of a different church." She giggled at the thought. "Would you think?"

I shook my head mutely. I was shocked to learn that Uncle Maurice wasn't a Jew any longer. I wondered what my mother would think about that. Would she be relieved or would she be upset because the change of religion would mean that Aunt Bettina's marriage wasn't such a step down socially after all.

"Why did he change? To a Protestant, I mean."

"Just decided, I guess." Sara sucked her index finger. "Mother's Methodist and he's Episcopalian. I told him I wanted to be a Jew, but he said I couldn't be one. He says I'm Methodist because my mother is. He says the Jewish religion says you are what your mother is because she's the garden in which the seed grows. I think that's funny. My father isn't a Jew anymore but he goes by the Jewish law. Don't you think that's funny?"

"I guess so."

"I think it stinks. I think it just stinks that Father stopped being a Jew. I think that's what made him mean. What are you? Your family? Your religion?"

"Mother's Methodist. Like your mother. And I'm Methodist too. Daddy's Baptist."

"So are they alcoholics?"

"Baptists?"

"No, silly!" Sara giggled. "Your mother and father? Aunt Martha and Uncle Howard?"

"Oh, no. Mother *never* drinks. She's a teetotaler. Father does, once in a great while. Maybe he would drink more often, but Mother makes such a fuss I guess it's not worth the trouble to him. Was your . . . Aunt Bettina . . . was she always a—"

"A drunk? I don't know. But it's most certainly because of Father. He has a mistress, my father. She's young. Twenty-three or so. I'm not supposed to know, of course. But everybody knows. *Everybody.* So, he's away a lot. Between his business affairs and his girl friends. To tell you the truth," Sara drawled, "I don't know which came first, Daddy's mistresses or Mama's drinking. I'm not really *positive* they're connected but I would think so, don't you? Anyhow, she's at least Father's third."

"Third?"

"Mistress. The third mistress I know about, anyway."

"Oh," I said, very impressed. I had never met anyone personally who I absolutely knew had a mistress. I wondered if I dared tell Mother about Aunt Bettina's drinking and Uncle Maurice's mistresses. Maybe she would make me come home. I probably could safely tell her about Uncle Maurice being a Protestant now. That probably wouldn't affect my own situation one way or the other.

"You know what I would like to do? I'd like to kill Linda Young. That's the name of Father's current mistress," Sara confided cheerfully. "But I guess somebody else would just take her place. I suppose in order to do any real good I would really have to kill my father if I were to kill anybody at all." Seeing the distressed expression on my face, she laughed. "Don't worry, I'm really not about to kill anybody this week. And Mama will certainly pull herself together soon. Before we leave for school next Monday. And we don't have to worry about her going shopping with us, either. I have all the charge cards. And we'll buy you oodles of pretty things."

I yawned.

"You're exhausted, aren't you?" Sara asked sympathetically. "Why don't you get into bed?"

I *was* tired. So tired that I was afraid I would fall asleep before I could properly think about all the events of the day, all the things I had learned about Aunt Bettina and Uncle Maurice. I climbed into bed, under the coverlet, and Sara left the room saying she would be back in a minute. My eyes started to close. They were *so* heavy. But then Sara came back, holding up a bottle of wine and two stemmed goblets.

"Don't you dare go to sleep on me! We're celebrating!"

I gasped. "Do you think we should?" I thought of Aunt Bettina and how alcoholism might be in our blood.

Sara must have guessed what I was thinking. She giggled. "Of course we should. We're not going to become alcoholics from one little bottle of wine. And besides, only weak people become drunks. That's what Father says. And he's very smart, you know. He may be a Protestant and he may be mean, but he's terribly smart. And you and I are not weak, are we? You and me and this little ol' bottle of wine are going to have us a good ol' time."

Two glasses later my head was swimming from the wine. Oh, Mother was right. One day in New York in the home of a former Jew and I had already sunk into the depths of iniquity. . . .

Sara put out the light and climbed into the bed beside me. "What's the fun of having your cousin with you if you sleep in separate rooms?" She wriggled around under the covers and in a couple of minutes I saw her satin pajamas go flying up in the air. She giggled. "I just adore sleeping in the nude, don't you?"

I had never slept nude in my life but I couldn't confess to that. "Oh, I do!"

"So take off your jammies, why don't you? There ain't nobody here but us chickens."

I couldn't help but take them off, but I was very embarrassed.

"Have you ever fooled around?" Sara asked.

"What do you mean?"

"You know. Play doctor with some little old boy? Or with a little girl? How about a little pickaninny? I thought all Southern girls fooled around with little pickaninnies."

I could only shake my head. I was so embarrassed I could have died.

"You never played rub-up with a boy at a party?"

I shook my head again.

"Didn't a boy ever touch your titty?"

"No," I barely whispered.

"Oh, my heavens! You are an innocent, little Marlena."

"Have you? I mean, did you ever . . . fool around with a boy?"

"Hardly. Once or twice. I told you—I don't know any *good* boys. Or men. Sometimes we girls fool around at pajama parties—just to see what it's like. Haven't you ever fooled around with a girl just to see what it's like?"

"No. . . ."

"Well, for goodness' sake, you've masturbated, haven't you?"

41

"No. . . ."

"Oh, my goodness! Haven't you ever even rubbed yourself with a pillow?"

"No."

"I don't believe you! And I heard Southern girls *did it to themselves* with a Coke bottle!"

"Did *what?*" I asked, but I had already guessed what Sara meant.

"Stuck it in their old vagies, in and out, just the way boys do it to you."

"That sounds terrible. I'm awfully tired, Sara. I think I'd like to go to sleep," I said.

"Don't you dare go to sleep on me, Marlena Williams. All my life I wanted a sister to talk to late at night, and now the first night I have my own cousin here you want to go to sleep instead of talking and all. You're just afraid I'll make you fool around just so you can see what it's like."

"I'm not afraid," I said but I was.

"Good. I'll make believe I'm the boy."

"Oh, no, Sara! I am awfully tired."

"Don't be a ninny! You have to find out what it's like sometime, don't you? How are you ever going to know anything if you don't get some experience? You just lie there and I'll make believe I'm the boy. . . ."

She leaned over me and tried to pry my mouth open with her thin, determined tongue, but I set my lips together.

"You're not cooperating, Marlena. Boys always try to stick their tongues in your mouth when they kiss you. Don't you know that?" Sara giggled. "Now just open your mouth and let me show you what they do."

I sighed and opened my mouth partly and Sara stuck her tongue inside my mouth and circled it around and around. It tasted of peppermint.

"Then they always try to touch your breasts. Always. You're supposed to protest, even if you like them. But they won't try that for at least the third date. So you're safe until then. This is what they do," and she started to stroke my breast. I was so embarrassed I wanted to cry.

"They always try to work on your nipples. The nipples are supposed to have an erotic reaction, you know."

"Please, Sara," I protested.

"Do you feel anything?" Sara wanted to know as she rubbed the nipple of my right breast with the palm of her hand. Much as I wanted to say no, I *could* feel my nipple harden under her hand and I did have a strange feeling *down there.*

Then Sara took her hand away and looked at my breast and screamed in delight. "Your nipple had an erection!"

I was so ashamed for my poor nipple.

"When that happens," Sara said with extreme satisfaction, "the boy usually takes it in his mouth like this and sucks!" She proceeded to do exactly that and when I moaned with discomfiture, Sara obviously took it as an expression of pleasure because she sat up and clapped her hands delightedly. "I just knew you'd like it. Now you know what fooling around is. Of course, that's just the beginning. *That's* not heavy petting. Heavy petting is down *there* . . . you know . . . but we won't go into that tonight."

Thank God, I thought with relief, and turned over, hoping Sara was ready to go to sleep.

"Of course you can't get a climax without getting touched down there."

"Of course . . ." I mumbled.

"But you can give yourself one by doing it to yourself."

"Do you?" I couldn't help asking.

"Masturbate? Sure. Sometimes at night I get pretty lonely. I think everybody masturbates sometime or other, but they don't admit it. They're lying when they say they don't."

"Lying isn't the worst sin," I said.

"And masturbating isn't either, so there. And I don't feel guilty about doing it, either."

"Of course not," I said, not wanting Sara to feel guilty. She had been so sweet to me. Again I felt my eyelids drooping.

"We're going to be best friends, aren't we, Marlena? Aren't you glad you've come north and we're going to go to school together?"

"Yes . . ." I said sleepily.

"Good . . ." Sara said contentedly. "Good night, Cousin Marlena."

"Good night, Cousin Sara."

5.

"I've always heard about Macy's. Can't we go to Macy's?" I pleaded with Sara.

"Don't be ridiculous, darling. Only clerks, secretaries, and tourists go to Macy's."

I wanted to protest that I *was* a tourist. I also wanted to see the Statue of Liberty, go to the top of the Empire State Building, see the Rockettes perform at Radio City Music Hall, and hear one of the big bands play at the Paramount. But Sara pooh-poohed all that. Maybe later on in the year we might go see the Rockettes and even go skating at Rockefeller Center if I insisted, just so I could write home about it, but right now we were too busy, Sara said. We had to go for our fittings for the school uniforms and then cover all the stores on Fifth Avenue and 57th Street.

It was already too late for the proper fitting of the pleated gray flannel skirt and matching blazer that made up the Chalmer's School uniform, the woman at Prazey's told Sara, instinctively realizing who was in charge. "All your schoolmates had their uniforms fitted in June. And the ones who didn't have them done then were in here the last couple of weeks in August. My goodness, your term starts next week," she tsk-tsked.

Sara did not bother explaining that she had been waiting for her cousin to arrive in New York. She just rolled her eyes, making me laugh. "Just do what you have to," she told the woman, "and send them over to my house by next Monday without fail."

The woman sniffed heavily. "Yes, *Ma'am*. But we'll only be able to have one set ready for each of you. We'll have to mail the others up to school."

I thought the blazer and skirt were very smart and rich looking until Sara complained, "They're not as nice as the uniforms we had at Tree's. We wore navy blazers there with plaid pleated skirts. Not as monotonous and dreary as these. But what's there to do? At least, we can wear either a white blouse or a navy sweater. And after classes and on Sundays we can wear what we like. And, of course, we wear dresses to dances and parties, if you can call them that. They'll be dreadful, I can tell you in advance. But we had better go shopping for party dresses just the same."

Going through Bergdorf's and Bonwit's, I watched with a trembling heart as Sara made extravagant purchase after purchase without pause or thought. At first I protested the items she bought for me—Mother and I had already bought the things I would need, and besides, Daddy had given me money so I could pay for whatever else I needed. But when I saw what a single white blouse cost at Bergdorf's I gave up and stopped protesting.

At four-thirty we were in Saks and Sara made me try on a black cocktail dress with a plunging neckline and a tulip-shaped skirt that allowed a long drift of leg to show. "Stunning," Sara pronounced. She herself had on a black taffeta with a low, square-cut neck and a bow that formed a bustle on the derriere. I assumed that we were just playing at trying on dresses, only Sara soon made it clear she was not playing. She told the saleslady we would wear the dresses out. The salesgirl looked faintly surprised but wrote up the sale, cut off the tickets, and we left the department in the new black dresses.

"Now—off to Cosmetics," Sara said.

She bought rouge, lipstick, eyeshadow, mascara, and whirled me off to the powder room. With great dexterity and speed, she arranged her own and my hair in upsweeps, made up both our faces with great red mouths, sultry shadowed eyelids, eyelashes heavy with beaded mascara.

I stared at myself in the mirror. I was almost unrecognizable. Why, I looked like a tramp! Like one of the girls who walked along the waterfront back home. *What would Mother say?* Then I looked down and started to laugh. Sara followed my eyes to see what I was laughing at; then she too shrieked with laughter. We were both wearing our penny loafers.

"We will have to fix this at once," Sara proclaimed and pulled me to the Better Shoe Salon. Soon we were both tottering on black, high-heeled suede pumps.

"Please, Sara, tell me, what are we dressed up for? Is this for Ginny Furbush's party tonight?"

That sent Sara into gales of laughter. "Don't be ridiculous," she said. "For that, we wear our velveteens, ribbons in our hair and those little patent leathers with the inch heel. That blue velvet dress you brought from home will be perfect."

At least I had brought *something* right from home, even if it was only a dress to be worn to Ginny Furbush's party. How did Sara know what would be perfect for what? She was only a couple months older than I, yet there didn't seem to be anything at all Sara wasn't sure of.

"What are we dressed up like this for, then?" I asked.

"We're going for cocktails, Marlena, silly puss. Don't you know it's cocktail hour in Manhattan?"

"We can't do that, Sara. We . . . we're not even fourteen yet. . . . Please, Sara, don't make us! I bet they won't even serve us!"

"Not even fourteen? Look in the mirror, puss. What do you see? I know what I see. A gorgeous, dark-blond eighteen-year-old stunner! That's what I see."

"Oh no, Sara. I don't look eighteen. I look like thirteen dressed up to look eighteen. Please, Sara, I don't want to—"

Sara looked at me pityingly. "Poor little cousin. She doesn't even want to have a good time. Well, I'm going to see that you have one anyway. And they *will* serve us. I've done it oodles of times."

"I won't know what to order."

"Poor itty-bitty Marlena doesn't have to worry. Sara will order for her."

"Where are we going?" I asked, sure that it was to my doom.

"Mmmm." Sara thought. "The Astor Bar."

"Have you even been there before?"

"Of course. A zillion times."

A few minutes later we were in a taxi and Sara was saying to the driver, "The Astor, my good man, and please make great dispatch."

45

"If you don't relax, Marlena, the bartender *will* know we're frauds and we'll be arrested."

Arrested? My God, I anguished, what would Mother say if *that* happened? She would pack me off back to Charleston and I would never see New York or Sara again. And I'd never even get to see Miss Chalmer's School at all. . . . I tried to smile and look as if I'd been in the Astor Bar before, even if not a zillion times. I took tiny sips of the sloe gin fizz that Sara had ordered for me. It tasted more like cherry pop than like something that would put me on the road to perdition, but still and all . . .

When I looked up from my drink, I saw Sara making eye contact with two men down at the end of the bar. They had to be at least thirty, I decided. It was all too clear what Sara had in mind. "Please, Sara," I pleaded, "don't do *that*."

"Don't do what?" Sara asked, not even looking at me. Slowly she opened her mouth, showing her pretty white teeth, licked her Joan Crawford lips with a pretty thin tongue, cast a sidelong glance at the frankly interested young men. "I'm not doing anything at all," she said as she cast violet-shadowed lids down provocatively. She raised them again, half-closed, with the red, wet lips glistening in invitation.

The men got to their feet and headed down the bar toward us. I jumped off my stool in panic and fled in search of the ladies' room. I stayed there until Sara came looking for me almost a half-hour later. When she saw the tears streaming down my face, she put her arms around me. "It's all right, honey. I wasn't going to *do* anything. I was just practicing."

"Can we go now?"

"Of course we can. Maybe tomorrow we'll try the bar at the Plaza. You'll just love the Plaza."

When the chauffeur delivered us to Ginny Furbush's, Sara instructed him to come back for us at nine-thirty. It was already eight o'clock, and I wondered if New York parties always lasted less than two hours. Was this big-city sophistication?

I watched Sara flit about the room—enthusiastically kissing the girls, exclaiming over their dresses, exchanging pleasantries, whispering bits of gossip. She was even nice to the little fourteen-year-old boys, all of whom seemed intent on appearing taller by stretching their necks like giraffes. Sara teased them, flirted with them outrageously, it seemed to me. And these were the same little boys she had called turds earlier in the day.

I felt my stomach cramp with nerves, my hands grow wet with perspiration. Sara made a big fuss about introducing me to everybody, cautioned the boys not to dare try anything funny with me—as if they were even thinking of such a thing. Then to make sure I would not

46

be a wallflower, she refused to dance with anyone until they had first danced with me.

I was self-conscious about my lindy hop. My breaks were different from those of these New York junior sophisticates. And when the band played the slow numbers, pretending that they were a three-piece Glenn Miller orchestra, I held myself stiffly away from my partners. It was enough trying to avoid any contact with any strange "hard-ons"—impossible to think of anything to say at the same time.

But I saw how Sara played the game. She draped herself over the boys' bodies, stroked their damp pink necks while humming along to the band, even allowed her pelvis to shimmy delicately against those of the boys.

Promptly at nine-thirty, as supper was about to be served, Sara made our good-byes, assuring everybody that we were "just dyin' to stay but Mama will break our little ol' necks if we don't get straight home."

Sara threw herself against the seat of the Cadillac. "God! Exhaustion! Boredom personified!"

"But, Sara, we were just about to eat. Couldn't we have stayed to eat?"

"If you had stayed to eat, honey, you would have had to sing for your supper," Sara giggled.

"How do you mean?"

"After supper comes the kissin' games. And on a full stomach it could only lead to disaster. Besides, I thought you wanted to go to the Paramount, didn't you? Tommy Dorsey's there with Frank Sinatra."

"Frank Sinatra? Really, Sara?"

"Really!"

"Isn't it kind of late?"

"Not in New York it isn't. They don't pull in the sidewalks in New York until five in the morning."

Sara disappeared into her mother's room as I got ready for bed. All the tensions of the day had left me completely spent. What a day! The black dresses, the theatrical makeup, the high heels, the men at the Astor Bar. And then the party. The Paramount had been the one event that had been only pleasureful.

I put out the light and pulled up the covers. Sara came tiptoeing in and crawled into the bed, cuddled up to me as if seeking warmth and reassurance. I realized her face was wet.

"Sara, are you crying? Is your mother all right?"

Sara would sooner have confessed to being a murderer than admit to tears. "Of course I'm not crying. Mother is okay. Sort of okay. Why

47

would I cry? I have you here, my own cousin, don't I? It's good to have my own best friend with me. As long as I have my own cousin, my own best friend, I'm never going to be lonely again."

"Me too," I said and closed my eyes. I was *so* tired.

Sara sat up suddenly, wiping her tears away with the back of her hand. "You know what? Tonight I think I'll teach you how to do it to yourself—"

I sighed. I had already learned that once Sara made up her mind to do something there was no talking her out of it.

6.

I awoke Friday morning wondering what was going to happen with the dinner party that my aunt and uncle were giving in my honor that evening. So far, neither had made an appearance and I knew that a large, formal dinner party required lengthy preparations.

I found Sara downstairs rushing about in a bright pink cotton shirt and boys' dungarees. I had never seen a girl dressed in dungarees. Out on the farms in South Carolina, girls who worked in the fields wore overalls, but in the city no girl ever wore pants except for tennis shorts or very proper Bermuda shorts accompanied by knee-high socks. Sara was talking fast and earnestly to the cook, checking out with Robert, the head butler, the dishes, the vermeil flatware, the Waterford crystal, everything that would be used for the dinner that evening.

"Can I help?" I begged.

"Yes, of course you can. Which set do you like best?" The choice was between plain white Lenox with a gold band or white and cobalt blue Spode with a narrow rim of gold.

"I like the white with the blue."

"Of course." Sara smiled. "Thank you."

"I want to *really* help," I said.

"Okay. Here are the flowers from the florist." Sara pointed to a huge white cardboard box. "And here are the vases. Can you arrange them? The big vermeil thing"—Sara indicated a large boatlike urn adorned with cherubs—"will be for the centerpiece for the dining table so make it especially gorgeous."

"Is your . . . is Aunt Bettina better today?"

Sara visibly tensed. "I think so. I told her I'd take care of things down here so she can take her time getting ready for tonight. She's nervous, you know."

I nodded.

Sara started to say something else, hesitated, then blurted out, "She's nervous about the party, about Father, not *you*, so don't feel—"

I nodded again.

"She just wants to look really well for him, you know, so he'll love her. And not be mad at her for being an alcoholic. It's all his fault anyway. I could kill him. Mother was . . . Mother's so beautiful, so sweet. . . ." She looked up to see that Robert was nowhere within hearing distance. "Maybe Mother was vain and weak, but Father . . . he should have helped her instead of turning his back on her and taking up with whores. . . ."

Embarrassed, I picked up a pink rose and examined it thoroughly.

"Let's make the dining-room table centerpiece all pink," Sara decided. "We'll use all the pink roses. You do that and I'll make an arrangement for the living room with all white flowers. And for the front hall, we'll use all yellow. How does that sound? I want the house to look especially beautiful for Mother. And I want everyone to think that *she* did everything. Okay, sweetie pie?"

"Of course, I understand."

"I really think you do. Sweet Marlena." Sara added a tall gladiola to her all-white arrangement and stood back to survey it critically, then picked up a white peony and stuck it in the white Limoges cachepot. "I've thought about it a lot, and I've decided it's all because Father left his faith. That made the difference, made him different. If he had stayed a Jew, he probably would have been sweet as sugar. He would never have taken a mistress. Don't you think?"

Bewildered, I just shook my head.

"Everybody knows that Jewish men make excellent husbands. They provide well for their wives and are always faithful. Did you know that?"

Without waiting for my answer, which was just as well, Sara went on. "It's true," she said with conviction. "I'm going to marry a Jew myself. But not one who's converted or about to convert, I can tell you that." Then she laughed. "But ah'm not about to do it until ah'm through having myself a good ol' time."

I marveled how all of a sudden Sara's "I's" had switched to "ah's."

"No siree," she continued. "Ah'm not about to marry until ah'm through having a ball. And don't you either, Marlena Williams, you hear?"

She stuck a white rose into the bouquet, stabbing it viciously into the center, backed up again, surveyed the arrangement from all sides. "Perfection?"

"Perfection," I agreed.

"Good." She carried the flowers off to the drawing room. When she came back she inspected my towering pink arrangement and pronounced it "Excellent!" and leaned over it, making a few corrections, pulling a flower here, straightening another. "I'm going to become a Jew myself, I decided. Officially. I'm going to get some instruction and be baptized into it, or whatever." She looked at my face and laughed. "You look so funny. Shocked. What's so shocking? I'm a half-Jew now."

"Are you going to do it just to spite your father?"

Sara laughed delightedly. "Aren't you the clever one? My little Charleston wise owl. I'm going to go up and see how Mama's doing now. She's really all excited about finally seeing you tonight. She loves you already. Do you know that? She's just crazy about you!"

We were setting out the placecards. "You look absolutely darling in that dress, Marlena. I'm so glad we bought it."

"I'm glad we're both wearing white gowns. Like we were twins."

"Mother's wearing white too. A Grecian style. From Worth's in Paris. A Worth gown never goes out of style. Did you know that?"

"Is she coming down soon?" I asked anxiously. I was almost as eager as Sara for Bettina Gold to be divinely beautiful tonight, composed, regal, in command of herself and the evening.

"The table does look gorgeous, doesn't it?" Sara asked as she lit the tapers in the vermeil candlesticks. "Mother will be down in a sec. She was putting on her emeralds when I checked a few minutes ago. The emeralds were Father's wedding present. He bought them for her in Paris when they honeymooned there. Isn't that romantic? Mother says he adored her so."

Sara tapped a placecard. "Here is old Mr. Rettinger. A nasty man. Let's fix his wagon and put him next to Mrs. Reinhart. She's a fat, ugly widow and she's looking for a new fish. Mr. Rettinger is such a pompous ass he really deserves to get her."

I had to laugh.

"And here's Teddy Lorrigan's card. He's Father's executive assistant. He's good-looking, fairly youngish and single, but he's bringing a date and I don't have her name. Still we can't have Teddy and his date sitting together. That's simply not done. But since I don't know who she is, I'll just stick her on the other side of pompous ass Rettinger. Poor thing. I hope she won't have too wretched a time."

I giggled. Sara *was* funny.

"You've done wonders with the table, Sara darling," a voice came from behind us.

We both spun around. Bettina Leeds Gold stood there like a queen from another land in her white Grecian gown that left one shoulder bared. She was a delicate vision, but, somehow, her edges were slightly blurred. "Marlena, my dear, sweet niece." She held out her arms to me and I rushed to her, all my shyness forgotten. I felt as if I already knew my aunt intimately.

Aunt Bettina was taller than I and she bent her head slightly to

50

kiss me. It was as if a butterfly had flown by, barely grazing my cheek. She *was* lovely, her pale hair piled on top of her head, a look of fragility about her, her face subtly made up, just a tiny bit of wear showing through. Sara stood to one side, watching us, guarded, apprehensive, protective.

I smiled at Sara, shook my head up and down in affirmation. *Yes, Sara, she's beautiful.* As beautiful as the pink roses would be tomorrow evening, I thought, a little less rosy, imperceptibly faded. Everything about Bettina was faded, exquisitely so, the blue eyes, the ash-blond hair, the unbelievably pale skin, everything like a powdery web—so light it could easily be blown away. The only vivid thing about Aunt Bettina was the emeralds she wore, glowing a hot green.

"I'm so distraught that I was too ill to greet you before, my sweet Marlena! I've been derelict in my duty. I hope you all haven't gone and told your mother on me. Dear Martha. So proper. She would never forgive me. But we'll get to know each other better, you'll see. I'll make up for lost time."

Everything seemed so unreal. My aunt seemed so unreal. I couldn't think of anything to say.

"You look super gorgeous, Mother. I just love you in that dress. Don't you, Marlena? We've finished putting out the placecards, Mama. Now we can all sit down and relax for a few minutes. Nobody will be arriving for at least fifteen minutes."

A look of consternation crossed Bettina's face, as if she had suddenly remembered something worrisome. "Your father, Sara. Maurice. He isn't here!"

"He is, Mother. He came home about an hour ago and went up to his room. He'll be down in a couple of minutes, I'm sure."

I was surprised to hear that Uncle Maurice was home. I had been waiting all this time to see him and now that he had come home, I had missed him. Actually, I was almost afraid to see him after all that my mother and Sara had said about him. Apprehensively, I glued my eyes on the doorway, waiting for the first glimpse of him.

My first reaction was one of surprise. No one had told me that my uncle would be so handsome, so distinguished looking. He didn't have a potbelly. He was not bald. He did not have a hooked nose down to his chin. He was deeply tanned, tall and broadshouldered. He had a shock of wavy black hair laced with gray, and a mustache and beautiful large teeth that flashed against his tanned skin as he smiled at me warmly. He looked rich, I decided.

He took my hand. "I'm glad to meet you, Marlena Williams. I'm glad you're here. I'm glad Sara has her own cousin for a friend. I've heard wonderful things about you."

I could not help but warm to him. I liked him! Then I felt guilty, disloyal to Aunt Bettina. "I'm happy to meet you . . . Uncle Maurice." I was confused; I didn't know what to think.

Maurice Gold kissed his wife on the cheek. "You look well, Bettina," he said, not even looking at her. Bettina's lightly rouged cheeks brightened.

He turned to kiss Sara, who turned her face away. Now it was Maurice Gold who flushed. He said, "Everything looks very lovely, Sara. You were right—we've managed quite well without a housekeeper. But I will have to see to hiring one now that you're going away."

"I can't take credit for the house or the table, Daddy. I was busy with Marlena. We were gone practically the whole day, weren't we, Marlena? Mother's done it all."

He smiled thinly. "Oh?" Then, "While we're waiting for our guests to arrive, I think I'll have a drink." He rang. Robert appeared. "I'll have a Scotch, Robert, please. Anyone else?" He looked around pointedly. He smiled at Sara and me. "Not you two. Wine at dinner should be enough for the two of you, I would think. Bettina? What would you like?"

Bettina looked down at her hands playing with a fold in her gown. "Nothing, thank you. Nothing."

"I'll have a ginger ale, Robert," Sara said quickly. "Make that three ginger ales, please." Obviously, she thought her mother needed a glass to hold in her hand.

As the guests started to arrive, Bettina and Maurice positioned themselves in the drawing room to receive them. Robert answered the door, and Clara, one of the downstairs maids, stood slightly to Robert's rear to accept the hats and wraps that he took from the guests and then handed to her. Sara and I stood several feet back in the entrance hall and Sara introduced me each time with the same words: "This is my Cousin Marlena from South Carolina. Marlena is a Leeds too, like my mother and me, you know. We're all Leeds girls from Charleston. Our great-granddaddy fired that first shot at Sumter that was heard 'round the world, you know."

I could barely keep from laughing. Sara's historical facts were somewhat askew but it didn't seem to matter since no one else noticed. Every now and then, Sara left her station to glance in on her mother in the drawing room. Everything seemed to be going smoothly. Aunt Bettina still had her glass of ginger ale in her hand and was mingling nicely with her guests. Then everyone had arrived and Sara and I went into the drawing room to mingle, too.

Like Sara, I kept an eye on Bettina. But she was keeping an eye on Uncle Maurice who was talking to the young woman Teddy Lorrigan had brought who seemed to be something of a femme fatale. Actually I had never met a femme fatale before, but I had read about them and Wanda Hale certainly looked like those I had seen in movies. She wore a lot of makeup and a slinky black satin gown, and when she had first arrived she had allowed her silver fox cape to slither off white, perfumed shoulders. Besides, she looked like Lana Turner.

I saw Sara watching them, too.

"He's *only* talking to her," I tried to reassure her. "He has to be hospitable, doesn't he?"

"But I think Mama's getting nervous. . . ."

Then we saw Bettina go over to Maurice Gold and Wanda Hale and we watched as she tried to cut into their conversation. She put her hand on her husband's arm and said something. He seemed to ignore her remark and sort of shook off her hand. She withdrew and before Sara could dash over and intercept her, Aunt Bettina, hands fluttering in space, took a glass from the tray a maid was passing.

"Let's go over and talk to Mother," Sara said. "Maybe I can talk her into giving up that drink."

We went over and Sara said, "Please don't drink that, Mama."

"I'm fine, Sara. Please don't worry. I'll just have a sip, a little sip. I *have* to have one little sip."

She turned away from us and said to Teddy Lorrigan who was standing alone, "It's very warm tonight. It reminds me of a Charleston summer evening. One really shouldn't entertain till October. In Charleston, one never entertained until well past September." She drained her glass. "Would you mind getting me another glass of champagne, Teddy? It's really very good."

Teddy did as he was told. He went and got the glass of champagne and came back with it and handed it over to Bettina. Then Maurice came over and said to Teddy, "Surely you know better than that, Teddy. Once Bettina starts drinking she ends up embarrassing us all."

Bettina paled, Teddy flushed, and Sara looked as if she might cry.

"I am always a lady, Maurice, and a lady never embarrasses anyone except, perhaps, herself."

With that Aunt Bettina drained her glass and Maurice Gold turned away in what seemed disgust.

Sara was beside herself. "Mama," she said, "I think you're getting tired. Won't you come upstairs with me? We'll go upstairs—you, me, and Marlena. We'll stay upstairs with you the whole evening, won't we, Marlena?"

"Yes, of course. Do come upstairs, Aunt Bettina. We can play gin rummy."

"You're a sweet girl, Marlena. Your father must have been a sweet man, God rest his soul."

"He hasn't passed away, Aunt Bettina," I said in a little voice.

"Oh? Of course not. I must be confused with somebody else. . . . Teddy? . . ." Teddy had disappeared. "Sara . . . I think I'd like another glass of . . ."

"No, Mother. Please. I know that that was a very humiliating remark Daddy made but please don't do this, I beg you."

"I have already suffered humiliations in the past, my darling. But a lady can rise above any humiliation. Marlena, please tell my sister Martha, that in spite of grievous circumstances, her sister Bettina acted like the lady she was brought up to be. Will you tell her that, dear?"

"Of course."

Robert approached. "Shall I announce dinner?" Not being sure to whom he was addressing his question, Mrs. Gold or Sara, he discreetly left off any term of address.

"Everyone!" Bettina called out. "Shall we go into dinner?"

Bettina barely tasted her appetizer, the *suprême de foie gras en casserole,* but she had a full glass of the Chablis Pouilly that was served with it. I knew the name because Sara had made me memorize the names of all the wines that were being served, and which went with what, just in case anyone asked me what we were drinking. I could barely keep my eyes off my aunt as I tried to chat with Philip Warden about the problems of the present-day South, as much as I knew of the subject, which wasn't a lot. Philip Warden was the youngest, handsomest man present, and Sara had been sweet to place him next to me instead of saving him for herself.

Sara, herself, talked to no one. She kept her eyes down and concentrated on mangling her food with her fork. For the first time since I had laid eyes on her, she seemed at a loss. Her mother was drinking and Sara didn't seem to know what to do about it. All of a sudden Sara was just a thirteen-going-on-fourteen-year-old girl at a grown-up dinner party.

Uncle Maurice had no trouble being charming to his dinner companions on his right and left. He chatted amiably, seeming quite smooth and urbane. Teddy Lorrigan, however, seemed to have trouble concentrating on the conversation of Georgette Pauley. She was telling him about her gall bladder operation and he seemed to find it other than fascinating. He kept glancing at Aunt Bettina too.

Champagne was poured for the oysters. (Sara had told me that it was necessary to serve champagne as the oysters themselves had been poached in champagne.) Bettina drank the wine and ignored the oysters. "My daddy always cautioned us to never marry out of our class," she told Ernst Lehman on her right.

Mr. Rettinger did not speak to Wanda Hale at all but did speak to Mrs. Reinhart, which was hard for me to figure out. Miss Hale, after all, was a beauty and Mrs. Reinhart had probably never been even passable. I supposed that he was afraid of Wanda Hale while he at least *knew* Mrs. Reinhart. And Perry Hodge, on the other side of the beautiful Wanda, did not speak to her either. But Sara had told me that *he* was in deep fear of his wife's wrath and hardly ever spoke to a strange woman, especially an attractive one. Miss Hale did not seem at all upset. She smiled and concentrated on her food.

Then the consommé was accompanied by the Bâtard-Montrachet and Aunt Bettina drank that too. "A very fine year, don't you think?" she inquired of the dinner partner on her left, a Mr. Dennis Rover, and upon saying the words she inadvertently emptied her glass in Mr. Rover's lap. Frederick, serving as footman, dabbed at Mr. Rover as discreetly as possible.

I wanted to do *something*, thought wildly about saying anything that would divert attention away from my aunt, but I could think of nothing. I looked at Sara but she stared into her soup. Uncle Maurice called down the length of the table in a somewhat loud voice, as if his wife's problem were deafness and not insobriety. "Perhaps you had not better have any more wine, Bettina. You seem a bit . . . indisposed. . . ."

"I'm just fine," a tearful Bettina called back. "Just a little accident. . . ."

"My fault, really," Dennis Rover said, obviously very embarrassed. A tremendous stain crept between and down his legs.

A wine Sara called a Mâconnais was served with the scallops of veal in caper sauce. I, determined now not to look at my aunt at all, marveled at this menu Sara had chosen. How did she know so much about these different dishes? I myself wouldn't have been able to think of anything more original than a ham garnished with pineapple slices and maraschino cherries or maybe, at best, roast turkey with giblet gravy. And the choice of wines? How did Sara know what wine went with what course? *Oh, poor, poor Aunt Bettina! If only the meal would be over.*

"Isn't everything delicious?" I said lamely to Philip Warden, who also seemed to be waiting for whatever would happen next.

Bettina sipped her Mâconnais and declared, "Frankly, Maurice, I don't give a damn," and slid down stiffly in her chair.

I heard someone say, "Scandalous!" I think it was Mrs. Hodge. I took a quick look at Uncle Maurice who was the picture of imperturbability, so much so it seemed almost arrogant. I got to my feet to help Sara and Robert take Aunt Bettina upstairs.

Sara and I put her to bed and sat with her until it was very quiet below and only the servants could be heard clearing away the debris. Then Sara went downstairs and I could hear her talking with her father. Their voices grew progressively louder and louder. Finally, I heard Sara scream, "I hate you! I hate you! I'll never forgive you!"

I tiptoed out into the hall. I saw Maurice Gold going out the front door. "You don't understand, Sara. You're just a child. When you get older, you'll understand. . . ."

"I'll never understand you . . . you Jew!" Sara screamed.

Poor Sara! I guessed that that was the only thing she could think of to say that might hurt her father and I supposed she wanted to hurt him very much.

When Bettina awoke the next day, it was clear that she was "not well." She rambled. At first she thought that Sara was still a baby and that she and her husband were still happy. Then she went back to when she was a little girl in Charleston.

"Martha," she addressed me. "Martha, you didn't have to take my pink hair ribbon—I would have given it to you if you had asked me. No, no, you don't have to give it back. You look right pretty in it. I want you to wear it."

Then she was herself for a while, complained that her head ached, that she felt awful. And where was Maurice? Would we sit and talk to her? Why didn't we show her the new clothes we had bought. Then she asked for her husband again. She seemed to have forgotten the events of the night before. Sara told her that her father was out. Business, of course.

"Of course," Bettina agreed.

Then she asked for a drink. She said that one drink would make the headache go away, would settle her nerves. "Please, Sara, please," she pleaded.

"Mother, you can't. Dr. Harris said—"

"Damn Dr. Harris, Sara. I never liked him, you know." She started to cry.

Again I felt sorry for Sara. How could she be expected to cope with all this? Uncle Maurice *was* a terrible man, to treat his wife so badly and then leave this burden on Sara's shoulders.

Sara did the only thing she could possibly do. She called Dr. Harris. And Dr. Harris called another doctor, a Dr. Annunzio, and then they both talked to Maurice Gold and it was all settled. Bettina was being sent to another sanitarium, a famous one out in the Middle West. And professional nurses would take her there in a private ambulance.

Bettina Gold departed Sunday morning.

Sara mourned the whole day through, seemingly inconsolable. "My fault. I should never have called in Dr. Harris. Mother never did like him. Now they've put her away for good."

"You don't know that it's for good, Sara. If that place she's going to is as good as they say, she'll get better for sure," I tried to console her. "And you did the only thing you could. How could you have gone away to school and left her here like that? Without anyone close to her to care for her. Your father—" I was going to say that Sara's father was not about to sit by her mother's bedside nursing her, but it certainly wasn't my place to say *that*.

"My father! If he hadn't said those things about Mama's drinking in the first place, if he hadn't humiliated her like that, Mama wouldn't have had to be sent away again."

I doubted that this was true but I said nothing.

"And if I weren't going away to school, then I could have stayed with Mother. We could have both stayed in the house."

"Don't you think your mother will stand a better chance of getting well out of this house, *out* of New York, away from—"

Suddenly, Sara beamed. "Of course. You're right. You are just the smartest. My little wise Southern owl. In this house she would never get completely better. I know the best thing for her would be to divorce Daddy. That's what he really wants. That's why he behaves like this. But Mother can't let go, I guess. Who knows? Maybe the doctors at the sanitarium will convince her that's the right thing for her to do. Yes, I guess it's for the best right now. Thank you, Marlena. And thank you for being with me. I don't know how I would have gotten through all this alone."

That night, Maurice Gold came upstairs to Sara's bedroom where we were finishing up our packing. He didn't look well, I noted with some satisfaction. His face was lined and grayish, not tanned and polished looking as it had been Friday night.

"I'd like to talk to you, Sara, in the library. Would you mind coming downstairs with me now?" he asked politely. "And I'll say good-bye to you, Marlena, now. Good luck at school. I'm sure you'll do very well there. Be happy." He held out his hand.

Feeling like a traitor, I took it. How could I not? This man would be paying my tuition.

Sara, wordlessly, went downstairs with her father. In a few minutes their voices rose and could be heard upstairs. I went out into the hall.

"You're despicable!" The soft voice was shrill.

Then Sara started up the stairs. Maurice Gold came to the foot of the stairway and called after her, "You'll understand when you get older. Just wait. You're only a child now. . . ."

I went back into the room, closed the door. I didn't want to look as if I had been eavesdropping. Sara came bursting in. "He wanted to make up with me. Can you believe that? After that horrible dinner. He said that in spite of our differences over Mother . . . everything . . . he wanted me to know how much he loved me. He said I could have anything I wanted. He's opening a checking account for me at a bank near the school. You're to have anything you want too. . . ."

"That's very generous of him."

"No. He just feels guilty. He wants to ease his conscience for the terrible things he's done to Mother. Oh, forget him. I'm going to try and not think about him ever again. Just remember one thing, Marlena. When you choose your man, be sure he's the kind of man that will love you when you're old, not just when you're twenty and beautiful."

57

"You'll be twenty and beautiful," I smiled ruefully. "I'll be twenty and medium plain."

"You're not plain. And you're going to be beautiful. I've decided that we're going to lighten your hair. We'll make you into the girl with the golden hair."

"Oh, Sara. What would my mother say?"

"We'll tell her it was an accident. That a bottle of peroxide accidentally fell from a shelf all over your head."

"She won't believe that."

"Well, then, too bad for her. It'll be too late by then, won't it?"

Such logic overwhelmed me.

"I guess we better go to bed. We have a long trip to Mass. tomorrow."

We prepared for bed. I saw Sara pull something out of a drawer. It was an empty Coke bottle. Sara *was* a little strange, I thought. What was she doing with an empty Coke bottle in her dresser drawer?

"Look what I'm taking to school," Sara said, making a determined effort to be gay.

"An empty Coke bottle?"

Sara laughed. "Remember what we were talking about the other night. How I heard that Southern gals used them instead of a boy's penis. . . ."

"Sara! You're crazy!"

"Let's try it out. Let's see if it really works—"

"Sara, will you please stop?"

"Oh, come on. Honestly, Marlena, sometimes I think you're no fun!"

"Tomorrow, Sara. When we get to school. I'm really tired tonight. Why don't we just go to sleep now?"

"No," Sara said. "I want you to do it now."

"Why must I?"

"Because it's fun. You'll like it. C'mon. Lie down and I'll do it to you just like I was the boy." She opened up her baby doll pajamas and held the Coke bottle to her and pranced around the room wildly. "How do I look?"

"You don't look like any boy," Marlena said.

"How do you know?" Sara asked. "Have you ever seen a boy with his peenie hanging out?"

"You're being horrible, Sara. I don't want to look at you."

"Ho ho ho, little girl," Sara said affecting a deep bass. "I'm going to fuck you."

"Will you stop, Sara?"

"Don't call me Sara, little girl. My name is Waldo," she said in the same deep voice. "Pick up your nightie, little girl."

"No, I won't," I giggled. I was terrified just the same.

"You will. Waldo says so!"

Sara struggled with me, pulling up my shortie nightgown with one hand, fumbling, pushing the Coke bottle at my vagina with the other.

"Will you stop, Sara?" I yelled, frightened. "You're acting like a crazy person! Sara, stop! You're hurting me! Oh, God! You're killing me!"

Sara suddenly withdrew. "I'm sorry, Marlena, I didn't mean— Oh, my God, Marlena! You're bleeding! Marlena! What have I done to you?"

I looked down. Terrified, I saw blood dripping from me, leaking down onto the pink striped sheet. Without thinking, I tried to cover my aching, bloody vagina with my hands as I sobbed.

"Oh, God! Dear heavens!" Sara cried. "Look what we've done! We've gone and busted your cherry!"

CHRISSY

1.

Chrissy Marlowe arrived at Miss Chalmer's School three days before the start of the fall semester. As Albert, her Aunt Gwendolyn's chauffeur, pulled up before the gray stone building modeled like a miniature Scottish medieval castle, Chrissy said wearily, "I think I'm going to reside in this building, Albert. You might as well take my bags in."

Albert looked at the somber castle, an intruder on the sunny landscape that Indian summer day, and said with sympathy in his voice, "Yes, Miss Chrissy," and opened the door for her.

Chrissy stepped out of the black limousine and looked around at the parklike deserted campus. It was clear that when she outgrew her square-cut chunkiness she would be an attractive young woman, but right now everything about her was square—even the bangs that hung almost into the black-cherry eyes, the hair straight and blunt-cut to just below the ears.

She was too warmly dressed in a heavy brown wool suit, but it was after Labor Day and Aunt Gwendolyn had not permitted her to take any light, summery clothes with her. In fact, Aunt Gwen had disposed of all the old things, and the only clothes in Chrissy's present wardrobe were the school uniforms, fall and winter wools and corduroys, and a few velvet dresses. She took off her jacket but was still too warm in the beige cashmere sweater. "I guess I might as well get this over with," she told Albert and went into the building, and he followed with her bags.

The office off the great hall that served as the school's lobby was hectic with the movement of secretaries and clerks, typing, consulting files. Someone told Chrissy to sit down. "Be with you in a few minutes."

She sighed deeply. "Just leave the bags right there, Albert. I'm going to have to wait for my room assignment. And you might as well go. I know Aunt Gwen's expecting you back tonight."

"Are you sure you'll be all right? I can stay with you awhile—"

"Oh, I'll be fine, Albert." She grinned at him, wanting him to know that she wasn't afraid, not even unsure. "I've done this umpteen times. I'm an expert."

Smiling, she was transformed into a very pretty girl. The smile showed her dimples and fine teeth. "I'll walk out with you, Albert, back to the car."

"You don't have to see me off," Albert laughed.

"I don't have anything else to do. They'll probably keep me waiting here all afternoon."

When they got to the car, Chrissy stuck out her hand to the chauffeur. "I guess I'll be seeing you at Christmas, Albert. In the meantime, take care of yourself. And be sure and stop in town and have a good meal before you start back." She felt a lump in her throat. At least Albert was somebody she had known for years. And there weren't many constants in her life.

Even though he knew his employer would not approve, Albert leaned down and gave Chrissy a big hug. She hugged him back. "Take care of yourself and don't smoke too many cigarettes." He winked at her. He would be sure to clean out the ashtray in the rear seat of the limousine before reporting back to Gwendolyn Marlowe.

"Okay." She grinned. "I won't, Albert."

She watched the car disappear down the road. She searched the landscape again for a figure, any figure, and, seeing none, kicked out at the gravel driveway, watched the pebbles scatter, went inside the building again, and slouched down in a chair.

"We have you in room three-ten. You're rooming with Maeve O'Connor. She hasn't arrived yet. You're early, you know. The other girls won't arrive until the thirteenth. You can go on up to your room now. Hoosier will bring up your bags as soon as he gets a chance. We won't have a full staff until the thirteenth. But your trunks are already in your room and you can start unpacking." The secretary smiled, a touch of derision in her voice. "We don't have the personnel to unpack for you, you know."

Chrissy had already acquired enough experience to recognize the petty ridicule of the envious, the resentment of the less socially endowed, and had learned how to deal with it—by acting with the arrogance expected of her.

"I simply *can't* unpack myself. You had better dig up a maid for me."

The secretary smiled with malicious delight. "I'm terribly afraid Miss Chalmer doesn't believe in a young lady not coping with her own needs."

Acting in a shocking manner or saying shocking things had become Chrissy's second line of defense. "Miss Chalmer had better watch her step. I just might decide to foreclose on her fucking mortgage. And tell me, what's to do around this godforsaken fucking place?"

The secretary ignored Chrissy's vocabulary. "The stables are open. You may also use the music room and the library. You *are* early."

"Do tell. Thanks so much. You've been a great help, young lady." Chrissy's voice was rich with sarcasm.

She turned away, not feeling nearly as confident as she made out to be. In fact, she was frightened. A new school was always frightening the first few days. She never got used to that hellish, scary feeling of being so goddamn alone.

"Hey, Carrie," the secretary called to the woman sitting at the next desk, as Chrissy went out the door. "Did you catch her? Do you know who that was? Chrissy Marlowe, the one from the newspapers, the tragic little rich girl." Her voice dripped sarcasm.

"You don't say." Carrie patted her jellyroll bun. "The poor little thing. How'd she act? Poor or rich?"

"Rich. Just like any rich bitch."

"Hmm. Remind me to cry into my beer for her tonight."

Chrissy trudged up the stairs to the third floor. Without actually knowing, she had figured out where to go from experience. The first floor was lobby and offices and chapel; the second floor housed dining hall, music room, library, and auditorium; the third floor was reserved for first-year students. She knew that the more stairs you climbed, the lower your year standing, except for schools in Maine where the ground-floor windows were snowed under. There was a red-brick building across the road—second-, third-, and fourth-year students were domiciled there, with the fourth-year students most surely situated on the first floor.

She hadn't needed that lousy secretary to remind her she had arrived three days before the start of the term. It had been convenient for Aunt Gwen to have her arrive today—not tomorrow or two days after.

Room 310 was austere. The rooms at boarding school were inevitably, painfully plain. She had heard from other girls that European schools frequented by rich Americans were a *bit* more luxurious, but not much. Chrissy guessed the austerity was in some way connected to building character in the children of the rich. She had been told that the schools in England the nobility attended were the worst of all for grim, bare appointments.

There were two narrow beds, two chests of drawers, two desks, two straight chairs. Without looking, Chrissy knew there would be two closets. It was considered sporting to take the better bed if you arrived first, but not the better closet. Accordingly, she lay down on one bed, then the other. One bed was almost imperceptibly less lumpy and she took that one for herself. Then she examined the two closets, and hung her suit jacket in the less spacious one. Not that she cared about being sporting. She just wanted to show to whomever showed up that closets were not important to her, that she didn't give a damn.

"I don't give a damn," she said aloud to the closet.

She lay down on the unmade bed, took out a pack of Lucky Strikes from her brown leather pouch bag, shook out a cigarette, tapped it on the back of her hand, and lit it with the gold lighter she had taken from Aunt Gwen's handbag before she left. She looked around for an ashtray. Of course there weren't any. Smoking was considered a major crime, especially in the rooms. But she had her own ashtray. She took it with her from school to school. She located the trunk keys in her purse, knelt, opened one of the monogrammed trunks, and fished around until she felt the square glass tray. It was crystal, marked with a large *M* cut into its surface. She had filched it from her Grandmother Marlowe's house four years before, when she had first taken up smoking.

Everything in Grandmother Marlowe's house had been marked with the *M,* even the toilet seat lids, though Chrissy had once heard a friend of her Grandmother Marlowe's whisper to another friend that *that* was terribly vulgar.

Red *M*s marked the bathroom towels, blue ones embroidered the sheets, gold or silver ones decorated the china, fancifully swirled *M*s engraved the flatware, and the stationery was embossed with tasteful dark gray ones. When she was very young and first came to live with Grandmother Marlowe, Chrissy admired the monograms, thought the display of the initial throughout the house a lovely custom. Later, when she discovered the Marlowe *M* also displayed on railroad cars and towering oil drums all over the countryside, on signs marking land developments and on the walls of banking institutions, Chrissy realized that the use of the monogram was more than a decorative flight of fancy. The Marlowes wanted to mark *everything* for their very own.

A discreet knock on the door. Chrissy expertly pinched out the burning tip of her cigarette with two fingers, knocking off the ash onto the floor without searing her flesh. She stepped on the ash, dropped the dead cigarette into the ashtray and shoved it under the bed with one foot. "Yes?" she called out, fanning the smoky air with her hand.

"It's Miss Chalmer, my dear. I've come to welcome you."

The door opened and a bird of a woman stepped into the room, small with skinny legs, bright little eyes that blinked sharply, a beaked nose. She sniffed at the air and smiled. "This room has not been aired properly." She went to the window and hoisted it wide. Tiny specks of dust rode the beams of sunlight.

"It's so pleasant to have you with us, Christina, my dear. I knew your grandmother. What a fine woman. And we had a Marlowe girl with us a few years ago. One of your Connecticut cousins, I believe. Or, perhaps, it was a Rhode Island connection? The Calvin Marlowe family? Your grandfather was a most distinguished figure. And I'm sure you're going to make a most distinguished record for yourself here at Chalmer's. Which reminds me—your roommate will be Maeve O'Connor. She's the daughter of the very distinguished writer, Padraic O'Connor. And little Maeve has never attended a boarding school before. I know you will help her accustom herself to the style of our school, take her under your wing, so to speak." She lifted one arm, chickenlike, to suggest what was to be done with Maeve O'Connor.

Chrissy wondered what poor Maeve's problem was that she was to be her, Chrissy's, roommate.

"Yes, Miss Chalmer. I'll do whatever I can."

"Good. Then that's settled. Now, have you unpacked your trunks yet?" the headmistress asked expectantly, although the clearly still packed trunks sat in the middle of the room.

"I was just about to do that," Chrissy said, looking down at the floor.

"Good. Good. Tonight you will eat dinner with me, since none of the other girls have arrived yet. Six o'clock, my dear, in my private dining room. Please be on time. And now, would you like to give me your pack of cigarettes, my dear?" She held out her hand, a tiny smile on her lips, a twitch of the beak's nostrils.

Chrissy dug out the pack of Luckies from her purse and wordlessly passed them over. She was not even surprised that Miss Chalmer had surmised that she had been smoking. Not with that beak. Nor was she alarmed. She had packs of cigarettes secreted throughout her luggage, stuffed into pockets of jackets and skirts, in shoes, in stockings and gloves, hidden among the folds of nightgowns and slips.

"Good. It's best to remove the temptation if one does not have the moral fiber to resist. But that is not to say, conclusively, that you do not have the moral fiber. We will find out more about that in the days to come, won't we, my dear? Six sharp, then." And she was gone, having flown out the door in a small burst of lifted, fluttering arms.

Without changing expression, Chrissy went to her trunk, lifted out a large pasteboard box, opened it, and withdrew another package of Luckies. She tore at the foiled corner of the fresh pack and withdrew a cigarette, lit it and, sitting on the floor leaning against the bed, blew several smoke rings.

Then she pulled the heavy box over to her. Besides more packs of cigarettes, the box held her most precious possessions, her most secret things—her newspaper clippings and her photographs. She sifted through the clippings again, for the thousandth time. These clippings were the story of her life, all the missing parts that she could not possibly know of without them; some of the clippings told of events she could not possibly remember. Some of the events she remembered well. She had collected these pieces of paper herself, slowly, with painstaking research and a lot of pain. And what the clippings didn't reveal, eavesdropping through the years had.

2.

They were a legendary couple—Christina Hatton and George Edward Marlowe. Christina Hatton was beautiful, charming, and her style had set fashions—it was said she managed to look both debutante and flapper at the same time. And George was handsome, dashing, the polo-playing heir of the Harding Marlowe branch of the Marlowe family, railroad people, land developers, American aristocrats.

Christina and George Marlowe lived in a French chateau on an estate in Long Island and *made* their name socially when they played host to the Prince of Wales (Albert Christian George Andrew Patrick David Windsor). Christina had had the entire grounds decorated with ropes of tiny little lights woven into the shrubbery; colored lights hung in the trees; ninety people sat down to a formal dinner and a thousand more were invited for after dinner to meet the prince and to dance to Paul Whiteman's Orchestra. And if this party weren't enough to establish the Marlowes as the foremost leaders of Society's younger set, the prince elected to be their houseguest for several weeks. To top off this coup was the fact that the prince, later known as the Duke of Windsor, deigned to go *nowhere* else socially. Newport Society had extended invitations, of course. Were not their facilities for polo the very best? But the gay young prince had completely eschewed Newport's invitations, including, notably, that of Christina's mother-in-law, Patricia Marlowe, who was in residence at her Newport estate, the Watershed, at the time.

Patricia Marlowe never liked Christina Hatton. She considered the young woman "wild," at the same time ignoring her son George's unsavory prenuptial peccadillos. First, there were those stories about Christina's grandfather and grandmother. The story went that Christina's grandfather, Horace Hatton, had married his wife right out of the *Louvre* a famous New York bordello of the mid-nineteenth century, known for its elegant appointments—indoor fountains, marble decor—*and* its staff of French beauties who had come to American shores to make their fortunes with their bodies. The *Louvre* was frequented only by the scions of New York Society—it was very expensive—and it was said that it was here that Horace Hatton first laid eyes on the beautiful Colette. After he married her, he *insisted* she had just arrived from Paris, the daughter of a duke.

There was more that Patricia Marlowe found objectionable in her daughter-in-law's pedigree. Horace Hatton's son, Jason, Christina's father, went West when he was eighteen, seeking adventure. Instead, he found gold and became richer than any Hatton before him. He also married the daughter of a miner who had literally discovered gold with his two bare hands A gentleman *never* made his fortune with his bare hands.

Despite his mother's objections, George married Christina amid great coverage by the press. Their wedding cake was five feet tall, the biggest wedding cake New York had ever seen.

The profligate life-style George and his bride immediately commenced did nothing to alleviate Patricia Marlowe's disdain for her daughter-in-law. As far as she was concerned, it was Christina who imposed the ostentatious spending, boozing, and jazzing about on an innocent George. It was Christina who encouraged George to spend his time on horses, sailing, gambling and dancing, even to cavort with people of the films and stage. It was Christina who generated all the hideous publicity the Marlowe family was receiving.

Worst of all, and this too was Christina's doing, George paid no mind to the family fortune and interests. Thus, the family business affairs had to be relegated to George's sister Gwendolyn's husband, Rudolph Winslow. This distressed Patricia Marlowe most of all. Rudolph, after all, was a Winslow and Marlowe affairs required a Marlowe's direction. Besides, Patricia Marlowe had no love for Rudolph Winslow, either.

When George and Christina's daughter, Chrissy, was born, Patricia Marlowe expected the young couple to settle down. But they went on with their usual behavior, and baby Chrissy was handed over to nurses, nannies and servants.

When Mrs. Marlowe complained to her daughter Gwen, herself the mother of three, about the way Christina was raising George's daughter, Gwen heartily agreed. She, too, disliked her sister-in-law, who was stunning and frivolous while she, Gwendolyn, was plain and shackled to a life of decorum and responsibility.

Then George had a boating accident and died, and the feelings of dislike Patricia Marlowe and her daughter felt for Christina intensified into a deep hatred. They blamed Christina for George's death. If she had not been so frivolous, George would have been less so too, would have been working, possibly, instead of boating without purpose. Then, instead of going into proper mourning and tending to her fatherless child, Christina was dashing about New York to cocktail parties, restaurants, the theater, and speakeasies with sundry unsavory men who were most certainly her lovers, and women friends who lived lives of equal disrepute.

When Patricia Marlowe and Gwendolyn Winslow cluck-clucked over Christina's suitability to raise the Marlowe heiress, Christina judged her adversaries well. She packed her bags and her daughter Chrissy, and shifted her operations to London.

Chrissy's own hazy recollections started with those London days. She was four then and there were some things she remembered. There were even things she *thought* she remembered from before that, from when her father was alive. Such as the wicker baby carriage. She could have sworn she recalled that wicker baby carriage; being in it, being wheeled around by her father. Then, later, she had come upon a photograph of her father laughing, with one hand holding on to the carriage, the other waving at the camera, and she realized that the recollection had been formed by the photograph, not by reality.

The actual memories *must* have started in London. She had hazy visions of her mother in splendid evening gowns—a black velvet with a hem of golden-colored fur, an emerald green satin gown with only tiny straps to support it, a red taffeta sprinkled with little shiny stones—kissing her good night as she departed for an evening of gaiety, leaving behind a memory of the delicious scent of gardenias. Later on in her life, Chrissy would occasionally detect the perfume's presence somewhere—in an elevator, perhaps—and a whole sea of images would crowd her memory.

She had never found out the name of that perfume . . . she only knew the odor conjured up a picture of her mother—green eyes, dark hair—kissing her, Chrissy, fleetingly. . . .

Chrissy's London days were filled with governesses, nurses, and music teachers, and a chauffeur who took her and the nanny for rides through the park. She could play simple pieces on the piano by the time she was five. And she could do simple recitations, too; little bits of poems with gestures and strong emphases. When visitors came for tea or cocktails, ladies in silk dresses and bits of satin hats or big hats with flowers, and slim gentlemen with ascots and mustaches, carrying silver-handled canes or riding crops or shiny top hats in the crook of their arms, Chrissy would be called into the salon to perform. She would do her recitations and the ladies would say, "darling," or "adorable," the dapper gentlemen would find her "jolly good" or "charming." But then they would take her mother away with them, and her mother would be gone, leaving in the usual flurry of fur and chiffon and perfume, and Chrissy would be alone again with the nanny or governess or maid.

Years later, the newspaper clippings would reveal to Chrissy that one of these dapper gentlemen who had come to the house and taken her mother about, was the Prince of Wales, the same prince who had once visited with her mother and father when they lived on the Island. Some reviewers of the social scene surmised that the torrid romance between Christina Marlowe and the prince had commenced back then while George Marlowe was still very much alive.

The newspaper clippings also disclosed that Christina eventually lost the prince to Wally Simpson, the American divorcée who brought on the abdication of the throne. Strangely enough, Wally Simpson had been Christina's friend, the two of them sharing the distinction of being Americans adventuring in England, and Wally's romance with the prince had only commenced when Christina went back to the United States to try to regain custody of her daughter. This became necessary after the Marlowes, Patricia and Gwendolyn, engineered the kidnapping of Chrissy one foggy spring day in London.

Chrissy was in Gramercy Park that afternoon with her nanny, Miss Poole, when Gwendolyn, accompanied by two oversized men with thin lips and derbies, materialized. Miss Poole would not have been a match for the grim, determined Gwendolyn, much less for the two burly professionals who accompanied her. And so, a few hours later, Chrissy was on a ship bound for America. Gwendolyn, displaying true American know-how and ingenuity, had laid her plans well. The timing of the abduction concurred perfectly with the departure of the *Queen Mary,* and with Christina's absence from London. Christina was with David, Prince of Wales, at Sandringham, the country estate of the British monarchs, some 110 miles northeast of London. Christina was not even contacted until the *Queen Mary* was well out of port and on its way to New York and Patricia Marlowe.

Chrissy didn't enjoy life in Grandmother Marlowe's Park Avenue house, with its painted ceilings, flowers and fruits in wreaths, encircling the Marlowe monogram. Grandmother Marlowe was a woman of stern manner and rigid etiquette, not given to shows of idle affection. She listened to the six-year-old's piano renditions and mannered recitations with grave attention, but not a "divine" or "charming" passed her lips. Rather, Chrissy was urged to do better, to strive for perfection.

The grandmother admitted to intimates that the child was "clever," but then, many children were clever, even those raised on the streets of the city, so to speak. A governess was hired to tutor Chrissy in all the subjects that Patricia Marlowe deemed suitable for a well-educated young lady.

The only good times in that house that Chrissy would be able to recall later, were when her cousins, Aunt Gwen's offspring, came to visit. They were older than she—the youngest three years older than Chrissy —but that didn't matter. Chrissy adored them and trailed after them, did everything they did.

The summer at the Watershed in Newport was better. The cousins were there almost the whole two months and with them their pets— the pony, Doolittle, the Scottish terrier called Terror, the one-eyed cat, Ralph, named in honor of a cockney groom at their Old Westbury estate who had one green glass eye.

The cousins and Chrissy could not have cared less that their summer "cottage" was an Italian Renaissance palace. The cottage was right on the ocean and they were allowed to swim for at least two hours a day in the presence of their private swimming instructor. They played croquet and blind man's bluff, and went sailing, accompanied by an old fisherman who lived in Newport the year round who was glad to earn the extra summer money. Of course, there were the boring daily music lessons, which took up an hour-and-a-half precisely and were held in the Grand Salon, called the Music Room for the occasion.

All four of the grandchildren participated, taking alternate turns at the piano and the flute. Chrissy passed the time waiting for her turn by studying the magnificent ceiling—it was part coffered, part coved, finished in silver and gold and painted in classical fashion with figures representing Harmony, Music, Song, and Melody. Then, there were two very grand chandeliers to study. One could spend hours trying to count all the pendulant crystals.

When Chrissy was seven, her mother arrived in New York to press suit for custody of her daughter. She filed charges of kidnapping against her mother- and sister-in-law but was persuaded to drop those charges in return for temporary custody of her child while the suit was being resolved. In order to show that she was prepared to offer a proper home for her daughter, Christina bought an estate in Old Westbury practically on top of the Winslows', and stocked it with horses, a Scotty dog that Chrissy named Mac, and a St. Bernard called Sam. Chrissy was enrolled in a day school nearby. Every morning for a while, her mother rose at eight to drive her to school herself, realizing that this would score valuable points in court.

Chrissy was ecstatic, happier than she had ever been in London or on Park Avenue, even happier than she had been at the Watershed in Newport. She had her mother, her lovely, sweet-smelling mother who laughed all the time, and *nobody* had as wonderful a laugh as her mother. She had friends at school and had a birthday party that was attended by all the girls in her class. The girls rode Chrissy's pony, and a trained monkey, dressed like a clown, danced with them, climbed a tree and pelted them with apple blossoms.

But after a few weeks, the country life palled on Christina and, needing more excitement in her life, she started inviting friends from New York to parties that lasted until dawn. After these parties she was not up at eight to drive Chrissy to school. And it happened sometimes that, through inattention, Chrissy was allowed to stay up all night too, until she fell asleep on a living-room sofa or, unobserved, under the circular stairway. So Chrissy didn't always make it to school on time, and sometimes, not at all.

But Chrissy did learn to mix drinks. Her mother taught her and her mother's friends thought it was an especially divine parlor trick.

Then Christina Marlowe's crowd tired of traveling to Old Westbury for their partying. It was all right for the occasional weekend but a bore to be doing constantly. It meant killing a couple of days—and all the restaurants, cabarets, and fun places were in the city. Soon, Christina herself was seen dancing all night at private clubs in the city, attending the theater, frequenting nightclubs, being photographed at the races. And, unfortunately, the staff at the house constantly changed, so that no one assumed the specific authority to see to it that Chrissy attended school every day, and thus she often didn't.

When the custody suit finally came to trial, the newspapers had a field day. Gwen Marlowe Winslow provided many witnesses, some of them servants who had served on Christina's staff, to testify that Chrissy was rarely sent to school, but knew how to mix an excellent martini. Patricia Marlowe testified as to how Christina Hatton had wooed her son to the dissolute life and to his final death. She failed to mention that before marrying the decadent Christina, George, at age twenty, had disgraced the Marlowe name by marrying a thirty-five-year-old black woman, a marriage that Patricia had had immediately annulled. Or that upon coming of age and into his inheritance, George had celebrated his twenty-first birthday by losing $200,000 at a gambling house.

There was testimony by friends of the Marlowe family of wild sexual orgies in London, Paris, and Cannes in which Christina Hatton Marlowe took prominent part. The judge was even shown certain pictures.

But Christina was not without friends to testify in her behalf. From London and Paris came princes and peeresses, dukes and baronesses to rally around their friend and attest to what a splendid woman Christina was—warm, generous, and witty—and how, when Chrissy was living with her mother in London, she was always at her mother's side. But the American court, caught in the gloom of the Depression, was not sympathetic to the sybaritic European royalty, and their testimony did more harm to Christina's cause than not.

Finally, near the end of the trial, Chrissy, dressed in a blue velvet coat with an ermine collar and a little ermine muff, was brought into the courtroom.

The judge took her to his chambers to talk to her in private. He asked Chrissy if she understood what was going on—that a choice was being made as to whom she would live with. He told her that her mother wanted her, as did her grandmother and aunt. Chrissy told the judge that she wanted very much to be with her mother. She told the judge how much she loved her beautiful mother—didn't the judge think her mother beautiful?—how she loved her pony, Wimpy, and her two dogs, Sam and Mac; how perfect life would be if they all could be together more, her mother, herself, the two dogs and the pony. Couldn't the judge tell her mother to stay with them all the time?

Judge Watley asked Chrissy if it were true that she played the piano very well, and was it also true, as he had heard, that she could mix a very good martini.

"Yes, sir. Very dry. And I can make a Manhattan too, if you would like. And I know card tricks. My mother's friend, Uncle David, taught me some really good ones. And I can recite too. Uncle Freddy taught me a funny one. Would you like to hear it?"

Judge Watley said he would and Chrissy recited for him:

> There was a young hermit named Dave
> Who kept a dead whore in his cave.
> He said, I admit
> I'm a bit of a shit
> But look at the money I save.

Judge Watley ruled in favor of Patricia Marlowe and Gwendolyn Marlowe Winslow. While they would bear joint custody and would jointly administer the estate of $3,000,000 Chrissy had inherited from her father, Chrissy would make her home with Gwen and Rudolph Winslow and the three Winslow children. But Christina Marlowe was granted visiting rights.

Christina broke down in court and cried. "I love her! I love her! Why won't anyone understand how much I love her?" Chrissy was to remember these words all her life.

Aunt Gwen and Uncle Rudolph led Chrissy out of the courtroom. She turned back and cried to her mother: "Mommy, when will you come visit me?"

Unfortunately, at that moment Christina was busy being comforted by her friends. She did not hear Chrissy's plea. And, so, she did not make a last and final contact with her daughter, who had to be forcibly restrained by Uncle Rudolph from running back to her mother.

Christina sold the estate in Old Westbury; it was of no further use to her. Finding life in New York both painful and boring, she returned to her old stamping grounds, London. Discovering the loss of her old beau, the prince, who had been taken by that common Wallis Simpson, Christina married a baron. Wilhelm von Steuben, who, though poor and not as much fun as George had been, was extremely handsome and descended from the Hohenzollerns. And he *was* brighter than the prince, but few people were not.

Christina wasn't quite sure whom she was spiting by marrying Willy, the Marlowes or the prince, but in the end it didn't much matter. Within three weeks, deciding that Willy was a bore in bed, she proceeded to cheat on him. And sorry that she had married him at all, she refused to give her husband the cash he needed to pay his gambling debts. Between the

71

cheating and the money, the baron was in a pique. Especially so about the money.

A year or so later, just days before Christina was to depart for American shores to take advantage of her visitation rights to her daughter, the baron resolved to avenge his dwindling honor. Whether he meant to shoot only Christina's lover of the day, the Earl of Wimbledon, upon finding Christina and the earl in bed together, or whether he meant to kill them both, was never firmly established. He fired two shots and both the earl and Christina, *flagrante delicto* in reversed missionary position, were killed instantly.

Had the baron managed to entrap the lovers in France or Italy, he would have fared better in the courts. But he killed the lovers in Christina's Mayfair flat and the English courts proved not as understanding of dishonored husbands as the Italian or French courts may have been. Besides, the baron was not a British citizen and the earl had had friends in high places. The baron was given twenty years.

In the meantime Chrissy had been happy at Aunt Gwen's, what with the three cousins, the ponies, the dogs, and the one-eyed cat. And if Aunt Gwen and Uncle Rudolph hadn't been exactly warm, they hadn't been mean, either. And Chrissy hadn't had to see Grandmother Marlowe too often—only during the summer at the Watershed, and for three weeks in winter at Palm Beach. But even then, the cousins' presence had helped. And she only thought about her mother once or twice a day and at night when she said her prayers.

There *was* something that puzzled her. *If* her mother had wanted to see her, why had she gone away to live? If she had stayed close by, they could have at least visited sometimes—the judge had said they could visit. And why did her mother hardly ever write to her? She, Chrissy, had written her mother loads of letters telling her about the school she went to, the games she played. . . . In return, she received presents and postcards but so few letters. And she was allowed to keep hardly any of the presents—the toys were judged by Aunt Gwen too young for her, or too old, and the clothes "unsuitable." But she had kept all the cards— the birthday card, the Christmas card, the picture postcards from Rome and Paris and the Riviera, and even one from Hong Kong.

That was one part of the puzzle. The other was that if Aunt Gwen fought for her in court, how come she didn't love her more? Aunt Gwen didn't smile at her or hardly ever, didn't kiss or hug her or tell her that she was an adorable baby. Were all adults like that? Did they love you only when they thought they might lose you?

When Gwen Winslow informed Chrissy of her mother's death, the little girl screamed and cried for hours. Later, when Rudolph Winslow returned from his trip, Gwen told him of the scene. "I can't understand why the child took it so hard. I'm sure she can hardly even remember her mother."

After two weeks of Chrissy's unrelenting mourning, Patricia Marlowe remarked: "It's the bad Hatton blood coming out in the girl. She'll have to be cleansed of it, one way or another."

Gwen frowned. "She'll have to go to boarding school, I think. They'll take her in hand. She'll learn not to be so self-indulgent."

Patricia Marlowe agreed.

Chrissy was sent to the St. Matthew School in upstate New York. She did not do well there. Sometimes she cried the whole night through. "Too emotional," was the headmistress's qualified opinion. "Perhaps a school in Europe?" she suggested.

Chrissy went off to the Hasley School for Girls in Baltimore. She lasted a year there, at the end of which Miss Hasley said, "Too head-strong. I feel that perhaps she would do better at another school. She's not really what we expect of a Hasley girl—a discordant note in our harmonious group, one might say." She suggested the Marlowes try a school in France. "They do place a different emphasis on things, you know."

Patricia Marlowe was very much against a European education. She had sent her own son, George, to Le Rosey, the school near Lausanne, and look what happened to poor George! All those foreigners. Germans and Yugoslavians and Russians and all kinds of flotsam. And they all majored in buggery, if you asked her. What had they taught George there but to gamble and drink? And George never did learn to multiply properly. Skiing was really the only skill he became proficient in.

"Besides, Gwendolyn, how can we send the child to Europe when war might be breaking out any day? She *is* poor George's child, after all."

Gwen laughed. "Of course, Mother. What *was* that woman thinking of? We could hardly send her to Europe. But *where* will we send her? It's going to be extremely difficult placing her after these dismissals."

"Don't be ridiculous, Gwendolyn. We are Marlowes."

Chrissy was sent north to a school in Maine. She was expelled in the middle of the year for consistent and unrepentant smoking. The New England Yankees were not amused by the spectacle of a child not yet eleven puffing away on a cigarette. But for a small endowment, they were persuaded to let Chrissy stay until the end of the school year.

Gwen Winslow was at her wit's end. What was to be done with the girl? Everything was going so well with her own children, Rudy at Exeter, Hardy at St. Paul's, Gwennie at Briarville in Virginia. "I will not ask Briarville to take her, Mother. I *will* not have Gwennie's education and peace of mind disturbed by Christina's problem child."

"Be quiet, Gwendolyn. I did not suggest you send Chrissy to Briar-ville. To the contrary. It's clear to me that the girl has to be more closely supervised by family. She has to be kept at home and sent to a day school."

"But that would be extremely difficult for me now, Mother. With the three children away, Rudolph and I were planning on all sorts of lovely things—perhaps a trip to Mexico. . . ."

Patricia Marlowe clamped her jaw tightly. "I was not suggesting she live with you and Rudolph again. I plan to take charge of the girl myself. But as for you and Rudolph going to Mexico, I don't think that would be particularly wise at the moment. With world affairs as they are, Rudolph would be better put keeping his nose to the grindstone for a change . . . and keeping his wandering eye on business."

"What *are* you talking about, Mother? After all Rudolph has done for the family! Sacrificing himself to look after the Marlowe affairs!"

"Poor Rudolph," Patricia Marlowe snorted, not nicely. There were stories about Rudolph she would have enjoyed filling her daughter's ear with but this wasn't the time. Right now, she had to take charge of George's child. Chrissy needed a firm hand, as George himself had.

Chrissy was enrolled in Wilton's in New York City. Wilton's was reputed to have a special way with the troubled children of Society's elite. Patricia Marlowe arranged a schedule for Chrissy to follow. She would be delivered to the Wilton's door by Mundy, the chauffeur, who would pick her up again at three and deliver her back to the Marlowe residence. Chrissy would then proceed with either her music lesson or music practice, depending on the day of the week, for two hours. She would then be permitted a free half-hour to change for dinner. Dinner would be taken with her grandmother, if her grandmother was not dining out. Dinner would be followed by a minimum of two hours' homework followed by a free hour to take care of personal needs, and perhaps a bit of reading. Bedtime would be at ten. She would have a religious class on Saturdays, which, hopefully, would teach her to conduct herself within a framework of strong moral strictures. Sunday, of course, she would accompany Mrs. Marlowe to St. John's. If for any reason Patricia Marlowe was not able to attend services, Chrissy would attend by herself.

Three weeks into September, Patricia Marlowe was off to Saratoga Springs where she took the baths. Many years before, she had made annual treks to Baden-Baden to take advantage of the thermal springs and to drink the *Friedrichquelle* that flushed the kidneys. But she had wearied of the place. Too full of foreigners, too German, too French, too decadent. Now she preferred the simplicity of Saratoga.

After Saratoga, Patricia Marlowe was off to visit her invalid sister in Louisville. She would not stay long—she detested Louisville, famous for tobacco, bourbon and the Derby, all odious, but duty called. Go she would, but always in the fall and never in the spring when the Derby took place. She had no wish to rub shoulders with the hoi polloi.

She was back in New York for a week before she departed for Bermuda. At least Bermuda was *civilized,* the service at the Princess was bearable, and there were no Jews. There was something to be said for that.

After Bermuda, she was in New York for a short while to attend the opera and the Philharmonic. She was, after all, on the Philharmonic's board. And she wanted to make sure that Chrissy was kept to her schedule. Then she was off to her Palm Beach cottage. Chrissy would come down when her school broke for Christmas vacation.

While Patricia Marlowe was absent from New York, the housekeeper, Mrs. Hubbard, was entrusted to see that Chrissy was kept to her schedule and the standards of the great Marlowe house were not relaxed. Every morning and evening Chrissy ate by herself in the fifty-foot dining room at the twenty-foot dining-room table, attended by two formally attired butlers. Throughout her meal, Chrissy amused herself by counting the people she disliked, by enumerating all those who had betrayed her. And her grandmother was not far from the top of the list. No longer did she wonder why her grandmother spent so little time with her. She no longer cared enough to wonder.

At Wilton's, part of the program included talks with a psychologist. While Chrissy spent these sessions for the most part in stony silence or answering questions in as few words as necessary, the psychologist's questions started her thinking more about her past. This was when she started her collection of newspaper clippings, at first unearthing a shoe box of them in a corner of her grandmother's wardrobe, then going to the public library and discovering a whole file on the Marlowe and Hatton families. She laboriously copied down everything she couldn't steal or acquire in some other way. Then she went through all the photographs in her grandmother's albums, appropriating those that included her father and mother. Those pictures, added to the ones she had received from the nice London executor of her mother's estate, made up Chrissy Marlowe's private album.

Chrissy behaved herself at Wilton's. She disliked the other "problem" children, the teachers, the psychologist, and she made no friends, but still she preferred staying there to starting somewhere else again. She would just bide her time until she was eighteen. Then, she would come into the money left her by her mother—five million dollars. She would get the three million dollars from her father's estate when she was twenty-one.

When spring came that year, it brought an influenza epidemic that carried off Patricia Marlowe. Chrissy stood at the gravesite stone-faced, stone-hearted, dry-eyed. She had been taught by her grandmother and her aunt that it was ill-bred to display grief, churlish, even craven to feel it.

Chrissy inherited another one million dollars, as did her three cousins.

Gwen Winslow was disappointed in that she only inherited $6,000,000 in actual cash. Patricia Marlowe had left the rest of her fortune to various charities that would honor her name. Gwen did, however, get the house on Park Avenue, the house in Newport, and the house in Palm Beach, as well as control of the Marlowe enterprises.

Either Gwen Winslow found her mother's death to be a liberating experience, or she was so stricken with grief that she suffered some sort of a breakdown. In any event, one week after she buried her mother, she filed for divorce from Rudolph Winslow. Had she finally discovered Rudolph's dalliances? Was she tired of his inept management of the Marlowe enterprises? Or had she just been waiting for her mother to pass on? Patrician Patricia would never *allow* divorce to sully the family name. One *controlled* one's husband, or even ignored him, but one did not divorce.

The answer was that Gwen had just decided she would enjoy life as she never had—the visitation of death had impressed upon her that it was later than one thought. She would rid herself of her unfaithful, annoying, and boring husband, of her Old Westbury estate and its responsibilities, of the burdensome Marlowe enterprises—of its control anyway. She would allow the Marlowe companies to go public, which would put Rudolph and the burden out of her life at the same time. She would be free, free, free—just as she was of her mother.

She closed up the house on Park Avenue. It required far too much time to run properly. She moved into a suite at the Plaza and went into a frenzy of redecoration, enlisting the aid of Lady Mendl, the decorator Elsie de Wolfe of international celebrity. Elsie's Art Deco was such a refreshing departure from the old-hat furnishings Gwen had always lived with.

She would, in a few months' time, lose twenty pounds, pare a half-inch from her nose, and have her face tautened. Eventually, she would become one of New York's café society, whereas before she had been one of the Old Guard. She would sit on the zebra-striped banquettes of El Morocco along with Brenda Frazier and Cobina Wright, Jr., and the other debs and post-debs of the times, who were all very much her junior. But if she were too old for this sort of thing, nobody would mention it. And certainly her young, handsome escorts would never dare mention it. She paid them too well for that.

In June Gwen Marlowe (she dropped the Winslow the day she filed for divorce) told Chrissy that she was through at Wilton's, that come fall she would be going to another boarding school as the Park Avenue house was being closed and it wouldn't do for a young girl to be living at the Plaza. As for Old Westbury, a developer was putting up a lot of little houses where the Winslow house had stood.

Chrissy stood stolidly, unmoved, apparently unshaken. She asked only about the animals—the dogs and the horses. "What have you done with them?"

"For the time being I've shipped them to Newport. We'll have to see about them later. Aren't you going to ask me what school will have you now?"

Chrissy pushed the bangs from her eyes. "What school?"

"If you're going to act surly, I don't know if I'll tell you at all."

Gwen Marlowe found the perfect school in Montreal. Her mother, damn her soul for getting her into this problem in the first place, would have been pleased. Chrissy's French was not what it should have been— due no doubt to the lack of continuity in her schooling. And those Catholics would know how to deal with the recalcitrant Chrissy. If Patricia Marlowe hadn't detested the Papists so, Gwen would have had no compunctions about putting Chrissy in a convent school altogether, but she was afraid to go that far—her mother might rise from her grave and spook her.

"And since you *are* going to school in Montreal in the fall, I think it would be wise for you to attend a French-speaking camp in Quebec this summer instead of wasting your time at Newport."

Chrissy said nothing, just pulled on her ear, rubbed at her black-cherry eyes.

"Don't do that!" Gwen spoke sharply. "Please." She consciously softened her tone. "Haven't you learned yet not to keep fussing with yourself? A lady does not touch her face, rub her eyes or her nose, or pick at her hair." And then with irritation, "And pull down your skirt. It's hiked up on the left side. Do try to lose a few pounds at camp."

In a patient, kinder tone: "I will give your best to Rudy, Hardy, and Gwennie. Perhaps we will find time for you to come down to Newport for a few days, after all."

Gwen had a momentary twinge of pity for the unsmiling girl. She *was* rather alone in the world. "At any rate, we will manage to do some shopping in the fall for clothes and you will come down to the city for that. I can see that skirt is already too tight. Shall I give your regards to Gwennie and the boys?"

Again Chrissy didn't answer.

She didn't give a stinking damn for her cousins. They too were on the list of betrayers; they too had forgotten she existed.

"Answer me."

"Yes. Give my regards."

It was easier that way. She was tired of fighting.

3.

L'Ecole de St. Jean Baptiste, named for the French Canadian patron, stood at the foot of Mount Royal, a gray limestone building in the Gothic shadow of the parish church of Notre Dame. Its headmistress, Marie Perigord, had hoped to be a nun but had not been able to withstand the physical rigors of religious life, and had turned instead to the tutoring of female children of the rich, but still in the service of the Lord. She ran her school as a combination of finishing school and convent. Her girls studied religion, French, art, music, embroidery, literature, history, English, mathematics and science, in that order, with a depreciating emphasis as one got to the end of the list.

Gwen Marlowe, upon making a large endowment to Marie Perigord's school in addition to the usual tuition (necessitated because Mademoiselle Perigord did not usually accept non-Catholics), had asked that since Chrissy *was* not a Catholic and *was* proficient at the piano (*her only accomplishment, for God's sake*), could they stress the music in her case, and let up a bit on some of the religious instruction? Since Mademoiselle Perigord was a woman of some principle—she had accepted Gwen Marlowe's endowment—she acquiesced. It was agreed that Chrissy would have private piano lessons with Mademoiselle Jacqueline Payot, in addition to the usual class music lessons.

The moment Chrissy viewed the slender, almost ethereal, Mademoiselle Payot, a yearning entered her lonely soul. Dressed in the usual black, adorned only by a rope of pearls creamy as her own skin, the thirtyish music teacher gave off a certain essence of elegant delicacy that vaguely reminded Chrissy of the days so long ago, the London days, the Mayfair salon.

The private lessons with the music teacher were the best part of Chrissy's day. No, not the best part . . . the only good part. Her only disappointment was that Mademoiselle Jacqueline, as Chrissy was permitted to call her, did not smell of gardenias. Her fragrance was the rose, the tea rose, perfect, voluptuary to the senses. It made Chrissy's head spin. And Mademoiselle was drawn to Chrissy. They were kindred spirits, *orphelines* in a cold world of strangers.

The other girls romanticized Mademoiselle Payot. They imagined her to have had a very great, very sad love affair. Her lover had been a sailor who had been lost at sea, went one version. Her lover had been so handsome that her younger sister had fallen in love with him and stolen him away, went another. Her lover, married, had left her to rejoin his wife for the sake of the children. None of these was too far from the truth. Her lover *had* left her for another, for the church, and she had never loved again. All she had now was her music and the young girls she taught, who loved no one but themselves.

In a way, it was natural for Chrissy and Jacqueline to turn to each other for comfort—the child who had no mother, no friend; the young woman who had no lover, no child.

Jacqueline would hug Chrissy when she came into the *salle de musique,* gladdened by her eagerness. Chrissy hugged back; she hadn't been held in she didn't know how long.

"Well, *ma petite,*" Mademoiselle would say, "who is your choice for today? Bach? Mozart? Chopin?"

"Oh, please, Chopin! I adore Chopin, Mademoiselle!"

"*Très bien.* Chopin it is."

As Chrissy played, the teacher draped her arm around the girl, touched her cheek, smoothed the bangs out of her eyes. When Chrissy did especially well, the teacher would kiss her in approval, in pleasure.

Chrissy was allowed to take outings in Mademoiselle's company. They explored the streets of Vieux Montreal, viewed the bronze sculptured monument to the memory of Maisonneuve, the city-founder, in the Place d'Armes, visited the Château de Ramezay and the Oratory of St. Joseph, took boat trips down the St. Lawrence and up the Saguenay. Chrissy was ecstatic.

In December, Chrissy received a note from her Aunt Gwen.

My dearest Chrissy,
Much pleased to hear from Mademoiselle Perigord that you are
doing well. At long last. This little note is dashed off to let you know that,
as I will not be in Palm Beach for the holidays, it will be best that
you remain at school. My suite at the Plaza is not that large and it was
all I could do to manage reservations for Gwennie and Hardy.
(You can imagine how full the hotel gets at this time of year.) Rudy
is going to Virginia to stay with a friend. Mademoiselle Perigord assures
me accommodations will be made for you to stay at L'Ecole. Or
perhaps you will be clever enough to manage to find a little friend
who will invite you home with her. That's what friends are for. Do
not be surprised if a little Christmas package finds its way to you.
Have a good holiday.

Love,
Aunt Gwen

Chrissy was neither surprised nor distressed. She ran to tell Jacqueline, who immediately said that she would ask permission for Chrissy to go home with her to her house in the city of Quebec.

Mademoiselle Perigord gladly gave her permission. It was always so sad to see the little ones left at the school for the holidays—it was so much better that they be in the bosom of their family . . . or friends. Besides, she had no wish to keep the big kitchen open.

Jacqueline Payot's house, left to her by her mother who had passed away several years before, was a quaint cottage on a narrow, winding street. It was all an adventure for Chrissy who had never seen anything like it before. During the day they wandered about, or took rides in the funny, little two-wheeled *calèche*. They went to see all the historical sites—the Plains of Abraham with the monuments to Wolfe and Montcalm, the City Gates and the Martello Towers, the Chapel of the Franciscans, the Church of Notre-Dames-des Victoires, and, of course, the shrine of Sainte-Anne de Beaupré where wonderful, healing miracles took place. And they would lunch at little restaurants, or the famed Château Frontenac, where Chrissy did the ordering, showing off her increasingly excellent French to an adoring Jacquie.

The nights were very cold and Chrissy shared the great bed in Jacqueline's room with its goose-down comforter and handmade quilts, cuddling up to her teacher's warmth. The second night Chrissy was there, Jacqueline unbuttoned her white flannel nightgown and put Chrissy to her breast.

"Suckle, *mon enfant*," she murmured, and Chrissy, dreaming that she was an infant at her mother's breast, put her lips to the rosy brown nipple and sucked voraciously, hoping, somehow, to receive from the creamy breast nourishment, nectar of gardenias.

She took her mouth away and looked at her mother's face. Jacqueline's eyes were closed, the lashes casting long shadows on the ivory cheek in the moonlit room. Jacqueline's two hands reached out for Chrissy's face, drew it to hers, and she kissed Chrissy full on the mouth, her small tongue pushing against Chrissy's teeth.

"My little darling," her mother breathed.

Under the goose-down comforter, Jacqueline's fast, adroit fingers removed Chrissy's long-sleeved nightgown. "*Maman's chou-chou*," she murmured and kissed Chrissy's tremulous body all over, the newly blossoming buds of breasts, the shivering belly, the parted thighs.

Soon Chrissy forgot the cold, soon her body quivered and shook and little sighs and cries escaped her open mouth. And the kissing . . . the kissing . . . all night long. . . .

"*Je t'adore.*"

"*Je t'adore.*"

The days were fun, sightseeing and exploring with her adored teacher, but Chrissy could hardly wait for the nights, for her "Mother" to come to her and love her.

Chrissy begged Jacqueline for them not to return to school. Why couldn't they stay here in the cottage forever? . . .

Jacquie laughed happily. "We will be back, my pet."

Madame Mignon, making her rounds one night, discovered that Chrissy was missing from her bed. She disliked wakening Mademoiselle Perigord but what else was she to do? She had not discovered Chrissy in any of the other girls' rooms. She could not bear the responsibility herself.

The headmistress was annoyed. "She must have had a nightmare and run to her teacher's room. I've made a mistake in letting that child grow so dependent upon the woman."

She put on her robe. "Come, we will go see if she isn't there. If she isn't, only God knows where we will find her."

The two women laboriously climbed to the fifth floor where the teachers were domiciled in small cubicles. The climb did not help the headmistress's disposition. "I will not have this nonsense going on, running to a teacher like a baby. I am dedicated to helping these girls mature into God-fearing, strong women, *n'est-ce pas?*"

"Oh, *oui,* Mademoiselle Perigord, *oui.*"

"I will punish the girl and give Mademoiselle Payot a severe talk, I promise you."

The headmistress tolerated no locks on any doors but her own. So when she heard little moans coming from within the music teacher's room, she flung open the door.

"Mon Dieu," escaped her lips as she fell back against Madame Mignon, who tried to peer over her mistress's shoulder.

"Mon Dieu," Madame Mignon echoed.

The girl and the music teacher were in the narrow bed together, the woman's mouth on the girl's convoluting lower half, the girl's hands reaching out, touching the woman's breasts, the girl's head flung back, her mouth open.

Mademoiselle Perigord literally threw Chrissy into her own small private chapel and told the girl to kneel before the figures of Christ and the Mother and to pray furiously, for she had sinned. She dispatched a telegram to Gwen Marlowe demanding the woman's presence immediately.

Three days later, news reached the school that Jacqueline Payot had returned to her little house and hanged herself from a ceiling beam. Mademoiselle Perigord sent that information along to Chrissy via the serving woman who brought in the food tray.

Chrissy had spent three days and three nights in the little chapel— the days kneeling numb and cold before the images of the Mother and Son, the nights on the floor, with a pile of rags to cover her, the headmistress's idea of a proper penance. When she heard the words telling her of her friend's death she turned to the silent, sweet-faced Mary and wailed: "If you're a mother, why haven't you helped me?"

Then, that afternoon Gwen Marlowe arrived in a proper snit. She had come by train since Albert her driver was off on a few days' leave and the train's service had been deplorable. Since she had taken her time about coming, Mademoiselle Perigord allowed her to cool her heels and fan her anger while the school, students and teachers, convened in the main chapel to pray for Jacqueline Payot's soul.

"I wish you to take this sinful child home with you within the hour. She must be removed from my school at once. You understand that this abomination cannot be allowed to spread. I have had her things packed. I will have everything brought down at once."

"My dear lady." Gwen Marlowe leaned forward confidentially. "It would not be beneficial to either one of us to have this story spread around. I think we can reach an equitable solution."

"Such as?"

"Such as let Chrissy stay until the end of the school year. A matter of three months or so. Frankly, I haven't the slightest idea what to do with her. I won't be able to place her anywhere this time of year. And think of this orphaned child. She needs your religious discipline. You, of all people, should want to save her immortal soul. Isn't that what you people call it? Restore her innocence and that sort of thing?"

"Please, Madame, spare me your condescension. I am not a fool."

"I'll sweeten the pot for you."

"You are talking of money, Madame?"

"Yes. A great deal of money."

Mademoiselle Perigord considered, then shook her head.

Gwen Marlowe sat back in her chair appraising the woman, her obstinacy. She would have to take a different tack.

"May I remind you that I sent you an innocent child? My poor orphaned niece was placed in *your* care. She was perverted in *your* school." Gwen narrowed her eyes. "I quake to think how the parents of your other little girls would take this information."

Mademoiselle Perigord studied her adversary, so polished in her black tailored suit and fox stole, her coquettishly veiled pillbox, her silk-clad crossed legs, taking her measure. "I hardly think you would wish to advertise your niece's perversion, Madame. After all, your name is well-known, even here in the provinces." She smiled faintly.

Gwen Marlowe was furious. She was failing; she wasn't going to get this stupid woman to change her edict. "You mean you got me up here just to accompany Chrissy home? You could have put her on ɪa train if that's all you wanted. You'd better think twice, Mademoiselle. I'm warning you. I won't take this lying down."

Mademoiselle Perigord stood up. "It is out of the question. Under no circumstances can I allow the girl to stay. It would be a situation . . . *impossible*," she said, using the French pronunciation. "*Impossible*. The whole school knows. It is one of those things that cannot be contained. If Christina leaves immediately, the girls will forget. If she stays, they will mock her, talk about it endlessly, even discuss it with their parents.

. . . No. I don't even know if my school will survive the *scandale* as it is. The sooner you leave with the girl, the better."

Gwen Marlowe cut her losses by getting the woman to agree to allow Chrissy the credits for the full term and to write her niece a glowing recommendation for the next school. In return, she agreed to say nothing more about Chrissy being ruined by L'Ecole de Jean Baptiste.

It could be worse. The little bitch could be pregnant.

"What about the woman?" Gwen asked curiously. "You've dismissed her, I presume?"

"Oh, *pardon*. I thought you were apprised. Mademoiselle Payot has chosen to commit another sin—she has taken her own life. She has hanged herself."

"Oh, my dear God!" Gwen's hand went to her temples. "Does Chrissy know?"

The headmistress shrugged. "Yes. I had her told this morning. I will have Christina's trunks brought down. I will call a car to take you to the station. I have already checked the schedule. There is a train leaving in two hours. Come with me now. I will take you to your niece."

They found Chrissy lying on the floor of the chapel in front of the altar in a pool of vomit. Gwen Marlowe looked at the figure crumpled on the floor and was overcome with remorse.

"What have you done to her?" Her voice shook. "The poor little wretch. She really *is* an innocent, you know."

"What have *I* done, Madame?"

Gwen Marlowe looked with curiosity at her niece, so stolid in her tweed suit, staring out the window of the train, her face inscrutable.

"What are you thinking, Chrissy?"

"Nothing."

"Do you have anything to say to me?"

Chrissy turned to her aunt, looked at her for a few seconds. "No," she said and turned back to the window.

Gwen Marlowe lit a cigarette and started to put the case back into her purse. Suddenly, she smiled to herself and held the case out to Chrissy. "Cigarette?"

For a bare second surprise flickered across Chrissy's face, and as quickly vanished. She took one and Gwen lit it with the Cartier lighter.

"Thanks."

"I want you to know, Chrissy, that I think this whole thing is a tempest in a teapot."

Again Chrissy looked faintly surprised, then once more she assumed the closed face.

"I know that many young girls form crushes on older girls or women. It happens quite frequently, especially when a girl is lonely, as I'm sure

83

you were. Mademoiselle Perigord is a provincial woman, an old-maid bitch. I'm sure this whole thing is very painful for you, and we won't mention it again, shall we? The less said, the better. It's *oublié* . . . forgotten." She gestured with a pale, red-tipped hand.

"But there *is* one more thing I'd like to say," she continued. "You'll be going to another school again in the fall. Right now I haven't the slightest idea where. But you can count on me—I'll find one. I just want to warn you against a repetition of this sort of thing. These things do get around and you'll get a reputation for—well, never mind. Just don't let it happen again. I'm sure you understand what I'm talking about. You were always bright, no matter what else."

Chrissy said nothing, simply stared out the window.

". . . and I'm sorry about your friend."

Chrissy turned back to her aunt, put her head to one side as if thinking. "She wasn't my . . . friend," she said enigmatically. "Not my friend."

It was dark outside and Chrissy said, "When are we going to the dining car? I haven't eaten in days."

It was Gwen Marlowe's turn to look surprised. "We can go to the dining car right now. God knows I could use a drink."

4.

It was Gwen Marlowe's good intention to keep Chrissy at the Plaza with her until it was time to go up to Newport for the summer. She really had no idea what else she could do with her for the few months until then and she did feel she should spend some time with her niece—try to help her with her problems.

To keep Chrissy busy and not completely dependent upon her own company, Gwen arranged for piano, dancing and art lessons, all at Carnegie Hall, which was conveniently near the hotel. She could walk there. If Chrissy was kept busy, hopefully she wouldn't get into any more trouble. And she herself would take tea with Chrissy every day—they would talk and perhaps they could work out some of the things that were disturbing the poor thing.

Gwen told all this to Chrissy. "I want to be your friend."

Chrissy smiled widely at her aunt and Gwen thought, she *is* quite pretty when she smiles.

But then Chrissy asked, "Why? Why do you want to be my friend? Do you want to get some of what Jacqueline Payot got? Is that it?"

Gwen Marlowe had always prided herself on never being shocked and not losing her temper—not terribly, anyway—but on this occasion she thought she would go out of her mind with rage. "You *are* a horrid child! You are revolting! And it's very evident that the rotten apple didn't fall very far from the mother tree! Worst of all, Chrissy Marlowe, you are very very *hard!*"

Hard? What's she talking about?

"And wipe that smile off your face, you revolting little bitch!"

Gwen Marlowe left the next day for Sea Island. Her best friend from her boarding school days, Emily Rogers, had been begging her to come down for a holiday. She didn't say good-bye to Chrissy, she couldn't bear to look at the awful child with her depraved soul. She left a few instructions with the maid.

For her part, Chrissy was glad that her aunt was gone and off her back. For a couple of days she went to her classes at Carnegie. On the third day that her aunt was gone, Chrissy found a discarded razor blade in the medicine cabinet in the gold and pink bathroom in the suite at the Plaza and slashed at her left wrist three times, then fainted at the sight of her own blood.

The maid heard Chrissy fall, rushed in, saw the girl's body on the tiled floor and called the hotel manager. The manager sent up the hotel physician, then called Gwen Marlowe at Sea Island.

"Oh, shitty-poo!" Gwen said inelegantly. "That stupid, wretched child!" she cried with irritation. "Why am I so cursed?" she asked her friend Emily and the handsome Colonel Hurd as they sat drinking rum and Cokes on the terrace. (Colonel Hurd was one of Emily's discoveries.)

She thought for a couple of seconds and decided. "I'll have to dash to New York immediately."

"Don't be ridiculous," Emily told her. "Obviously, that girl needs more help than you're able to give her. Professional help, I mean. Don't you agree, Jack?"

"Emily's right," Jack agreed.

"You can make all your arrangements from right here. We'll just call up this discreet little clinic in Atlanta which I've heard is the very, very best. Johnny knows somebody there. Johnny will call. And then you can have the girl sent down in a private ambulance. And you won't have to set one foot off the island."

"And you did promise you'd lead off the Founder's Day Ball with me at the Club Saturday," Jack Hurd reminded Gwen, surreptitiously running his hand up her leg so that Emily, at the bar, would not see.

"I did promise, didn't I?" Gwen smiled brightly, fluttering heavily mascaraed lashes. "All right, Emily. Have Johnny call the clinic and make the arrangements."

She placed her hand lightly on Jack Hurd's thigh and trailed her fingertips suggestively.

"Why did you cut your wrist, Chrissy?" Dr. Fielding asked in a no-inflection voice.

Chrissy grinned. "I guess I wanted to die."

"Why did you want to die?"

The grin faded. "I was tired."

"Tired? That's all? Tired?"

"Tired of me. Of being me. Tired of being."

"Despite everything, Chrissy, I want to do my best by you. Dr. Fielding has agreed that you should return to school. I've arranged for you to go to the Chalmer's School in Massachusetts. It's a very good school and at this point, believe me, it wasn't easy to get you in. Do try hard to make a go of it."

The Marlowe name hadn't been enough to get Chrissy into Chalmer's. Luckily, Miss Chalmer was in the middle of an expansion project—a new dormitory and a new playing field—and Gwen Marlowe didn't mind helping the cause. Chrissy was almost fourteen. Both she and Gwen had only to get through the next four years before they were relieved of one another. She was willing to do her part if only Chrissy would do hers.

They had a few days after Chrissy was discharged from the clinic in Atlanta to do whatever shopping was necessary for Chrissy and before Gwen herself left for Acapulco. It was a nuisance for Gwen—she had her own shopping to do, but she had made up her mind. She would do whatever was necessary for her niece, if it killed her. Finally, Chrissy was ready to leave. The bags were in the car. Albert was waiting. Gwen stuck out her hand to the blank-faced girl. "I'll look forward to seeing you at Christmas."

Chrissy smiled faintly, shook hands with her aunt.

There *was* something valiant about the girl, Gwen grudgingly admitted to herself. She grimaced slightly and leaned over and quickly kissed Chrissy on the forehead. Chrissy's reaction was almost as if she had been slapped.

She's feeling sorry for me, all of a sudden.

Well, she would show Aunt Gwen, Gwennie and the boys. She *would* last out the four years at Chalmer's. Maybe even graduate with distinction. She would show them all. She didn't need them. She needed no one at all. She would dance on Grandmother Marlowe's grave. She had read that expression in a book and liked it. She would dance on Grandmother Marlowe's grave and on Christina Hatton Marlowe's, too. Fuck them both in hell. And while she was about it, she would dance on Jacqueline Payot's grave too.

She felt like she was crying inside of herself. She was too unschooled to realize why she had so much hate for Jacqueline Payot. Nobody at the clinic in Atlanta had explained to her about the ultimate rejection of them all.

MAEVE

1.

Maeve O'Connor arrived Saturday, early by two days for the beginning of the term. Before Maeve came up, her luggage did.

Aunt Gwen had once told Chrissy that you couldn't always tell a book by its cover but you could almost always judge a person's station in life by her luggage. But there was nothing to learn from this set of neutrally tan leather bags except that they were a matched set, expensive and new, as were the two trunks. They bore no school or travel insignia. And *expensive* told nothing. Everybody who attended Miss Chalmer's was rich to a degree, except for the usual few obligatory scholarship students. And it was easy to pick out their luggage. Either all new and shiny and cheap, or worn, unmatched and cheap. But Chrissy already knew that Maeve O'Connor was not a scholarship recipient—Miss Chalmer had told her that she was the daughter of Padraic O'Connor, the famous novelist.

Chrissy groaned. Maeve O'Connor was probably an intellectual—a grind. Just what she needed!

"Yes?" Chrissy called out in answer to the knock on her door, ready to douse her cigarette if necessary.

"It's I, Maeve O'Connor," a low voice came through the door.

"Well, haul yourself in, why don't you?"

A slender girl ducked through the door as if she were trying to hide herself. But you'd never be able to miss her, Chrissy thought. Not with that blaze of red hair. She was a beauty. Chrissy wondered how old Maeve was—she looked older than the thirteen or fourteen all the first-year girls would be.

Golly! A grind and beautiful besides. We'll never be friends.

"You don't *have* to knock, you know," Chrissy said belligerently. "It's your room too."

"Oh, I'm sorry. That I knocked, I mean. I didn't know that you weren't supposed to." She held out her hand. "I'm Maeve O'Connor."

Chrissy's defenses were up. *So you're Maeve O'Connor. What am I supposed to do about that? Drop dead?*

87

"Yes, that's who you said you were when you knocked." Chrissy took Maeve's hand and shook it, without getting up from the bed.

Maeve laughed uncertainly. "I did give you my name before I came in, didn't I? Sorry."

Chrissy propped herself up, leaning on one elbow. "You're new at this, aren't you?"

"I'm not sure what you mean." Maeve frowned. "New at this school?"

"New at the whole business of boarding school."

"Yes, I am. Does it show?" Maeve smiled a sweet, sad smile.

"It shows."

Then Chrissy smiled her big, wide smile. At least Maeve O'Connor was no show-off, brimming with self-confidence. "Your luggage is new."

"Oh?" Maeve said, stricken. "Is that bad?"

"Oh, don't worry, we can take care of it. I'll show you," and Chrissy kicked and scuffed at the new luggage with concentration, dumped her ashtray over the bags and ground the ashes in with her heel. "Now no one will ever know."

Maeve laughed at this drastic solution with relief. She thought that she and this funny girl would be friends.

"And you have to stop saying you're sorry and act a little more nervy. Aggressive, kind of. Or the girls here will eat you alive."

Maeve looked frightened.

"Boarding school girls are a pretty tough lot," Chrissy said. "Everyone thinks schools like this finish you, refine you. Maybe on the outside. 'But inside these walls, baby, you got to be tough to survive!'" Chrissy spoke out of the corner of her mouth à la Edward G. Robinson.

Maeve laughed even though she had never seen an Edward G. Robinson movie.

"Will you help me, Chrissy?"

Chrissy was taken aback by this bald plea but she was pleased. "Sure I will. But how did you know my name was Chrissy? I didn't tell you, did I?"

"They told me downstairs. You're Chrissy Marlowe."

"Yes, that's me all right. I guess you've heard about me?"

"No, I don't think so. Should I have? Are you famous?"

"Sure. Don't you read the funny papers? I've been in the rags for years. I thought everybody heard about me. And you're the famous writer's daughter. I guess everybody's heard of your father. If you haven't been to boarding school before, what schools have you gone to? Day schools? Public schools?"

"No. I've never been to any school before. My . . . father"—she hesitated—"used to tutor me himself. And the last year or so I've been living with my aunt in Boston. She hired a tutor for me."

"How come you've been with your aunt? Your father's living, isn't he?"

"Yes, of course. He's living. He lives in Ireland . . . now. . . ."

"That's funny. I mean you living with your aunt too. I sort of live with my aunt. Only my father's dead. And so's my mother. Practically everybody I know is dead. How about your mother?"

"She's dead too," Maeve said mournfully and was appalled to see Chrissy burst out laughing.

"Why is that funny?" she asked, uncertain.

"It's just funny," Chrissy said, but she stopped laughing. "I guess the joke's on us. Why did your father go to Ireland? How come you didn't go with him?"

"I didn't want to," Maeve said. "I wanted to live with my aunt." She didn't want to talk about her father. She opened up both closets. "You've left the best closet for me. We'd better change."

"No. You're supposed to get the best closet because you came after I did."

"I don't understand. Why does that entitle me to the better closet?"

Chrissy laughed again, this time with real humor. "Because *you've* got the lumpy bed."

"Oh," Maeve said happily, "I'm so glad."

What luck! Maeve thought. She had this laughing girl for a room-mate! Aunt Maggie had said that she would make friends, that school would be fun, that it was better for her to board at a school so that she could get used to being with people her own age. Aunt Maggie was right.

"How old are you?" Chrissy asked, worried that Maeve was older than she.

"Thirteen. Almost fourteen. I was born on February twelfth, 1928. Lincoln's Birthday."

Chrissy laughed in delight. This was unbelievable! "My birthday is February twenty-second, 1928! Washington's Birthday!"

Then Maeve laughed.

"Hey," Chrissy said. "How about a cig?" She proffered the pack. "Only we have to be careful not to get caught. If necessary, be prepared to ditch it, even if it means jumping out the window with it."

Maeve looked uncertainly at Chrissy at first, then she knew she was supposed to laugh and she did.

2.

Maeve had never known her mother. Sally O'Connor died in childbirth and Maeve was raised in a house in Truro on Cape Cod by her father. She had never even met her Aunt Maggie until she was past twelve.

Aunt Maggie was her father's elder sister, older by one year, but they had been estranged and Maeve and her father had never even visited with her. Her father had hardly even made mention of her, or of his and Maggie's parents, for that matter.

Maeve and her father hardly ever saw anybody at all. Sometimes, a woman from the village would come to work for them, then go back in the evening to her own house. The woman would generally last with them for a while, then tire of the solitude and boredom of the days spent at the house overlooking the sea. Or her father would take a disliking to the woman and send her on her way. Then they would make do without anybody for a while, sharing the chores between them. It was not difficult; their house was sparsely furnished and their meals simple. They kept a few chickens for the eggs, and in summer tended a small flower garden. Her mother had started the garden, her father told her, because she had come from Ireland and liked tending the soil. How much her father must have loved her mother, Maeve thought, to have kept up the flower garden after she died. It was not easy to grow things in Truro —the long, cold winters cut short the growing season, the sandy soil was not fertile—only the scrub pine grew easily and the cranberries lent themselves to cultivation.

Every two or three weeks they would go to Provincetown to buy supplies, and once or twice a year they would go to Boston where her father would buy Maeve her clothes and a carload of books, and meet with his publisher. The meetings between the publisher and her father were as infrequent as the latter could make them. He tried to do whatever business needed doing by mail.

On their outings to Provincetown, Maeve would see other children playing games, or fighting with one another, or whatever children did, and she was curious about them, eager to talk to them, but her father discouraged that.

"We don't need anyone but ourselves. Isn't that true, Maeve?"

Maeve didn't want to hurt his feelings or make him angry, so she would agree. She was sickened on the occasions that he did get angry.

When they did go to Boston, Maeve always hoped that her father would say, "Would you like to visit your Aunt Maggie? Why don't we drop in on her and give her the surprise of her life?"

That was her fantasy, but it never came true. Instead, they visited all the museums, including the Abbott, which sort of belonged to them, she knew, but her father never explained exactly how. They lunched at Joseph's or at the Ritz Hotel on Ann Street, and took rides in the swan boats in the Public Gardens, and then they would go back to their house on the cliffs.

Maeve didn't miss the outside world too much because outside of the trips to town or to Boston, she knew nothing of it. She knew only the world of Tolstoy, Dostoyevsky, Chekhov, of Shakespeare, Kipling,

Dickens, and Mann. She was familiar with the lives of the people Lady Grey and the other Irish writers wrote about, and the old-time Yankees her own New England writers wrote of. She had read them all.

When she was very young, the mornings were spent on spelling, reading and arithmetic. Then, as she grew older, on geography, history, mathematics, French, and the simpler sciences. After lunch, her father would go to his study and write, and she would read. In the evenings, after dinner, they would discuss what she had read, dissect it, and she would have to defend her interpretations.

They would read Shelley, Keats, Lord Byron, Tennyson, and Oscar Wilde to one another. Except when her father was in one of his black moods, when he would not talk with her at all. Then, he locked himself in his study with his bottles and did not emerge for days. And she would go about her schedule as best she could.

She would tend the flowers if it were summer, walk the moors, telling herself wonderful stories about her mother and her Aunt Maggie, and about the fairies and elves that lived in the marshes. In winter, she went skating on the pond or made herself a snowman that talked quite fluently in a language known only to her and snowmen.

She would make herself little meals. But she knew better than to go to her father's locked door and offer him food. She had done that only once and when her father opened the door, she was terrified by what she saw and what she heard from his lips.

Only once, when her father was locked in his room, she had gone to Provincetown alone, catching a ride with a farmer who happened to come along in a truck, and she had spent a couple of hours there, walking around by herself, having an ice cream soda at a pharmacy, talking to some children she met on the street. When she had returned, her father was waiting for her, unshaven and drunk as a lord—she knew that phrase from her books—and he had sent her spinning across the room. She never went to town on her own again.

Maeve, mostly content in her life with her father, sensed, as she grew older, that something was missing from their lives. All her reading intensified this feeling. The books were full of emotions she had never felt, relationships she somehow missed. She worshipped her father, looked up to him, admired him. At the same time, she was frightened of him. She was never sure when he would break out in a torrent of rage, lash out at her, or maybe just lock himself up in the room. Sometimes he would even smash the furniture.

Every now and then a letter came from Aunt Maggie. Her father only tore it up without reading it. Once, when she was eight, Aunt Maggie came to see them. But her father would not open the door. Aunt Maggie called through the door: "You don't have to see me, Padraic. I only want to visit with Maeve."

Maeve looked through the window and saw a car with a driver waiting while her aunt kept knocking and knocking. Maeve wanted desperately to call out something to her, or to fling the door open herself, but of course she didn't dare. Finally, she watched her aunt go back to her car, a small person but with her head held high.

Her aunt came back again about two years later. This time her father came out of his room in a stupor and opened the door while Maeve watched with her heart beating terribly hard. Her father stared at the woman who waited outside and to Maeve, watching fearfully from behind, there seemed to be an air of bravery about her aunt. But Maeve could sense that in spite of the bravery her aunt was fearful too.

"I just wanted to see your daughter, Padraic." Her aunt spoke in a low, calm voice as if she were asking nothing out of the ordinary. "And I wanted to tell you that if it's difficult for you to raise her, I would gladly help in—"

"You?" Her father laughed drunkenly, bitterly.

And then Maeve heard her father recite from a poem he had read to her often. The poem came from a little book of anonymous poets that her father particularly liked. But he seemed to change many of the words:

> I crowned her with bliss and she me with thorn;
> I led her to chamber and she me to die;
> I brought her to worship and she me to scorn;
> I did her reverence and she me villainy.
> To love that loveth is no maistry;
> Her hate made never my love her foe
> Ask me then no question why—
> *Quia amore langueo.*

Maeve did not understand the poem at all but she saw her aunt flinch at the words. Then to her horror she watched her father spit full in his sister's face. Maeve trembled and started to wail and her aunt called out: "Maeve, hear me! If you ever need me you can come to me. Do you hear me? Just look me up in the Boston telephone book. Remember that, Maeve. . . ."

That night, when Maeve lay in her bed fully awake, she heard her bedroom door open. Her father was out of his room again. She wondered if the black mood was over. She hoped so. She had worried that Aunt Maggie's visit would have started him off on another cycle.

He stood over her and she could see his eyes shining in the dark, and they were the eyes not of the black mood but the eyes of a stranger. He got into the bed and pulled her to him, kissing her, first her face and then her neck, then his hands gently spread her. Maeve closed her eyes, waited expectantly with exhilaration for what she instinctively knew was happening. She was only ten, but she had read much. Somehow it had prepared her for this moment.

As Padraic entered her, her body arched out and up to him. The pain she felt mattered not at all. She was all senses, her body lived only for this moment, to be the answer for this man, her beloved, beautiful father who loomed over her, his eyes wild, his mouth seeking, his body so joyously hers.

———

Two years later, Maeve stood on her Aunt Maggie's doorstep and rang the bell.

Please, dear God, let her be here. Let her not be in the hospital or in Europe or anywhere but here.

If Aunt Maggie was not at home she did not know what she would do. Now that she had come to Boston, Maeve knew she could never go back to the house in Truro.

A big-boned maid came to the door.

"Is Miss O'Connor at home?"

"And who is calling?"

"It's I, Maeve O'Connor. Tell her I've come, please. I think she's been expecting me."

3.

Maeve was the third generation of the O'Connor family to be born in America. Her father's grandfather, Paddy (short for Padraic, Gaelic for Patrick), emigrated at the age of five with his mother and father from the village of Drumlish in Ireland in the year of 1850, during the Great Potato Famine. When the O'Connors arrived in Boston Harbor, they found themselves a home in a subcellar, where they doubled up with another family to share the damp, floorless space. By the time Paddy was ten, he was filled with rage at the subhuman conditions he and the other Irish immigrants were forced to live under, and he was consumed with ambition. He insisted on being called Pat since he realized that the name Paddy was associated with drunkenness and poverty—even the vehicle used to cart the drunk, brawling Irishman off to jail was called a paddy wagon.

He was a hod carrier at the age of eleven and a construction foreman at eighteen. By the time *his* son, Patrick, was born in 1875, Pat O'Connor had his own construction company and was determined his son would be a gentleman. In 1893, he sent Patrick off to Fordham University in New York where they tolerated the Irish better than they did in Boston. He admonished Patrick to avoid the drink, to control and channel the rage that seemed part of the boy's nature, to be both a devout Catholic and a lawyer.

But Patrick O'Connor, blue-eyed and dark-haired, fair of face, brawny and grown tall with the good food, knew better than his father where the money lay, and it was the money he was after. He studied banking and brokerage, and upon his graduation from Fordham opened up a brokerage house in New York with his classmate and good friend, Tom Malley. Within five years, through a complex maneuver, Patrick managed to corner a market, as the expression went, in railroad stock. With a couple of million in his pocket, and a well-established firm behind him, he decided it was time to go back to Boston, which was teeming with Irish immigrants, and the sons of the Irish immigrants who were starting to move up in the world and were not welcome at the banks of the Boston gentry. Patrick planned to open a bank specifically designed to meet their needs.

Patrick became successful and powerful enough to be invited (for business reasons only) to a dinner party at the home of the Abbotts, one of Boston's most prominent families, and laying eyes on Margaret Abbott, the daughter of the house, he decided that he would marry into the Protestant, First Family Abbotts. At twenty-eight, he had the money —now he would have the Abbott name and background for his own sons. He would have the blond, delicate Margaret, with her fine airs and the social position that came with her. No matter that she was plain— *all* Boston debutantes were plain. It was a well-known fact.

The first James Abbott was among the Puritans who landed in Boston in 1630, and although this group's bloodlines were better and bluer than the Plymouth Rock Pilgrims, the Mayflower contingency *was* earlier. Thus, some of the first James Abbott's great-grandsons and great-great-granddaughters were known to say unfactually: "We came over on the Mayflower."

That first James Abbott in America prospered in trade; his sons went into shipbuilding and their sons into law, silversmithing, shipping. By the time the Revolutionary War came along, the Abbotts were already rich, distinguished and highly respected. (Several Abbott sons were Tories, but this fact was later obscured by the family.) One Abbott rode with Paul Revere and one signed the Declaration of Independence while another was one of the signatories of the Constitution. A James Abbott was appointed a judge by George Washington.

By the time the nineteenth century rolled in, many of the early First Families had lost either their money or their social eminence, but not the Abbotts. They prospered, not only in commerce but also in medicine and law, and in the field of education—an Abbott was a president of Harvard. One was an activist in the antislavery society in the mid-1830s while another Abbott was an antiabolitionist activist—after all, the family did have money invested in the slave economy of the South.

But it was their commercial interests that really established the Abbotts as one of the very first families—not only in proper Boston but in the whole of the United States—for their fortunes were founded in such diversified fields. They were into shipping, railroads, hardware, even furs. The present James Abbott was a banker and the personification of all that was best in the family. His wife, Alice, was a Haight and therefore a member of the Society of Mayflower Descendants. She was in possession of records that *proved* her ancestors lived in the cabin next door to Miles Standish at Plimoth Plantation. She was also a member of the Massachusetts Society of Colonial Dames.

All in all, James Abbott was a Brahmin and tried to speak only to Lowells, Cabots, Lees, Higginsons and Wigglesworths, but that was not always feasible. He was forced on one particular evening to have Patrick as his guest, albeit he was Irish and therefore truly the scourge of Boston.

On her part, Margaret Abbott fell immediately in love with the big, darkly handsome Irishman. She was a secret romantic, and although she had been well schooled as to the attractions a suitable suitor must possess—money, an impeccable genealogy, preferably a third or fourth cousin as it was nice to keep Abbott money within the Abbott sphere, a Harvard education (with Yale as a poor second choice)—these requisites flew out of her head with amazing speed. Patrick O'Connor had money and intelligence but no other qualifications, not to mention his obvious deficiencies. But this made no difference at all to Margaret once she was exposed to Patrick's charm.

Although naturally taciturn and given to sudden, inexplicable angers, Patrick exposed only his charming ways to the infatuated Margaret. He spoke well and effusively, with a store of Irish stories and anecdotes. He smiled winningly, danced beautifully, and could even sing the heart-rending ballads of the wild Irish countryside. All this, coupled with his imposing figure, intense blue eyes, and a head of dark curling hair, was too much for prim Margaret who had never had her head turned with compliments before. The truth was, although a post-debutante, Margaret had never even been seriously courted.

Naturally, Patrick and Margaret had to court in secret. And not once did Margaret ever detect in the clever, artful Patrick a hint of the brooding, bitter, socially ambitious man that he was. He hated the proper Protestants almost as much as he yearned to be one of them. Readily,

Margaret agreed to marry him, dreaming only of a wedding night when she would be swept away on a wave of passion.

Neither Margaret nor Patrick felt any serious dedication to their respective faiths. The only question lay in who would sacrifice his Church for the Church of the other. Both were more than eager to make this sacrifice. Margaret desired to embrace the more mysterious and exotic Catholicism to prove her love; Patrick, on the other hand, was fiercely determined to become a member of St. Paul's where all the present-day Abbotts were members. He did not intend for a minute to allow Margaret to become a Catholic—he intended to convert himself the moment they were married. But he made one big mistake. He allowed Margaret to assume that he was going to convert to her faith for *her sake,* in a magnificent gesture of love.

And so, even as she courted in secret, Margaret became a Catholic in private. She took her instructions and was duly baptized. She planned to tell Patrick of her conversion only after their union, to present it to him as her wedding gift, her dowry.

In the meantime, Patrick planned the elopement. Much as he yearned for a large church wedding at St. Paul's, he knew there was no way to manage this. He would make it up to himself later, he promised himself. After the Abbotts came around. They were bound to—Margaret was, after all, their only daughter.

They went down to New York to be married. Tom Malley, his partner, arranged for Judge Parnell Reilly to perform the ceremony at the Malley residence on Fifth Avenue between Seventy-first and Seventy-second streets, right up the block from the Henry Clay Frick edifice. Tom and his wife, the gorgeous Bridget, also arranged for a reception for one hundred and fifty guests, gleaned from the judicial, political, legal and financial circles in which they moved.

Margaret was surprised by the luxurious life-style of the Malleys. Accustomed to the rather frugal and austere ways of the Boston upper-class, the Florentine *palazzo* was a cultural shock. And the food and drink served by a battery of servants at the reception reflected an opulence Margaret had never encountered. In Boston, one counted the guests and allowed exactly one glass of champagne per person. Here, the champagne flowed from a silver fountain, encircled by doves sculptured in ice. In the hollow of each dove was caviar. There were oysters on the half shell set out on silver salvers, cracked crab laid out on a bed of ice on vermeil platters, roast canvasback duck presented on Royal Copenhagen, smoked turkey on Spode china. Tom Malley and his wife Bridget obviously enjoyed spending the fortune they had so recently acquired.

Tom had thoughtfully arranged for the bridal suite at the Plaza for the newlyweds. The wedding night should have been everything Margaret dreamed of, but unfortunately she chose to inform her bridegroom of her gift to him, her conversion to Catholicism, before the marriage was consummated. Patrick's face darkened as the blood rushed to his head. He wanted to hit the innocent Margaret—she had made the worst kind of fool of him; she had destroyed his dream forever. He wasn't even able to ask her to renounce her newfound faith without revealing to her his real reasons for marrying her in the first place. Now he would have to reconcile himself to remaining a Catholic and therefore an outsider, unacceptable to anybody who was anybody in Brahmin Boston.

Patrick, in his fury, swept Margaret's carefully laid-out toilet articles from the dressing table to the floor and turned on his heel. He went down to the bar, and for the first time in his life got roaring drunk. Alone, upstairs in her wedding bed, Margaret was beside herself. She had no idea why Patrick had stomped from the room leaving her unfulfilled and desperately unhappy. She still didn't realize that her only desirability and appeal to her husband was her social standing and former Protestantism.

Patrick returned in the middle of the night. His bride lay in her virginal white nightgown—awake, waiting, trembling. He tore her nightgown from her, entered her without word or foreplay, achieved release in a matter of minutes. The whole thing was over before Margaret quite knew what was happening. Then she was more bewildered than ever. Was this the glorious wedding night she had dreamed of? In the morning, Patrick was sober but unsmiling. Although she didn't know it at the time, Margaret had seen the last of Patrick O'Connor's overwhelming charm. In the future he would, on occasion, use her body but he would never really talk to her again.

They left New York that very same day. Patrick was eager to confront the Abbotts and ascertain exactly where he stood with them. To his pleasant surprise, the Abbotts did not make the anticipated fuss. Faced with a *fait accompli,* they managed to convey their displeasure in a well-bred manner. Alice Abbott sank into a chair, sniffed, and delicately brought her handkerchief to her nose as if an unpleasant odor had been introduced into the house. James permitted himself a slight grimace, paced to and fro a bit in silent contemplation, said, "I see," then withdrew to his study to read his evening paper. Alice then excused herself and mounted the stairs to her bedroom.

Margaret and Patrick found themselves alone in the brown and wine-red parlor. Margaret tossed her head. "I don't care. I don't care what they think. We love each other. We don't need them."

"Let's go home," Patrick said and took his bride to the small town house on Commonwealth Avenue where he had been living since his return to Boston, and to bed. Patrick wanted and needed an heir as quickly as possible. Perhaps all was not lost yet, he thought, as he entered his wife. Margaret had *not* told her parents of her conversion.

Back in Louisburg Square, Alice and James prepared for bed. "They didn't even have a proper church wedding," Alice complained.

"He didn't even go to Yale . . ." James considered, "as some of these people do. . . ."

"What is the name of that bank of his?"

"The Dublin First National. . . ."

"Oh dear."

"Yes."

"Perhaps he can be persuaded to change the name, James—"

James thought about that. "That's a capital idea, my dear. I will discuss that possibility with him. It will give him a chance to show us what he's made of."

"I do wish she could have had a proper wedding, James."

"At St. Paul's?"

"And with a reception here in the house, James."

"Of course."

"Why can't we, James? It's really not too late."

"We'll do it, my dear."

"Do you think he can be persuaded to join our church?"

James smiled wisely. "I'm sure of it." He kissed his wife on the forehead and retired to his adjoining bedroom.

The following week, Patrick and Margaret were invited to her parents' home for dinner. Margaret's brothers, James and Paul, were also present along with their wives. Alice Abbott was cheerful through the consommé, the lamb chops and mashed potatoes and green peas and carrots. Finally, when the dessert was served, vanilla ice cream with chocolate sauce, she made her announcement: "We have made an appointment for Patrick to speak with Reverend Thayer about joining our church, after which we will choose a date for a wedding ceremony at St. Paul's, with the reception to be held here in Louisburg Square. What do you have to say to that, Margaret? Patrick?" she asked, confident of their gratitude and acquiescence. Her husband James's complaisant face complemented her words.

By the time Patrick had collected his thoughts, urgently whispering to Margaret, "Don't say a word about . . ." she had already risen to her feet. "That's impossible, Mother, Father. I am a Catholic too. I've already converted—"

Alice Abbott sank back into her chair, brought her handkerchief to her nose, and placed one hand on her palpitating bosom. As Patrick fixed his eyes filled with murderous contempt on his bewildered wife, the room was completely silent. Then Paul's wife dropped a fork on the rose carpet and Alice Abbott took the handkerchief from her nose and looked at her daughter-in-law sharply.

Finally James drawled, "I see. That *is* a horse of a different color."

Patrick got up and stalked out. Margaret, completely mystified as to her latest transgression, dashed from the room after him.

"Shall we have a brandy, Father?" Paul asked.

Patrick swallowed whisky after whisky at a tavern. Damn that flat-chested, thin-blooded Sassenach milksop! She had ruined it all! Why did she suppose he had married her? For her insipid face? That whiny voice? He could as well have married a lusty, full-titted Irish Catholic girl for all the good Margaret had done him! He went home to find Margaret waiting in bed for him. Seeing her looking at him with beseeching eyes, Patrick picked up a Windsor chair and smashed it against a wall.

Alice Abbott knocked at the open door of her husband's bedroom. He was sitting up in bed reading Emerson's *Essay on Friendship*.

"James, I've a splendid idea."

James put a bookmark in place, closed his book carefully, removed his reading glasses and laid them on his bedside table. "I presume you are referring to Margaret's little mess."

"I am, James, and do you know what I think should be done? Something very stylish, James. We are, after all, *both* descendants of a heroic band of people who came here in quest of religious freedom, are we not? Would it not be fitting for us to accept our Catholic daughter and son-in-law in true Christian fashion? With a flourish, James."

"I respect your feeling, as I always have, Alice. But exactly what is it you want us to do with a flourish?"

"Have a wedding at the Cathedral of the Holy Cross on Washington Street. It's a magnificent building and they do have a perfectly marvelous mural there."

"How do you know that?" James asked, a bit astonished.

"Oh, I happened to be in the neighborhood at one time—on an errand—and I went in. Out of curiosity, you know. The mural is of the All-Knowing and All-Forgiving Christ. A remarkable piece of work."

"Really?"

"Yes. And we could have a wedding full of pomp and ceremony. You know how these Papists love that pageantry. Then we can have a reception right here as we originally planned. No one would dare snicker behind our back. Don't you see, James? It's the only way we'll be able to hold our heads up proudly. And Margaret. Otherwise she'll have to go sneaking around down back alleys."

James permitted himself a snicker at his wife's choice of words. "Perhaps there is nothing else to be done," he agreed.

"And Margaret will wear the Haight wedding gown just as all the Haight brides have, ever since Plimoth Plantation."

James emitted another snicker. "My dear Alice, I know that the females in your family hold certain conceptions about that wedding gown but I can scarcely concede that that gown really dates back to the 1620's. Do you really believe that gown would have lasted nearly three hundred years? Nor is it likely the good people of Plimoth were ever able to lay their hands on the satin and lace that went into that gown. It was all they could do to cover their bodies with clothes warm enough to last through the winters. That gown probably didn't see the light of day until well into the eighteenth century."

"You are wrong, James. My own mother told me that Elizabeth Moore wore that dress at Plimoth Plantation when she married Peter Haight, and all the Haight girls wore it ever since. And I refuse to hear any more about it. Tomorrow, James, we will go talk to the priest in charge at the cathedral."

"Isn't it a bishop?"

"I have no idea. A cardinal, perhaps? Isn't that what they call those people?"

Thus, albeit a Catholic ceremony, Patrick found himself the participant of a wedding ceremony attended by the leading families of Boston. His mother and father were there, of course, along with his four red-headed sisters. And while a dozen or so O'Connor relatives and friends showed up at the church, none attended the reception at the Abbott home. Patrick felt he had paid only a very small price in return for his Beacon Hill reception. The Dublin First National had been renamed the Massachusetts Immigrants Mercantile Bank. He had also dropped the *O'* from his name. James Abbott had suggested that Connor sounded a bit smarter, if you will, than O'Connor.

Soon after, Margaret was with child. Patrick had been relentless in his lovemaking. Determined to impregnate his bride, he had bedded her not once, but twice and sometimes three times a day. She, of course, took the frequent incursions upon her person as proof of her husband's passion for her. Once pregnant, she was dismayed by his total indifference. Her mother, on the other hand, deemed Margaret's condition as a time for further action.

Days after learning of her daughter's pregnancy, Alice Abbott regaled her husband with a bit of gossip. "I was speaking with Cousin Jane today, James. Cousin Jane says that she is taking her mother to live with her in Milton."

"How nice for both of them."

"I don't think Cousin Jane thinks it's nice at all. It's something she *must* do. But that's beside the point. The point is Aunt Abigail's house. It will be vacant. I propose we make a bid for it immediately before anyone else hears a Louisburg Square house is on the market."

"To what end, my dear? Of course I do not doubt it would be a good investment. Property in the Square will certainly double in value within—"

"Really, James. You are being unusually obtuse. I am thinking of Margaret. Margaret, your daughter, who is carrying a Haight-Abbott within her. . . ."

James bit on the unlit pipe he held between his teeth. "A Connor, my dear, a Connor. A Catholic Irish Connor. Abigail will never sell her house to Irish Catholics. And what would the other residents of the Square say? They would be up in arms. We might even have another rebellion in Boston." He chuckled at his own little joke.

"Just leave it all to me, James."

One of Patrick Connor's dreams was now realized. He felt he had arrived. His first Christmas Eve on Beacon Hill held special significance for him. Everyone agreed that Christmas Eve on the Hill was a never-to-be forgotten experience. The caroling, the lighted candles in every window, the almost carnival atmosphere as, for the evening, windows were left undraped to reveal the dignified drawing rooms within the houses, the open-house champagne cup raised in friendship as the Puritan-costumed bell-ringers made their rounds.

But Christmas Eve notwithstanding, fury filled Patrick's heart when Margaret, brimming over with gratitude as the birth of her first child approached, hung crucifixes and holy pictures through their beautiful stately home. The woman lacked all taste, blending crucifixes with Federal brick. . . . The sight of her walking about his house with her rosary beads never far from hand gave him blinding migraines. On a few occasions he was so driven he tore her pictures and crucifixes from his walls and smashed them, pulled her rosary from her hands and stomped upon it. He was determined to wean her away from her religion and *force* her to accept her place in Society for both of them.

Their daughter was born in 1902 and christened Margaret Abbott Connor. She resembled her mother, plain, milk-white, and, even in her infancy, possessed of a longish Protestant nose. Although Patrick forbade it, his wife persisted in calling the baby girl Maggie, a nickname Patrick particularly abhorred. He had a redheaded sister called Maggie who was the personification of what Bostonians labeled as "mick." He himself called the baby by her full name, Margaret. His wife, he rarely called anything at all.

She not only irritated Patrick, she puzzled him as well. She did all the things he commanded her not to—even visited *his* family, including his sisters, although he told her in strong, bitter words that he would not have it. She smiled submissively, lowered her head in obeisance, murmured compliances, and then repeated all her offenses. This, in spite of her husband's ever-increasing violent rages. It didn't occur to Patrick that his wife's obstinacy was the determination of the converted zealot to redeem his immortal soul, to bring him back to his roots and to his Church.

Even as Margaret lay in her hospital bed the following year after giving birth to a beautiful son, she defied him. He had planned to name the child James if it were a boy. (Patrick had even mentally toyed with having his surname legally changed to Abbott, not an unprecedented action practiced by Irish immigrants who desired an English name of Boston prominence.) But Margaret filled out the form for the birth certificate in the hospital in Patrick's absence, and legally named their son the blatantly Gaelic Padraic, after *his* father, instead of her own. And then she had the gall to say she had done it to please him.

Padraic Abbott Connor was christened at the cathedral, with the elder Abbots standing by. Mad as it appeared to Patrick, Alice Abbott had become enamored of the pageantry of the Roman Catholic Church although she did not actually go over the baptismal line.

Finally, Patrick gave up on Margaret, allowing her to go her Catholic way. He installed a mistress in an apartment in Back Bay, a sensuous Portuguese beauty, renewed his ties with the brokerage house in New York, expanded his bank, and with his father-in-law's rather tepid assistance, intensified his efforts to scale the world that rightfully belonged to a millionaire, a son-in-law of the Abbotts, a resident of Louisburg Square.

James Abbott put him up for membership in the Somerset Club, but Patrick was refused membership. Even his father-in-law's attempt to take him to Harvard's Porcellian Club as a guest was frowned upon. The Brookline Country Club had some excuse for barring him too, and the City Club Corporation kept a waiting list even for sons of the First Families. The Union Club told James Abbott that in ten or fifteen years a vacancy might occur, and then his son-in-law might be considered. And although Alice and James were patrons of the Assemblies at which debutantes were introduced into Society, Margaret and Patrick's names were never on any invitation list.

Then, James Abbott dropped dead one morning while taking his constitutional. His family took immense pride in the huge attendance at the funeral. Fine funeral be damned, cursed Patrick, his only possible sponsor was gone.

Alice Abbott was so grieved by her husband's untimely demise, she became what could only be called an eccentric. Finding her own Church too unimpassioned, she found solace in her daughter's and she too converted to Catholicism. That done, she took to dressing very grandly, bedecking herself in the latest Paris fashions, and actually wore the family jewels in public. Next, she bought a brace of Great Danes, adorned them with dog collars studded with emeralds, and sashayed them down Tremont Street. Next, she shocked all of Boston by erecting a garish Venetian palace on a plot of land she owned in Back Bay. She closed up the house on Louisburg Square—she called it her Declaration of

Independence from the Brick. She was so bored with all the squabbles regarding the paving of the streets on the Square and the pride the occupants took in its brick-patterned sidewalks. As if to put the brick in its proper place, Alice had her new palace built around a marble-tiled courtyard. She added Italian gardens, lily pools, fountains, and, within, she placed a priceless art collection she bought up in wholesale lots, along with furniture, rugs, and tapestries that had originally belonged to English lords, Russian princes, French queens.

Then, Alice Abbott turned about and donated her palace to the city of Boston to serve as a museum in memory of her husband, James. She continued to live there on the third floor, but the palace was now the James Abbott Museum, reigned over by a commanding portrait of Alice herself, executed by John Singer Sargent.

Alice had, in effect, given away something close to twelve million dollars. Such generosity was unknown in Boston, where parsimony was regarded as one of the finer virtues. Alice's sons, James and Paul, were aghast over the loss of what would have been their inheritance, as Patrick was. Margaret thought it was extremely nice of her mother and she was delighted to take Maggie and Padraic to the Abbott museum, even if they were too young to appreciate its magnificence.

Patrick began questioning the quality of his life. True, he was living in Louisburg Square, but to what avail? His partner, Tom Malley, and his other friends in New York lived in mansions adorned with treasures as rich as those in the Abbott museum. They enjoyed the high life while his own was a model of austerity. He had married a wife as plain as a church mouse who made no effort to enhance either her appearance or their position in Society. Tom Malley, on the other hand, had married the woman he desired, the lovely Bridget, and she, born shanty Irish, had gladly assumed the fuss and feathers to which their fortune entitled her.

Even his children were as strangers to him. His daughter, Maggie, as plain and quiet as her mother, was already a devout churchgoer at five. His startling beautiful son, Padraic, was different from other children. He was given to violent fits of temper, very much like his father's, and showed flashes of great brilliance—he was already reading avidly at four. He was, for no apparent reason, hostile to his father, and Patrick, angered, could not fathom why. He clung to his mother's skirts and, in her absence, clung to his elder sister, Maggie.

Furthermore, Patrick had alienated himself from his own family, the O'Connors, and given up his mistress as not worth the trouble. Sex was not the driving force of his life. And every day the migraines got worse, constantly aggravated by his lack of social success. When he tallied up his life's score, he found the total minute and disappointing. In a last-ditch effort to make sense of it all, he decided to sire another child.

Maybe this time he would have the child that would really be his own. To this end, Patrick resumed intercourse with Margaret who was only mildly surprised at the new turn of events, having already come to terms with the fact that the husband she loved so much was not at all in love with her.

Patrick and Margaret's third child was named James Abbott Connor and was blue-eyed, fair-haired, and finally Patrick had the heir he wanted and could love. The new baby seemed of such a sweet nature all the Connor household was enamored of him, even the servants and especially the new baby's sister Maggie. But not Padraic. He was desperately jealous as his mother nursed the new baby, and as Margaret became more and more immersed in the care of the infant, Padraic turned for comfort to his sister. Maggie, mature beyond her six years, would compassionately allow the boy to suckle at her flat, tiny nipple as Padraic had seen the infant James do at his mother's breast.

Ever since their marriage, the Connors had spent the summers at the Abbotts' cottage in Nahant, a rather austere resort fifteen minutes from Boston. When Alice Abbott decided it was time for her to abandon bluestocking Nahant, she gave the plain salt-box cottage to her daughter and bought herself the fabled "Gold House" on Newport's regal Bellevue Avenue, with its back to the sea, from a Vanderbilt who had found Newport provincial compared to the attractions of Europe. Gold House was named for its ballroom, so lavish it was almost sinful. It had gilded walls and three chandeliers so heavy with crystal balls large as a child's fist that one servant, armed with a special ladder, did nothing but clean these chandeliers day in and day out. Splendid mirrors of Venetian glass were inset into the walls and the floor was of *giallo antico* marble, partially covered with Persian carpets that were rolled up when dancing was indicated.

Immediately, Alice Abbott started giving balls in competition with her neighbors, Patricia Marlowe on the one side, Caroline Schermerhorn Astor, the heretofore unchallenged Queen of Society—*she* had invented New York's famed 400—on the other. Alice Abbott decided that she would give the Astor woman a run for her money and the pretentious Marlowe woman as well.

While his mother-in-law did social battle in Newport, Patrick Connor found that, although he now officially owned property in Nahant and was due certain presumable rights such as membership in the Nahant Club, he still was not considered acceptable. Not only was he denied membership in the Club, he and his family were no longer even accepted as guests there without the sponsorship of Alice Abbott. In disgust, he sold his plain little house to his brother-in-law, Paul, who was then automatically made a member of the Club.

Then, Patrick, Margaret, and the children summered at Newport, staying with Margaret's mother. Naturally, the Connors attended those functions hosted by Alice Abbott but they were not invited to the other parties. Thinking that perhaps being a landowner here would bring him more respect, even if it hadn't in Nahant, Patrick bought Rosewood, one of the bigger mansions, when it came up for sale. He became the neighbor of Mrs. Astor, on her left. She immediately had the windows on that side of her house cemented over and all Newport buzzed with this insult. Next, Patrick's neighbors on his left had a brick wall built so high it completely obliterated the Connors' Rosewood from view. By summer's end, in spite of all Alice Abbott's efforts, Patrick got the message: Irish not welcome here. With malicious intent, Patrick managed to find a Jew to sell Rosewood to—if he could have, he would have sold it to a Negro.

He went back to Boston and brooded all through the gray winter. His wife left him to brood alone—she knew from experience that there was nothing to do for Patrick's black moods. And there was nothing she could do about his ever-increasing drinking. If she even spoke to him about it, he could go into a rage breaking furniture and china.

His depression deepened. His whole life was lackluster. He took little pleasure now in his house in Louisburg Square. He no longer proudly wiped his shoes each evening on the charming iron shoescraper that each house in the Square sported. He stood at his Bulfinch recessed window arch and looked out at the beautiful little park through his violet-tinted window panes, and instead of the joy of ownership he had previously felt, he found it all dreary. One day he thrust his fist through one of the window panes even though it was irreplaceable—the glass had been part of a shipment from England in 1818.

He couldn't bear to look at his wife or children, not even the impeccably named younger son, James. He was now only a reminder of the doors slammed in his face. And the nasty Padraic—he who shunned his father like the plague—was a reminder of the *reason* for all the shut doors. Patrick didn't give a damn how clever he was with all his precocious poetry! And Maggie—what was she but his wife all over again— delicately reproachful of his drinking, doggedly cheerful in the face of his ire, and dutiful. He could not forgive her her lack of beauty.

Then, in the spring, as the birds returned to the Hill, Patrick made a decision. He would go where he had friends. He still had his interest in the brokerage firm in New York. He would buy a house in New York and a place in Southampton for the summer near his partner, Tom Malley. Tom's brother, Tim, had a place there too, as did Tom's sister Lilly, who had married Justice Terrence Murphy. He didn't need Boston. Fuck Boston! Fuck all these white-livered Protestants! Fuck Louisburg Square and Newport and all the proper Bostonians!

Margaret Connor had some difficulty adjusting to Southampton.

True, the noveau-riche Irish there were devout Catholics, but their sybaritic, Cyrenaic hedonism was alien to her as life in a remote village in China would have been. But it took Patrick no time at all to feel at home. Here, as in Newport, summer cottages were cottages in name only and he acquired a magnificent house on the ocean with a salt-water pool, equipped with a marvelous invention that filtered out the sand from the ocean's water even as the water flowed in from the sea. Sandhaven sported two loggias, one above the other, that fronted on the water. The lower one consisted of three arches separated by pillars with Roman-Doric columns and was filled with potted palms and swept by sea breezes. The rear of the house faced a wide lawn with topiary, marble and bronze statuary, and a gazebo. All this was overlooked by the conservatory, which opened off the drawing room and led to a terrace with a marble fountain surrounded by dolphins, where the family breakfasted and lunched, not an easy feat since the kitchen was sublevel and several hundred feet away. A staff of thirty was needed and the third floor was given up to cell-like bedrooms to house them all. Margaret was kept busy overseeing the huge establishment, buying supplies for the household and striving to give personal attention to young James Abbott, who was only five and, unfortunately, not too robust. He did have his nanny, but Margaret was loath to leave the sickly boy too much to her care.

Margaret would have liked to spend more time with Maggie and Padraic too, but she could not manage it all. Maggie and Padraic had their own governess and Margaret knew that she could count on the mature Maggie to keep an eye on her stormy-tempered, antisocial brother. Margaret worried about the boy's erratic personality, but she forced herself to think of him as merely high-spirited. Besides, Padraic, with all his wildness and strange behavior, was not so far out of place in Southampton. All the youngsters there seemed to have a flair for outrageous acts. There was a multitude of cars in every circular driveway, and letting the air out of the cars' tires was considered a routine amusement. Even drowning someone's favorite cat in the pool was not looked upon as extreme. And locking up a little girl in a dark garage or stable for hours, while everyone hunted for her, was not considered anything more than a mischievous prank.

When Padraic tied one of Tom Malley's young daughters to a tree and whipped her bare behind with a birch branch, he blithely explained it away. He had written a play, Padraic said, and little Mary had agreed to act out a part of it with him. When Tom Malley went to Margaret to voice his dismay, she flushed and said, "I'm so dreadfully sorry, Tom, but I'm sure Padraic meant no harm. Why, he just went to Communion this morning."

Nettled, Tom then complained to Patrick that his son was a savage little beast who needed to be horsewhipped. Patrick laughed, "Just some high spirits, Tom, my boy. A chip off the old block, is all. . . ."

In the end, Tom laughed himself, both men had a drink and went off to play golf. But Stephen Malley, Tom's oldest son, decided he would punish Padraic himself, if no one else would. In an eye-for-an-eye fashion he tied Padraic to a tree and lashed him with a horsewhip. Only Maggie, who kept her mournful silence, saw Padraic slip out of the Malley stable several days later, leaving it in flames.

Patrick and his family joined the Southampton Beach Club. The extensive and prominent Murray clan had already broken down that barrier for the Irish who followed. It was hard for the Southampton Beach Club to resist them—the rich Irish families simply outnumbered their Protestant counterparts at the beach resort. The Murrays, the Cuddahys, the McDonnells had been well entrenched in Southampton for several years. In East Hampton there were more, older-money Catholic families. The Bouviers, while not Irish, *were* Catholic and they could trace their presence on American soil to one Eustache Bouvier who allegedly fought in the American Revolution and, though he went back to his native land, his son, Michel, returned to America in 1815 and founded a dynasty.

It was the best of times for Patrick. He was, at long last, in Society, and a Society that was a hell of a lot more fun than the stodgy, smug world he left behind. Southampton in the second decade of the century was a world of fancy cars, pools, stables, even polo fields. There was swimming and dancing and women in beautiful dresses who cared not if a jump in the pool ruined a seven-hundred-dollar organza dancing frock.

Patrick was invited everywhere in the Hamptons and he went, usually without Margaret. It was too strange a world for her. *Women went shopping in the daytime wearing an armful of diamond bracelets! One young woman daily swam and golfed with her constant companion, a handsome monsignor!* Still, Margaret could not complain that these people were not devout: Sundays the pews of the Sacred Hearts of Jesus and Mary Church were packed and practically everybody sent their children to Catholic schools dressed, of course, in clothes from the very best stores.

So, Margaret stayed home for the most part and if she heard the rumors and stories about Patrick's dalliances, she said nothing. On one occasion she did go to a dance and was deeply humiliated when she overheard one smart-mouthed matron say to another, "If that Patrick Connor holds the O'Brien girl any closer it will be a miracle if she doesn't get pregnant."

It was better that she stayed at home and prayed.

Life in the city went Patrick's way too. There, too, the Connors lived near the Malleys on Park Avenue and their children went to the same schools as the Malley brood: the boys to Georgetown Prep, the girls to the Sacred Heart Academy. And Patrick wormed his way slowly into the better clubs in New York. New York, after all, had the Jews to keep out—they couldn't concentrate on *everybody*.

Even the son that he didn't like very much, stunningly handsome Padraic, was a source of pride. The boy was considered a genius. At fifteen he had a book of poetry published; at sixteen, his first novel. It was decided that he would enter Yale that year. There was no point in his finishing prep school. Padraic was not at all sure he wanted to go to college altogether. He did not enjoy the camaraderie of his fellows— stupid, callow youths who enjoyed nothing better than trying to win athletic letters, sneaking away to get drunk, and brawling with one another. He had his books and his writing, his mother and adoring sister. What fucking need did he have of the pimpled dolts who leered over the corset advertisements in the Sears Roebuck catalog?

Padraic wrote a play, his first, the summer of 1919, about a soldier who came home from the Big War to find all his family relationships changed. He was supposed to leave for Yale in the fall, and he reasoned that if he could manage to get a production of the play he would not have to go to college at all and could stay home with his mother. That his prick of a father would be in residence too did not matter—his father was not around the house enough of the time to disturb him. And when he was at home, at least Padraic knew that he wasn't about to monopolize his mother's time.

Finishing the last scene of his play, Padraic hurried inside the house to look for his mother to read it to her. He found her finally in his brother James's room at the boy's bedside. James had a summer flu and had just fallen asleep so Margaret hushed Padraic as he ran into the room. "Later," she whispered, and motioned for him to leave. Padraic's deep blue eyes blazed with fury as he looked at his sleeping brother. Once again his brother had kept his mother from him when he needed her.

In a few days, James Abbott was recovered from his sickness and was allowed to go sailing with his brother who kindly offered to take him. Maggie intended to go with them, but she was delayed in returning from her shopping along the little main street in town. Learning that the two boys had left without her, she ran to the dock to await their return. In horror, but somehow not in surprise, she saw Padraic swim ashore alone.

Margaret never really got over her younger son's death. She tried to find solace in her Church, in the fact that he had gone on to a better world, but it was scant comfort. Somehow, she associated the "corrupt" life-style of frivolous abandonment in Southampton with the death of her son. If she had been a better person . . . If Patrick had been more devout . . . If they had never come to Southampton . . .

Margaret went back to her house in Louisburg Square with Padraic and Maggie, but without Patrick, who locked himself in a room with a case of Scotch and barely emerged. Margaret spent the next few months questioning her faith. Her mother had her "own" monsignor now who also lived on the third floor of the Abbott Museum and he tried to help Margaret accept the death of her son, but it was an uphill struggle.

When Patrick finally came out of his mourning room he found relief in the bed of Bridget Malley. A man who had lost a son to the sea and a wife to the Church had to seek solace somewhere and Bridget had been after Patrick for years. And she was still lovely. The affair started in Southampton and continued through the fall and into the winter in the city.

One afternoon in late December, as it started snowing, Patrick left his office, leaving Tom hard at work, and made his way uptown to Bridget's bedroom. Meanwhile, Tom developed a crushing sinus headache, due to the falling of the snow, and headed home himself. Unobserved, he spied his wife and Patrick in bed together. Calmly he went downstairs, retrieved his horse pistol from the library, then went upstairs again.

Tom intended only to shoot Patrick in the knee, which he had read was a particularly painful wound, but Patrick, spotting Tom, hurriedly started to pull on his pants and his knee was somewhere in the air close to his chest and Tom had never been a particularly good shot. He shot Patrick through the heart. Tom was sorry as hell; Patrick had been his buddy. The affair was hushed up and no charges were lodged, but Bridget was furious. Tom had made a fool of her, placing her in a humiliating position. Secondly, he had bloodied up her bed and not only did the bed have to be thrown away but everything in the room had to be replaced because it all had been decorated around the satin-upholstered bed. Besides, he had walked into the house from the snow and had not taken care not to sully her white carpeting.

Returning from the funeral, Margaret closed her Bible for the very last time and took to Russian literature. Maggie, never a favorite of her father, alone mourned while Padraic got falling-down drunk in celebration.

A few months after the death of his father, Padraic, who had never gone to Yale after all, won his first important literary prize, the New England Novelist's Award, for his novel *Brother,* about a youth who suffered the loss of a beloved sibling. Padraic wanted to share this celebration with his mother but she seemed uninterested; she congratulated him and went back to Chekhov. Padraic ended up getting drunk by himself. At the age of seventeen, he had won a major literary prize and discovered the comfort of the bottle. He also became victim to enduring migraine headaches.

On the occasion of one of these headaches, Maggie took Padraic into her bed, bathed his head with wet towels, caressed him, murmured words of consolation and, before she realized exactly what was happening, Padraic had burrowed his head into the space between her breasts and was trying to burrow his penis into her innocent vaginal orifice.

She immediately pushed him off. "No, Padraic, it can't be! You know that it isn't natural," she told him gently, not wanting to hurt him, sad really that she couldn't permit him this consolation. Angrily he left her. She went after him, eager to soothe away his suffering in some other way, not wanting him to be angry, knowing how anger only affected him adversely. She watched Padraic enter their mother's room and anxiously she wanted to see what would happen next, feeling guilty about her suspicions but unable to dispel them. *Would Padraic seduce her withdrawn, unworldly mother?* Minutes later, she saw Padraic leave in a fury, heard her mother's voice colored with cold contempt. Maggie breathed a sigh of relief but still she was worried how this rejection, coming after her own, would affect him. She had seen how Padraic dealt with rejection before.

It was only weeks later that Maggie discovered how Padraic had wreaked his revenge. Margaret, more detached than ever, came downstairs infrequently but Padraic was entering her room every afternoon and staying for some while. So one afternoon, not able to bear her suspicions any longer, Maggie slipped into her mother's room while her brother was there. There, with the draperies drawn against the sun, she saw Padraic administering a needle into her mother's arm, while Margaret herself lay back on the chaise, a dreamy smile on her lips, her eyes closed.

"Oh, Mother!" Maggie cried out. "No! You mustn't!"

Padraic laughed softly and Margaret, opening her eyes, turned to Maggie: "What do you know of what we mortals must do in order to endure! Go back to your Bible and leave me be."

Maggie went back to her room and decided that in the morning she would leave—she would go to her grandmother. And she would tell her grandmother what was going on—maybe her grandmother would know what to do.

Maggie carried one small suitcase with her. She passed her mother's room—the door was open. Padraic was standing at the window reciting a poem Maggie had heard him recite once before. She had asked then if he had written the poem but Padraic had only smiled and said it was an old English poem by an anonymous poet; he had just played with the words a bit, a sort of game.

> Why does your sword so drip with blood,
> Padraic, Padraic
> And why so sad are ye?

I have killed my horse so good, Mother
And I had no more but he.

Your steed was old and your stable's filled,
Padraic. Now say what may it be.
It was my father that I killed, Mother.
Alas, and woe is me.

What penance will ye do for that,
My dear son Padraic, now tell me.
I'll set my feet in yonder boat, Mother
And I'll fare over the sea.

What will ye leave to your babes and wife
Padraic, when ye go over the sea?
The world's room—let them beg through life
Mother, for them nevermore will I see.

And what will ye leave to your own mother dear
My dear son Padraic, now tell me.
The curse of Hell from me shall ye bear
Mother, such love you gave to me!

Maggie looked at her brother's red eyes. What a terrible poem, she agonized. What an ugly poem!

Padraic turned away from the window, saw her suitcase and laughed. "You don't have to go, loving sister. It's I who is going."

"Where is Mother?"

"Come here," he said and motioned for her to look out the window.

Maggie walked to the window and looked out. Her mother was dressed in the Haight wedding gown, sitting under the old oak tree, and talking. But there was no one else in the back garden but her. Maggie looked at her brother.

"What is she doing?"

Padraic laughed again. "She's disappeared into Chekhov and Tolstoy."

"Why, Padraic?" Maggie cried, horrified.

"Because she likes that world better." He smiled. "Doesn't she look happy?"

"I mean why did *you* do what you did?"

He looked at her quizzically. "Do you really have to ask?"

Maggie lay ill for several months. Alice Abbott placed her in the McLean Institute just outside of Boston and visited her every day. As soon as Maggie started to get better, she asked her grandmother about her mother.

"She's living in another world, Maggie. She's in her house in Louisburg Square but she thinks it's the country outside of St. Petersburg. She doesn't leave the house or her garden. I have a woman living with her who takes care of her and the house. But she's all right, Maggie. You'll have to take my word for it. She's seemingly happy. The world she's in now is a much more peaceful one than the one she left."

Maggie wondered about the drugs. What had her grandmother done about that? Alice Abbott must have seen the question in her granddaughter's eyes. She said, "I've taken care of *everything,* Maggie . . . I've arranged for everything."

"And Padraic, Grandmother? Where is Padraic?"

"He's gone away. He went first to Paris, then to Ireland. Since he won't get any of your father's money until he's twenty-one, I gave him a great deal of money so he'll be able to stay away for a long time. I thought it would be best for everyone."

There were so many questions Maggie wanted to ask her grandmother about Padraic . . . especially about why he was the way he was. Again Alice Abbott must have guessed what Maggie was thinking. She said, "There's an old Hungarian proverb, Maggie. 'Adam ate the apple, and our teeth still ache.' "

Maggie smiled wryly. "A Hungarian proverb from a proper Boston lady?"

"Not so proper these days, my dear. In order to spare you some worry I've had Padraic checked on. He's in Dublin now and he's put the *O'* back in his name. He's hanging about the pubs with other writers, a man named Joyce for one. And my reports says that he's been doing quite a bit of writing. Short stories. Essays. All brilliant but bitter. But they say many brilliant writers are bitter. Perhaps he'll find his salvation there in the land of his forefathers. Let him be, Maggie. Some people we just have to let be."

"Yes, Grandmother. I love Padraic but I don't want to see him."

"When you're completely well, Maggie, I'll be going abroad myself. I've always wanted to live in Italy."

"Italy?" Maggie was incredulous. "What will you do there?"

"I will make a pilgrimage first to the Vatican. Then I think I'll settle down in Venice or in Florence. I think a lot of the troubles people have are brought on by living lives that don't really belong to them. Your mother . . . Padraic . . . I think I was meant to be an Italian patroness of the arts." She chuckled softly. "And you, I think, are the proper Boston lady, my dear. I am going to turn over to you the custody of my museum."

"Me, Grandmother? Why me? I don't know anything about museums."

"You're an Abbott, my dear, more so than the rest of us. You'll learn. And I trust you to take care of it properly, the way I would myself. James and Paul would follow my letter but not my spirit. You will take care of my spirit. And you can live there too, on the third floor in my quarters."

"No, Grandmother. If you don't mind, I would rather live in your house in Louisburg Square. Is that all right with you?"

"Of course. I am leaving you that house, as well as the place in Newport. In fact, Maggie, I'm leaving you everything I own. But don't worry about the handling of the money. Paul and James will do that for you."

Maggie was shocked. *All of Grandmother's money?* "But what of Uncle Paul and Uncle James? Won't they be angry?"

"Don't fret about them, Maggie. They have their father's money. And as for Padraic, he'll have his father's and mother's. I've seen to that. I have control of Margaret's estate. I don't want Padraic to have to come to you for anything."

"But why have you left me *everything,* Grandmother? I can't possibly use it all."

"But you will know what to do with it. And now, enough talk of money. What will you do with yourself when you leave here? Besides living in the house in the Square and looking after the museum?"

"I'll go to school, Grandmother. I'll go to Radcliffe and study art and anthropology and all the things that will help me with the museum. And I will keep a watch on Mother. I won't intrude on her, Grandmother, but I can check on her every once in a while, can't I?"

"Of course, you *must,* Maggie. I am counting on you for that. And I think it's a splendid idea for you to go to Radcliffe. And while you're at it, find yourself a man. Not one of these stodgy proper Bostonians, either. Find yourself a man who can make you laugh." And she bent over and whispered in Maggie's ear so that the nurse who had entered the room wouldn't hear.

Maggie laughed softly, shook her head, and gazed over her grandmother's head toward the windows where the skies were gray and troubled.

"Did Grandfather Abbott make you laugh, Grandmother?"

"No, I cannot say that he did. But we had a chuckle now and then. But"—she smiled ruefully—"that's all that I was up to at the time."

Maggie put the *O'* back in her name too, as Padraic had, and did it for her mother, too. She went to Radcliffe and was graduated with honors, and each year she made a visit to her grandmother in Florence, who was disappointed when she heard that Maggie had still not found that young man who would make her laugh. She introduced Maggie to artists, titled noblemen, and American expatriates in the salon that she held two or three times a week but admonished her at the same time: "These men are to amuse, not to be taken seriously. When it is time to be serious, you'll know it and I won't have a thing to say about it."

On her trips to Europe, Maggie was always tempted to make a side trip to Ireland, but each time she talked herself out of the idea. She knew in the end that it would really be unwise for her to see Padraic—he was a keg of explosives best not tampered with. But she heard about him. And she read his two novels, both permeated with hostility toward the world. But, obviously, the hostility in his work did not affect its quality. Padraic was carving a reputation for himself not only in Ireland but in England and America, too. Only in his twenties, he was hailed by many as the foremost novelist of the decade and both the Irish and the Americans claimed him for their own.

In 1927 Grandmother Abbott died in Florence and her sons brought her body home to be put to rest in the Abbott plot. Dramatically, just an hour before the funeral took place, Padraic arrived. With him was a redhaired Irish girl. Her name was Sally Flanagan; she was just seventeen and Padraic introduced her as his wife. Sally Flanagan spoke English with a brogue so heavy she could barely be understood. A country girl, obviously uneducated and unworldly, she clung to Padraic like some shy and innocent fawn.

"I've come to bury me grandmother," Padraic told Maggie and his uncles with a beguiling smile. Then he asked sweetly if he could add his eulogy to the proceedings. James and Paul quickly acquiesced, proud to have their renowned nephew participate.

Padraic stood, beautiful with his long and wild mane of curls, a strange, poetic and romantic figure in a black suit and long flowing tie, and addressed the assemblage of mourners and the wind:

> Alice sat down below a thorn,
> Fine flowers in the valley;
> And there she had her sweet babe born,
> And the green leaves they grow rarely.
>
> Smile na sae sweet, my bonny Margaret,
> Fine flowers in the valley,
> And ye smile sae sweet, ye'll smile me dead,
> And the green leaves they grow rarely.
>
> Alice ta'en out her little penknife,
> Fine flowers in the valley,
> And robbed the sweet Margaret o' its life,
> And the green leaves they grow rarely.
>
> Alice Abbott's dug a grave by the light o' the moon,
> Fine flowers in the valley,
> And there she's buried her sweet babe in,
> And the green leaves they grow rarely.
>
> As Alice was going to the church,
> Fine flowers in the valley,

She saw a sweet babe in the porch,
And the green leaves they grow rarely.

O sweet babe, and thou were mine,
Fine flowers in the valley,
I wad clad thee in the silk so fine,
And the green leaves they grow rarely.

O mother dear, when I was thine,
Fine flowers in the valley,
Ye did na prove to me sae kind,
And the green leaves they grow rarely.

The assembled crowd knew not what to make of Padraic's oration.
"I thought the fellow was a novelist, not a poet."
"What kind of a eulogy was that?"
"I think it was disgusting, whatever it meant."
"The man is quite mad!"
Only Maggie knew the poetry was not original with Padraic, that he had adapted it from another poet of another century, that for some reason, it gave him more satisfaction to twist and turn the words of others for his own usage.

Padraic insisted on moving into Maggie's house with his seventeen-year-old bride. "Surely you wouldn't begrudge your brother and his bonnie bride a place to rest their heads. Besides, our grandmother must have left her house to both of us. Surely she did that?"

Hesitantly Maggie explained that Alice Abbott had left *her* the house, and that in time, he, Padraic would inherit their mother's house.

"Ah." Padraic smiled. "Do we have a mother, then? I was there, you know, at that house just three places down. There is a woman there all right, dressed like a Russian princess. She said to me, 'Ah, Andrei, you are home from the wars.'" He laughed so hard he almost fell out of his chair. "Of course, I could go there to live with my little bride."

Maggie knew she was being baited but still she had to protest. "Leave her be, Padraic, leave her be! She's suffered enough!"

He smiled. "You're a fine one to talk, Maggie. You who have stolen my inheritance."

"What are you talking about?"

"'You have stolen my birthright, Jacob, and for what? A mess of pottage?'"

"Don't you dare give me that, Padraic. I've taken nothing of what is yours. I don't *want* anything that is yours. What birthright are you talking about?"

"My Abbott birthright. *This house.* That other house down the street

115

where the Russian princess lives—that's an O'Connor house. What about my Abbott birthright? You are to have all of the Abbott money and the Abbott museum and the Abbott Newport palace. And I, poor orphaned Padraic, am only to have the O'Connor money. Tawdry, undistinguished money."

"Money is only money, Padraic. It is neither distinguished nor undistinguished."

"But you have all the ghosts that walk here."

"What do you want of me, Padraic? I will give you half of Grandmother's money if that's what you want, if it will make a difference to you. What do you want?"

"I want this house. I want the Abbott museum. I want half your heart. Cut it in two."

He stayed on, he and Sally. Maggie watched as he tortured the poor girl in different ways. He made her scrub floors as he sat and made critical observations. He mocked her brogue and her old-country ways. In anger or in drink, he struck the girl and Maggie knew that he was actually striking *her,* Maggie, tormenting *her,* Maggie.

Then Padraic would fondle his bride in front of Maggie, his hand stroking her breast, her legs, her buttocks, his hand playing with her genitalia. Or he would bare the girl's breasts and suckle at them as Maggie fled the room. One evening as the three of them sat in the drawing room, he forced his wife to the floor and attempted to copulate with her in front of Maggie's unbelieving eyes. As she ran out, she could hear Padraic's wild laughter coming after her.

Then Sally was with child and Padraic said to Maggie, "It will be *our* love child, yours and mine."

"Oh, yes?" Maggie asked, frightened. "And what of Sally? What of Sally?" And then she feared for Sally's life.

One day Maggie awoke to find them gone. In a few months she received an announcement in the mail from Truro on Cape Cod. Padraic and Sally O'Connor had had a baby girl, Maeve. A few days later, the mail brought a clipping from the *Cape Cod Times,* an obituary. Sally Flanagan O'Connor had died hours after giving birth to the daughter of the noted writer, Padraic O'Connor. A private burial service had been held.

Maggie cried that night, a haunting keening that sounded neither human nor bestial. She cried for Sally and for the newborn Maeve. In the morning she dried her tears. Her tears were of no use to poor Sally from the bogs of Ireland. There was only Padraic now, and his daughter. Maeve. Maggie knew what she must do.

For twelve years Maggie had waited to be called. She knew that the day would come when Maeve, in desperate need, would turn to her. And

116

she was ready. Even Maeve's pregnancy was not unduly shocking to her. Only a solution to the problem of the pregnancy was pertinent. Maggie searched her conscience and prayed silently for guidance. Incest was ugly; the product of this union might be even uglier. Was abortion the answer? She would have to find the proper doctor willing to undertake the procedure. And even if she did, was it right to abort the unborn life because it probably would be deformed in some way? What about the teachings of her Church? Could she risk the wrath of God? And what of Maeve's feelings? Now she was a child and looking to her, Maggie, for a solution. How would she feel later when she was an adult and fully understood all the issues? But Maeve was already four months pregnant. Might not an abortion be dangerous this late into the pregnancy? In the end, Maggie decided against abortion.

Having made her decision, Maggie laid her plans. Maeve would have the baby at home in Louisburg Square and at the time of birth the baby would have to be placed in an institution immediately. Maggie could not even take the chance of giving the baby out for adoption, there was so little chance of it being born normal. She bought a building in New York City as Boston was out of the question, and hastily arranged for the establishment of a Home for Special Children.

In the meantime, she would have to prepare Maeve for the traumatic events that would be hers to bear and she would have to do it, of course, in complete secrecy. Kathleen the maid was the only person besides Maggie who knew that Maeve had come to Boston. Kathleen, newly arrived in America, had left a lover back in Cork. Maggie gave the girl a dowry, a larger amount of money than Kathleen could have hoped to see in her lifetime, and sent her back to Ireland. Now only Maggie herself knew that Maeve O'Connor, a little over twelve years of age, lived in the house on the Square, awaiting the birth of a child. Only Maeve and Maggie, and, perhaps, Padraic too. Maggie guessed that Padraic would have concluded where Maeve had gone. But would he know why?

She carefully loaded the pistol that an Abbott had brought home from Gettysburg and waited for Padraic to come calling. It was a terrible sin to take a life, but Maggie was prepared to meet her maker and explain, if necessary, what took precedence. She had no doubts. The only hard part was: How did one take the life of someone one had loved so much?

She steeled herself to the weeping that issued every night from Maeve's room. But Maggie, whose instincts were usually right, was mistaken this time. She thought that Maeve cried for her unborn child. It never occurred to her that Maeve was crying for the beautiful Padraic, her father, her lover . . . that she yearned to feel his arms around her once more, to feel his body strong and hard against hers, to feel his lips upon her budding breast. It didn't occur to her that perhaps Maeve

117

had fled not out of fear nor hate, but only out of some subconscious, primal urge for survival.

And finally, one day, Padraic came.

"I'm here for my Maeve."

"Go away, Padraic. Go away and far."

"You've waited for years to steal my daughter. You've always tried to separate me from everything that was mine. You've always betrayed me."

"No, Padraic. It's *you* who have betrayed *me*. Betrayed us all. Mother. Sally. Now Maeve."

"Maeve? Betrayed Maeve? What in the devil's hell are you saying?" Wild eyes, part anger, part hurting, part madness, Maggie thought. Poor, mad Padraic. How she wished she could help him in his torment.

"Maeve's pregnant, Padraic."

That said it all, Maggie thought. She turned away from him so that she wouldn't have to look into those burning, dark blue eyes.

"Look at me!" he screamed. "Look at me and tell me the truth, you lying bitch!"

"I love you, Padraic," Maggie whispered. "I love you, God knows why, but I'll do anything to save Maeve from you. I'll protect her with both our lives if I have to. I swear it!"

Padraic struck her full across the face and she fell backward from the blow. He started for the stairs. Maggie knew then he would not fear her gun. She needed some other weapon.

"Stop, Padraic! One step more and I'll have you locked up in a cage where you belong—"

Now he believed her. He turned to look at her again. She cringed from the pain in his face, those eyes so blue. He turned and went toward the door. His last words to her were:

"May your soul rot in hell while the worms eat your guts!"

Maggie heard that Padraic had gone back to Ireland. With that settled, she made arrangements with her friend Dr. Gannon from the Abbott Children's Hospital to deliver Maeve's baby at home. She did all the work in the house herself so that there would only be four people who knew the truth and Dr. Gannon was sworn to uphold Maeve's secret.

Maeve's baby daughter took one full day and one full night to be born and, mercifully, Maeve was not conscious when the baby was finally delivered. Maggie took the seemingly perfect, rosy-faced, black-haired, blue-eyed child in her arms, bathed her and crooned to her as she rocked her. Then, going through the back gardens, Maggie carried the infant to her mother's house and left her there with Annie who took care of Margaret and asked no questions. Annie had already proved herself— she had kept Margaret's secret for years. In a few days, when Maeve was up and around, she herself would take the babe down to New York to the Home for Special Children. But in the meantime, she needed a place to keep the baby safe and hidden.

Maggie placed the baby girl in the arms of her great-grandmother, who rocked her and said, "Ah! Anna's little girl. How sweet she is."

Maeve awoke asking for her child and Maggie told her that the baby was already placed with a fine, childless couple in Ohio who would raise her as their own.

"Couldn't I at least have seen her, Aunt Maggie?"

"It's better this way, Maeve. She was beautiful and perfect and they, the father and mother, promised to call her Sally and they'll take very good care of her."

"What did she look like?"

"She had green eyes and red hair, just like you," Maggie lied. "Sally will have a good life, as you will. We just have to put the past behind us."

"And Father? What of Father, Aunt Maggie?"

"He's in Ireland."

"Will I ever see him again?" Maeve wept.

Maggie didn't answer. She held Maeve in her arms. For her part, though she loved her brother still, she hoped that neither she nor Maeve would ever see Padraic again.

FRIENDS

1.

Chrissy awoke in the middle of the night. Sleeping in a strange bed in a strange room was always difficult the first few nights at a new school. Then she realized what had awakened her. It was Maeve, weeping in the next bed. Poor Maeve. It was really hard on her. This was her first school, her first night away from home.

Chrissy spoke into the dark. "It'll be all right, Maeve. You'll see. It won't be so bad. We're friends and we'll make other friends. It won't be so bad."

But Maeve still cried. Chrissy felt an incredible sadness for her new friend. How well she knew Maeve's feeling, that "aloneness," like a wet, cold fog surrounding you with no place to escape.

Chrissy's first instinct was to go to Maeve's bed and comfort her, to tell Maeve she knew how she felt, being alone. But then Chrissy thought of how painfully it had all turned out that last time she had gone to a bed seeking comfort, giving comfort. No, she would not do that again. You could love a friend but never like that. She stayed in her own bed. Still, she had to find something, do something, say something to help Maeve, comfort her.

"I know what," she said finally. "I have a box of candy stashed away. How about I get it out and we have a little party? In the dark. We'll eat candy and smoke a couple of ciggies. Please, Maeve, okay? And we'll tell each other ghost stories. Did you ever hear that program on the radio— 'The Witch's Tales'? We'll see who scares the other one the most."

Gradually, the crying from the other bed ceased.

Maeve knew she could never tell Chrissy why she cried, that it was not because of being here in this room, at this school. She could never tell Chrissy whom she cried for. Still, Chrissy was already her dear friend.

"All right, Chrissy. But will you go first? You tell the first story."

"Sure. But let me get the candy first."

120

2.

It was already late into the afternoon when Sara and I arrived. It took Henry the chauffeur two full hours to unload the car and carry our luggage up to the third floor. Even though our trunks had gone on ahead of us, the limousine had been so crowded with suitcases, boxes, and garment bags, that we had been forced to sit up front with Henry.

Some of the other girls watched with a mixture, I guessed, of curiosity, envy, and amusement, as Henry brought up suitcase after suitcase, box after box, bag after bag. My cheeks burned as I heard their remarks.

"Well, at least there are *two* of them to share all that luggage."

"But I saw him bring in *four* fur coats. . . ."

"I don't care. My mother says it's in bad taste for a girl to have a fur coat before she's eighteen, or at least before she goes to college. Unless she's getting married."

"I think it's ridiculous. Especially since we have to wear those stupid uniforms most of the time."

"Dinner's at six. That gives us only a couple of hours. Do you think we should start to unpack?" I asked Sara.

Sara looked in the mirror over her dresser. She fluffed up her hair with the palm of her hands. "Uh-uh. Not in the mood. Too exhausted. We'll just pull out something to wear to dinner. Anything. Who cares? We could go out in the hall and get acquainted. See what's doing. See which creeps are going to be our neighbors."

Oh dear! I thought. I wished Sara would be more enthusiastic. I was nervous enough about meeting the girls who would be our companions for the next four years.

Sara pulled out a white leather cosmetic case from under a pile of suitcases and flipped open the locks. It was full of tubes and jars and compacts and lipsticks and little boxes thrown in harum-scarum. She picked out a small tortoise-shell box and opened it, spit into the little cake of dry black kohl, rubbed a tiny brush back and forth into the wetness, then applied the brush to the tip of her lashes. She picked out a lipstick in a gold case. It was bright orange and she applied it to her lips heavily, then took a tissue and wiped off nearly all of it. "I really like those five-and-ten-cent-store lipsticks better than this stuff. Westmore and Flame-Glo. They taste delicious."

"I thought we weren't allowed to wear makeup till our third year here."

121

"I've just used the tiniest bit. No one will tell the difference. Let me do you."

"No, Sara, I don't think so."

Sara smiled wickedly. "Marlena, come over here and let Cousin Sara fix you up."

"Why do I need it?" I asked, but went over to where Sara was standing just the same.

"Do you think I want all these dopey girls to think I have a washed-out cracker for a cousin? After all, we're the beautiful Leeds girls from South Carolina, aren't we, y'all?"

I was forced to laugh. There was nothing else to do with Sara but laugh. And submit.

"Now," Sara said, "we have to smell nice. I didn't read anything in the rules about not wearing perfume, did you?"

"No . . . but I'm sure it's not allowed."

Sara pulled out another case. It was full of large and small bottles of eau de cologne and perfume. She withdrew a big dark blue bottle and sprayed herself and me liberally. "Mmm." She inhaled the scent. "Delicious. *Evening in Paris*. It's cheap but I just adore it. Don't you?"

"Yes, I do, but you sprayed on so much—they'll smell us from a mile away."

"Complain, complain . . . You're never going to snare yourself a man, Marlena Leeds Williams, if you don't stop complaining."

There was a loud rat-a-ta-tat on our door.

"I guess we have a caller," Sara drawled. "A noisy one. Come on in, whoever you are."

A fat girl posed in the doorway.

"Slap your ass against the wall,
'Cause here I comes, balls and all!"

"Oh, Lordy! I don't believe it! Ginny Furbush! What are you doing here, Ginny?"

"Surprise! Surprise! When I heard you were transferring here this fall I told my mother I wanted to come here, too. But I kept it a big secret so you'd be surprised."

"Oh, Lordy, am I surprised! I can't begin to tell you."

"Pleasantly so, I hope! Hi, Marlena! How do you like it here?"

"I don't know. We've just arrived."

"Yeah, I know. The whole corridor is talking about all the luggage you girls brought. More than anybody else in the whole school," Ginny said admiringly. "Even more than Silky Burden. As a matter of fact, Silky doesn't even have a terrible lot of things and everyone knows the Burdens are richer than God."

"Is Silky on this floor?"

"Yeah. Down the hall. She's rooming with Jan Vanderbilt. Do you know her? I think she's awfully stuck-up."

"I know Jan from the Hamptons. She's not really stuck-up. She's kind of sweet. Just sort of reserved. Anybody else here I know?"

"You know Mimi Truewell, don't you? Her daddy's Rumson Oil. Her parents came up with her and they stayed for *hours*. They were afraid to leave their ittie-bittie baby all alone," she parodied.

"My God, Ginny! When did you arrive? You're already a walking encyclopedia of who's who at Chalmer's."

"Not really. There are two sisters here I haven't met yet. Their name is Dineen. Candy and DeeDee Dineen. They're from New Orleans. Half-French, or something like that. Some fancy family down there, somebody said. But their father is a movie star! He's supposed to be a dreamboat. Only their mother is married to Edward somebody, Wall Street, and they live in New York now. DeeDee's a soph, but she's living here at Main so she can room with her sister who's the frosh. They're both really beautiful, but stuck-up."

"Ginny thinks everybody is stuck-up," Sara explained to me. "We were just going next door to get acquainted with our neighbors. Who are they? Don't tell me you don't know, Ginny Furbush."

"Oh, I do. As a matter of fact I once went to school with one of them. Chrissy Marlowe. You know Chrissy?"

Sara shook her head.

"Are you sure? She's famous. She was in all the newspapers. Her aunt and grandmother snatched her away from her mother. You must've heard of the Marlowes. Her roommate is Maeve O'Connor. Her father's the writer—Pa . . . Pad . . . something. I never heard of him myself."

"Padraic O'Connor," I said. "I read one of his books. It was very difficult to understand. It was set in Ireland. He lives there even though he's an American. He's supposed to be one of the best living writers, but I thought his book was very . . . I don't know . . . kind of violent."

"You see, Ginny?" Sara said proudly. "My little cousin knows more than you do."

"I could die for shame," Ginny said, and sunk to the floor. Then she got up and said, "I gotta go. I have to look up somebody in Aldrich Hall across the road."

I giggled as Ginny exited.

Sara threw up her hands. "God! Who says you can get away from your past? C'mon, let's go next door and meet this Chrissy Marlowe. I *just* remembered who she is."

"You go ahead. I'll just get some things out for us to wear to dinner tonight."

"Are you sure? I told you I'm not going to let you be a weeping willow and wilt on the sidelines."

123

"I won't be a wilted weeping willow." I laughed. "I promise. And after you get acquainted you can introduce me. Okay?"

3.

"Come in," Chrissy called out in answer to the knock on her door. "This place is like Grand Central Station," she said to Maeve who was straightening the little piles of lingerie in her drawer. She was nervous each time their door opened. She was desperately hoping no one who had been at L'Ecole last year would show up.

She sighed with relief when Sara walked into the room. No, she had never seen this pretty girl before, she reassured herself.

"Hi, I'm next door. I'm Sara Gold from New York. Most recently, that is. From Charleston, originally."

"Hello. I'm Chrissy Marlowe. And this is my friend, Maeve O'Connor."

Sara went over to shake Maeve's hand. "You're the novelist's daughter. The one who's supposed to be the best living American writer."

Maeve smiled, puzzled. "How did you know?"

"Oh, I didn't. Ginny Furbush—I'm sure you'll get to meet her real soon—told us . . . my Cousin Marlena and me . . . that you were here and Marlena knew immediately who your father was. I bet you must be very intelligent."

Maeve was embarrassed but Chrissy answered for her. "She is." She was proud of her protégée.

"And you"—Sara went over to the bed where Chrissy was stretched out and sat down on the edge—"you're *really* famous!"

"Famous for being an orphan!" Chrissy mocked, but was pleased somehow to be recognized. "What about you?" she asked Sara. "Are your mother and father living?"

"Yes. My mother is and my father is, sort of."

They all laughed.

"Right now I'm sort of mad at my father, you see."

Chrissy sat up straight. "How come?" she asked. "What did he do? If you don't mind my asking."

Sara smiled disarmingly. "No, I don't mind. I know all about you, after all. About your aunt and mother fighting over you. I'm mad at my father because he was a Jew and didn't stay one. He *was* Jewish and now he's Episcopalian."

"You mean, you *want* him to be Jewish?"

124

"Well, that's what he's supposed to be, you know? I'm half-Jewish but I fully intend to become *all*. Officially, that is."

"I think that's very admirable of you," Maeve said in a voice that barely rose above a whisper. "Especially because of what's happening to the poor Jews in Germany and Poland and Austria. . . ."

Sara had never even thought about the Jews in Germany, Poland, and Austria. Embarrassed, she said vaguely, "Yes, of course. The Nazis." Then she said, "That's why I think it's so important to become one, officially, I mean. And I'm not afraid of the Nazis. I'm not afraid of anyone."

"Good!" Chrissy said. "I'm not afraid of anyone either. Have a smoke?" She offered the pack of Luckies.

"Oh, goody! You brought ciggies with you!"

"Yes. I came well prepared. Here." She pushed the gold cigarette lighter and the crystal ashtray at Sara.

"You know what I have in my trunk? A bottle of Sauterne. Why don't I get it and my cousin, Marlena, and we'll have a get-acquainted party."

"I don't think—" Maeve started to say.

Chrissy smiled a large smile. "Go ahead and get it. I think it's a divine idea."

"You know," Sara said, "when you smile you're absolutely beautiful." She turned to Maeve. "And *you* don't even have to smile. You're absolutely beautiful without smiling. I'll get the wine."

"This is my Cousin Marlena. She's from Charleston. She's a Leeds. We're both Leeds girls. And our great-grandfather fired that first shot at Fort Sumter . . . the one heard 'round the world, you know."

I looked down in embarrassment.

But Maeve said, "That wasn't the shot heard 'round the world. The shot heard 'round the world was—" She broke off.

Sara smiled. "Go on."

Maeve shook her head. "I'm sorry. I—"

"The shot heard 'round the world was fired at Lexington, Sara. The Revolutionary War," I told her, "not the War between the States. . . ."

Sara laughed. "Well, why didn't you say something before? You shouldn't let me go around making a little old fool of myself."

"I didn't mean to correct you," Maeve said. "I spoke before I thought."

"That's all right, Maeve," Chrissy told her. "Sara doesn't mind, do you? I told you Maeve was smart. She's always been privately tutored."

"I'll drink to that," Sara said gaily. She opened the bottle of wine. "Do you have some glasses? We only brought two goblets. We didn't have any more room in our trunks."

"Oh, I don't want any," Maeve said quickly.

125

"But you have to," Sara insisted. "We're going to drink to our friendship, the four of us."

"C'mon," Chrissy urged. She held two water tumblers. "You have to, Maeve. We're toasting all of us being friends."

I could see that Maeve was reluctant. "You shouldn't make her drink if she doesn't want to," I said.

"Is there alcoholism in your family?" Sara asked matter-of-factly. "Is that why you don't want to drink? My father says the Irish have a particular problem with liquor." Then she giggled. "My mother's an alcoholic and she's not even Irish. That's why Marlena is a tiny bit anxious about our drinking, too. She's afraid it runs in the family. But this is only a little wine. Nothing to fret about."

I studied my shoes. Sara *was* impossible.

"And *you* don't have to be embarrassed, Marlena," Sara said. "It's *my* mother who's the lush."

I could have died, but Maeve seemed impressed with Sara's honesty. "My father . . . does drink," she whispered, "but I don't know if he's an alcoholic. I don't know . . . I . . . oh, pour me some. This *is* a special occasion, isn't it?"

"Yes, it surely is," Chrissy agreed happily. "I'll get out the chocolates."

"All right. This time," Sara said, "since it is a special occasion. But after this we shouldn't be eating too many chocolates. It's terrible for the skin. And if we get all pimply and fat, we'll never get boyfriends. Men friends, that is."

She had already decided she would put Chrissy on a diet. She was at least ten pounds overweight. Without that ten pounds she would have a super figure.

Out of the corner of her eye, Sara caught Chrissy putting the chocolate back in the box. Good! She wanted the four of them, her three friends and herself, to be the most attractive girls at Chalmer's.

"We have to go down to dinner in a few minutes. We might as well finish off this wine." She refilled their glasses eking out the last drop from the bottle.

There was a gentle rap on the door.

"Girls, I've just come to say hello," a chirpy voice called.

"Oh, fuckers!" Chrissy jumped up from the bed. "It's *her,*" she whispered. "Old Chalmer. Quick! We've got to get rid of this evidence. . . . Damn!" She shoved the ashtray under the bed and fanned the air with flailing arms.

I grabbed the glasses and, opening a dresser drawer, tossed them in, flinching as I saw drops of wine stain a pile of nightgowns. Sara, holding the empty wine bottle and seeing Maeve fling the pack of cigarettes out the open window, immediately followed suit with the bottle.

"Come in," Chrissy called out as they heard the bottle crash on the

126

walk below. "Do come in, Miss Chalmer. Wow," she muttered under her breath.

The door opened and Ginny Furbush walked in, doubled over with laughter.

> "How ya douchin'?
> Ovary well,
> Cunt complain."

"Good grief," Sara wailed.

"Ginny Furbush!" Chrissy drawled. "I might have known!"

"Hi, Chrissy! Haven't seen you since Wilton's. I went to Tree's last year. It was better than Wilton's. *That* was a real nut house. Where did you go last year? Can I eat at your table? I'm supposed to eat with S. T. Stuyvesant but I can't *stand* her. She thinks she's better than everybody. How about it, girls? Pu-lease!"

"We'd be honored, I'm sure," Maeve said.

"*I'm* not so sure," Sara muttered under her breath.

"Tomorrow night we're lightening your hair," Sara told me as we put out the lights.

"I don't know, Sara."

"I do. We're having a mixer at the end of the month with that school across the lake, St. John's, and I want you to look ravishing. Not that it matters—it will probably be more *little* boys, legions of them."

"Maybe we'll meet some upperclassmen."

"That's the only thought that keeps me going."

We were silent a moment, each of us thinking our own thoughts. Then I said, "I like Maeve a real lot. She's really a lovely girl."

"She truly is," Sara agreed. "But I adore Chrissy. She's the funniest girl."

"I like her, too, but I think she's a little hard."

"Yes. Well, you'd be hard too if you went through what she has."

"I suppose. Sara, why did you have to tell them about your mother . . . about her drinking problem?"

"Why should I keep any secrets if we're going to be friends? Besides, I never told my darkest secret. That my father drove my mother into the insane asylum."

"Sara! It's a sanitarium. Not . . . you know . . ."

Sara laughed. "You can't even say the words, can you? You're a lucky girl, Marlena. *You* don't have any dark secrets, do you?"

Oh, but I do, I thought. *I have one secret that I've kept from you. I never told you how much my mother hates your poor mother. Or you, yourself, for that matter, Sara.* I sighed heavily.

"I feel so guilty," Sara said. "Here I've been having a good old time without even thinking about Mama lying right now in her asylum bed, miserable and friendless. Poor Mama. God has deserted her."

"I'm sure He hasn't, Sara. Just wait and see," I tried to reassure her.

"I think I'll say a prayer for Mama to my Jewish God, that's what I'll do."

———

Maeve lay in the dark thinking how frank Sara had been about her family. What a relief it must be to be so open, to have nothing to hide. Just like Chrissy. Her family history, sad as it was, was an open book, or so it seemed anyway. Maeve wished she could reveal everything, be open with her new friends. But she would never be able to enjoy the luxury of friendship without secrets. Her own secret was too horrendous even for deep friendship. It was Aunt Maggie's secret as well. To reveal it would be to betray Aunt Maggie. And her father. She could never do that to either of them. She loved them both too much.

She heard a stirring in the other bed. Was Chrissy crying? She made out the moving form in the dark. No, Chrissy wasn't crying. The slight rustling noise she heard was Chrissy, doing "it" to herself. Poor Chrissy. She hungered for love too.

Part Two

THE DEBS

Massachusetts

OCTOBER 1941

We had been at Miss Chalmer's for over four weeks already and were gradually getting accustomed. We had even made friends with some of the other girls. Ginny Furbush had attached herself to us even though Sara, whom Ginny particularly admired, teased her unmercifully. But Sara teased everybody. Sara *loved* the Dineen sisters—I guessed that was because they came from New Orleans and Sara loved everything Southern. Or rather, she *liked* Candy Dineen but was really crazy about DeeDee, the older sister. Sara and DeeDee were very much alike. DeeDee loved clothes, gossip, and talking about boys, just like Sara did, and they even fooled around in exactly the same way. Nobody else dared to go as far as Sara and DeeDee did, except maybe Chrissy. Chrissy was always ready for a good time even if she didn't smile much.

Sara worried a lot about her mother. She was on the phone to Kansas almost every day but she seldom got to talk to Aunt Bettina. But she did talk to a lot of different doctors and yelled at them and cried a lot and even begged sometimes. The phone was out in the hall and I was embarrassed for Sara because anyone who passed by could hear her. When she was really excited, the girls could even hear her in the rooms, I was sure. Luckily, Sara got over being upset quickly.

And Maeve was happy, I thought, even though she was kind of quiet. Every once in a while, she really went into a blue funk and her face was . . . well . . . closed. But I could see her making a conscious effort to shake it off. Every time we went down for our mail, I could see she was looking for a certain letter but it never seemed to come. I could tell that the letters from her Aunt Maggie that came two or three times a week were not what she was waiting for. I felt bad when I saw her face kind of fall. Was it a special boy she hoped to hear from or was it her father far away in Ireland? Sara voted for a boy and she was forever teasing Maeve about it. Then, at least, Maeve laughed and her sad mood passed. I thought she made a special effort to be gay for our sakes which I thought was a very nice quality. Maeve did have very good qualities.

Chrissy was probably the happiest one of us all, it seemed to me, even if she didn't smile much. It was as if she had cast off her past completely, had forgotten everything and everybody that existed before. Or tried to, anyway. She wouldn't even play in the school orchestra even though Miss Ritter, the music teacher, and Miss Chalmer knew that she was a very good pianist and her Aunt Gwen wanted her to study the piano. She was very good at drawing, too, and made wonderful caricatures, especially of Miss Chalmer. She was also an excellent "horsewoman." That was Miss Chalmer's word. Chrissy and Candy Dineen were probably the best horsewomen there. Maeve was good at tennis even though she said she had never played before, and I thought I would make the volleyball team. I was grateful that I was proficient at something besides studying even though Sara said that being proficient at volleyball was even worse than being an excellent student. Sara said that *any* form of physical activity was slightly déclassé, with the exception of dancing, and maybe sexual intercourse.

THE AUTUMN OF 1941

1.

"Miss Smythe has advised me that you will not participate in the physical education program, Sara. Now, we cannot tolerate this situation." Miss Chalmer eyed Sara over her wire-rimmed spectacles. "The school rules state quite precisely that every young lady must engage in the physical education program unless she is in some way incapacitated." She smiled brightly. "There is nothing in your medical records to indicate such a disability." She studied Sara from head to foot like a peregrine falcon appraising its prey. "And I see nothing about you that might preclude physical activity."

"I'm quite willing to go horseback riding. In fact, I'm quite fond of riding. And that *is* a physical activity, isn't it, Miss Chalmer?"

"We are talking about calisthenics, Sara. And team sports, such as field hockey and volleyball. Every Chalmer's girl must engage in a team sport, which encourages a cooperative spirit—an all for one, one for all spirit. And here at Chalmer's we also like to encourage the competitive spirit. A very important quality in today's world. We are, after all, preparing our girls to take their proper place in the world."

Proper place, meaning marrying somebody with enough money to contribute to the school's building program, Sara thought, but she only responded, "Yes, Miss Chalmer. Of course."

"We don't expect every girl to be a hockey player," Miss Chalmer enunciated carefully, "but every girl *can* play volleyball, can she not?"

"I suppose so." Sara knew that there was neither profit nor point to be gained by arguing with Miss Chalmer at this time—there were other ways of getting her way—a twisted ankle, a stubbed toe, painful menstrual cramps, maybe even a convenient swoon or two. She leaned over to shake hands with Miss Chalmer to show her willingness to be a good sport, and at the same time knocked over a carved jade horse that stood on the schoolmistress's desk. Serena Chalmer jumped and just managed to keep the little statue from smashing to the floor.

"Oh dear, I'm so sorry!" Sara cooed. "Goodness, I'm so clumsy. So darned uncoordinated, don't you know? But I will try to improve." Sara smiled charmingly and backed out of the room, desperately trying not to laugh in Miss Chalmer's face.

Maeve tried to interest Sara in playing tennis. Chrissy, lying on Sara's bed, had already agreed to give the game a chance. "I just started myself. You'll see how quickly you'll get the hang of it, Sara," Maeve urged.

Sara merely expressed disgust. "For God's sake, Maeve, what do you get out of it besides a good case of perspiration, a stiff elbow, or bulging muscles? Lordy, I can't think of anything less attractive than thick wrists."

"But I enjoy playing. When I was little I never got a chance to play with other kids. It's fun."

"Well, all right, if your idea of fun is getting all sweaty chasing a lil' ol' ball. But if I were you, I'd spend my time getting all that hair to behave."

"My hair?" Maeve's hand shot to the mop of blazing curls and her green eyes widened. "I didn't know there was anything wrong with my hair."

"Of course there's nothing wrong with your hair." Chrissy jumped to Maeve's defense like a protective hen. She glared at Sara. "I know oodles of people who would love to have all that curly hair."

"I didn't mean to offend," Sara said sincerely. "Your hair *is* gorgeous but there's enough for two people. If you'd set it in curlers after you washed it, it would be more manageable and tons more gorgeous."

Maeve looked puzzled. "Curlers? But my hair's already curly."

"That's what people simply fail to understand." Sara sighed with satisfaction. "If you set curly hair with the right curlers, you don't make it curlier; you just get smoother curls with more control. It will take out the kink and it won't curl just every which way. In other words, you'll be the boss."

"No, I won't," Maeve laughed. "You'll be the boss, Sara, and show me what to do. What kind of curlers shall I get? We can buy the curlers in town on Saturday."

"I already have the right curlers. We'll wash and set your hair tonight right after dinner."

"Thank you, Sara."

"Ho-ho . . . you'd best hold your thanks. You won't thank me tonight when you're sleeping on a head full of metal. It's pure hell! You probably won't catch a wink!" Then, smiling slyly, "Just like when you spend the night with a man."

"Sara Leeds Gold, you're just the biggest fabricator I've ever met up with at any school. I just fucking *know* you never spent the night with a man!" For emphasis, Chrissy blew a thick smoke ring.

Sara was annoyed that her word was being doubted. "Please don't blow smoke rings in my face. The smoke is bad for the complexion. And

134

please do refrain from using that nasty word . . . fucking . . . every two seconds. It is *so* unrefined. And how can you be sure that I didn't spend the night with a man?"

"For one thing, you've said yourself you don't *know* any men," Chrissy said logically.

"But that is not to say I haven't known a *few* for a *tiny* while," Sara explained with exaggerated patience.

"And where would you have had the opportunity to spend this whole night?" Chrissy asked, sure that she had stumped Sara.

Sara smiled sweetly. "You forget, dear Chrissy, that Mama was often 'away,' and Father was out of town a lot. More times than not I was all alone in the house."

"You *really* did spend the night with a man? You've really done *it?*" Chrissy asked. "Are you prepared to swear to the truth of your statement . . . swear to it on our friendship?"

"Oh, I never swear," Sara declared sanctimoniously. "I don't believe it's necessary between friends."

"You have to—"

"No, no," Maeve intervened. "She doesn't have to. She shouldn't be made to do something that's against her principles." *Oh, dear Lord, suppose they ask me if I'm a virgin? And I have to swear to it? Oh, no, please, God, don't let them ask me! . . .*

"Oh, poo, you sillies! No, I haven't spent the night with a man. Yet. But I fully intend to at the first opportunity."

Chrissy blew smoke out of her nostrils and watched it curl into the air. "I'm with you, Sara. You can call me Virgie for short, but not for long," she said blithely, but she wondered, where did Mademoiselle Jacqueline fit in? Had she technically lost her virginity then? A little? Totally? She wasn't sure. She had an urge to tell the girls about it. Would they laugh? Would they think her terrible? Maeve would be shocked terribly, for sure. Maybe she wouldn't want to be her friend anymore. Sara would probably think it was *très* interesting, a lark. Even exciting. She would certainly probe for all the details. She would dig and dig until she got them all. No, the best thing was just to wipe Jacquie Payot out of her mind as if she never existed, never lived, never loved . . . She was going to concentrate on boys—men. She would never love a girl that way again. Of course she loved Maeve, Sara, Marlena, but not like that!

I walked in, my arms full of books, followed by a perspiring Ginny carrying my overflow. Everybody looked very serious. "What's going on?" I asked. "What is everybody talking about?" I dropped my load of books on the bed.

Sara kissed me. "Our little bookworm. I do so worry about her eyes. We were discussing the problem of virginity, Marlena. So far, *I* have shamefully confessed to this terrible affliction, as has Chrissy. But now the rest of you have to confess too, or else under the threat of being excluded from our charmed circle, describe in vivid color the details of your deflowering, Maeve," Sara urged, "how about you? Are you virgin territory?" But she wasn't being serious. Everybody *knew* that Maeve was pure as the driven snow.

But still, Maeve flushed furiously.

"For heaven's sake, Sara, leave poor Maeve alone. Look what you've gone and done. You've embarrassed her." Chrissy draped a reassuring arm over Maeve's shoulder. "Maeve doesn't even think about such things."

"Yes, Sara," I cut in. I promised myself that if my cousin breathed one word about how my own hymen had been broken, I would never, never forgive her.

"Oh, all right. We'll leave Maeve alone. She will not be forced to utter the terrible words, 'I am pure . . . *Je suis très vierge*,' " Sara declared dramatically, stretching her arms heavenward. She turned to me and I gazed at her pleadingly. "And we will allow you the same privilege, dear Marlena. We will spare you the necessity of declaring yourself ignorant of a man's peenie-weenie."

Chrissy and Maeve giggled and I felt a surge of grateful love for Sara. She had not betrayed me after all.

Sara turned to Ginny who was, for the first time in her life, subdued. "All right, Furbush. Let's hear it from you. Has any man bestowed upon your large ass the largess of his ding-dong?"

Again the girls laughed even though Sara was being incredibly vulgar. She *was* funny! Only Ginny didn't laugh, Ginny of the vulgar limericks.

"Oh ho, what have we here? Speak, Ginny F., or forever leave our domain."

"Okay, I'll tell you. Only you have to promise not to tell my mother or Miss Chalmer."

"We are not about to divulge your secrets to Miss Chalmer. What a thought! Or your mother," Chrissy assured her. "For fucking sake, speak up!"

"I'm a fallen woman," Ginny declared matter-of-factly. "Cross my heart and hope to die."

Our mouths fell open. *Ginny Furbush?*

Sara's eyes narrowed. "Are you lying to us, Furbush? If you're not telling the truth—"

"I'm not lying, I swear it. My cousin, Theodore Taft Pepper, stuck it into me last Independence Day. It was at a party at our summerplace in Bar Harbor. Theodore Taft is my *second* cousin, not my first. But it was the first time for him, too."

"Oh, my Lord!" Sara breathed. "This is too heavenly. Who would have believed it? Our little Ginny. Now that's what I really call fireworks on the Fourth of July. And that name . . . Theodore Taft Pepper! . . . All right, Ginny, let's hear how you lost your own little cherry bomb in one big explosion." Sara removed a bottle of rosé from the bottom drawer of her bureau. "Now, Ginny, tell us, who made the first move? Eager, panting, little you or sweating, hot-with-desire Theodore Taft?"

2.

"It's my birthday next week, Sara," Mimi Truewell said, standing on one foot.

"That's extremely interesting, I'm sure, Mimi, but I have to wash my hair. So, if you don't mind—" Sara opened the door and waited for Mimi to leave. Since they had arrived at Chalmer's, Mimi Truewell had made a concerted effort to become an intimate of Sara and Chrissy, but they had politely but firmly rebuffed her as a pitiful social-climber who infuriatingly referred to herself and her schoolmates as "junior debs." "And as you're leaving, you can tell me why you are standing on one foot."

"Just practicing. It's not as important how *long* you can do it but the manner *in which* you do it. Gracefully. Ginny Furbush can do it nearly as long as I can but she's as graceful as an elephant. Would you care to see how long and how gracefully you can do it?"

"Certainly not. I haven't the least desire to stand on one foot, gracefully or not. So, hop on out, Mimi dear."

"Wait. I came to invite you to my birthday party. Mommy and Daddy are coming up this weekend to make me a birthday party. At the Blue Swan Inn in town on Sunday afternoon. I know the Inn really stinks, but it's the best this town has to offer. Mommy said I have to really limit my list of invitees but I really want you to come."

"Who else is coming? Any boys?"

Mimi Truewell found the impact of Sara's last question so stunning, she lowered the leg that was airborne to the floor. "No. I told you the invitation list is limited. Besides, I don't know any boys around here. Except for the few I got to dance with when we had that exchange dance with St. John's. Mommy said I wasn't to invite any boys because then I'd have to invite only as many girls as I had boys. And Mommy says it's more important at my age to have the best junior debs at my party."

"I see. I guess we'll come. It will be a respite from the revolting slop they serve here."

"We?" Mimi asked nervously.

"I'm accepting for Marlena too, so you can save yourself the trouble of hopping into our room again."

"The real trouble is, I *can't* invite Marlena. I told you the guest list is limited and Mommy says I should invite the girls who are . . . well, you know, the ones whose families she knows. I *am* inviting Chrissy and Maeve. My mother sort of knows Chrissy's aunt. They served on the same committee once."

Sara fixed the squirming Mimi with cold eyes. "What about Maeve? Does your mother know Maeve's father too? Or is it your father who knows him? I just bet they're best friends." She smiled nastily.

"No . . . I don't think so . . . but—"

"Oh, then I guess your mother's best friends with Maeve's aunt in Boston?"

"No."

"Really?" Sara drawled. "But still you're inviting her. It's mighty strange. Well, count me out. If my cousin isn't good enough for your dumb party at the Blue Swan, then your dumb party isn't good enough for Maeve, Chrissy, or me. None of us are interested in playing twenty questions about our family trees with Mommy and Daddy Truewell, who, I've heard, didn't get off the boat until 1919. My goodness, can that be true? Shocking! If word gets out, you'll be lucky if *anybody* comes to any party of yours ever again. But don't you worry, I promise not to breathe a word—"

"That's a big lie. Both Mother's and Daddy's families came here way back in the nineteenth century. And I wouldn't talk if I were you, Sara Gold. Everybody knows about your mother, that she's . . . Look, Sara, bring your cousin if you really want to. Goodness knows, I don't have anything against her. It's just that the guest list was limited to twenty junior debs!"

"Well, we're limited too. We don't go to all the stupid parties we get invited to. So take a big, fat, graceful walk on that one leg of yours, Mimi Upstart! . . ."

"I'd just love to sabotage her party," Sara confided to Chrissy. "It's not enough just not to go. Can you think of something really nasty we could do?"

"Golly, I sure can!" She lit a cigarette. Now that she was dieting, she smoked more than ever. In the few weeks they had been at Chalmer's she had already lost ten pounds. Her face had thinned and there were hollows in her cheeks that accented the doe eyes. "I have a really terribly terrific idea. We paint a swastika on *your* door when we are absolutely sure nobody's looking and then we put the blame on Mimi. Her father is one of those America Firsters and everybody knows *they're* anti-Semitic. And then *you* scream anti-Semitism, really loud.

138

Miss Chalmer is probably anti-Semitic herself but she'll be forced to take disciplinary action against Mimi. Isn't that a divine idea?"

Sara looked at Chrissy with admiration. "Divine. But how will we prove that Mimi did it?"

"Because somebody saw her do it. Me."

Sara threw her arms around Chrissy. "You are a darling. It's perfect! Only, don't tell Marlena. She'd be upset that we were doing this just because she wasn't invited to Mimi's party."

"And don't tell Maeve either. You know how Maeve is. She'd start to cry if she thought we were doing something mean to somebody, even Mimi Truewell."

"Our lips are sealed."

"It is hard for me to believe that a Chalmer girl would do something like this," the headmistress addressed both Sara and Mimi in her office.

"I didn't do it, Miss Chalmer! You've got to believe me! Why would I do such a thing? I never even thought of Sara as Jewish. I invited her to my party. I never would have invited her to my party if I knew she was— My father wouldn't have sent me here in the first place if he thought you took . . . you know. All I know is, I didn't do it!"

Oh, dear, Serena Chalmer thought, what am I to do now? These wretched girls. . . . She was damned whatever policy she proclaimed regarding Jews. "We would never exclude those of the Hebrew faith deliberately, Mimi. We do not practice discrimination against any group. Besides, Sara is not of the Hebrew faith; she is a Protestant," she said firmly. Maybe, if she just acted firm enough, she could confine and settle this thing, right here in her office.

"But that's not quite so," Sara offered sweetly. She knew exactly the dilemma in which Miss Chalmer found herself. "I am half-Jewish by birth and blood and all Jewish by inclination."

Serena Chalmer glared at Sara. Those people were all alike. . . . Given any kind of advantage they turned against their benefactors.

"That is not the information given us by your father, Sara," she pointed out acidly. "However—"

"However," Sara interrupted, helping the schoolmistress out, "that doesn't mean that I should be persecuted by having that awful symbol painted on my door." She started to cry. "I always dreamed of going to this school. I would never have believed that I would come to such a wonderful school and that such a terrible thing would happen to me. I might as well be living in Germany."

Serena Chalmer bit her lip in vexation. She wished both these despicable girls would fall through the floor and vanish from her sight.

"But I didn't do it," Mimi cried, gazing at the crying Sara in disbelief. "I didn't even know she was half-Jewish," she whined.

"She did too. I told her so myself. And she's called me a dirty Jew several times before this."

"Oh, I didn't! I *tried* to be friends with her! But I guess my father was right. He said you can't trust any long-nosed Jew."

"There, Miss Chalmer! You see?" Sara cried triumphantly and unloosed a fresh torrent of tears.

"That will do! A disgraceful situation! I am shocked, Sara, and disheartened that this has occurred at our school, an institution noted for both its high educational and moral standards. But, it is the word of one girl against another. I will have to investigate further and try to get at the truth. In the meantime, I want both of you to refrain from accusations and name-calling, and I insist that neither of you discuss this with anybody else until we have more facts."

Sara waited until Miss Chalmer finished, then smiled prettily. "But it is not just my word against Mimi's. I assure you I would never make any accusation purely upon conjecture. Mimi was *seen* doing it. Chrissy Marlowe saw her!"

Mimi was stunned. "But she couldn't have—"

"You mean Christina actually saw Mimi painting that thing on your door?"

"Yes, Miss Chalmer."

Damn! Now the situation was beyond hope, Serena Chalmer thought with disgust. Even if Sara and her friend Chrissy were both lying, which might very well be the case.

"Very well! We will go upstairs and confront Christina immediately."

Sara was terrified now that Chrissy would be caught smoking. At the speed the little old bird was flying, Chrissy wouldn't even have a chance to douse her cigarette. And Miss Chalmer was mad enough to expel Chrissy on the spot. "I am dreadfully sorry to have caused you all this trouble, Miss Chalmer," Sara practically shouted. "You do believe me, don't you, Miss Chalmer?"

"I'm right next to you, Sara, and I am not deaf. It is not necessary to shout."

The schoolmistress knocked once then barged into Chrissy's room, trailed by an eager Sara and a reluctant Mimi, who knew by animal instinct that she was playing against a stacked deck. Chrissy stood at attention while Maeve sat at her desk, chewing nervously on a fingernail.

Serena Chalmer slapped at Maeve's finger without thinking. "I do not understand, Christina, why, when you saw Mimi painting this swastika, you did not interrupt her. Why didn't you?"

Chrissy elongated her eyes—a trick she had learned by practicing before the mirror. "Oh, I wanted to, really I did. But the words caught in my throat. I was so upset I couldn't say a thing. I just went back to my room and fell on my bed trying to make sense out of the whole thing.

Why, when there's so much trouble in the world, why would anyone want to add to it—to pick on an innocent victim like poor, sweet Sara? I was raised a good Christian by my grandmother, Patricia Marlowe, you know, and I said to myself: 'Chrissy, this is an unchristian act. And tacky, besides.' "

"Exactly. Tacky," Sara breathed.

"She's lying, Miss Chalmer! They're both lying! Sara's just mad because I didn't want to invite her nobody of a cousin to my party!"

"How dare you?" Sara demanded with furious indignation. "My cousin is a Leeds of Charleston, as am I. Our forefathers fought in the Civil War to protect us from the likes of you, you . . . Yankee! You . . . Nazi swine!"

"Stop it, this instant!" Miss Chalmer snapped. "As you didn't see it, Sara, it's still the word of one girl against the other. Either Christina or Mimi is lying. But as we have no proof, we will all have to accept the situation and hope the guilty party's conscience will force her to confess."

"Oh, but I would never lie, Miss Chalmer," Chrissy said reasonably. "Grandmother Marlowe taught me it was a sin to tell a lie."

Suddenly, Maeve rushed forward and whispered, "Chrissy's telling the truth, Miss Chalmer. When Chrissy came back in the room and told me what Mimi was doing, I went out in the hall and saw Mimi just finishing up."

Everyone stared at Maeve.

"Why didn't you speak out before?" the schoolmistress asked.

"It's hard for me to condemn another person." Maeve gazed down at the floor to avoid Mimi's eyes.

"Very well. We have the word of two witnesses and I will have to abide by that. Your party will be cancelled, Mimi. I will telephone your father myself and explain the circumstances to him. You may count yourself lucky that your punishment is not more severe. Any repetition of such behavior will be much more severely treated, I assure you."

"Maeve's lying too! They're all in this together. I'm being framed. My father is going to be so mad! He'll probably take me out of this stupid school."

"To the contrary, I'm sure he'll be as distressed as I am that a Chalmer's girl could do anything so despicable. Now I think you had better go to your room and remain there for the rest of the day and evening. And I caution all of you not to repeat any of this to anyone. Under the circumstances."

Sara mouthed the word "Nazi" at Mimi as Miss Chalmer led her from the room.

Sara and Chrissy spun around and hugged Maeve.

"You saved the day!" Sara rejoiced.

"How come you lied?" Chrissy asked admiringly. "I would never have asked you to lie for us."

"Because I could tell Miss Chalmer didn't believe you. She thought you were both lying."

"Us lie?" Chrissy hooted. "What a notion. Sara, when you called Mimi both a Nazi *and* a Yankee, I thought I'd just about die. Why the long face, Maeve? We won!"

"I do hate to lie."

"But it was for such a good cause. We did it to avenge Marlena's honor," Sara said piously.

Chrissy punched her arm. "And because it was such fun!"

3.

"There's an announcement on the bulletin board," I informed Sara. "Thanksgiving dinner will be celebrated at school for those girls who have no plans for going home. I guess that means us."

"Not on your life. I don't intend to sit around for four days gobbling macaroni and cheese and Jell-O with carrot slivers when we could be somewhere else enjoying nectar and ambrosia."

"But what else can we do? It's too far to Charleston for just four days."

"We can go to New York."

"You haven't even spoken to your father since we got here."

"So what? We can still stay at the house. And even if he's there, I don't have to talk to him. We can go out for Thanksgiving dinner. Didn't you ever hear of eating Thanksgiving dinner in a restaurant? Lots of New Yorkers do that. We'll be able to go shopping and go to all the movies and shows we want. Just think—no Miss Chalmer, no supervision for four glorious days."

"I guess that part sounds good," I said unenthusiastically.

"Well, it's better than staying here with the rest of the goops, isn't it? And you've hardly even seen New York. You haven't gone to Radio City Music Hall or the Automat or the Planetarium or skated at Rockefeller Center, for God's sake!"

"It just won't seem like Thanksgiving having dinner in a restaurant."

"Oh, jeepers! If it's homey you want we'll eat at a Child's or a Schrafft's and you can see all the mommies and daddies and their rotten kids," Sara said with some asperity. "I know! We can eat at Child's Paramount and then we can go next door and catch the show. Maybe it'll be Harry James or Jimmy Dorsey or maybe we'll be able to 'swing and sway with Sammy Kaye.' "

"All right, Sara. That sounds like fun." I tried to smile.

"Or if you'd rather, we can have the staff serve us dinner at home and go out after. Wait a minute. I just bet Chrissy doesn't have any plans either! We'll ask her, and Maeve, too, if she doesn't plan on going to Boston. Just think—the four musketeers without anyone keeping tabs on us or telling us what to do."

"Don't you think you had better check with your father first?"

"No. If he's home, he *will* try to entertain us, but we'll ignore him."

Poor Uncle Maurice, I thought, even though I knew that he had earned this punishment by being mean to Aunt Bettina.

"Chrissy and I are going to Aunt Maggie's for Thanksgiving. It's only an hour or so to Boston and Aunt Maggie is counting on it so. There's going to be a big party—you can imagine the fuss they make about Thanksgiving in Boston. It seems there was a relative from my grandmother's side of the family that actually attended the first feast with the Indians. Can you imagine?"

"Doesn't it sound simply excruciating?" Chrissy glowed. "Though I'm sure I'll gain five pounds."

"You know, in all the years I lived with my father on the Cape it was just the two of us for holiday dinners." Maeve's voice trailed off and she was lost in a reverie for a few seconds. It was the first time she had volunteered mention of her father. "But this year, it's going to be *all* the Abbott relatives. And there are dozens and dozens of them."

"Sounds lovely," Sara said wistfully.

"You two are coming too. Chrissy and I were counting on it and Aunt Maggie would be very angry if she knew that you two had no special plans and didn't come home with us. Besides, Aunt Maggie's dying to meet both of you. You had better say you're coming or Chrissy and I will put you both to death by tickling."

"Sara?" I pleaded.

"Of course," Sara dimpled. "I've always wanted to see how the Yankees did things. But just promise me, Maeve—no macaroni and cheese, not one bite."

After Sara and I went back to our room, I noticed a change of mood in Sara. "Do you really mind going to Boston instead of New York?" I asked.

"No."

"Then what's bothering you?"

"I was thinking of Mama eating her Thanksgiving dinner all by herself. Poor Mama! To start out life in beautiful Charleston and land up all alone in a Kansas sanitarium."

"She'll get better. She'll come back, Sara. You'll see."

"Maybe. But *where* will she go when and if she does get better? That's the sixty-four-dollar question."

"You'll figure it out, Sara. You always figure out something."

"I aim to. Look, when we go to Boston, you wear my gray squirrel and I'll wear the beaver."

"Do you think we really should? Won't we look kind of—you know—showy?"

"Listen, honeychile, you want them thar Yankees to think we Southern gals are all hillbillies?"

"Oh, Sara," I said, full of admiration for Sara's spirit. "You *are* such a funny girl."

"I am, aren't I?"

Maggie O'Connor was a plain-looking woman, almost shapeless in a dark green wool dress and with a rather untidy bun, but she did smell of lilacs. I noticed Chrissy looking at her wistfully, as she hugged each of us in turn. It was almost as if Chrissy were trying to inhale her fragrance.

"Welcome to Boston, girls. I'm so pleased you came to share Thanksgiving with us."

I looked around. It was hard to believe that Maeve's Aunt Maggie, who was reputedly so rich, lived in this rather plain house. It *was* beautifully paneled and there was a lot of really lovely silver gleaming and a host of family portraits hanging on the walls, but I could see Sara looking unbelievingly at the furniture. It was unstylish and the colors were sort of dreary—brown and maroon velvet. But Aunt Maggie herself was sweet and warm, and I could see where Maeve got her well-bred manner, if not her looks.

We sat down to a late supper while Maggie told us about all the various Abbotts who would be attending the Thanksgiving dinner the next day.

"You know, I went to Newport when I was a little girl, when my grandmother was still alive. And I think I remember that there was a lady named Abbott living next door. Was that your family too?" Chrissy asked.

"Yes, that was *my* grandmother," Maggie laughed, remembering how unpopular her family had been with Patricia Marlowe. "And I went to Newport when I was a little girl and stayed in that very house. But, of course, that was years before you were born. And for a while we O'Connors had a house of our own there too, but then my father sold his house and we stopped going there for the summers. But I still own the Abbott house. I haven't opened it for years but maybe I will next summer. And all of you can come stay with us."

"That would be lovely, Aunt Maggie."

"Golly, Maeve," Chrissy sighed. "Wouldn't it have been great if you had gone to Newport when I was there, next door? We could have been friends then. You've never gone?"

"No. Never." Maeve turned to her aunt. "How is Grandmother, Aunt Maggie?"

"Well. She's reading *War and Peace* again and she's tatting a very large tablecloth. It's already thirteen feet long and thirteen feet wide."

"Thirteen by thirteen?" Chrissy repeated. "She must have a very large table."

"It's for the Winter Palace," Aunt Maggie said gently. "Maeve's grandmother lives in another world, you see."

Sara frowned, leaned forward. "What do you mean—another world?"

"A world of retreat where things are more peaceful and less threatening. A happier world for her."

"Would it be all right if I went to see her? And took the girls along, Aunt Maggie?" Maeve asked.

"If you stay just a few minutes and say nothing to upset her."

"Oh, we wouldn't say anything to upset her, Aunt Maggie," Chrissy blurted, then realizing that she had addressed Maeve's aunt as her own, added, "Oh, I'm sorry . . . Miss O'Connor."

"I would *like* you to call me Aunt Maggie, Chrissy. And you too, Sara and Marlena, if you would like. And I'd like all of you to think of this as your second home."

"Make that my *first* home," Chrissy laughed. "I really don't have another."

Margaret Abbott O'Connor sat in her drawing room with yards of lace tablecloth surrounding her as she tatted. Red-faced, round Annie who had admitted the girls, hovered protectively as they took their seats around the frail Margaret, dressed in a yellow satin ball gown with tiny matching bows caught up in a myriad of gray-white curls.

"How sweet of you to come calling, children. Are you the three sisters? No, of course not. How stupid of me. There are four of you, aren't there?" She pointed a finger and counted. "One, two, three, four. How strange. I thought there were only three of you yearning to go to Moscow," she said vaguely.

"That's a lovely tablecloth you're making," Chrissy commented, running her fingers over the lace.

"It's for the Palace. And I must hurry. We will need it very soon. There's going to be a wedding."

"Who's getting married?" Sara asked.

Margaret frowned. "I don't remember." Then she laughed softly. "It's one of the young ones. Anastasia, perhaps."

"It will be a lovely wedding, I'm sure," Maeve said.

145

"You must come to the wedding. I think the prince will want to dance with you."

"I hope he'll dance with all of us," Sara said.

"Oh, he will. He has lovely manners and he adores pretty girls. We must decide what you all will wear."

"What are you going to wear?" Sara asked.

Margaret looked confused. "I don't know." Then she brightened. "I know. I will ask Vronsky. He has such style. He'll surely know. He adores red. He will probably tell me to wear red. We will ask Vronsky what the three . . . no, four . . . of you should wear. Don't you think Vronsky has great style?" she asked Chrissy.

Chrissy looked at Maeve for help.

"Oh, yes," Maeve said. "I think so." She saw that Annie was getting nervous. "We just stopped by for a minute. We'll be going now."

We all kissed Margaret on the cheek and left.

Walking back to Maggie's house, Chrissy asked Maeve who Vronsky was. "Oh, he was Anna Karenina's lover. In the book. . . ."

"How long has she been like this?" Sara asked.

Maeve lifted her shoulders. "I really don't know. I only met her myself just over a year ago."

"But what happened to her? To make her like this?" Sara persisted.

"I don't know."

"What about your grandfather?" Sara asked. "Is he dead?"

"Yes."

"Was he mean to her?"

Maeve became upset. "I think so. But I really don't know. Why do you want to know?"

"I'd like to know, for my own reasons. Do you think you might ask your Aunt Maggie?"

"I'd rather not, Sara. We don't talk about things like that."

Later that night, as Sara and I lay in the twin beds in the room we shared, Sara said, "Can you imagine Maeve not knowing anything about her grandmother and not even trying to find out? Did you hear her? 'We don't talk about things like that.' How can you *not* talk about things like that?"

"Some people don't like to talk about things that are unpleasant, Sara. Some things are best left unsaid."

"Oh, poo! One thing I can't stand are people who are too polite to talk about things that really matter. There's *nothing* I wouldn't talk about."

"I know, Sara, but that's you. You like letting all your thoughts out."

Sara took a deep breath. "I guess so. It must be my Jewish blood."

I had to laugh. "You think *everything's* your Jewish blood. Do you really think there's so much difference between people? Whether they're Jewish or Protestant?"

"I certainly do. For instance, if it were me with that grandmother, I'd never rest until I got to the bottom of that particular kettle of fish. That's because I'm Jewish and Maeve's Protestant."

"She's Catholic."

"How about those Abbotts? They're about as Protestant as you can get. That makes Maeve half-Protestant, and that's the difference; it's the Protestant blood that makes her that way."

I giggled uncontrollably.

"What's so funny?" Sara demanded.

"You! You're half-Protestant too. I guess it's your Protestant blood that makes you that way, too."

"And you're *all* Protestant, Marlena Williams, and pig-headed to boot!"

The next morning we awoke at eight to find the house a beehive of activity. Preparations for the three o'clock dinner had started at six that morning and three tables were already set up horseshoe fashion in the Georgian dining room to accommodate the sixty-nine guests. Sixty-nine guests and all Abbotts, related by marriage or blood. Sara and Chrissy found that fascinating.

"We have to hurry with breakfast," Maeve urged. "We have a very special schedule planned for today. We're beginning with a traditional Pilgrim breakfast—beans, brown bread and fish cakes. . . ."

Chrissy emitted a groan.

"Because you're dieting, Chrissy, you don't have to eat the beans or the bread, but you have to at least make a stab at the fish cakes. Aunt Maggie's doing all this in your, Sara's and Marlena's honor, after all."

"Okay, okay, I will. Promise, hope to die. Then, after breakfast, what are we doing?"

"We're going to Plymouth to observe the 'Pilgrims' Progress' celebration. I've never gone myself but it sounds like wonderful fun. The local people dress up as Pilgrims and march up to the site of the fort on Burial Hill where the Pilgrims used to meet for worship. It starts at a quarter after ten, and since it will take us about an hour to get there, we have only an hour or so to get ready."

"It sounds lovely," I said as Sara rolled her eyes at Chrissy, who then jabbed her in the ribs with an elbow.

We had the Pilgrims' breakfast in the morning room and I noticed that *all* the help was Irish, each with at least some measure of a brogue. Back home in Charleston, all the servants were colored and in New York, at Sara's, they were all white, though made up of various nationalities. When I commented on this, Maeve explained that most of the help had

147

been hired only for the day since Aunt Maggie ran a very quiet, simple household with only two regular servants. But if she needed extra help, she always hired Irish immigrants since she believed they needed the work more than others.

Chrissy was not interested in a discussion of servants; it was the Abbott family she was curious about. She wanted to know the names of everyone coming and their relationship to each other.

Maeve laughed. "I'm not quite sure who's who myself. There's my granduncles James and Paul. Their wives, Helen and Dorothy . . ."

"What's their children's names?"

"I'm not sure. Cousin Jane, Mary, and Susan. And a Laura and a Lauren, he's a boy. But there are so many cousins, and cousins' children. There's John, and Peter, and James, and there's a Henry and . . ." Maeve threw up her hands. "You'll have to wait and figure it all out for yourself. A lot of the names are the same and I get them all mixed up. And some are blood relatives and some just married into the family. And these are only the Abbotts. Saturday, Aunt Maggie's having some of the O'Connor relatives over. My grandfather, Patrick O'Connor, never had much to do with his family, but my grandmother—when she was well—kept up with them and so does Aunt Maggie, a little anyway. Aunt Maggie's like that."

"How come she never married?" Sara asked.

Maeve flushed. "I don't know."

"You don't ask personal questions like that, Sara," I said, embarrassed.

"I have some Hatton relatives from my mother's side but I've never even met them," Chrissy broke in. "And I've got a bunch of Marlowes—two, three, four times removed—somewhere." She nibbled at the one fish cake she was allowing herself. "I do have three first cousins . . . Aunt Gwen's kids . . . but I hardly ever see them. If I never saw them or Aunt Gwen again, I wouldn't mind that either. But I'm dying to meet your relatives, Maeve. Aren't you, Sara?"

"Yes. But *I* have the best first cousin in the world." She smiled. "I truly hope you all get to meet her sometime."

"Very funny," I said. "But Sara does have a lot of relatives on her father's side, don't you, Sara?"

"Indeedy. Only they are Goldbergs and I don't know anything about them. My father wouldn't talk about them. But someday I'll look them up and I'll probably adore them."

"No, you'll probably be disappointed," Chrissy said, finishing up the last morsel of her fish cake.

"That's a mean thing to say," Sara said.

"Believe me, Sara. I'm an expert at relatives. Golly, I surely would love another fish cake but I don't dare."

We drove down to Plymouth in the big blue Buick touring car while Maggie stayed behind to supervise the dinner preparations. Reagen, the chauffeur, was a garrulous old-timer who commented on every point of interest along the way. We arrived in Plymouth right on time to see the modern-day Pilgrims gather near the famous Rock on the waterfront as drums rolled, and march up Leyden Street to the fort on Burial Hill. Then along with the rest of the observers, we joined the "early settlers" in the singing of Psalms.

"Aunt Maggie says these were taken from the Book of Psalms and translated from the Hebrew by somebody named Henry Ainsworth, and were sung by the earliest Pilgrims way back in Holland and then in Plymouth."

"Well," Sara said with satisfaction, "since they were originally in Hebrew I guess I can join in."

"We are going to have turkey at our dinner, but you know the Pilgrims really didn't eat turkey that first Thanksgiving," Maeve told us on the drive back to Boston.

"Really?" I marveled. "I didn't know that."

"They had venison, roast duck, goose, clams, eels, wheat and corn breads, leeks, watercress, wild plums, succotash, and homemade wine. I don't know why they didn't eat turkey."

"Golly, how do you know all that?"

Maeve, who had been speaking with enthusiasm, now lowered her voice. "I told you . . . I used to spend most of my time reading and studying. . . ." She seemed thoughtful. "Father used to tell me stories about the Pilgrims." Then her mood brightened again. "Today, we are going to reproduce practically everything they ate that first Thanksgiving. Except for the eels and things like that, of course. We're going to have roast duck stuffed with apples and raisins, goose stuffed with mashed potatoes and chestnuts—" Chrissy moaned, but Maeve continued; ". . . and Plymouth clam pie and creamed oysters. . . ."

"Pleeeasse, I think I'm going to pass out," Chrissy protested.

"Oh, just this one day you can eat. And we're going to have squash soup and corn pudding and sweet potato pudding and glazed onions and all kinds of pies—mince and pumpkin and cherry and cranberry tarts and Bradford Plum pudding served with rum sauce and—" Chrissy tried putting her hand over Maeve's mouth but Maeve eluded her, "named after the first governor of Plymouth."

"I really am going to swoon," Chrissy said happily. "I can always starve myself when I get back to school. There it's *easy* not to eat."

Chrissy conceded that it *was* hopeless trying to place and remember which Abbott was which, as she drank cup after cup of the eggnog made from the Harvard Club recipe, also an Abbott family tradition.

Uncle Paul said the formal grace, then Cousin Susan's little girl, Jennifer, recited the Selkirk Grace:

> Some hae meat and canna eat
> And some wad eat that want it
> But we hae meat and we can eat
> And so the Lord be thanked.

Everyone laughed and applauded. Sara whispered to me, "Lordy, did you ever?"

Then Maggie rose and announced that Uncle James would read from Governor Bradford's *Plimoth Plantation,* about that first harvest in 1621.

"Jeepers, do you believe this?" Sara asked me, but I ignored her. As Uncle James read on, Sara kept muttering under her breath. When he came to a part that told of a great store of wild turkeys, Sara raised her hand and called out, "If they had this great store of wild turkeys, why didn't they *eat* turkey on that first Thanksgiving?"

The assembled guests stared at Sara. *The girl from New York had actually interrupted James!* But then several other guests took up the chant, why then indeed had they not eaten turkey? Some insisted they *had* eaten turkey, after all, and a lively discussion took place until James cleared his throat emphatically and the voices, dissenting and agreeing, died down, and James finished his reading.

The serving of the dinner began and a large silver tray of bread was passed. Maggie explained to the girls that there were two kinds of bread—corn and something called Anadama Bread, so named because a New England farmer had a wife named Anna who was lazy and her bread reflected this condition, so that her husband was driven to make his own bread, all the time muttering, "Anna, damn 'er!"

I laughed. "Down home in Charleston we have Anadama Bread too, and we tell exactly the same story, only the farmer in the story is a South Carolinian." Then suddenly I was embarrassed. *Oh, golly, I've been rude. I've made Aunt Maggie look a fool! . . .*

But everyone else laughed too, as did Maggie. "I'm not a bit surprised," she teased. "Those Charlestonians are always trying to steal our Boston thunder."

Hugh Winthrop asked Chrissy if she would care to take a walk around the Square after dinner. Hugh Winthrop was an Abbott by way of his mother, Alva. He was seventeen, with wavy blond hair, pale blue eyes and a small, beaked nose. Chrissy did not find him in any way appealing. Actually, she didn't want to leave the warmth and the good cheer she felt emanating from within the house, the burning hearths redolent with pine cones, the noise level of familial good fellowship. But Sara was smiling at her encouragingly, and she knew that she had to start somewhere, with *some* boy . . . to wipe out some of the pictures in her mind that wouldn't go away no matter how hard she tried to wipe them away. *If I'm ever going to be a femme fatale, I might as well begin. And darn it—I'm going to be one if it kills me.*

They slipped out of the house, shoulders hunched against the cold, raw wind. A slight mist was falling.

"How do you like Boston?"

"It's all right."

They looked into houses they passed, rooms ablaze with light. Some of the families were still dining, one window revealed a group of beautifully dressed people toasting each other with silver mugs. A lady in a wine-colored dinner dress caught Chrissy's eye. Her fall of hair brought a vague image—another lady, a gray late afternoon in a London salon. . . .

Within a few minutes, they had made their way around the small Square then retraced their steps.

"How do you like that school of yours?" he asked.

"I've been to worse."

He snickered. "I'd just bet. I'll be going to Harvard next year."

"Really?"

"If I don't go into the Navy first."

She looked at him. He didn't seem old enough for that. Just a boy with pale, watery eyes. "Really?"

"Everybody says we'll probably be at war next year."

"I hope not."

He pointed at Maeve's grandmother's house. "Maggie's mother lives there. She's wicked cuckoo." He twirled his finger in the air and pointed it at his temple.

Chrissy shrugged. "I met her last night. I liked her."

"Yeah?" he said unbelievingly. Suddenly he grabbed at her on the deserted square and bussed her smack on the lips. When she didn't object, he put his arms around her and pressed his lips to hers again, this time slowly and lingeringly. Chrissy counted to herself. In *Rebecca*, Laurence Olivier had kissed Joan Fontaine for fifty-eight seconds. But then again, in *Pride and Prejudice,* he had kissed Greer Garson for only eighteen.

When he came up for air, Hugh grinned "You're a wicked kisser."

"Really?"

He dove for her again, this time grinding his bared teeth into her lips. What was he trying to do? Chrissy wondered. Split her lip? Draw blood? He tasted of pumpkin pie.

"We'd better go back," she said finally, running her tongue over her bruised lips. "Aunt Maggie will be wondering where we are."

As they trudged back, he asked, "Did you like kissing me?"

"Sure."

"If I invite you to our next dance, will you come?"

"Maybe. If they'll let me."

He opened the door and said with a dissatisfaction he couldn't pin down—after all, she *had* let him kiss her for as long as he wanted—"Don't you ever smile?"

Now that she was back in the house, safe and warm, she grinned at him, "Sure. All the time."

"Did you like my cousin Hugh?"

"Sure." She was not about to hurt Maeve's feelings.

"What did you two do out there?" Sara wanted to know.

"We walked around the Square, looked in other people's windows."

"Is that all?"

"No."

"What do you mean—*no?* What else did you do?"

Chrissy laughed. "Talked."

"You!" Sara pinched Chrissy's arm. "What else?"

"Okay. He kissed me."

Maeve looked a bit upset. She didn't want to hear any more, but Sara was curious, even excited. "Well? How was it? Is he a good kisser?"

Chrissy pursed her lips and closed her eyes. "Let me think. . . . I'd have to grade him a C-plus or maybe a B-minus."

Sara hooted. "Then I take it he didn't soul kiss you."

"Soul kiss?" I asked.

"You know, Marlena," Sara said slyly. "When they put their tongue in your mouth. Don't you know what that's like, Marlena?" While I blushed, Sara turned back to Chrissy. "Well, did he soul kiss you?"

"No, he didn't. What he did do was push his teeth into my lips so hard I thought he was going to make them into mashed potatoes."

"Mmmm . . . sounds very passionate. Did you feel passionate?"

"No! I felt pain."

"Did he feel passionate?"

"I don't know."

"Did he breathe hard?"

"I was too cold to notice."

"Does your cousin Hugh usually go around mashing girls' lips?" Sara asked Maeve.

Maeve stared down at the floor. "I don't know anything about him."

"Maybe it was his first time," I offered. "You know—like 'Andy Hardy's First Kiss.'"

"More like 'Cousin Hughie Meets Little Orphan Annie,'" Chrissy mocked herself. "He asked me to the next dance at his school."

"What did you say?"

Chrissy shrugged.

"Let's have some milk and cookies before we go to bed," Maeve broke in, eager to change the conversation.

"Oh, jeepers!" Chrissy cried. "Who could stuff anything else in?"

"But we have some really super cookies. Some of the relatives brought their specialties. Aunt Cindy made Joe Froggers and Cousin Ann made Snickerdoodles. . . ."

"That sounds scrumptuous. I'll have a Snickerdoodle," Sara said. "But first I want Chrissy to tell me how many times Hughie kissed her and did he press his you-know-what against her little old vagie."

Later, when Chrissy and she were alone in their room, Maeve asked, "You don't have to tell me if you don't want to, but what *did* you feel when Hugh kissed you?"

"Nothing."

"Nothing?"

"No feeling at all. I counted to see how many seconds it would last."

"Would you let him kiss you again?"

"Maybe. I think I'd rather try somebody else. Maybe I'd like it more, you know. Maybe I'd feel something. You don't mind, do you? I know he's your cousin and all."

"Third cousin, I think. I never even met him before. I don't care if you don't like him. But he must like you. He invited you to a dance."

"It doesn't mean he likes me. It just means I let him kiss me. He probably thinks I'd let him touch my breast or something next time."

4.

It was Sunday and we were relaxing, listening to records on Sara's phonograph. Chrissy lay on the bed, as usual, smoking. Maeve sat crosslegged on the floor while Sara sprawled in the big easy chair she had had shipped up from Sloane's in New York. I sat at my desk, trying to read amidst all the smoke, music, and chatter.

The door flung open and Ginny Furbush rushed in.

"Do you know how a mommy broom and a daddy broom make baby brooms?" Ginny asked.

"I'm breathless waiting for the answer," Sara drawled.

"They sweep together," and Ginny bent over in a paroxysm of laughter.

"Oh, God!" Chrissy moaned. "Where do you find these jokes?"

"I read a lot," Ginny said earnestly.

This set Maeve to laughing, I joined in, and even Sara was forced to smile.

"Hey, do you want to know something else?" Ginny demanded.

"Not another joke," Sara said. "Can't you see Marlena is studying?"

"The Japs bombed Pearl Harbor!"

"Where's Pearl Harbor?" Sara asked.

"Gosh, Sara. Don't you know anything? It's in the Philippines."

"No, Ginny," I corrected her. "It's Hawaii."

"Well, whatever. The Japs have bombed it. And the man on the radio says it means Roosevelt will have to ask Congress to declare war. Probably by tomorrow we'll be at war!"

Sara let out a howl of anguish, followed by real tears.

We all looked at Sara, impressed with her reaction. None of us had realized how sensitive Sara really was—none of us would have guessed that she would take this news so hard.

"Do you have a boyfriend that we don't know about?" Chrissy asked. "Someone you're worried will have to go to war?"

"Yes! I mean I'm worried they'll *all* have to go to war—all the boys and all the men that we won't even get to know now. Just when we were getting ready to meet some *real* men. Now, in the prime of our youth, we'll never get to have any experience . . . not until we're old and gray and by then, who'll care?"

5.

Less than two weeks after Pearl Harbor, Maggie O'Connor learned that she had a private battle to wage. Dr. Hepburn told her there was a lump in her left breast. She herself refused to believe the worst. They would perform the biopsy, it would prove benign, she was sure, and she would be able to go home in a couple of days. But it was only a week to Christmas, and Chrissy and Maeve were planning on coming to Boston for their eleven-day holiday. *If,* just if, the lump was not benign, she would not be coming home for several days or even weeks. She had to cancel the Christmas plans and without worrying Maeve. She would have to think of some plausible excuse. But where was the poor baby to go? Could she possibly prevail upon Gwendolyn Marlowe, whom she did not even know, to arrange vacation plans for the girls? No. From what Chrissy had revealed of her aunt's character, Maggie could only assume that the woman would look upon the request as an imposition. She would ask her cousin, Betty, her Uncle James' daughter, to take the girls in and provide them with a real Christmas celebration. Their home would be full of children and high spirits and the glow of holiday lights. Yes, a good solution. Betty would be pleased to be asked to help out and would require no lengthy explanations.

When Dr. Hepburn called and told Maggie that he had made arrangements for her to go into the hospital the following day, she told him that that would not do at all. She had things to do first—she needed the weekend and could not possibly check in until the following Monday.

"My dear Maggie, I thought I had impressed upon you the need for haste. If this goddamn thing turns out to be . . . The quicker we deal with this, the better your chances will be."

"I'm going to be just fine. I believe that God knows that I'm needed down here more than He needs me up there. Expect me on Monday, Sam."

"Goddamn it, Maggie, this may be cancer we're dealing with! What do you have to do that is more urgent than saving your life?"

"I have to go see my niece and explain to her that I won't be home for Christmas."

I was afraid that Sara would find out that my mother was not at all eager to have her as a guest for the Christmas vacation. Mother had said on the telephone: "It's mighty peculiar that a girl like Sara with that big fancy house and her rich, important father doesn't choose to go home to New York."

"But, Mother, I've told you. Aunt Bettina's in that clinic and it's too sad for Sara to go to New York. And besides," I whispered although there was no one around to hear me, "Sara and her father don't get along all that well."

"You never told me that before," Mother said, taken aback. Neither had I told her all the details of Aunt Bettina's illness and I hoped that she would not start asking questions about that now too.

"I can't talk about it now on the telephone, Mother, but we just *have* to have Sara for Christmas."

"Well, of course," Mother said. "Aren't we famous here in Charleston for our hospitality? And she *is* my niece, after all." Martha warmed up. "I personally have never believed in the sins of the father and mother being visited upon the children. Though being Bettina's daughter, she probably won't think we're nearly fancy enough."

"Sara's not at all like what you expect, Mother."

Mother was certainly going to be surprised when she saw how warm Sara was. Sara would probably hug her half to death. I smiled to myself just picturing it.

"Mother is just dying to see you," I told Sara.

"Aunt Maggie phoned. She's coming down this weekend and she's taking us all out to dinner Saturday night. She's already cleared it with

155

the school office. I wish I could tell you all it would be someplace grand but I guess it will have to be the old Blue Swan Inn."

"Is there any special reason she's coming?" Sara asked, applying Chen-Yu Mandarin Red to her toenails. It was a matter of not knuckling under—they weren't allowed to wear anything but colorless polish on their fingernails. At least her toenails would be red!

"Why does she need a special reason?" Chrissy asked, attempting a headstand. "She wants to see Maeve. Isn't that enough reason?"

"But you two are going there in a few days."

This set Maeve to worrying. Was something wrong? Did it have anything to do with her father, she wondered. Was he sick? Did he want to see her? Oh God, how she yearned to see him!

Maeve was relieved to hear that it was a friend of Aunt Maggie's who was so sick and not her father. *Thank you, Lord.* Though, of course, she was sorry for poor Melissa Thornton who lived in San Francisco and needed an old friend by her side. "Of course, Aunt Maggie, I understand. Of course you have to go to your friend if she needs you."

"So I've brought your Christmas presents with me today and I have presents for the girls, too. I hope Chrissy won't be too disappointed but I've arranged for the two of you to stay with Cousin Betty. You'll have a good time there and the whole family is looking forward to having you. And New Year's, there's a big party at the Ritz that Cousin Howard's club is giving—"

"Don't worry about us, Aunt Maggie. We'll make out all right. Except that I'll miss you. Oh, Aunt Maggie, I do love you so," she whispered. "I don't know what I would have done without you. . . ." Her voice trailed off.

"And I love you, Maeve. More than anyone in the world," Maggie said firmly, almost as if she were convincing herself. She hugged the child and wondered what was going to happen to Maeve if— *Please Lord, let me be all right for Maeve's sake.*

The Blue Swan Inn's dining room was filled with students and visiting parents, and everyone seemed to have chosen the Saturday night special of wiener schnitzel and potato dumplings.

"Ugh!" Sara wrinkled her little nose delicately. "Nazi food! You'd think they'd be ashamed with the war on."

"Golly!" Chrissy moaned. "Did you ever see anything so positively unappetizing looking?"

Maggie laughed. "I *was* thinking of having the schnitzel myself. Sort of a change from our usual New England bill of fare."

"Don't pay any attention to them, Aunt Maggie," Maeve said. "They

156

were born complaining. It's their style. Have the schnitzel and I will too."

"You'll be sor-ry!" Sara warned. "You'd be safer sticking to the roast beef. There's not too much they can do to spoil beef."

"That's what you think. They can make it taste like it just won the first race at Aqueduct. I think I'll just have a salad," Chrissy declared.

"Eat something substantial. You're getting too thin," Maeve said.

"There is no such thing as too thin," Sara said with assurance, studying the menu carefully. "Is there, Aunt Maggie?"

"I hate to sound like an old maiden aunt, but I do think growing girls need to eat."

"I love for you to sound like an aunt," Chrissy dimpled. "Just for that, I'll have the shrimp scampi."

"Ix-nay, easey-gray," Sara vetoed. "Bad for the complexion."

"You see, Aunt Maggie? All they do is ix-nay *everything* all day long," Maeve said lovingly.

Finally, the waitress took our orders and Maeve and Aunt Maggie told the rest of us how their Christmas plans had been changed. Quickly, I blurted out, "Why don't you and Chrissy come home with Sara and me to Charleston?" Then I wondered how my mother would feel about it. Two more "fancy" Northern girls?

"Oh, lovely!" Maeve cried. "I think that would be such fun. What do you say, Chrissy? Aunt Maggie, would that be all right? Do you think Cousin Betty would be hurt?"

Maggie smiled. "I think it will be just fine and I'll tell Betty that you had already made prior plans."

"I think it sounds divine." Chrissy felt her waist. "Christmas in the Old South. Just like Scarlett O'Hara."

"Chrissy is aiming for an eighteen-inch waist, just like Scarlett," Maeve explained to her aunt.

"Admirable, I'm sure. But don't forget that Scarlett had to be laced into that eighteen-inch waist. It probably wasn't very comfortable."

Tears rolled down Sara's cheeks.

"Sara, what is it?"

"I've decided I'm not going to Charleston. I'm going to go to Kansas to see Mama. I can't bear that she'll be all alone out there for the holidays."

No one said anything for a while, then Maeve offered to go with Sara and Maggie nodded approvingly. Then Chrissy volunteered to go too. "Shoot, I've never done anything better on Christmas anyway. I'd really like to go."

"No. It's something I have to do alone. Besides, reservations for the trains are hard to come by, what with the war and all. It'll be hard enough to get one reservation."

"Maybe you shouldn't go at all, Sara. It will be so painful for you," I said.

157

"I think she *should* go," Chrissy declared. "It's her *mother!* Fuckers! What's a little pain between mother and daughter anyway?" Then she realized what she had said in front of Aunt Maggie. "Oh, I'm sorry, Aunt Maggie. About my language. I'm working on breaking the habit."

"Good for you," Maggie said.

"I'll say," Sara added. "Someday, Miss Chalmer is going to hear her and then she's really going to be in trouble. Not to mention her smoking. Good heavens, you'd think she was raised in a reformatory or a home for wayward girls," Sara teased, but I guessed that she was trying to steer the conversation away from her going to visit her mother.

"Oh ho," Chrissy said. "And who keeps hidden bottles of wine that are going to get us *all* thrown out of school?"

"Nobody's going to get thrown out of school, I'm sure," Maggie said amiably.

"I still think Chrissy and I should go with you, Sara," Maeve said worriedly. "Marlena *has* to go home but we might be able to offer you some comfort."

"No, I really have to go alone. You see, Mama's a real old-fashioned Southern belle and she never likes anybody to see her when she's not at her best. 'Sara,' she used to say, 'don't you ever let anybody in your front door until your face is on and your heart is playing sweet music!' "

Martha Williams stood framed in the doorway in her good gray wool, waiting for her husband to bring the girls from the station. She had decided upon the gray wool because she wanted to give an impression of refined Southern womanhood to those two rich girls from the North— that Chrissy Marlowe with all her money and her lurid past. And that writer's daughter. . . . Her book club would not even review Padraic O'Connor's books, they were that filthy—all about lust, greed and homosexuality. Regardless of what Marlena said about how sweet Maeve O'Connor was, she herself was convinced that the girl would be snooty. Bound to be with a father so famous on one side and all those blue-blooded Boston snobs on the other. Well, she would show both girls that good breeding and gentility were not confined to the wealthy. But, all in all, it would not be an easy visit.

Daddy pulled the Dodge into the gravel driveway and we tumbled out of the car. Daddy followed behind and I saw that he was grinning from ear to ear. I rushed to Mother and threw my arms around her.

"Oh, Mother, I have missed you!"

"I've missed you, Marlena, but what's happened to your hair?"

My hand went to my head. I'd forgotten about my hair, forgotten that that would be the first thing Mother would notice.

"It's lighter! Several shades lighter! Marlena Williams, you've bleached your hair!"

"It was an accident, Mother. We were in the drugstore in town and somebody knocked a bottle of peroxide off the shelf and . . . it fell on my head—"

Mother looked incredulous. "What kind of story is that? How could a bottle fall off—"

"Mother, can't we talk about this later? I want you to meet Maeve and Chrissy. Maeve, Chrissy, this is my mother."

"Welcome to our home, Maeve, Chrissy," Mother said, graciously.

Maeve put out her hand and shook Mother's firmly. "Thank you, Mrs. Williams." She spoke so low that Mother had to lean toward her slightly to hear. "It's lovely of you to have us. You've made it truly Christmas."

I could tell that Mother was impressed with Maeve's manner.

Chrissy extended her hand. "How do you do, Mrs. Williams," she said coolly, as if basing her attitude on her perception of Mother's tone. But then, unexpectedly, Chrissy smiled so that her whole face lit up and showed how really beautiful she was, and how really sweet underneath it all. "I can't tell you how much it means to be here, Mrs. Williams. In a real home for the holidays."

Mother relaxed. "It's our pleasure, Chrissy, Maeve." And Daddy smiled at Mother, who started bustling around. She said, "I know how bad the service is on the trains these days and I knew you girls would probably be starving, so we have a little repast ready. Marlena, show the girls where to hang their coats and where the powder room is so they can freshen up. We'll eat and settle you girls in later."

We filed into the dining room and the table was set with the glazed blue and white Charleston Marsh Oaks pottery, Mother's second-best china, and the sideboard groaned under a platter of Mother's Charleston chicken (prepared with benne seeds and orange slices), a tureen of crab stew, bowls of black-eyed peas prepared with a dash of peppered cream and creamed mushrooms, and a big sweet potato pie, not to mention the pecan praline pie and the Gullah basket filled with corn bread.

Chrissy closed her eyes and held her stomach. "I think I've died and gone to heaven."

"You must have been expecting Sherman's army, Mother," I giggled.

"That's a terrible thing to say, Marlena."

"It *does* look like you were expecting a horde, Mrs. Williams," Maeve told Mother. "You can't imagine how good all that looks after weeks of the Chalmer's food."

Maeve and I looked on with disbelief as Chrissy piled her plate high. "Home cooking!" she sighed. "Did you make everything yourself, Mrs. Williams?"

"Well, Bess and I did." Mother smiled at Bess, who pushed more chicken on my plate before I had even started to eat.

While we ate, I saw Chrissy studying Mother. I wondered what she was thinking. Why was she studying her so intently, as if she'd never seen a mother before?

"Mrs. Williams . . . Mr. Williams," Chrissy called out. We all looked up with puzzled expectancy. "When we were in Boston for Thanksgiving, we all called Maeve's aunt Aunt Maggie. May I call you Aunt Martha and Uncle Howard?"

"You surely can, honey." Daddy beamed. "That would be uncommonly nice, wouldn't it, Martha?"

Mother was clearly startled by the question. "Of course," she said at first. Then she added, "I'd be pleased. But what about your own aunt? Perhaps she wouldn't like you to be collecting new relatives. . . ."

Chrissy sighed. "Aunt Gwen's not much of an aunt. I mean, if I could pick and choose, Aunt Gwen wouldn't be my number-one choice. Or even my hundred-and-one," she added.

Daddy broke into the conversation before Mother could ask any more questions about Chrissy's family. "Well, you'd better eat up, girls. Tomorrow is Christmas Eve and we've a big dinner planned. We have to clear the decks before the next batch of food hoves into view. . . ."

"It's hard to believe it's Christmas with all the camellias blooming outside. Imagine—camellias in December!" Maeve clapped her hands.

"December and January are the camellia-blooming months in South Carolina."

"And Mom's camellias always win a prize."

"But I've never won *first* prize, Marlena. Old Mrs. Renault always walks away with that."

"I think they give it to her out of custom," I defended Mother's camellias.

"The annual show is in Beaufort in January," Mother explained. "Then in May we always go up to Orangeburg for the Festival of Roses. You girls will have to come back in May when the place is just covered with roses."

"I think they'd probably like coming back in July more," Daddy said. "July's the Water Festival and that's really something to see."

"Okay," Chrissy said gaily, tossing her head. "We'll be back in May *and* July."

Everybody laughed and I said, "Then maybe we could drive up to Camden to see the steeplechases. Chrissy's just crazy about horses," I explained to my parents. "Oh, golly, if only Sara could be here!"

I realized that remark was a mistake because Mother looked at me hard. Her look clearly stated that *she* had yet to hear all about Sara and Bettina and Uncle Maurice. I avoided Mother's eyes. I dreaded that conversation.

160

"First, we're all attending services at St. Philip's on Church Street at five-thirty for the Christmas Eucharist. Then some of our friends and relatives are coming back here for Christmas Eve dinner. You don't mind, do you, Maeve, that the service is Episcopal?"

"Of course not. Aunt Maggie says that the Child was born unto us all."

"Good. Mother will be pleased. Oh, and to keep Mother happy, absolutely no Sloppy Joe sweaters or bobby sox or saddle shoes. Dresses and stockings and little heels, please!"

We filed into the pew, Mother first and Chrissy last, leaving Chrissy on the center aisle. Later, into the service, I was desperately glad that Chrissy was sitting the farthest away from Mother since she paid no attention whatsoever to the service. From the moment we sat down, Chrissy started flirting, actually flirting, with the cadet sitting on the aisle opposite her. He *was* cute, but Mother would certainly not accept that as an excuse, especially since the cadets from the Citadel Military Academy could not be considered real Charlestonians, even though they were known to have fought bravely and well in the War Between the States.

"Who *is* he?" Chrissy whispered to me, not taking her eyes off the cute boy in the adorable uniform, although the service had started.

"I don't know," I whispered back. "Just one of the cadets from the Citadel. Pay attention!"

"Don't you think he's adorable?"

I stared straight ahead. "Please, Chrissy! I don't think this is the proper time for this," I pleaded.

"He's much cuter than Hugh Winthrop, don't you think?"

"Shush! Everybody's looking! My mother's going to think you're awful!"

Chrissy folded her hands in her lap and didn't look at the cadet again until it was time for the Breaking of the Bread. But he kept grinning at her, and finally she gave him the benefit of her best elongated doe-eyed gaze.

Finally, the choir sang, "Good Christian Men, Rejoice," and it was over and I gave a sigh of relief.

While we waited for my parents to finish wishing the other congregants a Merry Christmas, I introduced Maeve and Chrissy to some of my former classmates, and Chrissy and the cadet, Ronnie Fielding, introduced themselves to each other.

The Christmas Eve buffet included a country ham, deviled crabs, lobster salad, veal birds, a chicken mousse, sweet potatoes in orange shells, chow-chow preserves, and a long row of desserts, including a black walnut cake and a pie of peanuts and yams. But Chrissy couldn't eat a thing. She was both too excited and anxious about the date she had made for the day after Christmas with Ronnie Fielding. Flirting was one thing, the actuality of a date was another. Now she was not at all sure he was even attractive.

Two days after Christmas, I was brave enough to tell Mother and Daddy the complete truth about Aunt Bettina. I had to because that was the day we received a telegram that Sara was on her way to Charleston. Maeve, Chrissy, and I were all upset—we wondered what had happened in Kansas to make Sara leave so quickly. She barely had had time to see her mother more than once, considering the traveling distance. Still, we had to laugh at the wording of her telegram:

COMING STOP WILL ARRIVE IN CHARLESTON GOD KNOWS WHEN ON THIS TERRIBLE TRAIN STOP WILL ADVISE YOU WHEN I GET THERE STOP IF I SURVIVE THIS TRIP AT ALL STOP PLEASE IF IT IS NOT TOO MUCH TROUBLE SOMEONE MEET ME STOP THOUGH GOODNESS KNOWS I HATE TO BE A BURDEN TO ANYBODY STOP I WILL BE QUIET AND NOT GET IN ANYONES WAY STOP YOUR SARA

Then I felt like crying. The telegram *was* funny but it was sad too. A mixture. Like Sara herself.

Mother was not amused. "Such ostentatious extravagance," she told me. "Is she trying to rub our noses in her profligate spending? The four-teen-year-old snip. . . ."

"Mother, please don't make up your mind beforehand to dislike Sara. She was only trying to be funny in the telegram so that we wouldn't feel sorry for her. Something dreadful must have happened at Aunt Bettina's sanitarium. Sara's really sweet."

"I have not made up my mind to dislike Sara. What a thing to say to your Mama. I always keep an open mind. I'm sure she's more to be pitied than scorned what with Bettina and that father of hers."

Daddy and we three girls went to meet Sara while Mother waited at home, putting out fresh towels, plumping up pillows that didn't need plumping, arranging a fresh bouquet of flowers for the dining-room table.

When we drove up, Mother was on the front veranda, smoothing her dress about her hips, patting her hair vaguely. Sara, wearing a glen plaid suit and trailing a brown fur coat, jumped from the car, dropped the coat, ran to Mother with outstretched arms.

"Aunt Martha! Oh, Aunt Martha! It was such a terrible trip and my Mama, she didn't even know me but for a few seconds. Aunt Martha. . . ."

Sara threw herself at Mother's ramrod-stiff body, thrust her blond curly head against Mother's thin bosom. "Oh, Aunt Martha," Sara said, "if you could see poor Mama, it would break your sweet heart."

I watched Mother's arms creep around Sara. I watched Mother struggle to speak, as if there were a thick, painful lump in her throat. "Don't you cry, Sara honey. It will be all right. We'll see to it that it will be all right."

Sara lifted her tear-stained face. "I declare, Aunt Martha, now that I'm here, I feel, I really believe, that it *will* be all right. You are so lovely, Aunt Martha. Just like Mama used to say—before she got sick. She used to say, 'My sister Martha, the most beautiful, sweetest sister in the whole world. Someday you'll see her, Sara, and you'll know I'm right.'"

Mother and Sara went into the house, arm-in-arm. We followed. Maeve was crying, but Daddy and I exchanged great big smiles.

"The train was full of soldiers but I didn't talk to them much."

"Why?" Chrissy demanded. "Have you gone shy, all of a sudden? Sounds like you missed your big chance."

"I was depressed. I couldn't think of anything but Mama. And besides, I didn't know a thing about them. They could have been sex maniacs, for all I knew."

"Sounds to me like you just lost your nerve." Chrissy smiled knowingly.

"Of course I didn't. I told you, I was just sick about Mama. I want to hear what you girls have been doing."

"Chrissy went frogging with a cadet from the Citadel."

"Oh, God, how awful!"

I laughed. "It just means going to the drive-in for hamburgers. It's a Southern expression."

"He had a car? He was old enough to drive?"

"Just a jalopy."

"Did you neck?"

Chrissy didn't answer.

"Well, I guess that means you did. Or did you go further than that?" Sara asked slyly.

Maeve and I leaned forward avidly. We hadn't asked Chrissy these kinds of questions about her date. But now that Sara was, we were eager to hear her answers.

"How far did you go?" Sara asked when Chrissy didn't answer her first question.

"How far do you think?"

"You petted! Tell the truth!"

"Sort of."

"What did he touch?"

"What do you think?" Chrissy was enjoying herself.

"Your titty."

"Yes. . . ."

"And down there, too?"

"Yes. . . ."

"And did you touch him too? Down there?"

"No."

"How come?" Sara asked.

"Because I didn't feel like it."

"How come?"

"I didn't like him very much."

"Not even after he touched you there?"

"Especially after that," Chrissy laughed. "But I guess now I'm the one with the most experience, aren't I?"

"I guess you are . . . so far." Sara tossed her head. "But you should have touched him there just to see what it was like. Don't you think so, Maeve?"

"I don't know." She turned red. "I'm sure she's got plenty of time for that. Who wants to take a walk along the waterfront?"

"Why not?" Sara said. "I want to see everything. I was just thinking —with Fort Sumter and Fort Moultrie here, and Beaufort not far away —this city is going to be a veritable gold mine of soldiers, sailors and Marines. If we ever get desperate enough, we know we can always go home to Charleston. . . ."

THE FALL OF 1942

Gwen Marlowe was indirectly responsible for the deflowering of her niece in September of '42—and, indirectly, Sara helped too. Gwen provided the occasion, the man, and the place. Having enjoyed her fling of self-indulgence in the years since her divorce, Gwen had been ready once again to take up the gauntlet of responsibility to society at large. With the advent of war, she had rushed into action with patriotic fervor. If the upper classes were not prepared to defend their privilege, who then would? She was at the forefront of committees to collect silk and nylon stockings, cooking grease, tin cans, waste paper, worn tires, even empty toothpaste tubes. She encouraged others to knit and roll bandages for the Red Cross. But the thing she did best was to organize luncheons and balls to sell war bonds and arrange benefits for the Navy, Marines, or whatever, or for the relief of something or somebody.

When it was decided to hold a Navy League benefit at the Plaza, concurrent with the opening of the Persian Room for the fall season, Gwen was the natural one to be chosen for the chairmanship. She lived at the Plaza and, besides, no one could match Gwen's energy or superb qualifications. She could always be counted on to bring in both the big donors and the famous. So Hildegarde the Incomparable, with her long kid gloves, would play the piano and sing her slightly naughty songs, and Gwen would fill the room with young beauties for the servicemen to dance with and to pretty up the affair.

Naturally, Gwen would have her own Gwennie come down from Smith and bring her friends, but this was also the perfect opportunity for Gwen to play hostess to her niece and those three schoolmates she had befriended. True, they *were* a bit young to attend such a party with red-blooded fighting men. Was Chrissy almost fifteen or was it sixteen? She couldn't exactly recall anymore. It was hard enough to remember the ages of her own children. Well, no matter—Chrissy and her friends *were* sophisticated, God knows, and mature-looking, with the exception of that mousy little girl from the South.

Besides, Gwen felt a little obliged to entertain her niece's friends at least once. Chrissy had gone to their homes for the holidays and had spent all of last summer at Southampton with the Gold girl, the one with the Jewish father. And her friend, Maeve, in spite of her surname, *was* a Boston Abbott and everyone was always going on about her father's work as if he were the Second Coming, or something. Yes, she would do it. No one would question the girls' ages. And even if they did, she was, after all, Gwen Marlowe, and there was a war on.

Gwen counted up. Gwennie was coming down with five friends and Chrissy and her three friends made ten in all. She would have to commandeer five rooms, at the very least, even though the management swore that no one would get preference other than a fighting man. "I need five rooms for the weekend," she told the manager, "and don't you dare tell me there's a war on!"

Chrissy, receiving the invitation, was not eager to go. Anything to do with Aunt Gwen bode little good. And she certainly wasn't eager to see that prig, Gwennie. But Sara wanted to go.

"*Anything* to break out of these walls, baby," she growled doing her imitation of Cagney. "And I'm dying to see Hildegarde entertain. I under-stand she goes around pinching all the boys on their fannies, and every time she sings "The Last Time I Saw Paris," somebody buys a twenty-five-thousand-dollar war bond in appreciation. Chrissy, I *want* to go!"

"You might as well give in now," Maeve laughed. "You know Sara never gives up until she gets her way."

Chrissy lay supine on top of the Plaza's prized satin comforter, her pale yellow satin evening gown gathered around her waist, her un-stockinged legs (her very last pair of prewar nylons having surrendered to runs the week before) spread and exposed. Her yellow panties lay abandoned on the floor while the new yellow sandals, purchased the day before on a quick run to I. Miller's, dug their spiked heels recklessly into the comforter, as a dress-jacketed, bottomless Ensign Corky Towne just four months out of Princeton, crushed her, furiously trying to crash through her vaginal membrane.

Chrissy was determined to go all the way this time, even if it killed her, and the way things were going, it was a very valid possibility.

Sweating and panting with frustration, Ensign Corky Towne offered: "You could blow me."

"What?"

"You know, French me! Suck me!"

"Oh."

"Then I'd do you," he promised. "Some of the fellows don't like to dive the muff, but I don't mind. I like it."

Chrissy was unfamiliar with his phraseology but she fully gathered his meaning and she smiled a secret smile. How surprised Ensign Corky would be to learn that she was an old hand at that particular method of love-making. She probably could teach him a few things.

"No," she said flatly.

She was not going to leave this room a virgin, technically speaking, not if she had to keep Corky Towne here all night. He might have assumed that it was his mournful, touching tale of going off to die for his country some day soon that had brought her to this room, this bed, to lie passionately beneath him so that he might not go off to war, and maybe death, unloved. But it was not so. Kissing, necking, petting—heavy and otherwise—with various members of the opposite sex had not aroused any particular feeling within her. Was this because she always stopped short of penetration? Tonight she would find out. Tonight she *would* be penetrated.

She kissed him, placing her mouth wetly on his, sticking her tongue in his mouth and running it about inside in what she imagined to be lascivious fashion, ran her hands over his buttocks encouragingly. "Try a little harder," she whispered, blowing in his ear. *That* was supposed to drive them wild.

She wormed her hands in under him where his penis tried valiantly to enter her, and stroked him. He groaned, gave another, more forceful thrust, and then *she* groaned, not in passion but in a flash of pain, as he finally entered her. Immediately upon contact with her deep inner warmth, he exploded and collapsed his full weight on her body.

One of Ginny's limericks flashed through her head:

> Thank you kindly, Sir, she said
> As he broke her maidenhood.

She waited, perhaps a half-minute, and then said, "Excuse me, please. Would you mind very much getting off? I really must shower."

"Did you?" he asked, exhausted.

"No, but you did."

"I'll finger-fuck you," he offered. "Or I'll still muff-dive you."

"No, thank you just the same. You'd better go on downstairs before you're missed. I'll come down in just a jiff."

"Are you sure?" he asked sheepishly.

Getting up from the bed, unzipping the back of her dress with one hand, she didn't answer him. The dress, already crushed, fell to the floor. Seeing her standing nude, the thin body with the small hard breasts tilted provocatively up and outward, Ensign Towne became hard again.

"I bet I could make you come this time," he offered.

Again she didn't answer, went into the shower. She didn't turn on the water until she heard him leave, closing the door behind him. Then she turned the faucets on full force, carefully keeping her hair out of the stream of water. With her eyes shut, as the loving warm water washed her body clean, she caressed herself until she felt the familiar shudders, wave upon wave upon wave.

When Chrissy reentered the Persian Room, the band was playing "Chattanooga Choo Choo," but she was hardly in the mood to jitterbug. Sara rushed up. "Where *were* you?" she asked Chrissy breathlessly. She had only just managed to break away from the grips of three uniformed men, all of whom had tried to impress her with their war records. "Your Aunt Gwen's been looking for you for the last half-hour. I think she wants to introduce you to some people. The Harrimans or somebody. . . ."

Gwennie Winslow came up to them. "Have you heard the latest? They're going to graduate Yale Class of forty-three this December! And they say that three-quarters of Yale's undergraduates have *already* enlisted," she complained. "Why, there practically won't be *anybody* left at Yale—"

"My goodness," Sara said cheerfully. "And what's Smith without Yale?"

Gwennie looked at Sara blankly then stalked away.

"Now, back to you," Sara said. "Chrissy Marlowe, did you go upstairs with that ensign, the one with the leftover acne problem?" She gingerly touched Chrissy's hair. "Mmmm . . . slightly damp. What've you all been up to, honey chile?"

"I declare, Sara Leeds Gold," Chrissy mocked Sara's accent, "you're worse than Ellery Queen."

Sara looked at Chrissy hard. "Chrissy?"

"Yep. The Marines have landed at last."

THE WINTERTIDE OF 1943

1.

Maggie O'Connor had lost her right breast the Christmas of 1941, and her left the following year. Now, just a year later, they, the army of doctors, wanted her to go back into the hospital again—for a checkup, they said, and some of those X-ray treatments, just to be sure. But Maggie knew that she was losing her private battle. She only wondered now how long it would be before the disease terminated its tour of duty. She had so much unfinished business. Her war work, the hospitals that she toiled in behalf of, her mother, and, always, Maeve. Each time she felt the tidal wave of anger rise within her raging against her fate, she begged the Lord to forgive her and went to her church to pray for more time. She needed more time badly, so that she could see her mother to her final rest. Who would take care of her mother if she herself went first? And, dear God, what of Maeve? She was strong and she was good, but only a child certainly, not mature enough to understand all that she would have to contend with. And Maeve's baby. Who would check on her every now and then? *Not Maeve.* She could never tell Maeve that her baby wasn't perfect and living happily with a family that loved her. And Padraic. Maggie had had no communication with him. Of course, she was well aware of his work that continued to come out of Ireland—every novel brought him more acclaim. She herself did not understand how the critics found his work so meritorious—to her it was so full of hate, almost to the point of being incoherent. But that was beside the point. After her death, would not Padraic come to claim Maeve? Or would Maeve seek out Padraic herself? They had not spoken of him, but she sensed that Maeve loved him yet, mourned for him. . . .

Oh, Padraic! What would become of him? The world knew him only as the reclusive genius, and the world was ready to forgive its geniuses their eccentricities, their idiosyncrasies, even their falls from grace, for it was the eccentricities, the falls from grace that made them more interesting and colorful, the idiosyncrasies that set them apart from the rest of humanity. But to her, Padraic was far beyond the eccentric. His

169

genius was mixed with madness. Was it in their blood? Had he been doomed from birth to bear this oppressive yoke? And if and when the rest of the world discovered it, what then? Who would be there to protect Padraic from the wolves come to tear him apart?

No, she couldn't give in. Not yet. What had that saint, F.D.R., said, when they had asked him to run for still another term? The poor tired man, so sick, had told the world, ". . . and in this war I have as little right to withdraw as a soldier has to leave his post in the line . . ."

She would have to fight; she could not leave her post in the line.

When Maggie came home from the hospital for the third time, she was resigned to the fact that she had, at the very most, two years. She would have to make the most of them. Uppermost in her mind was to prepare Maeve for her death. She had to make Maeve realize the full extent of the threat Padraic posed. And she would have to get her affairs in order so that Maeve could take over custodianship of the museum, the hospitals that were Abbott charities, and her grandmother, with the least amount of trouble. Poor baby! Not yet sixteen and soon with so much to bear.

Maggie decided to open the Newport house for the summer. She and Maeve would have time to talk and be together. Sara and Chrissy would probably join them for most of the season while, she supposed, Marlena would most likely go home to South Carolina.

Maggie sent her '42 Packard Clipper to pick up the girls. She had bought the car the year before in a kind of thumbing-her-nose-at-fate gesture, for '42 had been the last year any new cars would come off the assembly line for the duration, and at the time, she was not really sure whether it would be her last car for all her time to come.

2.

I could barely keep the tears back saying good-bye to Sara, Maeve, and Chrissy. Maeve made me promise I would come up to Newport for at least two or three weeks and I asked Sara to promise to write to me at least once a week, revealing everything. "Especially if the cat jumps off the roof!"

Sara giggled. "What do you mean by that?"

"That phrase is now used by the military, Sara, to signify a landing of troops has taken place. And the soldiers are using it to signify a landing of you-know-what. . . ."

"Well, if you-know-what happens, or even if my cat breaks his neck, you'll be the first to know. In the meantime, for goodness' sake, have yourself a good old time down there with all those boys crawling around the place and, if *your* cat jumps off the roof, just send me a picture postcard saying, 'In like Flynn,' and I'll get the idea."

Maeve and Sara were filled with excitement as they drove down Bellevue Avenue with its emerald lawns and summer palaces. But Chrissy was quiet. Seeing Grandmother Marlowe's house again was going to be excruciatingly painful. She always tried to shut those days out of her mind, tried not to think about her grandmother, her mother. *Oh, fuckers!* She couldn't believe that after all these years she could still feel the pain, miss her, her face, her perfume, her voice:

"Who is Mommy's sweetness?"

"Isn't she the dearest baby?"

And then she remembered the, "Run along, precious." "Nanny is waiting for you, darling baby." "I haven't time to read that story, dear bunny." "I'll see you tomorrow, sweet lamb." And the fucking courtroom. "Mommy! Mommy!" She heard the child calling in her head as if it were someone else.

Maeve took her arm. "We're here, Chrissy. I'm sorry this is so painful for you. Is that your grandmother's house? The one that's all boarded up?"

Chrissy shrugged. "It's Aunt Gwen's now. But it doesn't matter. It's only a house." Sometimes she hated her mother's memory so much. And if she hated her, then nothing else from the past mattered anyway.

But the tension was still there, even after Maggie welcomed the girls, and asked: "Would you like to see the house?"

Sara looked around the great ballroom. "Now *this* is really something! Our place in Southampton doesn't come any way near this for absolute splendiferousness. I must say, Aunt Maggie, you gentiles certainly know how to live!"

And they all broke out into laughter, even Chrissy.

Maeve hugged her. "And I must say, Sara, you Jews certainly know how to make a girl laugh."

Maggie found Chrissy in the library curled up on the oversized Italian Renaissance sofa. "You look comfortable. And it isn't easy to be comfortable in here. These rooms are magnificent but certainly not cozy." She saw that Chrissy had been crying. "Why didn't you go down to Bailey's Beach with Maeve and Sara?"

"I don't know. I didn't feel like it. I was reading."

"Anything good?" She came over and picked up the book lying on the sofa. It was *The Well of Loneliness* by Radclyffe Hall. "It's no wonder you're so down in the dumps. It's a sad, depressing book, isn't it?"

"Have you read it? It's about lesbians."

"Yes, I know."

"Do you think it strange that I'm reading it?" Chrissy asked, somewhat defensively.

"Not at all. I've read it. It's an exceptionally fine novel. Of course, it's received a lot of notoriety because of its context. . . ." Oh, dear, Maggie thought, this poor child is worried, concerned about . . .

"You don't think I'm a . . . one of them . . . just because I read the book?" Her tone was slightly belligerent.

"Oh, Chrissy dear, of course not." The girl was troubled. "I told you—I've read it myself. The book is . . . disturbing, I know. But you mustn't be upset."

"I *might* be one," Chrissy blurted out, relieving some of the pressure she felt. "I'm not sure." She started to cry again.

Maggie took the girl in her arms, and soon Chrissy blurted out the whole story, how she mourned for her mother, the incident with her music teacher.

"Oh, Chrissy"—there were tears in Maggie's eyes too—"you were just an innocent child, caught up in a situation. Of course it doesn't mean you're a lesbian. You were lonely, starved for affection, and you needed someone to take the place of your mother. It was natural you would turn to this lovely lady who was such a good friend to you. And . . ." She faltered. How could she explain away the *teacher's* behavior? *She* had been no child. "And your friend was lonely too, and she lost control of the situation. It was she who was the adult . . . it was she who should have—" Maggie faltered. Then she said: "Yes, it *was* wrong. But it wasn't your wrong. Your friend Jacquie forgot her true responsibility to you because of her own need for love. I think she took advantage of a confused child in order to gratify her own needs. I think she was just weak. And the poor thing, she paid the price in a very terrible way, didn't she? But she did pay the price. Let it rest, Chrissy. Don't go on paying. . . ."

"But how can I be sure I'm not a . . . you know, one of those? I *love* my friends, Maeve and Sara and Marlena. I love you, Aunt Maggie."

"Thank you. And I love you. But there are all kinds of love. And thank God for that. The love you have for your friends is a beautiful thing. And I pray to God that it will sustain you and them for the rest of . . . your lives."

"But I never seem to meet a boy I can love."

Maggie laughed softly, smoothed Chrissy's shiny hair. "You're just a girl, Chrissy, just a girl. You will . . . you will. Just give yourself a chance. You'll find a man you love. And then you'll love your children."

"My mother didn't love me," Chrissy said bitterly.

"I'm sure she did . . . in her own way. Oh, there are many manifestations of love, Chrissy. Accept the fact that she loved you and let it go at that. Letting go of the past is what sets us free to go on with our lives."

Chrissy put her head on Maggie's bosom. "Oh, I do love you! You've been like a mother to me."

Oh, Chrissy. You'll have to let go of me too.

The four of them were in the kitchen preparing dinner.

"This is fun," Sara said, fluting a radish rose.

"I'm glad you think so, Sara. I was afraid you would think it was terrible of me to invite you here for the summer without sufficient help to run the place. Poor Betsy. Even with most of the house shut down, she's being run ragged. But I don't think anybody in Newport was able to get all the help they needed this summer, what with the war plants going night and day. And that's as it should be."

Maeve was peeling potatoes. "When we were over at Hammersmith Farms, Jackie and her sister Lee were doing the hedges. Their mother's a stickler for topiary."

"I've never met Janet Auchincloss. I don't know many people in Newport. Jackie doesn't go to Miss Chalmer's, does she?"

"No," Sara answered, carefully scoring a cucumber. "She goes to Miss Porter's in Farmington, Connecticut. But we're friends from the Hamptons. Jackie's father's people, the Bouviers, are in East Hampton. They have a lovely place there. 'Lasata.' But her mother married Hugh Auchincloss and they live in Washington now and come up here for the summers. Maeve met her at our place last summer. Jackie's father is *very* handsome, isn't he, Maeve? Of course he's not as handsome as your father is. *Nobody* is. Imagine having a father that handsome, and famous, too. We're dying to meet him, aren't we, Chrissy?"

Maeve glanced quickly at her aunt and Chrissy caught the look they exchanged. She had long sensed that there was a problem between Maeve and her father that involved Aunt Maggie too, but unlike Sara she never probed.

Maggie dried her hands on a towel carefully. "One of these days I'm sure you will. When he comes home from Ireland."

"In the meantime, Aunt Maggie," Sara said, "I wish you'd convince your niece to be more social."

Maggie smiled. "What's the problem?"

"Jackie's mother is having a lawn party to entertain some servicemen —it should be lovely. They overlook the bay. But Maeve won't go. She's

173

becoming more and more impossible. She was bad enough at school, always refusing to go to the dances, but it's unpatriotic not to entertain our fighting men, isn't it, Aunt Maggie?"

Maeve's scarlet cheeks betrayed her once again. "I never know what to say to boys . . . men. And I'm not a good dancer. I'm just . . . uncomfortable. I don't have to go just to please you, Sara," she blurted in a rare burst of resentment. "Do I, Aunt Maggie?"

Maggie looked pained. She knew this was one of the problems plaguing Maeve, this fear of men. Or was fear too strong a word? "No," she said softly. "You don't have to go to please Sara. But maybe you should go to conquer that feeling of . . . discomfort—" She looked deep into Maeve's eyes. She had to be careful of her words in front of the others. "When I was a girl, I used to be shy with boys. Then I learned that they were just boys, not some strange creatures. There were all kinds, most nice, some grand, some just as shy as I was. And I learned a boy could be as good a friend as a girl and as easy to talk to. I think you should make the effort, Maeve."

There was so little time left. She had to push Maeve into the world as fast as she possibly could.

Sara finished painting Maeve's and Chrissy's legs with the liquid stockings so that the three of them had the same orangey-colored legs. "Now you draw on the seams, Chrissy, since you're the artist in the family." Sara handed her her eyebrow pencil.

"Oh, golly. Suppose I don't get them straight? Okay, here goes. I'll do you first, Sara." The first seam she drew was fine, the second one wavered up the calf and then veered off to one side. Chrissy giggled. "Sorry, Sara. You're going to look a bit crooked. You don't mind, do you?"

"Of course not," Sara said bravely. "Who needs straight legs anyway?"

"I think I'll go seamless," Maeve said, trying not to laugh at Sara's leg.

"Me too." Chrissy grinned.

"You could cold cream me and start all over," Sara said.

"Why bother? Nobody's going to look at your legs anyway."

"Oh, gee, thanks a lot, Chrissy Marlowe." She wet the tip of her finger with her tongue and streaked Chrissy's leg. "Guess you just got yourself a run, sweetie pie."

"You mean old thing. I'm going to give you a run!" She wet the tip of her finger and ran after Sara who ran out of the solarium shrieking.

Maggie came running in. "What's going on?"

"Just Sara and Chrissy horsing around."

Maggie watched the girls leave. She would lie down after they were gone. She *was* getting more tired every day.

They looked so pretty in their sundresses and their high-wedged sandals. "Don't sneak any cocktails," she called out, teasing.

"We'd never get away with it with Jackie's mother. She's strict," Chrissy yelled back.

"We'll probably get teetotalers' punch. Ickey!" Sara mumbled, smoothing her dress out on the car seat so she wouldn't arrive at the party wrinkled. "I fully intend to sneak a cocktail into my punch."

"Do you think Aunt Maggie is all right?" Maeve asked the other two. "She seems kind of tired."

"She *is* losing weight," Chrissy said. "But what's wrong with that?"

"Can you imagine what he had the nerve to say to me then? 'What are you saving it for? Aren't you afraid it'll turn green with mold?'" Sara told the story with a great show of indignation.

"Oh my Lord!" Maeve tried not to laugh, but Chrissy shrieked, "That's disgusting but it is funny."

"If you think that's funny, you should have heard what he said when we were leaving! 'Will you be my pen pal? Promise me you'll write.' First he tells me my vagie's green and moldy, then he wants to be my pen pal. . . . Did you ever?"

"Oh my Lord!" Maeve said again and the three went into yet one more paroxysm of laughter.

Ryan, the combination chauffeur-gardener-handyman, looked into his rearview mirror to see what was going on. You never knew with these rich kids. What the dickens did they find to laugh about all the time? he wondered sourly.

"Where's Betsy?" Sara asked when she discovered Maggie changing the bed linen in Maeve's room.

"She's lying down, poor old thing. She's got the rheumatism again."

"Let me help you. You look pretty poorly yourself."

"Oh, I'm fine, Sara, but I'm always glad to have some help. Here—you put on the pillow slips. Why aren't you at the Casino watching the tennis matches?"

"I hate tennis."

"But it's fun at the Casino, Tennis Week. I was only a very tiny girl when I used to come here, but I can still remember my grandmother —she was a very great lady—going to the matches. She used to wear the Casino's colors—green, yellow and white and a pin—a little tiny flag set with diamonds, emeralds, and pearls—a replica of her boat's flag. The boat is long gone but I still have the pin. I'll have to get it out one of these days and give it to Maeve. But tell me, is your lack of interest in tennis the only reason you didn't go along with Maeve and Chrissy?" Maggie asked shrewdly. They went into the room Chrissy and Sara shared and began stripping the beds.

"Not exactly," Sara said. "I wanted to think about something. You see, I received a letter from one of my mother's doctors. He wants her to divorce Father but every time he mentions it to her she grows agitated and goes off on another— He wants me to start writing about it to her slowly . . . in stages, you know."

"And aren't you willing to do this?"

"I don't *want* to, not really. It would be all over then, for sure. The end of us as a family."

"But if the doctor wants this, he must want it for a good reason. He must think it would help your mother get well. And that's the important thing, isn't it?"

"Yes. . . ."

"And you aren't really a family now, are you?"

"No. . . ."

"You don't even see your father, do you?"

"No. . . ."

"Perhaps if there were a divorce and your mother did get well, you and your father might be friends again . . . with the bitterness out of the way. Then you could have a relationship with your mother and with your father. You'd be more a family than you are now."

"You make it sound so easy, Aunt Maggie."

Maggie laughed softly, picked up the used sheets and dumped them into the basket.

"I know it's not simple, Sara. Saying good-bye to the past is sometimes the hardest thing we must do in life. But sometimes we have to amputate a limb to save the body. And sometimes if we save the body, then we can save the soul."

Sara nodded thoughtfully. Then she asked, "You're a devout Catholic, Aunt Maggie. And I know the Catholic Church doesn't condone divorce. And yet you're saying that it might be best for my mother to divorce my father."

Maggie nodded her head. "Yes. I'll tell you a story. I have a very wise friend. He's a doctor and an Orthodox Jew. He left Poland just a step ahead of the Nazis and finally managed to get here by way of Shanghai. And I asked him jokingly what he found to eat in Shanghai because I knew he only ate kosher food. And he told me that while the Torah says a Jew must not eat non-kosher food, it also says, most importantly of all, that he must do everything and anything to stay alive. Life, above all. That's why when Jews toast each other, they say *L'chaim*. To life."

Sara looked at Maggie, her eyes filled up, and she threw her arms around the woman's neck. Maggie hugged her. "There you are, Sara. Your Catholic aunt has given you a lesson in being a good Jew."

What a coward she was, Maggie berated herself. She had tried to help

176

Chrissy, she had advised Sara. But here it was, nearly the end of August, and still she had not spoken to Maeve. She could delay no longer.

Sara and Chrissy, in rolled-up dungarees and too-big shirts, had gone off to ride at Hammersmith Farms. Maggie was alone with Maeve.

"Shall we walk along the beach?"

Maeve nodded, apprehensive. It was not like Aunt Maggie to ask her to stay behind when the others would be having fun. She wondered immediately if it was her father Aunt Maggie wanted to discuss. Was he sick? Had he returned to America? Did he want to see her? Oh, she wanted to see him so badly but she was afraid.

"Your father's an atheist," Maggie began, "so of course he didn't raise you in the Church. And I have not really tried to— I thought the time would come when you yourself would want— But we have run out of time. And I'm sorry—the Church would be such a comfort to you now. . . ."

"Aunt Maggie, why are you talking this way? What's wrong? Is it father?"

"What I have to say to you concerns your father in one way. Maeve, I want you to be strong. I'm not going to be with you for too long now here on earth . . . but my spirit will be with you always."

Maeve sank to her knees, her red hair wild with the sea air. "What are you saying, Aunt Maggie?" Then, "No! I don't want to hear!" And she covered her ears with her hands.

Maggie fell on her knees too, put her arms around her niece and held her fiercely to her breast. "Maeve, oh my Maeve, honor me by accepting with peaceful resignation that which the Lord wants. . . ."

"I can't! I can't! I need you! Tell me you're not going to die!"

"I can't do that." She covered the girl's face with kisses. They rocked back and forth together in the sand as the sun shone down on them. But there was a sharp breeze coming up from the sea.

When the girl calmed down, when her sobs became only sniffles, Maeve told her the contents of her will. "The money part will not be difficult, dear. Paul and James and their sons are trained to take care of money and you will be able to rely on them. You will be the chief trustee of the institutions your great-grandmother and I have founded, but there again you have people you can rely on until you feel ready to assume some of those responsibilities. It's your grandmother I am most concerned about and—"

"And Father?"

"Yes. Your father. Two things I will ask you to do for me. One, is to care for your grandmother, to see to it that she has whatever she needs. Your grandmother is happy in the world she has created for herself. She cannot have too many years left. I want you to see that she remains . . . content. For that, she needs her house, which she has, of course, and someone there to care for and administer to her. Now there's

Annie. Hopefully, Annie will be there until Mother no longer needs her. If not, you will have to see to it that she is replaced by someone equally trustworthy."

"I will, Aunt Maggie, I promise."

"But there's something else she needs to keep her happy in her dream world. . . ."

"Yes?"

"Morphine, Maeve, morphine."

The word sunk into Maeve's consciousness. Her grandmother an addict? A dope fiend? That's what they called them in the comic books. That's all she knew about the people who took drugs . . . scary people with grotesque faces and long taloned fingers. But her grandmother wasn't like that. She was a little old lady in old Russian ballgowns.

Maggie watched the play of expressions on Maeve's face. "It's the morphine that keeps your grandmother happy in that world of fantasy. Don't be too distressed about this. If it weren't for the sweet dreams the morphine provides, your grandmother would have to spend the rest of her days in an institution, tortured and . . . unhappy. She's a sick woman, Maeve, and morphine is but a medicine."

"But what will I do? Where will I—?"

"Dr. Gannon provides the drug. He's been helping us for many years. And Annie gives it to your grandmother. That's why, if she leaves, she will have to be replaced with care. And if something happens . . . if Dr. Gannon goes . . . he will have to be replaced too. You understand."

"Dr. Gannon? The same Dr. Gannon who delivered my baby?"

"Yes."

"He is the keeper of our secrets, then?"

"Yes."

"Was Dr. Gannon in love with you, Aunt Maggie?"

"We're good friends. The other . . . it was a long time ago."

"But why didn't you . . . you and he . . . marry?"

"I suppose if I had loved him enough I would have married. But I guess other things came first."

Maeve started to cry again bitterly. "You gave up everything for me, Grandmother, and Father, didn't you?"

"I gave up nothing. You have been the best thing in my life, Maeve O'Connor. That's why you must be very brave and strong and carry on."

"With or without Father?" She had come to the heart of the matter and Maggie did not try to deny it.

"Without him, Maeve. Most definitely without him. I'm sorry, my darling, but for your own sake, you must not even see him. I think he will try to get you back, to have you live with him. But you mustn't. What you and he shared was wrong, a terrible sin. You were a young girl but I think you knew that instinctively, didn't you? That is why you

178

left him and came to me when you . . . needed help." She didn't want to mention the baby if she could avoid it. "I know you still love him—"

"Oh, Aunt Maggie, I do, I do! I dream of him all the time. I want him to come to me, to take me in his arms. I want him to love me again. . . ."

Maggie was not sure just how Maeve meant this and she chose not to ask. "Your father is, in many ways, a great man. They call him a genius, Maeve, and that he is. So we can't judge him by ordinary standards. It is his genius that places him apart from ordinary men and it is that difference, in turn, that makes him the great, extraordinary artist he is. No, we can't judge him. He's a wild creature who must live in his own habitat. Like Mother, he lives in a world unknown to us, a place of strange dreams. And from all that come the wonderful words and thoughts and ideas. But genius creates and at the same time, it can destroy. It may very well destroy him in the end. There is nothing we can do to save him from his own genius, but it is your duty, Maeve, to God, and man and, eventually, to my memory, to see to it that you are not drawn into his quicksand. I don't think he knows right from wrong. He would make you unhappy, Maeve, without even trying. He is so filled with anger—at all of us. You, me, Mother. The anger is there, in his writing, in his reactions to life. We just have to leave him his anger but not get in the way of it. . . ." If she hadn't frightened Maeve, then she had not accomplished anything. "I know it may be the most difficult thing in life you will have to do, but you must keep yourself from him. Promise me, Maeve!"

Oh, this is too much to bear. I must lose you, Aunt Maggie, and now I have to swear not to love Father.

"I don't know if I can, Aunt Maggie. I'll never love anybody else. I'll never love another man. . . ."

"You will, Maeve, you will! You must accept in your heart that it cannot be, once and for all. Say good-bye in your head, say good-bye in your heart. Pity him, love him as your father, but say good-bye and move on. Promise me, Maeve!"

"You ask too much!"

"I love you, Maeve, and I'm dying. That gives me the right to ask too much."

"How long . . . how long will you be with me, Aunt Maggie?" She had no tears left.

"Maybe two years. A bit more or a bit less. I spoke to you now because I wanted to give you sufficient time. . . ."

"All right, Aunt Maggie. I promise."

Good-bye, Aunt Maggie. Good-bye, Father. There would be no one left for her. Only the friends.

"I love you, Aunt Maggie."

179

3.

Sara came out of Grand Central Station and blinked in the sunlight. It had been such a wet and cold fall, she found it hard to believe the sun was actually shining. *Hello, sun!* It was such a nice day maybe she would walk over to her father's office instead of taking a cab.

She turned right and headed toward Madison. On the corner of Madison and Forty-second Street, a construction worker whistled at her, a lovely blonde in a beaver coat. She knew that in her almost-high black heels she looked older than her almost-sixteen years. And her new hairstyle *was* glamorous; the wave over one eye looked even better on her than it had on Veronica Lake.

As she approached the Gold building near Forty-ninth, she wondered for the umpteenth time what it was her father wanted to discuss with her, something so important that he had actually talked Miss Chalmer into letting her come down in the middle of the week. She looked up to the top of the building before she went through the entrance doors. Her father's own building. Was she still her father's own daughter? She didn't know anymore.

Her father had a new receptionist, Sara noted at once. This one was very decorative if one didn't mind the Max Factor orange and the bleached yellow pageboy.

"Oh, yes, Miss Gold, your father's expecting you. I'll have Miss Peters show you in."

"You needn't bother. I still know the way."

Maurice Gold rushed to the doorway to greet her. He bent his head to kiss her, but Sara turned her face aside and his lips brushed her cheek.

"You look wonderful, Sara. It's so good to see you. You look all grown up."

"You saw me about five months ago, Father. I haven't changed that much."

"But you have, somehow. You look older."

"Look, Father, I'm just in town for the day so if you have something to discuss with me, we had better get to it."

Maurice Gold rearranged his expression. His palms were damp with anxiety. How could a not-quite-sixteen-year-old make him feel so inadequate? But Sara had always managed to do that to him. Maybe he just cared too much. It was obvious she didn't give a damn about him.

"I've made a reservation at the Stork for lunch. I remember how you always loved to go there. We might even fool them into giving you a drink today. You certainly look old enough," he laughed.

Sara said nothing.

"It's difficult to start. . . ." He smiled at her entreatingly. "We used to be able to talk. Can't we try, Sara?"

"You took care of that, Father. Why don't you just begin at the beginning?"

"I've met somebody, Sara. . . ."

"So what else is new?"

"This time it's different, Sara. This is somebody I want to marry."

Sara's mouth opened slightly in surprise, her lashes fluttered nervously. Then she managed to close her face again and she smiled, "You already have a wife, remember? She lives in Kansas in a sanitarium where you've stashed her."

"Stashed her?" He chuckled mirthlessly. "You sound like somebody out of 'Gangbusters.' " He smiled, trying to establish some contact with the past when they had not lived in a state of hostility. "I remember how you always liked that program. You refused to go to bed until it was over. That, and the 'Lux Radio Theater.' "

"Yes. And 'Grand Central Station.' Don't digress, Father."

"Look, Sara, you have to accept that I'm not solely responsible for your mother's breakdown. I've tried to explain that to you countless times. Sometimes marriages don't work out and it's nobody's fault. In this case your mother's own basic instability made her unable to cope with a not unusual situation. Normally—"

"There is no 'normally,' Father. There is only my mother alone out there in a strange and frightening world."

Sara not only looked like an adult, she sounded like one. A very bright adult, Maurice thought sadly. There was nobody in the world like his Sara. Christ, if he could only have managed to keep her his little girl. But it was already too late for that.

Sara watched her father assemble his thoughts again for another tack. She believed he loved her. She *guessed* he loved her. And he was *so* distinguished looking. She even felt a tiny bit sorry for him—he was trying so hard to convince her not to hate him. But she could not allow herself to feel *any* compassion for him—she had to be strong for her mother's sake and her own.

"So, Daddy," she said, "tell me true. Who is the lucky lady? Anyone I know?"

"No. She's English. A war widow. Her husband was killed at Dunkirk."

"Then what is she doing here? Why isn't she in England rolling bandages or whatever?"

"She was visiting friends here when the war broke out."

"How fortunate for her. Why didn't she try to get back to England? There are ways. Wasn't it her duty to go back to the homefront and keep the home fires burning while her brave husband was getting himself killed at Dunkirk?"

He ignored her sarcasm.

"Violet has two children. She didn't want to take them back to London with the bombing and all."

But Sara didn't hear the last sentence. Children? Her father loved a woman named Violet with children. She felt the pain through her heart.

"How old are they?"

"Stewart's six and Gillian's eight. Stewart is named after his father. Stewart "Pip" Wilson. He was titled. Violet is *Lady* Wilson." Maurice couldn't keep the pride from his voice.

"I see," Sara said.

"What do you see?"

She smiled, wetting her lips with her tongue, they were so dry. "I see why you want to marry her. A Lady, a *real* Lady. So what do you want from me, Father? My permission? I don't give it. But you're a grown man." She laughed. "Luckily you don't need it."

She rose, put on her coat.

"Sit down, Sara. We've more to talk about."

She took off her coat, sat down again, looking more now like a child dressed up in her mother's red-collared black suit, too thin for the broad, movie-star shoulders.

"I want to divorce your mother."

"So I've gathered. What the hell do you want from me? See a lawyer."

"You've become tough, Sara. I'm sorry about that."

"Being your daughter's taught me how to be tough. But don't let it bother you. I know how to be soft when I need to be."

"First, it's almost impossible to divorce a woman in a sanitarium without her consent. Second, I want your mother to accept it, so it won't affect her detrimentally any more than—"

"It already has?" Sara finished for him. "It's a bit late to worry about that now, isn't it?"

"Strange as it may seem to you, Sara, I still care about your mother in a certain way."

"Tell it to the Marines."

He bit his lip. "Look, Sara, I've spoken to your mother's doctors. They're of the opinion that your mother *should* be divorced from me, that she won't get better until she's left the past behind."

She heard him out, did not reveal that the doctors had told her the same thing. And she wasn't going to tell him that, with Maggie O'Connor's help, she had made up her mind that divorce was in her mother's best interest and that she was prepared to persuade her mother to do just that. And, incidentally, she wasn't going to tell him that she did not *feel* tough, as he had accused her, not inside. *Inside I'm crying, Daddy.*

"The doctors have tried to talk to your mother about this without any success. They think *you* can persuade her. They think you're the only one she'll listen to."

No, she was not about to tell him that she had already started the groundwork in her letters, that she was going out to see her mother again in a couple of weeks—her Christmas vacation—and would very likely clinch the deal for him at that time.

"So, Papa, you want me to be your bearer of bad tidings. Or your Brutus, in a manner of speaking?"

"No, not Brutus. For her own good, Sara."

"Oh. More like me playing John Alden to your Miles Standish, only we're talking divorce, not marriage."

He was losing his patience. "Call it anything you like. Will you do it? For your mother, not for me."

Sure. She would be doing the right thing. And everybody would stand to gain. Mama would get a new chance at life. Violet, the Lady, would gain a rich new husband, and her father, an aristocratic wife, and Stewie and Gillian would get a new daddy to replace the one they had lost. Only she would be a loser. She would lose a father in this pretty little exchange. Sara did not like being a loser.

"Okay," she said.

He was surprised. "You mean you'll do it?" Somehow he had expected a bigger battle, a major encounter.

"Yes. What's the deal?"

"Deal?"

"Deal. What do I get out of it? Mother gets well. You get Violet. Stewie and Gillian get you. What do I get?"

"What do you want?"

Everything. Whatever I can. You have to pay for everything, Father. You of all people should know that.

"First of all, Mother has to get a settlement. And I have to get my settlement too."

Maurice Gold was affronted. "I *intended* for your Mother to have a comfortable allowance for the rest of her life. And you *always* have had every goddamn thing you wanted. A family of six could live a year on your monthly allowance. Did you think I didn't intend to provide for you? Goddamn it, Sara, you're the chief beneficiary in my will!"

"For now." Sara smiled bitterly. "What happens to me when you decide little Stewie and Gillian are more child to you than I am? What happens when Lady Violet bats her pretty blues and Sara's out in the cold? No, Father, I don't intend to be a figment of circumstance."

"A figment of circumstance? What kind of a phrase is that? What do they teach you in that school?"

"They teach me mathematics. Three into one is one-third. I want you to add up everything you have, what's in the banks, bonds, stocks, every little old piece of property, every building, every company, and I want it formed into one large corporation. You're not a private company anymore, Father. You're going public. There are going to be three shareholders—Mother, me, and you. But I want to be fair with you, Father, so I'll give you thirty-four percent and Mother and I will only have thirty-three percent each. This way you'll be the majority stockholder."

Maurice Gold looked at Sara with astonishment. Where had she come from, this child, this Regan, this Goneril? And where had she learned all this business about corporations and stockholders? When? He looked at her and he thought he knew her—violet blue eyes, golden hair, face as sweet as an angel's. She had always been mature, clever, dexterous, and capable. But this? This mind sharp as a steel trap? And as cold?

He played with his gold Mont Blanc. Idly, he asked: "And who will be president of this corporation?"

"You, Father, of course. You'll be the majority stockholder. And if you behave yourself and don't try to gyp us, Mother and I won't combine our votes to push you out. Oh, and one thing more. I want the house in New York and the place in Southampton. I think that just about does it. Oh, and Marlena's education. You're already committed to paying for that, and her debut expenses, of course."

Maurice Gold's rage was tempered by his admiration for his daughter's acumen.

"I don't think you're being very fair, Sara. Everything I have, everything I own, I got by myself. I sweated for everything and now you want me to give away two-thirds of it. One way or another, you're going to end up with your mother's share so if we split it up fifty percent for me, twenty-five percent for your mother and twenty-five percent for you, you'll end up with fifty percent anyway."

"No, Father, I don't think so. That would mean that after Mother dies and you die and Violet leaves her share to *her* own, I would be left with half of everything and Stewie and Gillian with the other half. Since you were *my* father once, my *real* father, that would make me very sad. Then I would certainly need a lot of money to comfort me. Look, I know this is a big decision for you. Would you like some time to think about it?" she asked in a commiserating tone. "But just keep in mind what will happen if you don't agree to what I want and Mother doesn't agree to the divorce. You've already lost me; you'd lose Violet the Lady, too. And you'd have nothing but money to keep you warm. Which is foolish. Even with only thirty-four percent you're still going to have a tremendous fortune. Plenty for Vi and the kids. Really."

Maurice Gold laughed ironically. He did not have the heart to do battle with Sara, and as she had pointed out, he had already lost *her*. He *needed* Violet. "All right, Sara, you win."

184

"Good, Daddy. Only make sure when the accountants and the lawyers add everything up, they include *everything,* every last little old thing. Because I'll certainly have everything checked and double-checked."

Maurice Gold wanted very badly to smack his daughter hard across her superior little mouth. Not yet sixteen and she thought that she had everything figured out. But she had a lot to learn. She didn't even realize that she had just won the battle with him not because she had outsmarted him but only because she *was* Sara and he loved her. She was going to learn the hard way that life could cross her up no matter how clever she was. And now with the way things were, there was no way he would be able to soften the blows for her.

"Shall we go to lunch now?" Sara asked brightly. "You can tell me all about your new family."

Maurice Gold decided to make one last effort, a fool's effort, but he would make it. "Maybe they can be your new family too, Sara. Give yourself and them a chance. You can afford to be generous. You're walking out of here with an incredible fortune. Do it, Sara. Maybe you'll even get to like Violet and the children."

"Oh, Father, I don't think so. These pushy foreigners, you know. They think they can just walk in and take over everything, our country, our money. . . ." *Even our fathers. . . .*

Maurice Gold stood up angrily. He had given away his money to Sara but now she had gone too far, like the spoiled little brat she was. "You've turned into a bitch, Sara. You turn my stomach and I don't want to have lunch with you after all."

I turn his stomach? What does he think he does to me?

"That's good. If I'm a bitch, what does that make you? You're the one who turned your back on everything and everybody!" She burst into tears. "You turned your back on your whole family! On being Jewish! On Mother! And now on me, your little girl," she said piteously.

Maurice Gold turned white. "I never turned my back on you. *You* made it turn out like this! For the rest of it, I did what I had to do! You don't know anything about it. You're still wet behind the ears and you've always had everything. You don't know what it was like to come here, a poor, ignorant Yiddel who couldn't even speak the language, with all the doors shut in his face. . . ."

"But that's the point, Daddy." She wiped her tears, blew her nose into a tiny handkerchief, a gesture that for some reason made Maurice Gold want to cry. "You didn't have to do it your way. Do you know how many Jews came to this country as immigrants, made great fortunes and became great men *without* turning on their families, without becoming *goyim?*" she spat out.

Maurice Gold was stunned. Where had she learned that word? How was it that it came out of her mouth with the same quality of derision his father had used?

185

"Otto Kahn founded the Metropolitan Opera. He gave five million dollars to it! And he even subsidized the Abbey Players in Dublin and helped George Gershwin. And Adolph Lewisohn. He was a Jew too. He founded Lewisohn Stadium so everybody could hear wonderful music for free. And there's more. Lots of them. Maybe it was their fathers who made the fortunes, but none of them became gentiles to do it . . . they remained Jews and did good things. . . ." She ran down.

Dazed, Maurice Gold realized she must have studied up on all this. A maze of unrelated thoughts raced through his head. How she used to sit on his knee in a long nightgown and beg him to tell her a story. How, sometimes, she would be waiting at the door for him when he came home and would scream, "Daddy!" and jump into his arms.

"They were great men and they didn't have to marry ladies with titles or buy their way into Society. But you—you're handsome and tall and rich and you're the littlest man I know, Daddy. How I wish you had been one of the others . . . so I wouldn't have to be ashamed to be your daughter."

She picked up her fur coat and her pouch handbag and walked out the door.

Coming out of the building, she wondered where to go. She wasn't ready to go back to school yet. She walked quickly as if she knew where she was going, carrying her coat even though it was very cold. She walked down Broadway. A young man huddled into a suit jacket and wearing pegged pants stood near the curb, observing the scene. "It must be jelly because jam don't shake like that," he called to Sara.

She looked up. "Four-F," she hissed and hurried past the Hotel Taft. Then, on impulse, she turned back and entered the hotel. Someone had told her about going to see Charley Drew at the Taft; he played the piano and sang risqué songs. She could use a drink! She walked into the room named after its star performer and sat down at a little table near the piano.

A waiter came over to take her order, never doubting that she was of legal age.

"A Manhattan, please. A bourbon Manhattan with two cherries. When does Mr. Drew come on?"

"Not until five, Miss."

She glanced at her watch. It was only ten past two. She shrugged. *"C'est la guerre,"* and the waiter nodded compassionately.

The room was crowded with soldiers, sailors, marines. A husky young marine smiled at her from across the room. A corporal wearing a Purple Heart ribbon tilted his head upward at her, silent, asking. The waiter brought her drink. She sipped.

"Buy you a drink?" Some kind of an army man came up from behind.

186

Sara looked him up and down, finally decided to answer. She smiled at him. "I already have a drink."

"You can always have another." He showed teeth that needed attention.

She considered sending him on his way. But said. "All right," and drained her glass. He sat down and motioned to the waiter.

"My name's Walter Hannigan. Lieutenant," he added.

"Chrissy. Chrissy Marlowe." The first quick drink had gone to her head and giving Chrissy's name seemed terribly funny to her. She giggled. "By all means, Lieutenant," she drawled intimately as if that were his name.

The waiter brought the drinks. Lt. Hannigan raised his glass. "Here's looking at you, sweetheart."

"I'm not your sweetheart . . . yet."

"Yet," he repeated.

"Are you on your way to war, Lieutenant, or have you been?"

He considered, wondering which story would have the most impact. "Leaving. Tomorrow. Can't say where," he said sadly, mysteriously.

"Poor Lieutenant," Sara murmured, lowering her eyelashes over the glass.

After an hour of half-romantic, half-sexually insinuating conversation, Lt. Hannigan announced that he already had a room booked at the hotel, no small achievement. Every place in town was full up.

"Why don't we go upstairs to my room for a while? Then when this guy comes on, this Drew, we can come down again."

"I hear Mr. Drew sings 'Roll Me Over' in very droll fashion."

He looked at her carefully. Was that an answer?

> Roll me over,
> In the clover,
> Roll me over,
> Lay me down
> And do it again . . .

She sang in a low, husky tone and the Lieutenant guessed *that* was answer enough. He rose to his feet, threw a five-dollar bill down on the table and said, "Okay. Let's go."

"Go where?" she asked innocently.

"Up to my room."

"Why would I want to do that?"

"What've we been talking about?"

"I haven't the faintest idea what *you've* been talking about."

He sat down again. "What are you, anyhow? A C.T.?"

"A C.T.?" she considered. "What's that? A cute thing? Yes, I guess I am at that."

187

"Cock teaser, that's what," he said meanly.

"Lieutenant. I'm being kind to you. Don't you recognize jailbait when you see it?"

"What are you talking about?"

"Jailbait, soldier. I'm underage. If one of your Military Police came along you'd be in big trouble just drinking with me."

He looked at her for a few seconds, the truth sinking in. He got up from the table. "You might be jailbait, honey, but you're still a C.T."

She had wasted the afternoon. She wished now that she had gone to Toffenetti's for lunch and had the fried shrimp platter. It was touristy there and garish, but warm and cheerful. Then she could have gone to the Strand or the Capitol. She could have felt her heart leap with excitement, as it always had, when they opened the voluminous curtains and with a great play of the horns, the bandstand rose up from the depths and came forward, forward, forward. . . .

She didn't know who was playing where. Maybe she could have seen Jimmy or Tommy Dorsey. Maybe Helen O'Connell would have sung, "Green Eyes," or Frankie, "I'll Never Smile Again," and she could have squealed and swooned along with all the other kids playing hooky that afternoon, from the Bronx and from Brooklyn and across the river from New Jersey. Sara cried a little bit.

Maybe she should go have coffee somewhere now. Yes, she would go over to Lindy's and have coffee and cheesecake. Cherry cheesecake.

But when Charley Drew sat down at the piano at five, Sara was still there. She went over to the piano. She liked Charley's looks. Young-middle-aged. Squarish and tanned, or was that pancake? A smiling, world-weary countenance. Sara sighed. "Play it, Sam," she said. "Play it again."

THE DWINDLING DAYS OF 1944

1.

Chrissy was performing her obligatory turn at student-waitressing, a turn that came only about once every three weeks. It was Miss Chalmer's way of paying lip service to the concept of each girl developing a well-rounded sense of responsibility. Actually, Chrissy rather enjoyed the chore—once she had the pleasure of dropping a wedge of Boston cream pie in Mimi Truewell's lap. But as Chrissy served the salad, centering each plate with careful exaggeration, she went into a faint and slid, amusingly enough, right into Ginny Furbush's lap. At first, everyone thought she was clowning and Ginny attempted to push her off onto the floor, but then they realized it wasn't an act.

They took Chrissy to the infirmary where Nurse Robbins took her temperature and pronounced her seemingly well enough. Miss Patrick, Miss Chalmer's assistant, offered to drive Chrissy into town to see Dr. Forman but Chrissy begged off. "I just got nauseous from the smell of the food. I feel really super. Can't I just go back to the dining hall and have a cup of tea?"

Miss Patrick and Nurse Robbins exchanged looks. Everybody knew that Chrissy Marlowe was practically starving herself—no wonder she had fainted.

"You'd better start eating, Chrissy," Miss Patrick said. "Or you'll be fainting every day. You hear?"

"You can become seriously ill if you don't eat. You're a growing girl," the nurse added.

"God, I hope not. I might start growing sideways."

"All right, Chrissy, go on back to the dining hall. But eat something, for goodness' sake."

"I knew you were getting too thin," Maeve said. "No wonder you fainted."

Chrissy lay in bed, pale. "Maeve, I think I'm pregnant."

"Oh no!" Maeve's hand went to her face almost as if to ward off a

189

blow. "Oh, no, you can't be. You're not even seventeen," she said foolishly.

Chrissy smiled woefully. "I think I am. I'm almost a month late."

"What will we do?"

"Go get Sara, will you? She'll think of something."

Sara took charge immediately, for which we were all grateful. "First thing, we have to get you to a doctor and see if you're definitely pregnant. Then we'll know where we stand and what has to be done. And for God's sake, get up from that bed. What are you trying to do? Rest up to keep yourself from miscarrying? We'll go to New York this weekend to see a doctor—we'll say we're going to visit your Aunt Gwen. I'll make an appointment with some doctor—it doesn't matter who. I'll pick out a name from the telephone book, somebody near my house. . . . Just in case, start falling off the bed right now."

"Oh, Sara, I don't think I can. I feel too weak."

"Don't make her," I said, and Maeve sat next to Chrissy on the bed, as if to protect her.

"If she doesn't start dragging her ass around, she's going to feel even weaker."

"Sara!" I protested, shocked both at Sara's language and attitude.

"Don't *Sara* me!" She shoved Maeve aside and grabbed Chrissy's arm and pulled at her until she half fell off the bed, then let go and Chrissy landed on the floor.

"Now get yourself up, get back on the bed and roll yourself off, again and again. Maybe we can get that period going and save ourselves a lot of grief."

"Jeepers, Sara! You haven't even *fucked* anybody yet. How do you know what to do?" Chrissy asked, frightened by Sara's businesslike, hell-bent attitude.

"Because *I'm* not a little old asshole, that's why. I wouldn't open my legs until I knew which end was up. Oh, golly, why didn't I take you to Marg Sanger's while there was still time?"

"Who's Marg Sanger?" I asked.

"Oh, I declare! You're all a bunch of sad sacks. What's the use of all your studying, Marlena, if you never even heard of Margaret Sanger and birth control?"

"No . . . I never did. But I do remember something. I remember overhearing Bess talking. You've got to take a hot bath and drink a mixture of quinine and mustard and if that doesn't work, you've got to jump off the roof."

Chrissy started to cry.

Dr. Bedemeyer confirmed that Chrissy was pregnant. He gave her some preliminary instructions and Chrissy let the nurse set up another appointment for her. "What now?" Chrissy asked Sara.

"I found out there's something we can get from a drugstore. Ergot something. But I think we have to find an under-the-counter pharmacist."

"Isn't that a poison or something? I could lie down underneath a train too."

"I think you'd best go see your Aunt Gwen."

"I just said it. I could lie down underneath a train."

"I'll go with you."

"You don't have to. You can wait downstairs in the lobby."

"Chrissy, I'll stay with you."

"No. But later, when I'm dying, I'll be glad to have your company."

"Chrissy, we're in this together."

"You mean you're going to help me raise the little bastard?"

Sara laughed. "It's a good thing Maeve and Marlena aren't here to hear you."

Sara waited downstairs at the fountain in front of the Plaza while Chrissy went upstairs by herself to face her aunt.

"You look divine, Chrissy!" Gwen pecked her cheek. "You *are* skinny, aren't you? Marvelous! Your arms are like sticks. I love the look!"

Chrissy swallowed. "I'm pregnant, Aunt Gwen."

Gwen Marlowe looked at her for a few seconds, then sucked in her cheeks. "I see," she said. "Who is the father? Anyone you should marry?"

If the father were a Whitney or a Rockefeller, was Aunt Gwen prepared to shove her down the aisle?

"I don't think so." The truth was she wasn't sure who the father was. Since Ensign Towne there had been quite a few "experiences," as Sara called them. Chrissy herself looked on them as *experiments*—somewhere, sometime, there had to be some boy or man who could awaken *something* within her.

"I see. Well, Providence moves in mysterious ways. This is marvelous in a way. I've just been asked to be on the board of the Knickerbocker Home for Unwed Mothers. It's a fairly new project. It was a problem, you know, with all the soldier boys going off to war and leaving little loaves baking in a lot of unwed ovens. We will tuck you in there, under an assumed name of course, and you can give me a day-to-day report on how things really work there. Nothing like an insider's eye-view. Then we will arrange for adoption and no one will be the worse for wear. You'll have to miss a term at school but—"

"I'm not going to be a fucking guinea pig for your Unwed Home. I want an abortion!"

"Really, Chrissy. Your language is getting to be a bit tiresome. I'm afraid it's a little late for what you want. An abortion is out of the question."

"Why is it out of the question?"

191

"I will not traffic with illegal butchers."

"Sara says you can get a legal abortion in Cuba or Puerto Rico."

"There is a question of morality. There are those of us who consider it murder to take the life of an unborn child."

"Oh, stick it, Aunt Gwen!" Chrissy turned to go, tears welling up.

"I beg your pardon. I don't think I understood you correctly."

Chrissy wiped at her eyes, brushed back her hair with one hand, drew herself up haughtily. "Blow it out your barracks bag!"

Chrissy found Sara staring at the bronze nude holding the basket of fruit that graced the Plaza's fountain. Chrissy chuckled morosely. "She's called the Fountain of Abundance. Just like me."

"We'll go to Cuba," Sara said. "Maeve, can you speak any Spanish?"

"Not very much, a few words. I don't know how to say 'abortion' in Spanish."

"I'm a goner," Chrissy wailed. "They'll probably give me a lobotomy instead."

"Why don't we ask DeeDee Dineen what to do? She's very sophisticated," I suggested.

"We don't need any more cooks for this stew," Sara said decisively. "I *knew* all that French they teach us here was a waste of time. We'll go to Puerto Rico. They speak a lot of English there."

"This is turning into a circus," Maeve said. "I know what we have to do." Her high color had paled. "Aunt Maggie."

"But she's so sick." I shook my head. "How can you bother her?"

"I think she would still want us to turn to her if she knew we were in trouble."

"Look, Maeve," Chrissy sighed. "It's no good. If my Aunt Gwen who goes to church only on Easter Sunday to show off a new hat thinks it's immoral, how is your Aunt Maggie going to feel about it? She's a devout Catholic."

Even Sara agreed. "It does seem an awful lot to ask of her."

Maeve looked at her friends. They didn't know what it meant to give birth to a child then give it away. They didn't know what it was like to lie awake at three in the morning wondering where that baby was or what she looked like or whether the baby was happy. She *had* to ask Aunt Maggie for help.

"Aunt Maggie has connections with doctors. And she's a loving, strong woman who believes in helping. *That's* her real religion. She's the logical person to go to."

2.

Maeve's glance swept the library. It was so warm here with the fire going, comfortable, reassuring. Late November, late afternoon, one could really appreciate this room on a day like this. The gray days of autumn. Winter. Can spring be far behind? the poet asked. Would Aunt Maggie even live to see the spring? She looked so much frailer, even though it had been only three weeks since Maeve had last seen her. She had been sure that it was the right thing to do—to come to Aunt Maggie. Now she wasn't that certain. Did she really have the right to disturb Aunt Maggie? Did the living take precedence over the dying?

"What is it, Maeve? You look like you have something very weighty on your mind."

"I do. But I was just wondering if I had the right to—"

"You have all the right. What is it?"

"Aunt Maggie, Chrissy's pregnant."

"Ah." Maggie nodded her head. "Poor child. She has a strong need for love."

So Aunt Maggie *did* understand.

"And you want her to come here—to bear her child, as you once did?"

Aunt Maggie did not understand everything, after all. "No, Aunt Maggie, we . . . Chrissy doesn't want this child. We . . . I . . . want you to help her. Get a doctor . . . maybe do it here—"

"An abortion? No, Maeve! You ask too much!" She fell back in her chair as if from exhaustion.

Maeve felt like a monster pressing on but she had to. "You didn't do it for me—do it for Chrissy."

"A baby is a gift from God, Maeve. It's a sin to destroy a life."

"No, Aunt Maggie. It's a sin to allow a life to come into a world where it is not welcome."

"But every child is welcome in God's world. Somewhere there is a home, a loving home, waiting for Chrissy's child. A home that hasn't been blessed with a child. We would find it."

Maeve shook her head. "How can you be sure? How can you know for sure that wherever that baby went, it would find a happy home, that the people were good, that they wouldn't turn on it, wouldn't—" She shook her head. "No! If you don't know where the baby is, if you can't see for yourself, you're never sure!"

Maggie realized, of course, that Maeve wasn't talking about Chrissy's baby at all. And she still couldn't tell Maeve the true whereabouts of her own child because Maeve would never again have even a moment's peace.

"Was I wrong then, Maeve?" Even without knowledge of the child's abnormality, did Maeve judge her wrong? She closed her eyes. "Tell me that I was wrong and I will arrange for a doctor, arrange for Chrissy to have her abortion in this house. Tell me that it is *more* moral—for there are no absolutes in this world—to end an unborn life than it is to allow a mother to give her baby away not knowing where . . . how . . . whom—" And what answer would Maeve give me if she knew of the baby's abnormality?

Maeve tried to squeeze her tears back. Oh, she needed the strength to hurt Aunt Maggie so cruelly in order that Chrissy could have another chance . . . would not have to bear the torment that she herself had . . . did. . . .

"You were wrong, Aunt Maggie. Forgive me but you were wrong."

The afternoon turned to dusk, then to dark. Maggie and Maeve sat without switching on the lights, Maggie in the chair, Maeve on the floor with her head in her aunt's lap.

BEGINNINGS AND ENDINGS OF 1945

1.

Maggie, lying in bed, as she did most of the time now, heard the news over the radio—President Roosevelt, the valiant warrior, was dead. She was stricken with sorrow for the country. As for the President, he was with God. As she herself would be very soon. She would not make Maeve's commencement exercises. That was two months away but it could just as well be two years away as far as she was concerned. She could scarcely eat anymore and was growing weaker every day. The doctors wanted her to go to the hospital so that they could stick tubes into her, prolong her life a bit longer. For what? She would rather be buried weeks before Maeve's graduation so that her presence, neither here nor there, wouldn't be hovering over the proceedings, casting a spell of gloom for Maeve. And she was determined to die here, in Louisburg Square, and not in the hospital. But not until she had performed one more deed. *Just time for one more transaction, Lord.*

She had sent a cable to Padraic to come to her on her deathbed. She never doubted that he would come. The dramatic impact of the very word *deathbed* would send him rushing to her side. And she knew where to find him. She had always known where he was.

Oh, how she mourned for his lost soul. . . . Padraic—nature's jest. She had read everything he published; she had never stopped being surprised at the imagery and beauty of his words since there was so much hatred revealed at the same time. His work was beauty torn from the depths of despair, out of the dregs of his wretched humanity.

How the Old Enemy must have laughed the day Padraic was born. Would he laugh on the day Padraic O'Connor died because he had died at the hands of his sister, Maggie, who never stopped loving him?

That was pretty ironic. "You always kill the thing you love," Oscar Wilde said and *there* was a man for ye who knew something of the darker side of life. But old Oscar knew how to laugh, too.

Oh, dear God, her mind was wandering. She was disoriented. Like her mother. It must be the drugs they gave her for the pain. Like mother, like daughter. But on the day Padraic came, she would take no drugs. She would have her wits about her that day. She had failed Maeve once —had allowed her to give birth to poor, marked Sally because she herself had been a coward—unwilling or unable to disobey the edict of her Church. But she would not fail Maeve this time. This time, she, Maggie O'Connor, was prepared to do murder for the child of her heart.

She still had the pistol with which she had once threatened Padraic— this time she would use it. She secreted it in the drawer of her night table and waited. Any day he would come. In the meantime, she fingered her silver and pearl rosary, read her book of meditations, *Imitation of Christ,* over and over.

Then one afternoon, only a few days later, she heard a ruckus from downstairs. Her heart constricted. The raised voices—Betsy trying to make Padraic wait while she announced him.

But Padraic would announce himself. "Maggie!" His voice thundered through the house. "Maggie, me love, it's your brother!" and she heard him bound up the stairs. Then he stood in her doorway, tall and majestic as she remembered him. Strong and carnivorous, or was that only in her imagination? And still so dashingly handsome. Dorian Gray. And like Dorian Gray, elegantly dressed in the black suit that was almost Edwardian, and with the flowing tie that marked his style.

He pulled a chair to her bedside and sat astride it, even that with a flourish. "So you are dying, Maggie." Not a question. And not gloating either. But his eyes were burning. It always mystified her how his blue eyes managed to burn like that, as if they were red-hot coals. "And you have summoned me here to ask my forgiveness for you have trespassed against me."

Maggie closed her eyes. He believed it still—that he was not the sinner, but the sinned against. Perhaps he was not evil but only mad, like his mother. But she could not argue, and to what point? Soon, he would be dead.

"You turned my mother from me, as my father did. And then, very deliberately, you stole my daughter away so that I would be left alone in this lonely place. There is no place to go, you do understand that, Maggie?" he whispered softly. "There is only ugliness and the grotesque. On all sides of me there are gargoyles with laughing faces. And I am alone. Without mother, sister, daughter, lover. Oh, yes, there are the critics—those who laud me and acclaim me"—he laughed—"but they don't even understand that which they praise. Nowhere is there any understanding. There is only betrayal. And you, Maggie O'Connor, I do not forgive you." He took a silver flask from his pocket and drank. He rose from his chair and paced. "No, I do not forgive you. I curse you to damnation!"

He sat down beside her again, leaned over, and smiled sweetly into her eyes. "I damn your soul for eternity. And now that you are going, I can reclaim my Maeve. I will take her back to Ireland with me and together we will roam the moors."

"You're insane!" Maggie gasped and her hand went for the drawer of the night table.

He grabbed her hand quick as a snake and held it fast. With his other hand he lifted the flask to his mouth. "Insane? But they say I'm brilliant, the most brilliant writer of the century. If I am insane, then what are they who call me brilliant?"

She jerked her hand from his with a suddenness and tried to pull the drawer open. But he was quicker than she and stronger a hundred-fold.

It was he who opened the drawer and removed the pistol. He loomed over her with the gun in his hand. He uncocked it and looked into the chamber. She closed her eyes, wished fervently that he would use the pistol on her and then they could come and take him away and lock him up and Maeve would be free.

He put the gun to her temple.

"You wish that I would use it on you, don't you? You, Maggie, who would kill your brother. No, Maggie, little sister, little Cain. Lie there and die in your own time. I can wait."

When he was gone, Maggie writhed in torment. She had wanted to spare Maeve the whole truth about her father. Now she could not even do that. She would have to speak to Maeve again . . . quickly.

He had time. Waiting time. Where would he wait? he wondered. Truro, that was in some ways like the Ireland he loved? No. Louisburg Square! What better place than the house where he was born? What better person to pass the time with than the dear old mother who had given him life? And while he waited and passed the time, he would start the most important book of his career. A fascinating woman, his mother. He would sit with her, explore the labyrinthine depths of her mind, follow the winding, curved, distorted, grandiloquent complexities of her brain. Perhaps it would bring him the Nobel? .

The bastards called him the greatest living writer, didn't they? Greater than Faulkner, greater than Hemingway, that ass-fucking poseur. Anyway, they hadn't given the prize to him and old Ernest was four years older than he was. And they hadn't given the prize to Ernest's buddy, Fitzgerald, either, and now they never would. Old Scotty was moldering in his grave with his brain, they said, pickled from the drink. Well, he had been weak. Weak men shouldn't drink. Anyhow, he had always considered Scotty a lightweight. *Not in my class. Not in O'Neill's, either.* Even though O'Neill had never written anything as good *after* he won the Nobel. O'Neill had been forty-eight when he won it. He had six years to beat O'Neill's record and be the youngest writer ever to get it. He had no doubts at all that he would. And this book that he was going to write now, with Mother's help, might just turn the trick.

He used not the doorbell but the old brass knocker, pounding away furiously until the woman, Annie, came running.

"And what's the fuss about?" she demanded.

"Tell Mrs. O'Connor she has a caller."

"I'll be telling her no such thing; Mrs. O'Connor doesn't have callers."

"Doesn't she now? Not even when it's her son longing to lay eyes again on his old murther?" Padraic's eyes danced.

"Bless me, is it Mr. Padraic then?"

"Yes, it is I returned from over the seas. And it's glad I am to see that my mother has such a sweet darling caring for her."

Annie blushed. It had been a long time since she had heard such words addressed to her.

"Will you be staying long then, Mr. Padraic? It's time soon for Mrs. O'Connor's medicine."

"Yes, I'll be staying. Staying for quite a bit. I'll be taking some of the worry off your shoulders. I'll be giving me mother her medicine. What's your name, me girl?"

"Annie."

"Well then, Annie, would you be so kind as to get us some tea and a bottle of brandy to go with it while I say hello to my mum? And, Annie, not a word to anybody about me being here. Not even to my sister. Especially not to me sister. Not for a while. I'll be planning a surprise, you see." He smiled winningly at the old woman.

"It'll be our secret, Mr. Padraic. You can count on me. I'll be getting your tea now." She started off for the kitchen. "You go right on in. But Mr. Padraic, sir, about your mum. She's a bit—"

He laughed. "Yes, Annie, I know."

Only a bit, was it?

He went into the drawing room. Margaret sat working her needle in and out of the petit point she held in her lap. She was dressed in a magnificent wine-colored velvet gown, with flowers encircling her gray head.

"Anna!" Padraic called. "Anna Karenina! How beautiful you are!" He rushed to her and took her hand and covered it with kisses. "Yes, Anna, it's your Vronsky, come home to stay."

2.

"You wanted to kill my father?" Maeve cried out, almost at the point of collapse. "You, who believe in God?" She ripped at her own wild hair in agony.

"He's sick, Maeve. In his sickness, he can be . . . almost evil. And the lambs must be protected."

"No, no, no . . ." Maeve sobbed, raking at her own face with her fingers. "It's only the drinking that does this to him. Don't you see?"

Maggie shook her head, told Maeve how jealous the young Padraic had been of his brother, James, and how, subsequently, James had died at sea so mysteriously.

"But that is only suspicion on your part, Aunt Maggie. It could be all your wicked imagination. Don't you see that?"

Then Maggie told Maeve of how Padraic had introduced their mother to drugs, how her mind had deteriorated until she lost touch with reality completely and became as they knew her now.

"But, Aunt Maggie, you yourself told me she became withdrawn after James's death. And more so, when Grandfather Patrick . . . You told me that she was already strange, had even given up her religion. . . ."

"Withdrawn . . . strange, yes. But that is not the same as being a drug-addicted madwoman. Padraic did that."

Maeve, on the verge of hysteria, searched for answers. "But, Aunt Maggie, are you sure that Father introduced Grandmother to the drugs? Maybe it was the other way around. She was strange and unhappy, maybe she sought solace in the drugs, and encouraged Father to join her in her escape from reality. . . ."

"No," Maggie said fiercely.

"I think you're wrong, Aunt Maggie. Why do you want to believe the worst?"

"Maeve, listen to me. He was obsessed. He hated her. He thought she had betrayed him. He thinks everybody betrayed him. Even you. . . ."

"Me?" *Oh, no, not me. . . .*

"Yes, you. Even you," Maggie said sardonically. "Even you, the daughter he slept with."

But it was no use, Maggie saw. No use to even bring up her suspicions about Sally's death at the time of Maeve's birth. Whatever she brought up Maeve would still waver. All she had done was fill her with doubts, with torn loyalties, to drive her to the brink of—what? A breakdown? She could not fail. She had to use her last, her very last, weapon. She had to use a lie, God forgive her, to convince Maeve of the danger that was Padraic. She threw off the covers. "See!" She pointed to her wasted body. "See what he has done!"

Her shrunken form was covered with the black-and-blue bruises she had inflicted upon herself that morning, before she had sent for Maeve. "Before he left, he raped me!" she whispered, her voice dying away to a hoarse whisper. "Now you *know* for sure what your father is!"

God forgive me! I have lied for Maeve's sake and for Maeve's sake only!

Maggie's lips moved silently and Maeve wrongly assumed that she was praying for Padraic's soul.

"*. . . I confess to Almighty God, to Blessed Mary, ever Virgin, to Blessed Michael the Archangel, to Blessed John the Baptist, to the Holy Apostles Peter and Paul, and to all the Saints, and to you, Father, that I have sinned exceedingly in thought, word and deed . . .*" She struck her breast three times.

"*. . . O My God, I am heartily sorry for having offended Thee, and I detest all my sins because of Thy just punishments, but most of all because they offend Thee, my God, Who art all-good and deserving of all my love . . .*"

Throughout Maggie's silent Act of Contrition Maeve kneeled at her aunt's bedside and prayed for her father's soul. Then Maggie said, "Send for Father Andrew, Maeve."

"Oh, no! Oh, not yet, Aunt Maggie, not yet!" Maeve sobbed hysterically.

"I must be ready."

"Please, Aunt Maggie," Maeve begged. "Not yet, please. . . ."

Maggie smiled weakly. "Just in case, Maeve. And the prayers won't go to waste."

The priest came and Maeve watched, quiet now, as he made the sign of the cross with holy oil on her aunt's forehead and asked for mercy for her soul.

When the rites of Extreme Unction were completed, Maeve turned to the priest. "Can we pray for my father, too?"

Maggie had left instructions that the Requiem Mass exhibit joy rather than sorrow, to reflect the knowledge that death was only the beginning of life with God, and that the celebrants of the Mass wear white for hope eternal rather than black for sorrow. She also requested that as much English as possible be used, instead of the Latin, so that everybody would understand the celebration.

Maeve sat in the front pew with her friends, Sara, Chrissy, and Marlena. The uncles, James and Paul, had remonstrated that the front pew was only for family but Maeve insisted that the friends *were* her family and her uncles had desisted. What did they know of these papist rites anyway? But they were pleased that the principal celebrant was the Archbishop himself—that their niece had been accorded the highest respect as befit the position she had held in Boston Society and in the Catholic lay world.

The Archbishop circled the coffin twice, first sprinkling it with holy water, then swinging the incensory that held the burning charcoal and the fragrant substances, reciting. ". . . may the angels take you to paradise . . ." Maeve felt a shudder course through her body. ". . . may the martyrs come to welcome you on your way . . ." She turned in her seat, searched the rows of mourners. *Is he here?* ". . . may the choir of angels welcome you . . ."

She was sure that she sensed his presence and she was frightened. Had he come to pray for Aunt Maggie's soul? Or his own? Was he present at all?

3.

It was incredible! Victory in Europe and a letter from Dr. Julian . . . both on the same day! Dr. Julian wrote that Mama was greatly improved! Sara ran to the phone in the hall. She just had to speak to her mother. And to Dr. Julian. Find out exactly what was happening there. Did "greatly improved" mean Mama was cured? Would Mama come marching home soon, along with the boys from the European front?

But the telephone lines were buzzing with the news from Europe and Sara was not able to get her call through. She had to tell somebody! She went to look for someone with whom to share her news.

She found Chrissy in her clothes closet, celebrating V-E day all by herself with a bottle of red wine.

"What are you doing in the closet, for heaven's sake?"

"I heard Miss Patrick going down the hall. Have some wine. It must be called Vino Rotgut. But once it's down, it's all the same."

"I've heard from my mother's doctor, Chrissy! He says she's greatly improved!"

"Well, that *is* wonderful news, Sara. I'm so glad for you . . . and your mama. Here, have a slug."

Sara sat down on the floor of the closet and put the bottle to her lips.

"Will she be coming home, Sara? And when?"

"I don't know yet. But I think it's going to be soon, real soon." But where was home? New York? She and Mama could set up housekeeping together in their house. Another couple of months and she would be through with school for good. They could redo the house . . . it would be fun for both of them and it would give Mama something to keep her

201

busy. But the house would be full of memories. Maybe they should get a different house. But New York? Would Mama be happy there? Could she? Actually, Sara thought, there was only one place for her Mama to be.

Chrissy was just a little bit drunk. Hazily she asked, "Where is home, Sara?"

Sara laughed. "Home is where the heart is."

Chrissy shook her head. "I guess I don't have any heart."

"Of course you have a heart, Chrissy darling. It's big and beautiful, a sort of be-bop heart."

Chrissy giggled. "What's a be-bop heart, Sara?"

"It's different from other people's. It's got a different beat—more exciting, new. . . ."

"But if home is where the heart is, Sara, where's my be-bop home?"

"Don't worry, Chrissy. We'll all find a home."

Sara was not worried. She would find a home for Chrissy and she would find one for Mama, too.

"I should have applied to colleges," Chrissy said. "That's somewhere to go. It's funny. Marlena is the only one of us who's going to college and she's the only one of us who has a real home."

"Yes," Sara agreed. "That little old house in Charleston really is a home. . . ."

"But Sara," I protested as I watched Sara pack two white matching suitcases, "you haven't even got permission to go to Charleston."

"Poo, who cares? We're practically graduated already. Commencement is only a few weeks away. I can't be expelled now."

"But it *is* only a few weeks to commencement. So why are you going to Charleston now? I didn't realize you were *that* crazy about my mother. . . ." I said wryly.

"Of course I am. I'm also crazy to see the camellias in bloom."

"The camellias bloom in December and January, not in May," I pointed out.

"Then I'm crazy to see the calla lilies in bloom."

"The roses are in bloom." *What was Sara up to?*

"Sara, why *are* you going to Charleston now when we're graduating and then going to Charleston in only a few weeks?"

"You know, you look adorable in those rolled-up dungarees, Marlena honey. But don't let old Serena Chalmer catch you! She'll have a fit."

"Aunt Martha, I have the most wonderful news. Mama is getting better! I just had to come down here and tell you the news myself. After all, you and Uncle Howard traveled all the way to Kansas all these years to see her. I just bet that was one of the main reasons Mama got better."

Martha smiled at Sara's enthusiasm. "I'd be happy if that were the truth, Sara. But I'm more inclined to think it was getting rid of your father that did the trick, no insult to Maurice Gold intended."

"Well, of course, that was a factor. But I can't tell you how much it meant to Mama having you come to see her, Aunt Martha. A couple of times she said to me, 'Sara, my sister Martha loves me. My sister Martha forgives me for all those years I didn't go see her. She understands why I was so negligent and doesn't hold it against me. She's the most wonderful sister in the whole world!' "

Martha set out a black walnut layer cake and poured tea into fragile flowered cups. "You do go on, Sara," Martha said, but she was pleased.

"Oh, black walnut cake! It's wonderful to be home here in Charleston. Heaven!"

"When do you think they'll be letting Bettina go?"

"Two, three months . . . as soon as I figure out where to take her. After all these years in that gloomy place, it's got to be someplace wonderful, where the sun shines and people love her." The tears rolled down Sara's cheeks. "We have the house in New York, of course, but Mama was *never* happy there. She always said, 'Sara, I haven't had a happy day since I left South Carolina, excepting for the day you were born.' "

Martha sat upright in her chair. "Well, I certainly don't think New York is the right place for her to be. My goodness, no, with all those unpleasant memories. . . ."

"I agree completely, but what else am I to do?"

"You can bring her here to Charleston, that's what you can do. Right here to the old Leeds place. The sun shines here, Sara, and there are people here that love her."

"Oh, Aunt Martha, do you mean it? Never in my wildest dreams did I ever— Oh, when Mama hears about this, I bet she'll be well enough to leave tomorrow. If you're not the best aunt in the whole world, then surely I don't know who is. . . ."

4.

Serena Chalmer watched the men setting up the chairs for the afternoon's ceremony through the window of her office. Thank God the sun was shining so the commencement exercises would be outside, as was traditional. Tradition was one of the most important components of a school like Chalmer's.

The girls were strolling the grounds with parents, grandparents, siblings. The headmistress spotted Marlena Williams and Sara Gold with Marlena's parents. At least *they* had shown up. It was a personal disappointment to her that Gwendolyn Marlowe had not found it convenient to attend her own niece's graduation. She had looked forward so to having her—and the woman had the gall to send her chauffeur in her place.

And the other parents knew that Padraic O'Connor's daughter was among the graduates. His absence was sure to be commented upon. She had hoped that Mr. O'Connor could be persuaded to be their speaker for the day. That would have been a coup, considering the man's literary reputation. But all their prodding could not make Maeve reveal his whereabouts. She found it very strange that Maeve would not know where to reach him. All things considered, those three—the Gold girl, Maeve, and Chrissy Marlowe—were her biggest disappointments in this year's graduating class. At least the cousin, the Williams girl, was going on to Radcliffe.

Everyone knew that the supreme test of a school such as Chalmer's was how many of their graduates were admitted to the seven sister schools. When Sara, Maeve, and Chrissy all refused to file applications for college, Serena Chalmer was appalled. She could understand Sara Gold's not applying; the girl didn't have a serious thought in her head. But Maeve O'Connor? Such an intelligent girl. And they had not even been successful in persuading her to enter the Association of Preparatory Schools' annual poetry competition. And Chrissy Marlowe could easily have gone to Smith. Unlike some of the other girls, there would have been no question of her acceptance. Gwen Marlowe had gone there, and Chrissy's cousin. She would have been an "inheritance"; they would have had no choice but to take her. All in all, she had to admit that the "Terrible Three" had been more problem to her than not, and she was not sorry to see them go. Especially that snippy Gold girl. Everytime she laid eyes on Sara Gold, her skin began to get an itchy feeling as if she were about to break out in hives.

The men rolled out the red carpet on which the girls would walk down the middle aisle in pairs, then they laid it up the stairs to the raised platform where the lectern was already in place. Janey "Pony" Manning Hastings would be their speaker today, instead of Padraic O'Connor. Janey had just published *A Social History of Westchester County*. Janey *was* a graduate of Chalmer's and the girls had nicknamed her "Pony" because horses had been all she had talked about. And because of her long face with the overly large front teeth.

Well, Serena Chalmer thought, it was time to put on her processional robe and go out and mingle with the guests. Another year, another crop of young faces.

All the girls were dressed in white—a Chalmer's tradition.

204

"I adore white," Sara said, "but I just hate it when everyone is wearing white—like we were all a bunch of Brides for Christ."

"Sara!" I admonished her, and squeezed Maeve's hand for comfort and Maeve smiled back at me gratefully.

"What do you think of Aunt Gwen sending Albert to attend my commencement instead of coming herself?" Chrissy asked cheerfully. "Isn't it divine? I've always adored Albert." But I wondered if Chrissy's cheer was sincere.

"The worst part of this affair is that awful grenadine pink punch and those neon-colored petit fours they're going to serve when the exercises are over. I think they must have saved them from last year's grad," Sara whispered loudly.

"Shush! They're about to begin."

Maeve turned around in her seat and scanned the faces in the audience. She wasn't sure why she did it or whom she was looking for. But in the last row of the semicircle of chairs she spotted a man who looked somehow familiar—had she seen his picture somewhere? A distinguished-looking man with a lot of gray, wavy hair and a mustache, whispering to the plain, pleasant-looking woman beside him. Maeve leaned over, whispered, "That man, sitting in the last row, next to the lady in the blue dress and turban. Doesn't he look familiar?"

We three turned around. I gasped and Sara said, "Don't look now but that's dear old Dad!" She smiled curiously. "I guess that's Lady Violet next to him. She's not about to win any beauty prizes, is she? He had an awful lot of gall to bring her here."

"Please don't make a scene, Sara," I begged.

"I have no intention of doing that. *I'm* a lady! Now, everybody shush! Everyone's staring at us. Pay attention, girls! This is your commencement!"

Sara shook hands with her father, her stepmother.

"So nice of you to come, Father, but you needn't have troubled yourself."

"It wasn't nice of you not to invite me yourself."

"Let us not get into a discussion, Father. Marlena is bringing over Aunt Martha and Uncle Howard to meet you, though I'm sure Aunt Martha would rather not. But they've been wonderful to me and Mother. Please try to make a genteel impression."

Violet Gold looked pained but said nothing.

I made the introductions and Mother was civil, Violet Gold was cordial, my father was pleasant, and Uncle Maurice was charming. He recalled that he had made Mother's acquaintance before, when he had first met Bettina. Mother just inclined her head.

"Did you know, Father, that we're all going to Charleston for the summer? We're bringing my mama home at last."

There were tears in Uncle Maurice's eyes. "I'm so happy for you, Sara."

"It's Mama you should be happy for."

Maeve and Chrissy came up with Chrissy's aunt's chauffeur just then.

"Everybody! I want you to meet my friend Albert. He came all the way from New York to see me graduate. . . ."

5.

Sara went to the sanitarium, took Bettina back to the Leeds house on Meeting Street, and spent the summer days joyfully watching her mother bloom again like the delicate flower she was. Sara knew she had done the right thing—this was where her mother belonged. Perhaps, after a while, when her mother was really strong and secure, they could buy their own house, someplace really close by. In the meantime, Aunt Martha and Bettina were getting along beautifully. Martha was the big sister, protective and bossy, Bettina the petted, adored and adoring little sister. A perfect arrangement for now, Sara thought. Later on, they would see.

Maeve and Chrissy went to Newport for the summer and once a week Maeve would go into Boston to check on her grandmother. Dr. Gannon brought the medicine, Annie administered it, and her grandmother tatted, embroidered, did the petit point that she was so skilled at, read Chekhov, had conversations with the family of the Tsar. The world did not intrude at all into the house on the Square. No radio played, no newspaper was read, no mail came, the war had never happened. It was peaceful there. Annie seemed a bit nervous now and then and Maeve guessed that this was because she was no longer used to callers. Only infrequently did Margaret O'Connor's brothers come visiting, and then they did not even stay for tea. But Maeve liked going there—it was a temporary haven from the world, there in that house where time stood still.

From there, she would go to Maggie's house, her own house now, and go through all the papers that were as much a part of her legacy as the money. There were some small details to see to, little decisions to be made—the hospital, the home, the museum. Things were slow in the summer but in the fall she would really have to take up her responsibilities, even though Sara was counting on the three of them taking up residence in her house in New York and preparing for their debut. As if there were any necessity for a debut. Debuts were for children who had not yet tasted of life. And she and Sara and Chrissy had had enough experience already to fill a lifetime. Debuts meant parties, dances, nightclubs, and balls. It meant a continual exposure to men. And that was the last thing Maeve wanted—to meet men, dance with them, touch them, be touched, love or be loved. No, she wanted no debut. Sara would be disappointed, but Maeve knew where her place was and it wasn't New York.

In Newport, she and Chrissy swam, sailed, played tennis, rode. Lovely. But Chrissy needed more. She was always restless, she needed parties, needed the attention of boys or men, whoever was around. It seemed to Maeve an almost physical craving. Like her omnipresent cigarettes. But then, afterwards, it was always the same. After the dancing and flirting, the kissing and the petting and the consummation, Chrissy was abject, depressed, distressed. Sometimes crabby, sometimes even zombielike. Then, the very next day, she wanted to go again, someplace, any place where she would meet somebody new.

"Please, Maeve," she wheedled one afternoon when there was a cocktail party she wanted to attend. "Come with me. Why don't you want to go with me? Sometimes I think you're terribly afraid of men. They don't bite," she giggled. "Unless you really want them to. But if you're not careful, you'll end up an old maid just like your Aunt Maggie."

"Chrissy Marlowe! That's the meanest thing you ever said. To call Aunt Maggie a—"

"Oh, don't be mad. I didn't say anything so awful. Aunt Maggie *was* . . . I mean, she never did marry. That's all I meant to say."

"Aunt Maggie was too busy . . . too busy taking care of everybody else. She didn't spend her time just thinking about herself the way some other people do."

"I apologize. Okay. I'm sorry. Now will you come out and play with me? Two rum and Coca-Colas and you won't feel a thing. Really, Maeve, it's the first time that's the hardest."

6.

"Do you think we should redecorate?" Sara asked Chrissy, looking over the drawing room of her town house. "I do plan for us to entertain. What do you think?"

"I think people will think it's strange for two seventeen-year-olds to be living in this house alone and entertaining by themselves—"

"Do you think we need a chaperone? We could always ask your Aunt Gwen to come stay with us, if you think we need someone—" Sara mocked.

"But really, Sara, how *are* we going to debut? Don't we need somebody to sponsor us? Make the arrangements? Your Aunt Martha was adamant. She wants Marlena to come out in Charleston and she says that if the rest of us will come down there, she can sponsor all of us, but it *has* to be Charleston. And your mother's there too. Don't you think—"

"No, I don't. Even Marlena doesn't want to debut in Charleston. She says going back and forth will take up too much of her studying time. Charleston is a nice place to live, but there is nothing, but nothing, like a New York debut. And if you'll leave it to me I will arrange everything. It's only September so I still have some time to arrange things. I've decided we'll debut at the Waldorf—there's a Cotillion there every year around Christmas when some of the city's finest young ladies make their bow. That's us, just in case you didn't notice. In the meantime, we go to all the parties, do the clubs, and go to all the other debuts. In New York! Now that the horrible old war is over, New York is really swinging. This is a wonderful year to debut!"

"I only wish Maeve was here. I can't believe she's going to stay in Boston and not debut with us."

"But, Chrissy honey, what can we do if Maeve doesn't want to debut? I guess it's because her aunt just died a few months ago. And she and Aunt Maggie had planned on her making her debut in Boston and now . . . you know . . ."

"But I was *counting* on you, Sara, to talk Maeve into coming to New York. I hate to think of her alone in Boston. I don't know what she does there all by herself. She's getting morose, I think."

"But with Marlena nearby in Cambridge? They do see each other."

"Oh, I don't think they see each other that much. Marlena's busy with her studying. After all, her college just started. Poor Maeve. She's so alone. And she'll never have a date if we're not there to force her to. Good God, don't you think she's a little young to bury herself with museums and hospitals and taking care of that crazy grandmother of hers?"

Sara perched her new black and white striped hat on her pale yellow head, looked into the mirror and cocked her head to one side. "Do not worry your tiny mind. I have the feeling that before long, Maeve will get mighty homesick for her two sweet old pals and will get her little ol' ass down here." She turned to face Chrissy. "It comes with a matching bag. What do you think?"

"Not bad. Let me try it on."

"Oooh," Sara cried. "I think it looks even better on you. I wish I had your looks."

"*My* looks? You're the pretty one."

"Maybe. But *you're* the stunning one."

"Sara, do you really think Maeve will come to New York?"

"I have that feeling. Now, do you want to see the other hat I bought? It's very mature."

7.

Padraic had almost come to the end of his novel, *Fragments of the Great Shattered Whole*. He was disturbed—he needed a better ending for the book than the one he had outlined. He had been here since May, studying his mother, talking to her, getting inside that crazed brain of hers. This book had been an experiment, a brilliant one—it would make his mother's brain immortal—he had interred it there within the pages of his novel. Yes, Margaret and her brain would be part of the legacy he would bestow upon the world. But still—something was wrong with the ending. . . . And he had no more patience to ponder it. Usually, he took much longer with a novel, but he wanted to be done with it. He was restless, eager to reclaim his Maeve and cross the sea, back to his Ireland where he felt a kinship with the earth, the moors, the sea. Maeve, Maeve, Maeve . . . living but three doors down. He was convinced that in her innermost being she *knew* he was there, waiting. They had always shared this silent communication. Yet when Maeve came to see her grandmother, she sat there so calmly, talking Margaret's gibberish with her, as he listened upstairs, sharing conspiratorial glances with the fool, Annie, who had kept his secret these many months. Did Maeve not really sense that he was close by?

He poured a little of his prized absinthe into a cordial glass and sipped. It was not easy to come by, especially here in Boston. He laughed. He always managed. He always had his resources. . . .

He had grown fond of absinthe in his youth, in those early days in Paris. He knew what they said about it, that it rotted the brain. He laughed again. That might be true for the weaklings, the cowards, the ignorant. For him, absinthe sharpened the senses until he was aware of subtleties in the universe to which ordinary men were not privy, the true shape and color of things. And when the migraine came upon him, it was the only thing that helped the searing pain.

No, he couldn't delay anymore. He had to be off. He could suffer Margaret the loon and Annie the fool no longer. He took another sip of the liquor. *What could he do with that ending?* Margaret was the key. Margaret was the substance of the book; she had to be its ending too. . . . But of course! It was the only possible solution. . . . There was no other. Margaret would redeem his book and he would redeem her immortal soul. She was of no further use to him; she was of no further use to herself. She had been child, wife, mother . . . and had failed dismally in all those roles. Not only would he forgive her for her rejection of him—he would send her off in a blaze of glory! His book would be a classic and Margaret would live on as one of the most famed characters in literature—as memorable as Anna Karenina herself!

———

Annie was off to market; Padraic had assured her he would take care of their charge. He rushed into Margaret's room where she lay dozing, dreaming who knew what dreams, the dreams of the drugged being very special. He smiled fondly at her and gently shook her.

She awakened, looked around her vaguely.

"Where am I?" she asked.

"In Moscow, my sweet."

"Oh, I thought it was Petersburg."

"Perhaps it is."

She relaxed against the pillows.

"Is it time for me to dress for the ball?"

"No, Anna. You are to meet Vronsky down at the railway station. You are eloping together."

"But what of my little boy? Surely I cannot leave him."

"He will follow. Later."

"Are you sure? I couldn't leave little James behind."

Padraic's fond smile faded and a bitterness, reflected in the set of his lips, took over.

"I promise you, Anna—you and little James will be together— Now, you must hurry and dress. Or you will miss Vronsky."

She looked frightened.

"Miss Vronsky?"

"Yes. You are to meet him at the depot. You must dress in your most beautiful gown . . . no, your most beautiful traveling attire. After all, you and Vronsky will be traveling . . . away together. Now, let us see. What shall you wear?"

He threw open her closet.

He chose a bottle green velvet suit with a train.

"Ah, yes! You will be quite lovely in this. And you must look your loveliest for your lover, *n'est-ce pas?* If you are at your loveliest he will never leave without you."

Dismay and confusion crossed her face.

210

"Leave without me?"

"Yes, if you are not in time he might think you weren't coming and leave without you—"

"Leave without me," she repeated.

"So we must hurry, you see. Here, let me look at you." The jacket was askew, wrongly buttoned, the skirt twisted to one side. "No, no, this will never do." He rebuttoned the jacket, straightened the skirt. "There, that is much better. Magnificent. Truly magnificent . . . no one could doubt your beauty. Certainly not Vronsky."

"Vronsky?"

"Yes, my dear, your lover Vronsky. We are meeting him at the depot. Remember?"

Margaret wrinkled her brow trying to remember.

"And now for your hat." He removed a large-brimmed picture hat from the shelf. It too was bottle green velvet. "Here, let me put it on for you." He lightly smoothed her unarranged, matted hair with his hand and placed the hat on her head, touched the tail of the great white plume lovingly. "There, you look charming, Anna. . . . No one would say you were not at your most charming. . . ."

She smiled sweetly. "Thank you, Pad—" She stopped, looked about her uncertainly.

For a moment *he* looked confused.

"What did you say?" he demanded.

"I said we must hurry. I do not wish to miss Vronsky."

"Of course," he said and his mouth twisted.

He placed her in the shining Pierce-Arrow carefully as if she were fragile glass.

"But what is this carriage? I don't remember it. Do I?"

"It's a horseless carriage, Anna. You went to the ball at the Summer Palace in it just a few days ago."

"The Summer Palace? But it is not summer, is it?"

"It will be, Anna, it will be."

The railroad station was crowded. He tried to hurry Margaret through so as to attract as little attention as possible. At the same time, he had to make sure that his scene was complete.

"Ah! Here we are. Now we must find Vronsky."

He looked up and down the platform. "I do not see him."

She looked worried. She looked up and down the platform too. "I do not see him."

"Hmmm. I wonder if he has left without you."

"Left without me? Why?"

"He might have thought that you had changed your mind. That you didn't love him?"

"Didn't love him?"

"But you do! You love him and you want to go away with him, don't you?"

"Oh, yes. I must go away with him."

He looked up and down the platform again. "No." He shook his head. "I don't see him. Perhaps *he* changed his mind. Yes, I think so. He decided that he didn't love you and he went away without you."

"No!" she cried.

"Yes! I think he has abandoned you!"

"Oh, no!" she cried.

Several people were staring at the bizarre picture they made. Padraic smiled at them, spread his hands, as if asking for their compassion. To Margaret he said, "Ah, yes! I think that is the truth. Vronsky is gone . . . gone. . . . I think he has forsaken you!"

Margaret sobbed, and a train pulled in. Now he must move quickly, he decided. Too many people were staring.

He dashed up and down, stopping at each car's entrance, looking into windows.

"No! He is not on this train! He is gone! But we will take one last look—at the first car down the way. Come quickly, Anna! Hurry! Before the train pulls out!"

He grabbed her hand and pulled her down the platform toward the first car. The train made a roar as it prepared to leave. Margaret stumbled, her face a picture of anguish but Padraic pulled her forward.

Again the train roared. Padraic frantically ran up to all the windows as Margaret, now very frightened, watched him.

"No! He is not here! All is lost! Vronsky has left you . . . he has gone! All is lost! You are forsaken, you are alone! Anna, there is nothing left! . . ."

And then Padraic was gone, disappeared into the crowd.

The train started up. Margaret was utterly confused now, *lost, forsaken, alone.* . . . She looked all around her, saw only the white-faced staring strangers. Vronsky? Where was he? She spun around—there were no familiar faces . . . nobody. . . . Terrified, she saw the track in front of the now slowly moving train yawn up in front of her. *Vronsky! Where are you? Why have you forsaken me?* She hesitated. Did she hear someone call her name? . . . Where, oh where was Vronsky? . . . *Quickly, before it is too late . . . Anna! . . .*

Maeve threw open the door of her grandmother's house. "Annie, Annie!" she screamed. "Where are you? What have you done?"

Annie came shuffling out of the kitchen, her splayed peasant feet slapping in felt slippers. "And what it is I'm supposed to have done, I'll be asking."

"Grandmother . . . how could you let her leave the house?"

The old woman was confused. "But she's upstairs—resting. . . ."

"No, she's not! She's dead! She went down to the South Street Station and fell in front of a moving train. . . ." Maeve sobbed.

"Oh, sweet Jesus . . . may the saints preserve us. . . ."

"Why did you leave her alone? Why didn't you wait until Betsy or I came and—"

Annie bit her fingernails. "But I didn't leave her . . . you mustn't blame me, Miss Maeve! *He* was here."

"He? . . ."

"Yes, Miss Maeve . . . he's *been* here all along."

They both looked up toward the landing at the top of the stairs. Padraic stood there, looking down, impeccably groomed, graced with his extraordinarily smooth countenance. Maeve felt her blood freeze.

"It was him, Miss Maeve, it was him . . ." Annie blurted out.

"Oh, my God!" Maeve whispered. "You've done this! Murderer!" she screamed.

A black scowl crossed his face and he came down the stairs slowly. Maeve backed away, more so as he came closer. Annie, seeing the black look of him, went running out of the room, out of the house.

"The blatherings of an old cabbagehead. Pay her no mind."

Still, Maeve backed away.

He stopped, his face very dark. "And would you be believing that ninny instead of me who is the deepest part of you?"

"Don't! Don't! I know *everything* about you."

"What do you know, Maeve me darling? That you and I are a part of one another unlike any other two people who have ever lived."

He put his arms around her and her body shrunk as if resisting on its own.

"I have loved you; you have loved me; you are part of my flesh and blood; I am part of yours." His voice caressed her.

She felt as if she would swoon in his arms.

"We have known each other forever, you and I, through endless time."

She realized then that he was drunk. Not the unshaven, disheveled drunkenness she remembered, but besotted all the same. With drink? With drugs? Or with the madness?

She broke loose. She could not trust her own body not to betray her, her body that still wanted him.

He held out his arms to her. "Come back, little Maeve. I have always loved you, loved you so much, as no one has ever been loved—"

"Too much! You have loved me too much!" she cried out. "You've sinned and you've made me into a sinner—"

213

His face clouded with the black look she remembered of old. "Are you saying that you will not come with me?"

"I'm saying that I don't ever want to see you again!" *Oh, God, help me!*

She saw all the rage in the world in his face.

"Bitch!" he denounced her. "Daughter of a thousand bitches!"

Would he strike her down? Would he kill her there and then? She wanted to run but was powerless to do so. Would he pursue her forever to the ends of the earth?

She fainted and when she came to, he was gone. *Where to?*

Margaret Abbott O'Connor had been born into Episcopalianism, had converted to Catholicism, had withdrawn into nothingness. In death, her brothers Paul and James reached out and pulled her back into their Episcopal world and she was buried as all the Abbotts had been buried in America since the seventeenth century.

Maeve stood at the grave site along with her friends, terrified. Terrified that Padraic would reveal himself here and would demand to eulogize his mother in his Padraicesque eloquence. She dared not even look up for fear of what she would see.

There was no question now of her staying on in Boston. She would never know where he was—in Grandmother's house or standing in a crowd next to her. Or had he gone back to Ireland? Wherever he was, she couldn't be alone. She had to go to New York, be with Sara and Chrissy.

She would live with them in Sara's house, but would they be able to protect her from the blood in her own veins, the strain of madness that ran in that blood, in her father's blood, Grandmother Margaret's, even her grandfather's? She had never known her Grandfather Patrick but he too was given to the black rages, she had been told. How could she ever marry? How could she give birth to innocent babies, not knowing for sure if she would pass that madness on to them? And what of her baby, Sally? Was she mad too, wherever she was?

8.

"Chrissy, must you chain-smoke?" Aunt Gwen fanned the blue white film filling her sitting room. Now that she no longer smoked herself, she couldn't bear the atmosphere other smokers created. "And must you drape yourself all over that chair? Sit up! Sit up!"

Chrissy cast a dirty look at Sara who sat upright in a black silk dress imprinted with a huge hand-painted flower. The look plainly said, "Do you see what you've gotten me into?"

Sara ignored her and continued her practiced speech. ". . . so naturally I thought you would be the logical one to sponsor our debut since my mother is in Charleston in delicate health and Maeve's aunt has passed away and . . ." Sara decided to lay it on with a heavy hand. ". . . no one else has your clout in Society. After all, Aunt Gwen," she said, even though she had never received Gwen Marlowe's permission to call her that, "a Marlowe *is* a Marlowe. . . ." She smiled sweetly, daring to be corrected.

The guile of the girl! Pushy, like the rest of her kind.

"And what of your father, Sara? He moves about quite a bit in *certain* social circles, does he not?"

Sara hesitated. Should she mention the fact that she and her father did not see one another?

"In certain social circles, yes. But he does not have *your* credentials, Aunt Gwen."

"I see. I will explain my position to you, Sara." She pointedly ignored Chrissy who struck a match to still another cigarette. "I have discovered that I no longer believe in Society as we know it. It is no longer *relevant*. The winds of war have swept all that away. We must all do something that is relevant with our lives. I myself have become a photographer. I was seriously thinking about becoming a sculptress, but Gert Vanderbilt Whitney did that years and years ago, and I wanted to do something that was completely original. . . ."

"Oh, very original," Chrissy muttered.

"As I was saying, Sara," Gwen continued, pointedly ignoring her niece's interjection, "I have become a photographer. A beginner to be sure"—she laughed modestly—"but a serious one, nevertheless. It is art that is relevant, Sara. It is art that lives on through the centuries taming the beast that lives in all men. I am, at this very moment, turning Marlowe House into a museum, for the art of today, for the future cultivation of art, for all to enjoy . . . the little people too. . . ." She finished somewhat lamely.

Chrissy sat up. The Marlowe mansion, Grandmother Marlowe's great house, was to become a museum? Aunt Gwen was actually giving it away, just like that? She looked at her aunt with grudging admiration.

"Golly, Aunt Gwen, that's really keen."

"*Keen?* Really, Chrissy."

Chrissy sighed. "Do you think we could have a little drinkee?"

Gwen Marlowe consulted her wristwatch. "That would be nice but I really don't have the time."

This was their cue to leave, Sara knew, but she was not about to give up yet. "That's very admirable. I think that's just wonderful ·. . .

the photography, the museum . . . *divine!* But how much could our little debut interfere with that? You don't really have to *do* anything. All you'd have to do would be to make a few phone calls."

Gwen smiled patiently. "But you have missed the point I was trying to make, dear child. I do not believe in *haute* Society anymore. Therefore, I do not believe in debuts, which are the official bow into that society. A debut is an archaic custom, my dear. Pagan rites!"

"I must say I'm very disappointed, Aunt Gwen. Chrissy *wants* this debut, *she* believes in the Old Order. Don't you, Chrissy?" She didn't give Chrissy a chance to answer. "And what difference can one little debut make to the relevance of Society? You do admit a certain responsibility toward your niece? She is an orphan, after all, and you're the only one she has."

Oh dear, she is pushy. Still, it couldn't hurt to give a party . . . just a party and nothing more.

"Very well, Sara, I'll tell you what I *will* do. The museum will be opening in a couple of months. November. We will make the opening party of the Marlowe Museum in Chrissy Marlowe's honor." Then she smiled and added: "And in your honor too. And that sweet little Irish girl. Is there anybody else you'd like to include?" she asked, her voice ripe with irony.

"Yes. My Cousin Marlena. She's at Radcliffe."

"Yes, of course. But I want you to bear in mind—this is in no way to be considered a bow into Society. It is just a party, the opening of the museum, in honor of Chrissy and her little friends. A white tie affair, of course."

It wasn't what she had hoped for. Still, it was something, Sara comforted herself. She rose, "Christina, come. We'll be in touch then, Mrs. . . . Miss? . . . Marlowe . . . Ta, ta." She wiggled her fingers and pushed Chrissy in front of her.

"I won't say I told you so," Chrissy said in the elevator.

"I do not regard this as a defeat. A party at the new Marlowe Museum is not without a certain cachet. Let us go to the Oak Room and celebrate with a drink."

"Let's. After Aunt Gwen, I need a double."

They settled themselves on bar stools.

"I guess I will have to do the debut myself," Sara said thoughtfully.

"But Aunt Gwen's party—"

"Is only a party. It is not a debut. Debutantes can have a lot of parties given in their honor. But they are only in addition to—"

"I see." Chrissy nodded solemnly.

"Do you know who works at the Plaza now? Serge Obolensky. Prince Serge Obolensky. He's the public relations director. And he's a real White Russian prince, through and through."

"Really, Sara. You're a walking edition of *Information Please.*"

Sara ate her maraschino cherry. *Public relations director. . . . Now that's an idea.*

Sara swung into action. Without any further dawdling, she hired Miss Hortense Greenway, herself of impeccable social lineage, who "managed" debuts. Miss Greenway would arrange for the presentation ball, the Debutante Cotillion to be held in the Grand Ballroom of the Waldorf-Astoria. She also assured the girls invitations to all the other important coming-out parties and balls. They would be on all the right lists. And Miss Greenway worked with the Cotillion people to see that the proper "eligibles" made up the all-important stag line.

"And it would be good if we had a series of parties given in your honor. You supply the sponsors, I supply the guest lists."

Sara had the museum party sewn up, which made Miss Greenway very happy. "And we can have Maeve's uncles and their wives come to town and give a party. They're the Abbotts of Boston, you know."

"Excellent!" Miss Greenway enthused.

"I don't know if—" Maeve mumbled.

"We'll send out the invitations in their names, and if they choose to come, we'll be delighted to have them," Sara said. "Isn't that right, Miss Greenway?"

"Absolutely."

"And my family are the Leedses from Charleston."

Miss Greenway was not quite sure she was familiar with the name or the lineage. . . .

"My mother and my aunt will give a tea dance at the Carlyle, I think. You just send out the invitations in their name, Miss Greenway," Sara said firmly.

"Of course, my dear. I'm sure all New York will be delighted. . . ." Her voice trailed off. "And how about your father? He is married to a titled English war widow, is he not?"

"Forget my father, Miss Greenway. He is not . . . *relevant.*"

Miss Greenway nodded her head, not at all sure what Sara meant. But Sara understood completely what it was she wanted of her father. She wanted him to read about her wonderful debut in the papers, and all the wonderful parties she attended. She wanted him to see her name plastered all over.

Next, Sara hired a public relations firm to make sure that their names made the columns, both Society and Broadway.

"Why, Sara?" Maeve asked, not at all eager to be in the public eye. "What's the point?"

"We're doing this thing, the debut, the whole shebang, right? So we might as well be stars. Remember Brenda Frazier—she came out in thirty-nine, I think. She was very glamorous and her pictures were simply everywhere, and Cholly Knickerbocker, you know the column . . . well, Maury Paul was Cholly then and he *adored* Brenda and he gave her lots of space in his column, and then he named her Debutante of the Year. I've decided that the three of us should be the Triplet Debs of the Year. I'm afraid Marlena will be left out because she won't be making the party and nightclub scene, though I'm going to try and persuade her to make as many parties as possible. But can't you just see our picture on the cover of *Life*: The Three Debs of 1946—a blonde, a brunette, and a redhead! Cute?"

"Divine," Chrissy agreed. "The only trouble is *Life*'s covers are in black and white."

"Are they?" Sara asked. "Well, that will be another first. For us, they'll use color."

"Can't you leave me out of it?" Maeve asked.

"No, not on your life," Sara chortled, proud of her pun.

"Don't worry, Maeve. Just because Sara says it will be so, doesn't necessarily mean it's a *fait accompli*. She doesn't even know Cholly Knickerbocker." Then she clapped her forehead. "Heavens to Betsy, do you?"

"Not yet," Sara purred, "but I will. The new Cholly is Igor Cassini, one of those White Russians, and I think we'll get to know him very well. I intend to make that my very next project."

"It seems to me that you're putting an awful lot of energy into this, Sara."

"But, Maeve"—Sara's eyes were large—"what else is there to do?"

I came down from Cambridge for as many parties as I could manage but it was never enough for Sara. As Christmas approached and with it, at least, *our* formal debut, I was worn out. I told Sara that it felt like we had been out for ages.

"Don't be ridiculous! It's only the beginning. The forty-five–forty-six debutante season isn't over until through the spring of 1946."

9.

Of course, we all wore white. Chrissy's strapless dress was composed of tiers of ruffles, tier after tier, so that the skirt moved like a bell. Sara's dress was strapless satin and followed the curves of her body. Maeve had at first chosen a bateau-necked model of crepe de chine but

Sara had flatly rejected it, insisting her dress had to be strapless too, so Maeve settled on a creamy-white velvet with a bustled effect in the back. My mother had picked out my dress. It had a satin bodice with a sweetheart neckline and a bouffant skirt of seven layers of net. And we all wore long kid gloves that reached almost to the shoulders. When we posed for our picture, all together, I was disconsolate; I was practically the only girl debuting who did not show at least *some* bosom.

Maeve tried to console me. "You look like an antebellum Southern belle."

"A real Scarlett O'Hara," Sara chimed in.

"How come I feel more like Melanie Wilkes?" I pouted, trying to pull down the front of my neckline.

First there was the promenade, with each girl escorted by two young men. And there was a ratio of three men to every one girl for the stag line. Since I had not attended that many coming-out parties, I found it all terribly exciting, but Sara sighed, looking the stag line over. "The same bunch as usual and there are still a few boys in uniform. Nothing new."

I noticed with particular interest a naval lieutenant with brown slick hair, who, marvel of marvels, was smiling at me. "Who is he?" I whispered to Sara.

"That's Johnny Grey. He just got back in town. And he's positively staring at you. What a coincidence!" Sara smiled archly. "I heard he's going to Harvard Med. He did his pre-med before he went into the service. You'll be practically neighbors."

"He's cute," Chrissy said, but her attention was elsewhere. There was that Gaetano Rebucci again, the one from California. Dark wavy hair and the white teeth of a movie star. Sara had scoffed at him, said he resembled a gigolo. But Chrissy thought he was sexy.

"For God's sake, Maeve, smile!" Sara commanded. "This is your debut, not your execution!"

"Are you sure?"

"No, not really. But I don't think they shoot you just for trying to enjoy yourself. Look at Chrissy over there. She's trying. She keeps trying."

"You're the most beautiful girl in the room." It was Gaetano Rebucci's usual line but this time he thought he meant it. Those black eyes, that mouth. "I'd love to have my mouth on yours this minute . . . this second . . . mmmm," he moaned seductively as they danced. "Feel it? Do you feel my mouth on yours? Mmmm. . . ."

"Tell me more about your family in California."

What was with this babe? He talked sex and she wanted to know about his family.

219

"What do you want to know? There's Grandpa and Grandma Rebucci, Mama and Papa, my brothers Reno, Aldo, Guido and Rocco, and my sisters Anna, Marie, Gina, and Philomina. And there's a bunch of uncles and aunts and cousins and a million babies. Napa Valley's crawling with Rebuccis."

"It sounds glorious!" Chrissy's black-lined eyes shone and the dark-lipsticked, pouty mouth widened into her rare but brilliant smile.

"Brrr, it's like a meat freezer in here," Rodney Blacker mocked Maeve's reticence, shivered with exaggeration, hunching his shoulders up into his neck. "How come those Irish eyes aren't smiling?"

He was rewarded with a tentative smile.

"Tell me about the vineyards. Did you pick grapes when you were a little boy?"

"Not exactly," he laughed. "We've thousands of wetbacks for that. Hey, haven't you ever heard of Rebucci Wines?"

"No, I don't think so. Should I have?"

"Well, it's not exactly French wine, but we're probably the biggest name in wine in the U.S. of A. And after the vines are picked clean, we have the biggest party in all California. All the grapepickers come and half the Valley. Jesus, it must be even more people than that, because if you counted all the Rebuccis, we must be half the Valley all by ourselves."

Chrissy shivered in delight. She could just see it—all the children, the families, eating and drinking wine, dancing and laughing. . . .

"Tell me more!"

He kissed her neck. "I will. Upstairs."

Chrissy smiled again, her eyes meeting his in promise. "Do you have a room here?"

"A room? Baby, I've got a suite."

"Sara, you're driving me crazy. Look what you're doing to me. Do you feel that?" Bud Lasseur pressed his message home.

"Will you cut that out? My heavens!" she drawled. "This is supposed to be a samba!"

"Careful. Don't tear my dress."

"We'll get you a new one. Hundreds of them," Gaetano Rebucci murmured, expertly pulling down the back zipper.

"But it's my debut gown. I'll never have another."

Guy's skillful hands unhooked the strapless bra. As it fell to the floor, his lips reached for the rose-tipped breasts. But Chrissy bent down to retrieve her dress, picked it up tenderly and laid it on a chair. She would save it for her daughter's debut, the beautiful daughter she would have someday.

"C'mere, baby." He lifted her onto the Waldorf's pink silk spread and pulled off her panties. Chrissy closed her eyes. Tonight had been her debut. Maybe tonight it would be different.

My new friend Johnny Grey and I went to the buffet together to help ourselves to black bean soup and cracked crab. Maeve came running up followed by a slightly tipsy Rodney Blacker, precariously balancing a newly filled glass of champagne. "Hey, come back, my wild Irish rose!"

"He won't leave me alone," Maeve whispered to me. "Have *you* seen Chrissy?"

In a romantic semidaze, I shook my head. "Maybe Sara has."

"No, Sara's been looking for her for the last half-hour. She's just vanished into thin air."

She just *had* to feel something this time. She would! She would! Finally, his mouth found her mound of Venus and yes . . . yes, she did . . . oh, yes, she did. Oh, it felt good, good. . . . Her fingers clawed at the black waves of his hair. A little sigh of pleasure passed her lips. It was the first time she had managed to feel *that* again . . . other than the times she had done it to herself.

Her arms went around his neck. "Now tell me more about your family. Tell me about Grandpa and Grandma Rebucci."

He laughed and inserted himself in her again.

"Soon, baby, soon."

And soon he asked, "How would you like to meet them yourself?"

"Really? You mean the whole family?"

We received the telegram the next day. Sara ripped it open.

"Quick, Sara. What does it say?"

"Oh, my Lord! She's gone and done it. She's eloped with that gigolo!"

"You mean she's married? Our Chrissy's married?" I asked incredulously.

"I'm afraid so. Damn her!"

221

"But she hardly knows him," Maeve worried. "Why do you think she did it?"

"I don't know," Sara said. "But I'm madder than hell at her! She's ruined all my plans!"

"What plans?" I asked.

"Chrissy, Maeve, and I were going to be the Triplet Debutantes of 1946 since, of course, we couldn't count on you, Marlena," Sara said accusingly. *"You're* so busy ruining your eyes at Radcliffe." She threw herself down on the couch.

I laughed. "And you *still* can't count on me. I *am* returning to Radcliffe in two weeks as soon as Christmas vacation is over. You two will have to be the *Twin* Debutantes of the Year. And right now I'd better be off. I'm going to the hotel to see Mother and Daddy before they go back to Charleston."

"Well, hold your horses, will you? I'm going with you. I want to see Mama too. I'm happy at least that *she* made it up here for the debut, even if Chrissy just *barely* made it before she eloped. . . . But before we go we have to have some champagne."

"But it's only eleven o'clock," Maeve protested.

"So what? We have to toast our married friend, Chrissy Marlowe Rebucci." Then Sara giggled.

"What's the joke?" I asked.

"Imagine what Aunt Gwen is going to say when she hears that name! I think I'll call her up and give her the good news, just in case she hasn't heard."

THE YEAR OF THE DEBUTANTE 1946

1.

Maeve and Sara waited for word from Chrissy. In four weeks there had not been a call or a note. Sara guessed that the couple was in California, but she didn't know exactly where. She made a call to the Rebucci Wineries hoping to gather some information, some clue, but she found out nothing.

"Do you think there's something wrong? Do you think Chrissy got married and forgot all about us?"

"Oh, Sara, Chrissy wouldn't do that. They must still be on their honeymoon."

"Yes, well, I have a feeling this honeymoon is going to be a short-lived one."

"Why do you say that, Sara?"

"Just a hunch."

But Chrissy's letter, when it finally arrived, refuted Sara's intuition.

Dear Maeve and Sara,

Sorry I have not been in touch sooner, but everything's been so exciting, so divine, I just haven't had the time. Guy's family has been so wonderful to me—it's just as if I were one of their daughters. Mama Rebucci is one of those lovely old-fashioned ladies who believes that a woman's place is in the kitchen taking care of the babies and seeing that everybody's happy and well-fed. Well-fed! I must have gained ten pounds already. There are servants, of course, but Mama Rebucci supervises everything and makes the spaghetti sauce herself. She says no self-respecting Italian woman would let anyone else make the sauce! And she's teaching me! By the time you two come to visit, I will have all the techniques down pat and will treat you to a meal that I've prepared myself . . . the sauce, the antipasto, everything.

Papa Rebucci calls me Little Christina. He's kind of stern and gruff but I think he's fond of me. I think the whole family, all of Guy's brothers and sisters, like me. And everybody wants to know when I'm going to have a baby. Grandmother Rebucci says, "Soon you'll have the bambino, Christina," almost as if she were foretelling the future. And I would love to have a baby immediately, if only not to disappoint Grandmother Rebucci. But Guy says that there are enough little Rebuccis running around already and that we should wait at least until we have our own house. Aldo, Guy's older brother, and his wife Josephine have four children but they still live here. All the others have houses of their own on the property. It's a huge estate—big enough for twenty houses. Aldo talks about building his own home, but Guy says that Aldo's a real mama's boy and will never leave home. Guy is not like that at all. He's anxious for us to have our own place but I think he's waiting for Papa Rebucci's permission, or something like that. And Papa Rebucci's waiting for Grandfather Rebucci's permission. That's the way it is here. And I love it. Between you and me, I don't care if we never move out. I could live here forever.

I think the Napa Valley with all the vineyards is the most gorgeous place I have ever seen. And our house is a Spanish hacienda and compared to Grandmother Marlowe's place in Newport, it is almost plain, but ever so much more warm and beautiful.

I can't wait until you two come out here and see what real living is like. My dream is to stay here and have ten babies and have you two and Marlena living right here near me.

I love you,
Little Christina

Maeve had tears in her eyes. "Doesn't she sound divinely happy?"

"Do you think so?" Sara mused. "I think it's mighty funny that she raved about Mama Rebucci and about cooking spaghetti sauce and about California and about having babies, and she hardly said a word about Guy except that he wants to move out of the big house and needs Papa's permission. It's probably more like he's waiting for Papa to dole out the money."

"Oh, Sara, you always look at the darkest side of things."

"That's not true. I'm the one who always thinks we're going to have a wonderful time and meet somebody wonderful. You, on the other hand, never want to go out. You're always convinced you'll have a terrible time and that you'll never meet anybody wonderful at all."

"But it's true, isn't it?"

"But that's because you don't let yourself have a good time. While everybody's doing the conga at El Morocco, you *sit*."

Suddenly, Maeve grew frightened. "Sara, do you think it's going to be like this always? What's going to happen to us? Will we spend the rest of our lives sitting at El Morocco and the Copa?"

"Of course not. We go there *now* and try to have a good time. *Later* we'll do something else."

Maeve wrote:

My dearest Chrissy,

You sign yourself Little Christina and I think that's lovely, but I can't call you anything but Chrissy. That's what I called you that first day at Chalmer's when you became my dearest friend and that's how I'll always think of you.

California and everything and everybody there sound wonderful and if I could, I would jump on the first plane possible and come out and see it and you. Only Sara will not allow it. I am some kind of debutante-love-slave and Sara promises me my freedom only if and when we are officially known as *the* Debs of '46. In the meantime, Sara sees how many balloons she can catch at the Stork, and when she finds a $100 bill inside she's so delighted one would think she was a pauper.

Besides going to lunch and parties, we shop! Oh, how we shop! Mostly party dresses to be sure. But also afternoon dresses and tea dresses and suits to go to luncheon in. And hats. Sara is very big on hats now. And, of course, shoes and bags. And scarfs and jewelry. And, as usual, with our Sara, if I don't go along with her, I never hear the end of it.

Personally, I think this whole debutante scene is overrated, and every day I tell myself I should go back to Boston and do what Aunt Maggie intended me to do, but I put it off from day to day. Besides, Sara would kill me. Marlena is very much involved with college and *very much* involved with that Johnny Grey who's at Harvard Med. I think Marlena's in love.

I'm very happy for you, Chrissy darling. And we will come out to see you very soon. Sara sends her love and says she will not write. But she will phone.

Love, Your Maeve.

Dear Sara and Maeve,

We are moving to Los Angeles! It is very involved, but Guy and his father had sort of a falling out and then sort of an agreement. Papa Rebucci wanted Guy to become involved in the business but Guy simply could not see himself "stomping the grapes," as he puts it. So, finally, it was decided that he would go into the sales end of the business, for which, I suppose, he is better suited. Then Guy thought he should be manager of sales, but Papa Rebucci said he could not start at the top, and besides, Uncle Vito's son, Vic, has been in the business for years, and he wants to be the top man in sales, so . . . So Guy said he would go to L.A. and be the regional sales manager there, which really broke Mama Rebucci's heart because she wanted us to stay with her in the big house. And to tell you the truth, I am not thrilled to leave here, but Guy is. I think he would really rather be the regional sales manager in L.A. than top man and stay here. But I suppose Hollywood will be great fun. I hope you two will get off your fannies and come out here to visit me.

Lovingly, Chrissy.

"I see she's not calling herself Little Christina anymore," Sara observed.

"I think she's really heartbroken, don't you, about leaving that big family."

"Well, disappointed, to say the very least. I guess the honeymoon *is* over."

"I hope not. Poor Chrissy."

"We've a very nice house even if it is only rented. It's in what they call the Hollywood Hills," Chrissy told Sara over the phone. "I wish you and Maeve would get the hell out here and visit me. We've plenty of room. Four bedrooms and five baths."

"How come you didn't buy a house of your own?"

"Because, believe it or not, Guy's only making two hundred dollars a week. And that's it."

"But I don't understand. I thought the Rebuccis were the wine kings of America. Aren't they loaded?"

"Papa Rebucci is. And Grandpa Rebucci. But Guy doesn't have a dime of his own and I guess he won't until he settles down and really becomes involved in the business. To tell you the truth, Sara, and don't breathe a word to anybody, we're living on my money."

"Really, Chrissy! Do you think that's wise?"

"I don't think I have a choice. I mean, one night at the Trocadero and Guy's check is blown. And night after night . . . the Coconut Grove . . . Mocambo . . . lunch for twelve at the Derby."

"Well, if Guy is only making two hundred dollars per, why is he buying lunch for twelve?"

"Business. He has to take people out so they'll buy his wine."

"I really don't want to be a troublemaker, Chrissy, but that's just crazy. If Guy takes people out for lunch, or for the evening, that's a business expense and Rebucci Wineries are supposed to pick up the tab."

Chrissy laughed hollowly. "Not Papa Rebucci. He says Guy is a spendthrift and no one's getting drunk on French champagne on his

226

California wine money. Besides, he's mad at Guy. He says Guy should do less drinking and more selling."

Sara laughed. "He's got a point."

"Never mind that. When are you two coming out? I'll give a party for you and I'll invite Bogey and Betty. We're pretty good friends with them. Bogey and Guy had a drinking contest the other night at a place at the beach. Bogey got loaded really fast and hit somebody and then Guy had to defend him from this beach bum and they called the cops. It was lots of fun."

So why aren't you laughing more, Sara wondered.

"That does sound like fun. More fun than the rhumba breakfast at the Stork every Sunday. People bring their kids and dance while the kids eat their eggs. Can you imagine? That's what *we're* doing for kicks these days."

"So why do you do it, Sara?"

"Why does anybody do anything, Chrissy?" *Why are you paying that gigolo's bills?*

After they hung up, Sara repeated the conversation to Maeve. "What did I say when I first laid eyes on Mr. Rebucci?"

"You called him a gigolo. But really, how was anyone really to know? How could Chrissy have known?"

"You have to develop an instinct. You have to *know* before you marry a man that he will adore you, treasure you, and take care of you. And never marry anyone that won't."

"But can you be sure, Sara? Can you ever be sure?"

Sara thought about her mother. Mama had been sure. Sara shrugged. "You sure as hell should give it a try."

In March, they had their photographs taken by Jerome Zerbe, the Society photographer, and when Sara didn't see their pictures turn up anywhere in the tabloids, she fired Bill Doll as their press agent and hired Count Rasponi. "He's more Society-oriented," she assured Maeve.

Maeve worried about Bill Doll's feelings.

"In this game, Maeve, you have to be ruthless. We just weren't getting enough coverage. Besides being in Cholly's column a lot, where have we been? In Leonard Lyons' only once in the past month, in Kilgallen's twice, and in Winchell's not at all."

"Somebody told me it's terribly hard to get into Winchell's because he demands five gossipy items about other people before he gives you one mention."

"Well, that's the publicist's problem, not ours."

Maeve would have preferred to be in *no* columns. "All in all, Sara, wouldn't you say we've had pretty good exposure?"

"Not enough. It's never enough." She wanted to make sure that her father saw her name every time he picked up a paper. Let him know that she had done it all by herself.

Maeve held the newspaper behind her back. Sara, painting her fingernails, wanted to know what she was grinning about, like some rufous green-eyed Cheshire cat.

"You've gotten your wish. Here—" She handed Sara the paper folded to the Knickerbocker column.

There were their pictures, hers and Maeve's. The caption read: "Twin Debs of the Year . . ." Sara sighed.

"It's really peculiar that Igor Cassini had the idea of *twin* debutantes just like you did. I mean, every year there's only been *one*. It's almost like a little *birdy* had been whispering in his ear. Don't you think it's peculiar, Sara?"

"Yes, indeedy. Now, *Vogue* and *Harper*'s will really be after us to pose for them. But I'm sure you'll be more in demand than I will."

"Me? Why?"

"You're tall and red-haired, just like that new model we saw in *Life*. Only tons more beautiful."

"Oh, fiddlesticks, I'm not half as beautiful as she is. I'm not beautiful at all."

"Oh, for God's sake, Maeve, I *hate* when you're so modest. If you'd ever let any guy closer than ten feet, you'd find out how beautiful you are. You'd probably be the most sensationally popular woman of all time, like a . . . Lillie Langtry or . . . a . . . Madame Pompadour."

"What nonsense you talk, Sara!"

Sara looked at her speculatively. "I think I've discovered your secret."

Maeve's hand went to her throat and her heart lurched. "What secret?"

"It's not that you don't *like* men; you're afraid of them. Scared to death of them."

"You're talking rot again."

"You *act* as if you're frigid. But I just don't believe it. Underneath, I think, you're sizzling with passion."

Maeve laughed. "You speak in such excesses, Sara. What about you? You act like you're a steaming cauldron, but you haven't had any more bottom-line experience than I have. Maybe it's you who's afraid of men, underneath that sexpot exterior."

"Me? Afraid of men? I'll chew them up and spit them out for breakfast. I'm just waiting for the right man, for the big time, that's all. But I do think that you and I *will* have to speed up our action. I suspect that even my retiring little cousin is sleeping with her beau."

"Marlena?" Maeve was incredulous. "I don't think Marlena would— Not without being married!"

"I'll bet she's spreading it for old Johnny. He won't graduate for years, so they can't get married. And she's so crazy about him. All he'd have to say is, 'How do I know you love me if you don't prove it?' to have Marlena knocking herself out proving it."

Maeve sighed.

"Well, don't be upset. You know what they say—'Use it or lose it.' "

"I don't think that that's scientifically correct," Maeve giggled.

"I hope not, sugar."

Sara threw the newspaper in the wastebasket.

"Sara! What are you doing? After all your campaigning to be Deb of the Year, aren't you even going to save the clipping?"

"Maeve, me darling, tomorrow morning *this* is yesterday's news. Cold mashed potatoes. Now that we have been named Debs of the Year for 1946, *the season* is officially over. The new season has begun and there's a new bunch of pretty faces coming up. I think we can now be officially called *post-debs*. And I just hate being post-anything. We'll have to think of something else to do."

"Such as—"

"Oh, we'll think about that in the fall. Let's plan for the summer. It will sneak up on us before we know it and anybody caught dead in New York in the summer should die of shame. We'll go down to Charleston for a while—I have to visit with Mama—and then we'll go up to Newport and then down to Southampton. There's going to be a few good parties there. Then we'll head out for California to see Chrissy. How does that sound? But first, we really should finish up our debutante season with a reunion lunch, even if it's not a full year. You, me, Marlena. I'm sure we can manage to tear her away from her Johnny for a few hours, don't you think?"

Maeve giggled. "I'm not sure about that! They're inseparable. . . ."

"Mmmm . . . I hope he's good enough for Marlena. I hope he doesn't break her heart."

"Oh, Sara, why do you have to always think the worst? Have a little faith."

"Okay. A little. Very little."

"Oh, you!" She gave Sara a little push. "Wait one minute, Sara. Why can't we try and get Chrissy to come in for our reunion lunch? I really can't wait till late August or September to see her!"

"Why not? That's a wonderful idea. We'll have the reunion at the Cub Room and we'll even take a picture with that cracker bastard, Sherman, just for the record. And then I'm going to slap him across the face and never enter that place again, that fucking anti-Semite!"

"Sherman Billingsley?" Maeve was shocked. "How do you know?"

"It's all over town. Common knowledge."

"So why have we kept going there? We should have stopped the minute you found out."

"Don't be ridiculous, Maeve! How could we have been important debs without being seen at the Stork? But now, thank God, we don't have to go there anymore."

2.

Chrissy came in for the reunion, thinner than ever, and wan. Maeve hugged her ecstatically. "I expected to see you fat from all that spaghetti."

Chrissy smiled faintly. "I haven't had a strand in months. Guy doesn't even work for his father anymore. I guess he's the black sheep in his family."

"What does he do now?" Sara wanted to know.

"He plays. I guess you'd call him a playboy. And I'm his little playgirl," she mocked herself.

"But I thought you'd be all bronzed and athletic-looking. The real California girl," Sara chided. "Instead you're especially pale and delicate-looking."

"I was always pale and I was never athletic-looking. Did you expect me to develop muscles?" Then suddenly she burst out, "I just had an abortion . . ." and started to weep.

"Oh, Chrissy, baby." Maeve hugged her.

"But why?" Sara demanded. "Your letters . . . your calls . . . you kept harping on how you were dying for the little bambino."

"Guy . . . it was Guy. . . . He said all his life he had been up to his ass in babies crawling around. He threatened to walk out on me if I had the baby."

"Then why didn't you let him?" Sara asked in a perfectly reasonable way.

Maeve and Chrissy stared at Sara as if she had said something revolutionary. Chrissy sat down as if the weight of Sara's question was too heavy to bear standing up. "What would I have done then? I would have had a baby without a husband."

"So what? If it was a baby you really wanted. You *were* married this time, the baby would have been legitimate. And you didn't have to be alone. You could have always come here, to us, with the baby. You knew that. . . ."

"But Guy—"

"Clearly it was a question of which you wanted more—Guy or the baby," Sara said, trying to get to the heart of the matter.

"But I married Guy to have babies, to be part of a big family."

"So now you have Guy and no baby."

230

"But if I had had the baby and no father for little Guy—that's what I planned on calling him if it were a boy—I . . . we . . . the baby and I still wouldn't have been part of a real family."

"So now you have Guy and no baby," Sara repeated. "Are you and Guy a real family?"

The three women sat in silence for a minute.

"It's really funny. A couple of years ago I had that first abortion and I felt only relief . . . such incredible relief. I never thought about it being a *real* baby. And now . . . I can't stop thinking about it for a minute. I keep seeing it in my mind . . . fat, cute, gurgling . . . and I feel so empty, so empty. . . ."

"Look, Chrissy," Maeve suggested. "Why don't you stay for at least two or three weeks? You need a rest. We're going to Charleston first, and then Newport—"

"Mmm, sounds heavenly," Chrissy sighed. "Guy won't even notice I'm gone. He'll be too busy tangoing up Hollywood and down Vine, which is the only vine he gets to see these days."

"Hey, that's pretty sharp," Sara chortled.

"It is, isn't it?" Chrissy cheered up.

Then Sara asked, "How's the sex?"

"Sara!" Maeve remonstrated.

"Oh, hush up, Maeve. We're all adults now."

"I don't mind talking about it." Chrissy sat up from her slump. She lit a Nat Sherman pink cigarette with a lipstick-red tip. "I made up my mind to elope with Guy when I had a climax that night at the Waldorf. It was the first time that . . . you know. I thought, jeepers, it must be love! And that's the way it was all the time in Northern Cal."

"Love amongst the grapevines," Sara interjected, but Chrissy ignored her.

"But the moment we left, the orgasms stopped. Of course, by then, Guy was acting like I was"—she groped for words—"a one-night stand."

"What do you mean?" Maeve asked anxiously.

"Well, it's hard to explain. It's as if there's no sense of sharing . . . it's sort of empty . . . it's like I'm just a body now and the sex's a sporting event. After we went to Southern California he never even said, 'I love you,' anymore."

There was a large silence in the room and then Sara said, "You really do need a vacation. As soon as Marlena comes down, we'll have our official luncheon and then we'll all head down to Charleston."

I couldn't wait to tell the girls my news.

"See?" I pointed to the tiny gold pin on my lapel. "I'm pinned. I'm engaged to be engaged!"

The girls hugged me and Sara said, "You do seem different. You look positively dreamy! It really must be the rosy bloom of love! But why didn't you get Johnny to come down with you? We *really* have to get to know this guy now that he's engaged to be engaged to our little Marlena."

I *was* a little embarrassed that Johnny hadn't come with me—first to New York and then to Charleston—to really get to know my family. But he had said he had all these dates lined up to play tennis and really couldn't break them. And, after all, he *had* met everybody, hadn't he? Mother and Daddy and the girls. . . . Still and all, I was a tiny bit chagrined. His tennis matches didn't seem that all important. . . .

Then I explained to the girls that after the couple of days in New York and then three, *only* three, days in Charleston, I would have to return to Cambridge.

"Oh, look at her!" Chrissy hooted. "She can't be away from her Johnny for more than a few days. . . ."

Chrissy was teasing of course, but I thought I detected a bit of wistfulness there, a touch of envy.

It ended up that I stayed for a week in Charleston. My mother insisted upon it. And she was a bit miffed that Johnny hadn't come with me. And also that I planned to spend the whole summer in Cambridge. But how could I not with Johnny there? I tried to explain to Mother that medical students couldn't afford to take time off.

Sara, Chrissy, and Maeve spent three weeks there. Sara, of course, wanted to spend the time with Aunt Bettina. She looked pretty good, I thought, and seemed really well. Sara said that when she was more settled herself she would take her mother to live with her—that was her ultimate dream. . . .

As the girls packed to depart Charleston, Maeve and Sara for Newport, Chrissy to go back to Hollywood, Maeve noticed that Chrissy was very depressed. "Why don't you come to Newport for a few days first?"

"Why . . . yes, I think I will," Chrissy answered immediately. "I'd really like to get some riding in. I have nobody to ride with in California."

The three spent three weeks in Newport. When it was time to leave there for Southampton, where Maeve and Sara were slated to attend several coming-out parties, Chrissy decided that it really wouldn't be nice if she didn't at least go to Candy and DeeDee Dineen's party. "After all, we were such good friends at school. They'd be hurt if I didn't show up, don't you think?"

"Absolutely!" Sara agreed. "Don't you think, Maeve?"

Maeve appeared thoughtful. "Yes, I do."

After three weeks in Southampton and after the Dineen sisters' coming-out, Chrissy got up one morning and asked: "Who's for six weeks in Reno?"

"Reno?" Maeve repeated.

"I think that's a really peachy idea," Sara said. "I've heard of the most divine dude ranch there with the handsomest cowhands around."

"Are you sure, Chrissy? Are you truly sure?" Maeve frowned. "And have you discussed this with Guy? Surely he must have something to say—"

In way of answer, Chrissy shrugged.

———

The women left the courthouse, all three dressed in full-skirted white sundresses with white ballerina slippers. They had spent the last six weeks in plaid shirts and dungarees, but this was a special day.

"Now you're supposed to throw your ring away," Sara said. "Do you have it on you?"

Chrissy rummaged in her bag and then they found an almost dried-up creek and leaned over the crumbling wooden railing guarding the shabby body of water.

"I guess this will do as well as anything else," Sara said.

"You don't *have* to, Chrissy, if you'd rather save it," Maeve whispered.

But Chrissy hesitated only a second, and then they all watched the gold circle disappear beneath the dirty water.

"Now let's have a drink."

"Golly, let's," Chrissy said, still staring into the water. "Let's get stinko."

They spent the afternoon in the lounge at Harold's Club. Chrissy had several drinks, Sara two or three, and Maeve nursed one the entire time. They discussed Maeve's near teetotalism and Maeve finally admitted that she didn't drink because her father did—a lot. It had been a long time since anyone had even mentioned Maeve's father.

A trio played country music and a cowboy with an aged leathery face came loping over. It was clear that he had had one too many, and when he smiled, he showed rotted teeth. "One of you gals want to take a turn around the room?" Chrissy leaped to her feet and Sara and Maeve watched in amazement as the cowhand whirled Chrissy around and then bent her over in a back-breaking dip and she stumbled.

"Oh, Lordy," Sara breathed as Maeve gasped.

They came back to the table and Chrissy introduced Luke who

grabbed a chair, sat, and proceeded to whisper dirty nothings into her small, flat ear.

"Do you smell something nauseating?" Sara asked Maeve, wrinkling her nose in distaste. She hoped Luke would take offense and his leave.

When this didn't happen, Maeve got to her feet. "We'd better go back and pack our things, Chrissy. We're leaving first thing in the morning."

Sara got up too, but Chrissy stayed in her chair giggling at something smutty Luke had just said. He glanced up at Sara and Maeve, then said to Chrissy, "Why don't you and me take off, honey, just the two of us, and leave your little old gal friends to fend for themselves?"

"Yes. I think that's a super idea." She got up and linked arms with the wizened Luke.

Maeve looked at Chrissy, so young and clean-looking in her white dress and ballet slippers, and she couldn't bear for her to go off with the horrid old man.

"No!" she cried and grabbed at Chrissy's arm.

"Oh, for heaven's sake, Maeve!" Chrissy snapped. "I'm sick to death of your goody-goody act!" She pulled her arm away and allowed Luke to walk her out, his arm around her waist.

Sara and Maeve sat back down and Sara ordered another round as Maeve quietly sobbed.

"Oh, Maeve, don't. She didn't mean anything, she was smashed!"

"I don't care what she said to me. It was him! He was so revolting! How could she?"

Sara shook her head. "I guess he's what she needs this afternoon. A kind of a cleansing agent."

"Cleansing agent? But he's filthy!"

Chrissy took off her dress and her silk panties and laid them on a chair. Luke looked at her nude body and shook his head. "You got the smallest titties I've seen in a month of Sundays."

He straddled her and, sitting, rode her hard, holding on to the small breasts as if they were reins. He battered, thrust, and rammed until he came, his sweat dripping onto her body.

"Would you mind dismounting now, cowboy?"

He did so and laughed. "You're nothing but a bag of skin and bones like an old nag I used to own."

Chrissy picked up her panties, wiped herself with them then threw them onto the dirty sheet. "You're not such a hot fuck yourself, old man," she said dispassionately as she slipped on her dress and slippers.

3.

"Oh, your father has a new book out, Maeve!" Chrissy said, holding out the book-review section from the Sunday *Tribune*. "His review is on the front page."

"Yes, I know. I read it."

"It's a fantastic review . . . I think. I don't exactly understand everything the reviewer is talking about. One minute he calls the book the work of a god and the next he refers to the 'deviations of a crazed reverie.' . . . Did you understand what he's talking about?"

"Not completely. But I don't think my father would find it exactly thrilling. I don't think he would be happy unless the reviewer said the novel was worthy of the Nobel Prize."

Maeve knew how obsessed her father had been with the Nobel—even when she was a little girl. Would *Fragments of the Great Shattered Whole* contribute to his winning the prize next year? Well, she had no intention of reading the book.

Still, it was a way of hearing from him. And she was grateful for that. The uncertainty of his silence had been nerve-wracking. Was he playing a cat-and-mouse game? Had he sworn vengeance upon her? She wasn't sure anymore. All she knew was that she felt his presence everywhere throughout the silence. And, lately, she had had the sensation of being followed. Was she too going mad?

4.

It was November—almost a year since their debut—and Sara was bored with nightclubs and parties and the types of men she met. It was all so repetitious. But it was mostly for Chrissy that she was concerned. Her affairs were becoming more reckless—she had even taken up with a mobster of sorts for a month or so. And Maeve seemed at such loose ends.

"It's really high time we did something with ourselves," she proclaimed. "It's almost the new year and we're going to be *nineteen!* Why don't we start the year off by doing something different? I intend to enroll at the Dramatic Workshop at the New School in January. I've always loved the theater. It will be such fun! Stella Adler teaches there and she's a disciple of Konstantin Stanislavski who founded the Moscow Art Theater. It's a whole new concept in acting. Don't you think that sounds exciting?"

Maeve smiled. How like Sara to embrace something new so completely.

"And I want you to come to the New School, too, Maeve. They've got wonderful writing courses. I'm sure you could be a great writer. It must be in the blood!"

"No, Sara," Maeve said firmly. "I am definitely *not* interested in writing. I've been thinking about what to do myself, and I've made up my mind to enter nursing. There *are* classes starting in January, I think."

Sara blanched. "Nursing? Scrub floors and empty bedpans?"

"Yes, that too," Maeve told her. "But there's more to nursing than that. Nursing is caring for people, helping."

"Heavens to Betsy, nurse away if you must. It must be the Abbott Protestant ethic buried deep in your Catholic soul. Now we come to you, Chrissy. Do you think you'd like to study music or art?"

Chrissy laughed. "Must it be either/or?"

"Those are your two talents and one should utilize whatever talents one possesses."

"All right. I'll choose art."

"Very good. You can attend the Art Students League on West Fifty-seventh. That's definitely the best place for you. I've been talking to people about it. I know some of the café regulars who go there. It's unstructured and they have some very fine teachers. And besides, it's so close to the shops. You can always dash into Bendel's for a bit of shopping."

Chrissy suppressed a smile. "Do register me."

"Which hospital do you think I should enroll at?" Maeve asked with a straight face.

"At this moment, I haven't the slightest. Who would know about hospitals, really? But I'll look into it. Flower Fifth, maybe? Or Payne-Whitney?"

Maeve had been only teasing and Sara had responded off the top of her head, giving the names of hospitals that might be considered fashionable, but inadvertently she gave Maeve an answer. Payne-Whitney? The emotionally disturbed? Mental health was the very field to which Maeve was inclined.

"Well, then, it's all settled, isn't it? I'll be an actress, Maeve will be a nurse—if she must—and Chrissy will be an artist. Heavens! We're really going to start the new year off with a bang!"

SEASON IN NEW YORK 1947

1.

Maeve met Dr. Gregory Carey on a professional level, in a manner of speaking. She had finished dispensing bedpans to those patients on the corridor, working from the north end to the south. Then, pushing the aluminum cart, she retrieved them again. Coming out of Room 311, she slipped on something wet on the tiled hall floor. She placed the pan on the cart, gave it a shove down to the next room and went to wipe up the floor. When she heard the clash and clatter of metal, she looked up. She had just hit a doctor with her cart!

Dr. Carey was most gracious about being bumped and splashed. He was a large man with a beautiful mane of silver white hair, and his gray eyes laughed at her discomfiture but were warm all the same.

"Doctor, I don't know what to say. . . . Oh, dear, can I wipe you off? I . . . please forgive me."

"All I have to do is take off this white coat and I'll be as good as new . . . that is, if I shed about fifty years at the same time."

What a charming man, Maeve thought, as he walked away smiling. And that voice . . . more like a Shakespearean actor than a doctor.

"He's one of the best psychiatrists in the city," Jilly Dayton, one of the older nurses, told her. "When you hit 'em, you really hit 'em!"

Chrissy was ecstatic. Art school was ever much more fun than going to lunch, shopping, and partying. Not that they still didn't go out in the evenings, but now it was the days that were more important, filled with excitement. And she was finding out that her artistic abilities were more than a "knack." She was really good. She took anatomy in the morning with George Bridgman and painting in the afternoons with Robert Brackman. It was glorious! She was so grateful to Sara. Imagine, little Orphan Annie Chrissy Marlowe studying with the great Brackman!

And she absolutely adored the ambiance. Each day when she came home she had a new story to tell the girls. "Suzy is this model that works at the League, the most incredible wreck. Well, in between sittings, she walks around nude underneath a flowered kimono that barely covers her bulk. Today, she was sitting on the steps with us, having a cig, with her legs spread apart, and the wind blew her kimono up. Well, there was the most incredible traffic jam on Fifty-seventh Street and one truck driver, catching Suzy with her v.j. exposed to the winds, went berserk and nearly drove right up on the sidewalk. It was hilarious!"

Sara realized at once that she had no real urge to act professionally. But it was a romp mixing with theater people after the dreary sameness of the café society crowd. Not that there weren't other debs doing exactly what she was. Especially the dibs and dabs of modeling. And enrolled at dramatic schools, making the rounds of all the auditions, not really wanting major roles, but just bits of parts, enough to make them part of the theater world so they could drop names, sit at Sardi's or Toots', exchanging gossip, enjoying the exotic life.

Soon after Sara started the Workshop, she met a young man who just dropped in on class, a former student who had already had real parts. She knew that he was special the second he walked into the room, even though he was dressed rather slovenly in a leather jacket, a soiled T-shirt, and rumpled chino pants. First, because Stella made such a fuss over him, calling him a "little puppy thing," and then because everyone else just stared and stared—even in his sloppy garb his was a commanding presence. And last, and certainly not least, he was the handsomest young man she had ever seen. They went out for a drink together and then he rushed off somewhere to see a friend about a friend and stuck her with the check.

Sara went home annoyed but beguiled. She couldn't wait to tell Maeve and Chrissy about her new friend.

"His name is Marlon and he was wearing one red sock and one green and he's absolutely the most gorgeous thing I've ever laid my little ol' eyes on."

"And you didn't cohabitate?" Chrissy asked primly.

"Of course not," Sara said demurely. "You know I don't indulge in non-kosher cocks."

I heard all the New York stories by way of the telephone and hurriedly scribbled notes, but I was not at all envious. I had Johnny! And of course I was well into my second year at Radcliffe, though I still didn't have any idea what I was going to do with my Bachelor's degree.

I was an English major as who wasn't at Radcliffe. Actually, I was more concerned as to my status with Johnny. I was still engaged to be engaged and what I really wanted was an engagement ring on my third finger, left hand.

The feeling of being followed persisted. Unnerved, Maeve jumped whenever anyone came up behind her. She dropped things, couldn't concentrate on her work at the hospital. Spotting Dr. Carey in the cafeteria one day having a cup of coffee with several colleagues, she wondered about asking him for some kind of psychiatric help. She waved to him, not daring to go up to him—he nodded and smiled at her with his lips and his eyes.

Dare she consult him? Would it be proper? Why not? He was in private practice and she would be a paying patient. She went to the public telephone and looked up his office number. She would call for an appointment this very minute before she lost her nerve.

The doctor was actually glad to see her, she could tell. He even rose from his chair, came out from behind his desk, took her hands, and ushered her to her seat. She was dressed up for this visit. Was she too formal in her forest green velvet suit and the white ruffled blouse? Would he think it strange? Foolish? What?

"Is there anything in particular you're disturbed about, Maeve?" his voice soothed.

"Yes . . . I think . . . I feel somebody is following me. But when I turn around, there's . . . nobody there."

"But then you're still not convinced?"

"No . . . yes . . . I don't know."

"Do you have anyone in mind you think may be following you?"

"Yes. I mean no . . . I don't know. Maybe my father," she whispered.

"Ah. . . . Suppose you tell me something about your father."

But she could say no more, the words froze in her throat.

She told him instead about Aunt Maggie, how she had loved her, that she had died.

When the session was over, Dr. Carey proposed that she see him twice a week for the time being. "But you're not to worry. I'll tell my secretary that you're to be extended professional courtesy."

"No. . . . I mean I can pay whatever it is, Doctor."

He smiled. "A student nurse?"

"I . . . I can pay. I'm . . . independently wealthy. Isn't that how you say it?" She laughed to cover her embarrassment at talking about money.

"I see." He was making the connection—the name, the money, the rumors he had heard at the hospital. "But you shall still receive the professional courtesy." He chuckled. "You should see all the wealthy doctors' families I treat who *insist* on professional courtesy."

They laughed together—a very nice sensation. Maeve left, thinking how good it was that she would return in three days.

Much to Sara's dismay, Chrissy discovered Greenwich Village and the Bohemian life. It was so tacky!

"What's so great about the Village?" Sara demanded. "It's been there all your life. When I went to day school, the kids used to go down there to see the fags. Or on somebody's birthday the parents would take a bunch of us to the Village Barn and order us Shirley Temples. It's a place you go occasionally for a laugh; you don't practically *live* there."

"A lot of the kids do live there," Chrissy said, shaking her gypsy earrings. "It's where a lot of today's art is happening. And the music! The parties!" She whirled about in her long, gypsy skirt. "Compared to the parties in the Village, the ones we go to are tepid tea."

Sara groaned. Actually, she had to concede that the bright red scooped-neck blouse with its billowing sleeves was complimentary to Chrissy's coloring, the gypsy accents not unattractive. But when Chrissy wore her artist's beret and a beat-up old Army jacket, Sara couldn't bear to look at her.

"If you must—go! But please, Chrissy, be careful. Don't get in any trouble."

Chrissy drew herself up, bestowed upon Sara her haughtiest glare. "I beg your pardon, Sara Gold?"

"Is it true they smoke marijuana in the Village?" Maeve asked. "I hope *you* don't."

"Oh, God! Oh, fiddle-dee-dee! You two are *too* much!"

Very early on, Marlon made a half-hearted attempt to get Sara into bed. She tried to explain that she had to be sure first, and she wasn't.

He waved a desultory hand and told her that it was okay—that she really wasn't his type. And then he smiled at her in a very ingenuous way and asked her if she would like to learn to play the bongos.

Maeve had been going to Gregory Carey for several months, and she thought that she might be a tiny bit in love with him. She sensed too that he felt something for her as well. Or was it merely compassion?

240

Did he look upon her as a child? She knew that he was losing the objectivity psychiatrists had to maintain, as well as his patience.

"You've talked about your aunt and you've talked about your friends. You've even talked about the pet raccoon that belongs to Sara's friend, Marlon. You'll talk about anything but you refuse to talk about your father. We are not going to make any progress until you do. Do you understand that, Maeve?"

She understood but she was helpless. She couldn't; she just couldn't.

Finally, Dr. Carey suggested that they discontinue their sessions for a while. It was nearly summer. Perhaps after the summer she would be ready, more willing to open up to him.

Maeve was disconsolate; he *couldn't* dismiss her. "I need you!" she pleaded.

"But I'm not helping you." He turned his back on her. "This is very painful for me, too, Maeve," he almost groaned. *"That's* what is wrong. I'm losing my professional detachment. We both need some time."

2.

It was hot that summer in New York, and sticky, but Chrissy stuck to her classes at the League and her nights in the Village. Maeve buried herself in her work at the hospital, putting in more hours than were on her schedule. Unmourned by Sara, Marlon had departed for Province-town to try and talk Tennessee Williams into giving him a part in his new play. "He has a mother fixation anyway," Sara dismissed Marlon blithely.

And then Sara found Willy Ross, or maybe it was the other way around. Big and clumsy, homey and homely, Willy's thespian talents were comedic, and he had had several roles in major productions, but not leading roles. "He'll never be a matinee idol," Sara giggled, "that's for sure."

Chrissy wondered just what it was Sara saw in Willy. She herself saw only the comic face and the dry, wry wit. Maeve detected the big, sweet heart reposing in the ungainly body and the kindness to small creatures, children, animals, and young women alike. As for Sara, she knew that he was Jewish and gentle, funny and loving, and didn't pressure her into any commitment, physical or verbal. "And he adores me."

"But do you adore him?" Chrissy asked.

"Is it more important to adore or be adored, after all?" Sara countered.

"Shouldn't it be a little bit of each?" Maeve really wanted to know.

They all came down to Charleston to attend my engagement party, Willy included. He, of course, especially wanted to meet Bettina. Mother was pleased with my match, Daddy was very proud, and I wore a mauve strapless gown and, for once, felt very, very beautiful—as pretty as a bride.

Johnny looked *so* handsome and I ran back and forth showing everybody my diamond engagement ring. I loved it even though it was not exactly large. I heard Sara tell Maeve it *was* on the small size but Maeve reproved her. "As if that matters—it's the size of their *love* that counts."

Then Sara asked how much Maeve knew about love and Maeve asked the same thing of Sara. Chrissy, having already wed and lost, seemed to take a jaundiced view of the whole thing. But I gathered that Sara was not completely happy with my choice while Chrissy sort of sat on the fence. As for Maeve—I think she just believed in *love*.

I saw Aunt Bettina, who seemed well if a bit ethereal, watching Sara with Willy and heard her tell Sara, "He really loves you and he has a gentle soul."

Sara kissed her mother. "I know, Mama. I know that. But I'm not sure. How can I be sure?"

Bettina shook her head helplessly. Apparently, she thought she was not the one to say, under the circumstances. She, I guessed, had once been so sure herself.

But *I* was sure. Surer than I'd ever been of anything. And for once I didn't care what Sara thought, or anyone else, for that matter.

We all went up to Newport for Jackie Bouvier's debut at the Clambake Club. The guests danced to the strains of the Meyer Davis orchestra in a beautifully decorated, flower-filled room. Jackie wore bouffant tulle, and her younger sister, Lee, made her appearance in a pink satin strapless gown with long black gloves and stole the show.

"No matter what you do, there's always somebody who's gonna upstage you," Willy growled, and we all laughed.

"If she were my baby sister, I'd wring her sassy little neck," Sara said. I knew that Sara wished that she herself had a little sassy baby sister.

A couple of weeks later we met at the Colony for a second annual reunion lunch, even though Chrissy, Sara, and Maeve lived together and saw each other every day and I had seen them all every two or three weeks that summer.

"I'm sure Cholly Knickerbocker will proclaim Jackie Bouvier Deb of the Year for 1947, and you know what that means," Sara lamented as we sipped our champagne. "It means *we're* old hat, we're passé. . . ."

3.

It was fall, and Maeve gathered her courage and called Gregory Carey.

"Maeve! I've been thinking about you!"

"Dr. Carey, I've been thinking too. About us. Can't we be friends? Not patient and doctor. Just Maeve O'Connor and Gregory Carey, friends?"

She heard his low chuckle. "I thought you'd never ask."

Almost immediately, they were spending all their free time together. Walks in Central Park on Sunday afternoons, plays, concerts, the museums, dinners in little French restaurants. And Maeve's fears started to evaporate. She no longer thought about being followed, she went days without feelings of anxiety, a week without thinking about her father even once.

"Well, have the Marines landed?" Sara asked Maeve one night when she returned home at two in the morning.

For a moment Maeve tried to figure out what Sara was talking about, then, realizing, she blushed. "Of course not!"

"What do you mean, 'of course not'? A man of fifty spends all his time romancing a gorgeous young redhead. It's not incomprehensible that he would want to go to bed with her. Do you think he's queer?"

"Honestly, Sara, you make me ill. Can't two people have a relationship based on companionship and friendship without sex?"

"Not if they're man and woman."

"What about you and Willy?"

"Willy's waiting, that's all. It's not that he doesn't want to—he's just not the type to press. But the sex is *there!* And don't you fool yourself about Greg Carey. Maybe *you* don't feel the sex thing, but if he's normal, *he* does. Maybe he's waiting for you to start seeing him as a lover, not a surrogate daddy."

"How do you know how I see him, Sara?" Maeve asked, her voice so deathly quiet Sara almost didn't hear her, so deathly quiet Sara realized it was a very important question.

"I don't know, for sure. Maybe we have the same fixation, you and I, Maeve. But *I* make sure to stay away from older men."

Maeve went to bed. She thought about what Sara had said. Did Greg want her in that way? What kind of a fool was she? Of course he did. She had been an ostrich, hiding her head in the sand. Sara was clever. And Sara was more honest with herself than she was. Sara knew what both of them, she and Maeve, were all about.

She had felt so secure with Greg. A fool's paradise. Now she was no longer secure. What now, then? Would they be lovers? When? The more she thought about it, the more she realized that this was what she wanted, too. She needed him. She was ready. Everybody needed love, didn't they?

When she called Greg the next day, there was an urgency in her voice but neither of them said anything other than to make plans to meet for dinner at the La Belle Fleur, a favorite restaurant, at seven. Still, somehow she knew that he knew what she was thinking about.

Maeve sat staring at the phone for a half hour after she had spoken with Greg. She couldn't go to the hospital, she wouldn't be able to concentrate. She called in, said she was ill. Maybe she was; she felt as if she had a fever. She put a hand to her cheek. It was burning.

She took hours to dress. She wanted to wear something special. But nothing too dressy. Not too seductive, too obvious. A short dress? A long dress? She put on, then discarded, a long, black chiffon. Too sexy. A midcalf bright blue velveteen? No. It made her look like a co-ed. A long evening skirt with a white silk blouse. Did it transform her into a prim schoolteacher? Finally, she settled on a day-length black wool scooped out in front and in back, a dress that followed the lines of her body closely. And perfume. Not too heavy. White Shoulders? Je Reviens? Just a spray, not too much. Not overwhelming. Was she nervous? Or just . . . anticipatory?

He held her hands across the table. Obviously, she had transmitted to him that this was a special night. He was smiling at her in a different way. But the smile was not reassuring.

He ordered champagne.

". . . I thought we might see a movie tonight . . ." she found herself saying, like a fool.

". . . your eyes are especially green tonight, Maeve . . . glittering . . . like green glass. . . ."

"I thought maybe *The Hucksters*. Ava Gardner's in it. I do like her. . . ." Her voice trailed off.

He smiled into her eyes, a knowing smile. "Yes . . . you look different tonight, Maeve. You look like a . . . a woman." He poured more wine into her glass.

"And Clark Gable's playing opposite her. Do you like Gable? They say he's a man's actor as well as a woman's."

"Stop chattering, Maeve. It's all right."

He made her feel like a silly schoolgirl. She could feel herself blush at his words.

The waiter brought the *escargots aux champignons*. She couldn't even bear to look at them, but Greg ate with relish.

"When you called me in September I knew then . . ."

What did he know?

"While you were my patient, it was out of the question. . . ."

Of course. Out of the question.

"I sent you away because it was an impossible situation. But I knew you would be back . . . like this."

He planned it this way. Is that what he's saying?

"I was only waiting for you to get over your childish fixations."

You're not such a good doctor, after all, Dr. Carey. Fixation, yes. Childish, no.

"But I knew this night would come."

Oh, Sara, Sara! You were right again.

She wished Sara was sitting here right now, to tell her what to do.

"And your unhealthy dependence upon your friends . . . Immature . . ."

The wine was going to her head, confusing her. Was he saying she should depend upon him? That he should take the place of her friends?

The waiter brought the tournedos Queen Anne. The aroma of the butter brandy in which the meat was sautéed nauseated her.

"You're not eating," he reproved her. "You have to keep up your strength!" Now his voice was insinuating. She couldn't believe this was her Dr. Carey.

She found no words with which to speak but she didn't have to. He threw down his fork. "Of course you can't eat, darling! You're ready, aren't you? Impatient! Forgive me. I wanted to conceal my own . . . shall we say, zeal?"

She felt weak. *Zeal!*

He called for the check, helped her on with her wrap, pressing his fingers into her shoulders, brushing her neck with his lips. Shivers ran down her back. *Shivers of desire?*

They were in the taxi and he gave the driver her address. She wondered why they weren't going to his apartment. Had she told him Sara and Chrissy would be out?

He took the key from her bag and opened the door. Fervently, she hoped somebody would be home although she knew that they wouldn't be. He guided her up the stairs. Why didn't she speak? Tell him she wasn't sure. But she hadn't the will, the audacity. From the first, she had treated him like some awesome god. Even if she told him she had changed her mind he wouldn't believe her. His kind always believed you meant something different from what you said.

He kissed her at the top of the landing, and she collapsed weakly into his arms. But it was only her knees betraying her, not her passion. Why didn't she simply tell him that she wasn't weak with desire but with fear.

He undressed her lovingly, competently, while she lay on the bed whimpering like a small beast at bay. He undressed himself rapidly, but took the time to drape his clothes carefully over the back of a chair. *Is this, then, passion?*

She saw the gray flesh of him, the slack skin, the white hair covering his chest, the flaccid thighs. She could not help but notice that the only thing hard about him was the very thing she could not bear to look at. She turned her face away. She felt betrayed. *Oh, Dr. Carey, you should know fathers are not supposed to fornicate with their daughters. . . .*

He was standing over her. She had to say something. Voice her objection. Hadn't he been the very person who told her to give voice to that which was disturbing her.

Dr. Carey, I don't think I really want this. I only wanted you to be strong for me, to be the Heavenly Father on Earth for me. Not—my lover! Yes, I loved my father in that way and, yes, maybe I am frightened of sex with anybody else. I just know that I don't want to make love to you. I . . . can't. . . .

She jumped out of the bed, pushed past him, ran for the bathroom, locked the door, retched into the bowl.

I'm not leaving this bathroom until you leave. Oh, I am sorry. I did mislead you. I thought I wanted this, too. But you should have known better, Greg. You're the doctor.

Then she was overcome with shame. How ridiculous she was—hiding in the bathroom like some child, waiting for the big bad wolf to go away all by himself. *I have to face this.*

She wrapped herself in a bathsheet and went back into the bedroom. Greg still didn't understand what was going on; he lay in her bed under the sheet. He smiled at her encouragingly, held out his hand. She took the hand but said, "I'm sorry, Greg. I . . . I was wrong, I don't want . . . this. Forgive me. Just say I'm not ready."

She was grateful that he didn't make a scene, didn't get nasty. He only kissed her hand. "No. Forgive *me*. . . ."

She retired to her dressing room so that he could dress gracefully, with dignity. When he was ready to leave, he knocked on the door. "I'm leaving, Maeve. Don't feel any guilt, please. The responsibility is all mine."

She wondered all the same, after he had gone, with whom the ultimate responsibility lay.

THE WINTRY DAYS OF 1948

1.

It was a bleak wintry day and Chrissy and Sara sat around that Sunday morning reading the papers. "Bonwit's has some new imports. Do you want to go shopping with me tomorrow? You never did get any Diors. I think you'd find the New Look infinitely more flattering than your Village Look," Sara told Chrissy. "Do you think you're through with your Village phase?"

"I'm through," Chrissy said flatly.

Sara looked up from the paper. "What is it, Chris? What's wrong?"

"Remember that silly little ditty we used to chant at school? So-and-so has the—" She clapped her hands three times.

Sara stared at her. "I hope you don't mean what I think you mean."

"I do."

Tears came to Sara's eyes. Chrissy looked like a little girl this morning, no makeup, baby doll pajamas, the ebony hair slicked back into a pony tail. She looked so *clean,* dammit!

"Have you seen a doctor yet?"

Chrissy shook her head.

Sara got her address book and thumbed through it. "Here. . . ." She scribbled down a doctor's name and address. "This is the doctor everybody's going to these days for that."

"How do you come to have his name?"

"You know I have the addresses for everything. As soon as I hear a name people keep using, a skin specialist, a hairdresser, a doctor—I write it down just in case."

"It came in handy this time, didn't it?"

"I'll go with you tomorrow, if you like."

Chrissy nodded. "Please. And, Sara, don't tell Maeve, all right?"

2.

Willy began to press for marriage. "Sweet William," Sara called him, after the flower, but she would not be pressed. She did love Willy, but something *was* missing. "Excitement . . . *la grande passion* . . . *je ne sais quois*. . . ." she told the girls. She even read the Kinsey Report, hoping for an answer. But the report gave only cold statistics, no explanations.

Then, one March day on a modeling assignment, she found the answer. Also posing for the cold-cream ad was another actress-student-model, Grace Kelly, one of the five "Society types" the advertising agency had specified that day. Sara had become friendly with Grace after they kept bumping into each other on their rounds of auditions and modeling jobs. Grace told Sara that she had just come from an audition at the Gramercy Playhouse, that they had been looking for someone to play the role of a prostitute but that, of course, *she* didn't think she herself was the type. Sara agreed. Grace wasn't the type, not with her patrician, cool beauty. Then Grace suggested that perhaps Sara wanted to try out for the role and Sara thought she was only *half* teasing. Grace told her that the playwright was new but the script really seemed good, terribly strong and very emotional.

"I *will* give it a try. I wouldn't mind playing a tart. After all, that is the test of a true artist, *n'est-ce pas?* Being able to do something completely foreign to his true nature. I just don't want anything too major at this point. I don't like to have to learn too many lines. I'm going to trot on down there as soon as we're through here. But, Gracie darling, you've got tons too much rouge on. Here, let me wipe some of it off. We don't want people to get the wrong idea, do we?"

Sara didn't get the part. Still wearing the Chanel suit she had worn for the cold-cream layout, Sara made Jack Blatt, the producer, groan. The director, Carl Canfield, vaguely wondered why an obvious "jeune fille" was trying to do a Brooklyn waterfront whore with a Vassar accent. And Rick Green, the author, wanted to know where this Park Avenue dilettante had come from—didn't they have enough problems? But he sent word to Sara as she was leaving that if she cared to hang around until they were through, he'd buy her a cup of coffee. Personally, he went for Park Avenue blondes. And while Sara never drank coffee— it was dreadful for the complexion—she hung around. She sort of liked Green's dark, brooding good looks.

It was a whirlwind courtship—days hanging around the cold theater, evenings spent in hot bistros. After a week, Rick and Sara decided to marry.

"Aren't you being a little hasty?" Maeve asked.

"Marry in haste, repent in haste," Chrissy said dolefully.

"There's nothing to wait for. I've been waiting all my life. I've found just what I've been looking for. Rick is Jewish, good-looking, ambitious, and brilliant. And exciting! He's going to be one of the brightest stars in the theatrical firmament. I just know it. And he *is* sexy. Don't you think he's sexy?"

"Does he adore you?" Maeve asked, remembering Sara's own admonition.

"Of course!"

Maeve had the distinct impression Rick Green adored only himself.

"We're getting married in two weeks. I'm announcing our engagement in the *Times* this Sunday and we'll have the wedding here in the house two Sundays after that. I'm going to hire one of those wedding consultants to take care of everything, the invitations, the caterer, the works. The color scheme is going to be gold and green—for our names. Isn't that darling? The ceremony part will be private, just you two, Marlena and Johnny, Mama and Aunt Martha and Uncle Howard, Rick's parents, and Jack Blatt, Rick's producer. But there'll be about five hundred for the reception. I've found the sweetest little rabbi . . ."

"Rabbi?" Maeve asked in surprise. "But you've never officially converted. Don't you *have* to? Don't you have to take instruction?"

"When I spoke to Rabbi Hirsh—he's Reform—he never even asked me if I was official. He knew my name was Gold and he simply assumed . . . Rick assumes . . . and I don't see any reason to stir the pot. Rick's parents are sweet old-fashioned Jews and I don't want to start anything. Mama's not about to say anything, and Uncle Howard and Aunt Martha won't dare, and you two won't, so who's to know. I *have* a Jewish name, you know. All I have to do is add an *h* to Sara. Well, for God's sake, Maeve, stop looking at me like that. Don't Catholics have this thing—Baptism of Desire? It's enough if you're planning to become a Catholic, so that in case you die before you're baptized, you're still considered a Catholic. Well, it's the same thing. . . . Call it *Conversion* of Desire, if you like."

Chrissy giggled and Sara giggled back.

"Now, if this leaks out, I'll know who the stoolie is, Maeve O'Connor, so button your lip. I don't want to hear another word about it. Now, are you two going to help me with the plans and the shopping for the trousseau?"

Maurice Gold called Sara after seeing the announcement of her engagement in the paper.

"I'd like to give you away, Sara."

"Oh, Father, you gave me away a long time ago."

There were a few moments of silence.

"Uncle Howard is going to give me away."

"I see. May I attend your wedding then, as a guest?"

"No, Father. I appreciate that you'd like to be there, but you'd only upset Mama and neither of us want that, do we?"

More silence.

"Well, then, may I tender you my very best wishes for your happiness?"

"Certainly. Thank you."

"I hope your Rick Green is the very, very best."

Did she hear a break in her father's voice?

"You know, Sara, I love you. I've always loved you. . . ."

"Not enough, Daddy. Not enough. . . ."

No one did question Sara as to her Jewishness. She signed both the civil license and the religious one without blinking an eye, and only Aunt Martha raised an eyebrow but kept a stony silence. Everything went off smoothly and the Society column editors noted the witty, namesake gold-and-green color scheme.

As Rick Green's play was very much in rehearsal, the couple decided to defer the honeymoon until after the play opened to rave reviews, at which time they would take off for Paris. But Sara had reserved the bridal suite at the Waldorf, feeling very sentimental about the hotel where she had made her bow. And for the special occasion, she bought an eight-hundred-dollar bridal nightgown with matching peignoir. She fully expected the chiffon and lace creation to be ripped from her body with a mad passion.

Rick Green was very much impressed with his wedding, the mansion that was now his too, and the unbelievable guest list. Dorothy Kilgallen and her producer husband, Richard Kollmar, were there, along with Ed and Sylvia Sullivan, and the entire cast from *Streetcar*, all friends of his bride. Puffed up with pride, and the envy of his old friends from Brighton Beach, he drank with everyone. If anyone remonstrated with him he threw off the offending hand with a fury. It was *his* day. He had married an heiress, and a hell of a looker, too. The first of *his* days. The big one would be of course the opening night, and ever since he had started with Sara, Jack had been talking about moving the play up from off-Broadway to the big street itself.

As a result of Rick's rejoicing in his good fortune, he was quite drunk by the time he arrived at the Waldorf. And he was quite ignorant of Sara's plan of operation—the wedding night according to Hoyle.

Sara was still unpacking her overnight case, removing her wedding-night finery, when she noticed that Rick had already peeled off all his clothes and was flexing his shoulders and arms in the mirror. She looked at him and was overcome by his olive-skinned beauty. "Rick, darling . . ." she breathed.

"You ready?" he slurred. "Take off your damn clothes!"

He was impatient, she thought, and shivered in anticipation.

"Just a minute, sweetie. I have to put on my little ol' nightie," and she headed for the dressing room.

"Fuck it! Just take off your clothes."

So be it, she thought, and dropped the nightgown. It was more exciting this way. "You take off my clothes," she said shyly, a first for Sara.

He made a face and tore himself away from the mirror. He fumbled with her suit buttons and gave up. "Take 'em off yourself," and flopped down on the bed flat on his back and stroked himself.

Sara watched him, horrified. What was he doing to himself on his wedding night, for God's sake?

She stripped herself of her clothes. "What are you doing, Rick?" she asked coolly.

He laughed drunkenly. "Getting myself big for m'little bride."

Sara went over to the bed and stood there naked and, she hoped, beautiful, and waited for the inevitable, "Sara, you're so lovely you make my heart stop." But he didn't say it. Instead, he was examining his penis with an intense curiosity as if he had found a disturbing pimple. When he looked up, he said, "Whatcha waiting for? Get on top!"

She was perplexed. What about the foreplay? Didn't he realize she was new at this game? Didn't he realize that she had been saving herself for him?

In a few minutes, he cried, "Jesus Christ! Inexperienced on stage, inexperienced in bed! Just what I didn't need tonight!"

"Maybe we should have had a dress rehearsal," Sara quipped.

She was thinking of shutting down the play after the opening night. But she would look such a fool. She got up and went to take a shower. Maybe they would have another run-through when he sobered up.

Rick Green was considerably disconcerted when he realized that he was expected to share Sara's luxurious home with Chrissy and Maeve.

"Jesus Christ! You'd think two of the richest broads in the country could afford to have their own places!"

Sara tried to explain reasonably that Chrissy and Maeve had no real family, no real home of their own, no place to go other than this house, where the three of them had lived together as a family.

"Poor little rich girls!" Rick mouthed with penetrating sarcasm.

251

"Drop dead!" Sara drawled sweetly.

"Get them out of here, Sara. I'm warning you. This is our house now, yours and mine." He didn't need that sanctimonious bitch Maeve around, watching him with those reproachful eyes every time he raised his voice. Or the superior Chrissy Marlowe with her slightly amused derisive smile.

"Careful, Shakespeare, or you'll find *yourself* out on your ass. . . ."

When Sara was first making her plans for the wedding, Maeve had discussed with Chrissy their moving out, the two of them, and getting their own apartment.

"Newlyweds should be alone and this *is* Sara's house."

"Why don't we just wait awhile and see?"

"But why, Chrissy? Wait and see what?"

"Well, it's almost May. Why don't we wait and see if this union makes it to December? And then if it does we can start the New Year with our own place. . . ."

"You certainly are taking a pessimistic view—"

"No, Maeve, not a pessimistic view. Just a realistic one."

When the quarrels started slowly but gained momentum with each passing day, Maeve again suggested to Chrissy that they move out. She, for one, was uncomfortable listening to Sara and Rick squabble.

"It would be stupid for us to move out now. The way things are proceeding, why, before we even signed our names to a lease Sara might be on a plane to Vegas and asking us to come along for the ride."

It was not long before the fighting started in Rick and Sara's bedroom the first thing in the morning, followed them down the stairs into the dining room for breakfast, into the library or drawing room after that, through the halls and out the door, and picked up once again in the evening the moment they walked into the house.

Sometimes Maeve could see that Rick was fighting for control, would back off from Sara. When she mentioned this to Chrissy, trying to give him *some* credit, Chrissy said, "Big deal! He knows a good thing when he sees it—when his eyesight isn't blurred from his drinking. He's just trying to hold on to what he's got."

It *was* worse when Rick drank. He was a surly drunk. It wasn't long at all before the fighting was more than nasty words and slammed doors. Furniture crashed and once it was a plate of soup hurled across the dining-room table. Servants left and new ones came. It was only a matter of weeks before the word was out that if you worked in the Gold-Green household you had better learn to duck.

"Now how long do you give this marriage?" Chrissy asked Maeve.

252

Maeve was thoughtful. "I don't know. I've seen a lot of people in trouble at the hospital. Some marriages last fifty years, feeding on hostility, anger, violent quarrels. Some people can't live any other way."

"You're not suggesting that our Sara is one of those people?"

"No, of course not. But, Chrissy, you know as well as I do—you never know what people really need—you never know what they're capable of—"

Maeve knew instinctively that the breaking of furniture and dishes could be a prelude to worse—it might be only a matter of time before Rick and Sara became physical toward one another. They were already the talk of both café society and the theatrical crowd, referred to as the "Battling Greens" in the columns. Winchell started it and Gardner and Lyons picked it up. The morning Sara came downstairs with dark glasses on, although it was raining outside, Maeve clutched her heart.

Chrissy wouldn't let Maeve speak. "This thing has to run its course. We can't interfere. In the meantime, knowing our Sara, I can't wait to see the other guy." She noted with satisfaction that when Rick came downstairs, his handsome, sulky face was crisscrossed with Band-Aids and red angry welts.

In nightclubs such as Leon and Eddie's or the Latin Quarter, Sara and Rick Green were considered part of the nightly entertainment. But at the more formal Colony, after they overturned a table, dishes and all, they were asked to leave.

One morning, as the four were eating breakfast, the butler brought in the mail. Opening a letter addressed to her, Sara found a bill in the amount of $972.43 to cover the breakage of a mirror in the bar at the Riviera. Sara, slightly hung over, tried to recall when they had been at the Riviera, and how the mirror had come to be broken.

Rick smiled maliciously. "That's the night Jack asked you to make an investment in the play, since it was decided to go to Broadway with it, and you said no, and I said you were a tight-assed, penny-pinching bitch, and you threw your old-fashioned at me, glass and all, and I ducked."

"Since one might assume you're the man in the family, you take care of it," and Sara made a paper airplane out of the bill and sailed it down to Rick's end of the table.

"Since you wouldn't part with any of your fucking shekels to invest in the play, you cheap-assed broad, pay the fucking bill yourself," and he soared the paper airplane back at her. His aim was poor and it hit Maeve instead.

Maeve excused herself from the table, but Chrissy sat there waiting. *Go get him, tiger!*

Sara hurled her teacup and once again Rick ducked and the cup and contents landed on the Aubusson. The rug was thick and soft and the cup did not break. Chrissy looked at the cup, at Rick's poisonous smile and at Sara's face, ugly with venom, and decided she didn't care for the set of Sara's once-rosebud mouth. It was now a thin, straight line with the corners turning down and it was beginning to harden into place. Maybe it *was* time somebody said something.

"Sara," she said after Rick had gone. "Your marriage is losing its charm. To quote some wag, I hope the fucking you're getting is worth the fucking you're getting."

It was almost the beginning of July when Maeve decided to take a leave of absence from her nurse's training instead of continuing through the summer. She was restless and nervous, and in her state of mind she couldn't help herself, let alone others. She begged Sara to go with Chrissy and her to Southampton, to Newport, even to the Mediterranean. "We could charter a boat and sail for a couple of weeks. *You* need the rest too." She meant it—even though Sara's marriage was not much more than two months old, it had taken its toll. Sara's nerves were honed to a fine edge.

"Come on," Chrissy urged. "It *is* summer and you always said anybody caught dead in New York in the summertime should be shot."

Sara laughed. "Did I say that? I say a lot of things. Anybody who listens to me is a fool. But I couldn't possibly leave Rick all by himself when he's having such a bad time with the play." She smiled maliciously. "They've already put off the opening twice. And now they're scheduled to open right after Labor Day and he's got to rewrite practically the whole play, poor thing. No, I wouldn't miss a minute of this for anything. But you two run along without me. Anybody caught dead in New York in the summertime is a rotten egg."

Chrissy and Maeve decided they wouldn't go without her. They couldn't leave her alone in the house with Rick. Anything could happen. The three girls did meet Marlena in Charleston in time for the Water Festival in July, which served as their reunion for the year. Other than that, and the occasional weekend in Southampton, they were all there, the three friends and Rick, in Sara's beautiful town house, all of them waiting for the long, hot summer to be over.

3.

The morning newspapers carried only the reviews of the play, *The Nights Are Damned*. The afternoon papers carried the reviews of the play *and* a review of the drama that unfolded at the play's opening-night celebration at Sardi's.

The curtain had fallen on *The Nights Are Damned* around ten-thirty and Sara Gold Green, seductive in shimmering black satin and flashing an armful of diamond bracelets, had entered Sardi's with Chrissy Marlowe and Maeve O'Connor, at about twenty minutes to eleven. Chrissy and Sara flashed big white smiles as if photographers were about to take their picture, while Maeve ducked her head, as if in fear that they would. Sara flitted about kissing cheeks, while Chrissy and Maeve sat looking at one another with nervous expectancy. Five minutes later, Rick Green came in with a scowling Jack Blatt. No ovation, Rick Green bitterly noted. The bastards could have at least stood up and clapped, as they had for Porter when *Kiss Me Kate* opened. *Fucking, ungenerous bastards!* Vincent Sardi came up and put his arm around him for a second. *Damn white of him, considering he is getting paid for this party.*

"Darling!" Sara called to him. "We're opening the first bottle of champagne! Come quickly! I wouldn't want you to miss that first pop!"

Carl Canfield, the director, came in with the glum cast and some of the assemblage stood up and valiantly clapped hands. *Oh, they'll do it for the actors, that bunch of shits. . . .*

"You'd better sit down, Sweetie," Sara said, smiling brilliantly. "Or everyone will think *you think* they're applauding you."

Some of the cast from *Brigadoon* drifted in and Sara dug into her prime ribs.

"How can you eat?" Green demanded of Sara, as somebody called out, "Review on the radio . . . not *too* bad!"

"Try the cannelloni," Chrissy urged Maeve. "Heavenly!"

The Daily News came in first.

"Rag!" Rick spat before he even read the first words, ". . . Gobble, gobble, gobble—"

Then the *Times* came in and everyone silently passed the papers along. Only Sara kept eating as she read, "This night was truly damned . . ."

The crowd immediately started to disperse. A few hangers-on tried to drink up and grab a bite of the food before they left.

"It's you!" Rick turned on Sara with venom. "Ever since the day I met you my luck's soured! *You're* bad luck, you bitch!"

Sara stood up, picked up her white fox wrap. "Oh, I don't know, honey. I'd say I was lucky. First, I had the good luck *not* to get a part in your misbegotten play. Then I had the good luck *and* the good sense not to put any money into the staging of your little old asshole of a play. I'd call that luck!"

Rick got to his feet, picking up the knife Sara had used to cut her prime rib, and with an upward thrust, plunged it into her belly.

Maeve and Chrissy found Sara sitting up in bed putting on her makeup. "These damn hospital beds are the most uncomfortable torture racks ever designed to make people sick. Will you two please bring me some of my lovely lacy pillows from home so that I can sit up without breaking my back?"

Maeve laughed with relief. "I know you're all right if you're complaining. We brought you some of those pecan rolls you adore."

"Goody."

"Who sent you all these magnolias?"

"Willy Ross. Wasn't he sweet after I treated him so miserably? Magnolias in New York in September. They must fly them up from Charleston."

"When are you getting out of here?" Chrissy asked. "I want to make reservations for Vegas. Or do you have to stick around to press charges?"

"Oh, I wouldn't dream of pressing charges. It would be so . . . *niggardly* to press charges, don't you think? Rick has enough problems."

"In that case, I'll make the reservations for—"

"It will take six weeks in Vegas. I'm thinking more like Mexico." Sara blotted her lips.

"What's the hurry?" Chrissy asked. "*I* could use six weeks in the desert after these last few months."

Sara stared pensively into her makeup-case mirror. "Do you think I've aged from my experience? Tell the truth." Then, without waiting for an answer, "What do you think of a quickie divorce in Mexico and then a year in Paris?"

"Paris!" Maeve said. "What a wonderful idea. Do you think we could?"

"Who in the world can stop us?" Chrissy demanded. "Why *not* Paris?"

"You know, we did everything all wrong," Sara said. "We should have gone to Paris for a year *before* we made our debut. That's how it's supposed to be done. So we have to rectify our error."

"Golly!" Chrissy sat down on the bed. "Just think—if we had gone to Paris before the debut, everything would have worked out differently. Just think of the mistakes we could have saved ourselves. . . ."

Maeve thought of Greg Carey, then she said cheerfully, "Look at it this way. Who knows what other mistakes we would have made *instead* and didn't?"

Part Three

THE WOMEN

New York

NOVEMBER 1948

We had a bon voyage party in their stateroom, drank Piper Heidsick, nibbled stuffed shrimp and poached oysters, and sang bits of old songs that had been big in the early half of the decade, songs like "Tangerine" and "Green Eyes" and laughed a lot and cried a little. I couldn't help but think, "It's really *their* world! . . ." But then I wasn't sure. God, I hoped it would be! For Sara and Chrissy and Maeve. And for me, too. And yet I was not convinced that it would.

I looked back over the past few years and it all hadn't been bad, but it all hadn't been good either. We toasted the future, of course. "To the very golden future!" Chrissy said, and we all cheered.

Then the ship's horn blew and it was time for me to leave.

"Ernest, Scott, here we come!" Sara breathed.

"What about poor Zelda?" Maeve asked wistfully.

"Quick!" Chrissy said. "Let's toast Zelda!"

And we did.

"Sure you won't change your mind and come along with us?" Chrissy asked. "You can just not get off the ship. . . ."

I laughed and shook my head. I had Johnny, didn't I? The ship's horn blew again and I walked down the gangplank and waved from the dock.

They stood at the railing waving back, laughing with excitement and looking so glamorous and beautiful in their matching ankle-length sable coats over white flannel trousers and white cashmere sweaters that they fairly took my breath away and the other passengers couldn't help but stare.

I waited until the ship was out of sight. Would I ever regret not having taken Sara up on her offer—the trip to Paris as a pregraduation gift? It *was* exciting for them to be going off to the city of light, but I had wonderful things waiting for me too—my graduation, my marriage.

Finally, the ship was gone—off the horizon. How long would it be, I wondered, until I saw my friends again? What adventures awaited them across the sea? Would they find happiness, the answer to their dreams? I made a silent toast minus the champagne. *To all our dreams!*

PARIS 1948-1950

1.

I had been back in Cambridge over a week and had not yet seen Johnny. He had all kinds of excuses . . . mostly that he had to study—always a valid excuse for a medical student. I accepted the excuses but I was hurt. And apprehensive. Doubts began to assail me. I had no doubts about my own love for Johnny. Had I not proven that over and over again? I had ceased keeping count as I used to in the beginning. Monday afternoon at three. Saturday morning at eleven. Tuesday night in the back of the Pontiac. Wednesday afternoon—time for only three kisses and no more. Oh yes, over and over again I had proven my love, had given of my loyalty and devotion. No—it was Johnny's love that I was beginning to doubt. Had he grown distant, detached of late, or was it only my imagination just because he wasn't dying to see me? Surely, if he were, he could have stolen away for an hour to see me—even medical students had an hour for love, surely.

Then, finally, he called and asked if I would like to take a walk. Then I was positive something was terribly wrong. A young man in love who hasn't seen his sweetheart in almost two weeks doesn't ask to see her in public.

We walked and I listened to him tell me in so many words that I was not quite good enough for him to marry. Oh, he couched it in nicer terms. He was, after all, Harvard. He told me it was really me he loved but he had to think of his career. A young doctor starting his internship with only his good name, a pleasant face, and a personable manner must think in different terms. "You do understand, don't you, Marlena, my true love?"

And then he went on to tell me that he had been seeing someone else for the past few months. A Boston debutante, plain of face, but with a bankable Brahmin name and Boston "in-trust" money. He was going to marry her, and after he finished his internship, he would command a proper Brahmin practice and a house on Beacon Hill. I looked at his Jon Whitcomb profile and I was sick with his betrayal. I thought that right then and there, in Harvard Square, I would bop him right on his beautiful nose.

I thought of Sara. What would she say when she heard that a Leeds girl from Charleston cuts no ice in Boston, especially if she is genteelly impoverished to boot? And having had her debut at the Waldorf didn't make a twit of difference to an ambitious young doctor with his eye on the Hill.

There was, I knew, a certain prescribed etiquette for broken engagements. If the girl breaks off the engagement, she gives the ring back. If the boy does, she is entitled to keep the ring for her trouble. She goes home, brokenhearted, and wraps it in tissue and puts it away in a corner of a dresser drawer. Later, when the pain starts to fade or if her heart is mended by a new sweetheart and a new ring, she digs up the old one, removes the diamond from its Tiffany setting, and has it reset in a cocktail ring surrounded by small rubies, or in a dinner ring circled by tiny emeralds.

But standing in front of Nini's Corner with happier faces than mine rushing past, I could think only of throwing the ring in the Charles River. Or scratching an X on Johnny's downy pink cheek with the sharp edge of the diamond, marking him forever. Instead, I pulled it off my finger, threw it in his face and ran off down the street.

I spent the next few days in bed in my little room. I didn't go to my classes and I barely ate anything. I just kept going over it—over and over—in my mind until I thought I would go crazy. I hadn't thrown my ring in the Charles—maybe I should throw myself. But I was only indulging myself. I knew down deep that I would never do such a thing. No, I would stay in school and graduate like the good little girl I was. I concentrated on that until I was too numb to feel any more pain.

Then I grew ashamed of myself. Where was my self-respect? So I got up and dressed myself and went to the Square to get something to eat. Tomorrow I would go back to class. I bought a newspaper on my way back to my room. It must have been fate that I had chosen that day to get up from my bed and go back out into the world and buy that newspaper, for there on page three was an Associated Press release from Paris. The headline read:

American Heiresses
Take the Ritz by Storm

Sara Gold, recently divorced from playwright Rick Green; Chrissy Marlowe, who divorced Gaetano Rebucci of the California wine family some months ago; and Maeve O'Connor daughter of noted novelist, Padraic

O'Connor, were seen lunching at the
Ritz today. The 1946 New York
debutantes, dressed alike in matching
white silk shirts, gray flannel trousers
and sable coats, were the recipients
of much attention from the Parisian
ladies also at lunch. Chalk one up for
American fashion know-how. Our very
own princesses have outchiced the
French at their own game!

Of course! I would place a call to Sara. It would help to share the
hurt, the humiliation and the shame. It would help to talk to Sara and
to Maeve and Chrissy.

"That bastard!" Sara emphasized. "Poor baby! Are you sure you
don't want to join us here?

"No," I said bitterly. "I might as well finish up and graduate so at
least I have something to show for the last few years. But you three
aren't wasting any time either, I see. You're in Paris only a little while
and the papers here are already carrying an article about you."

"Whatever are you talking about?"

"Hold on a minute. I have it right here. I'll read it to you."

"Heavens," Sara said when I finished. "Isn't that the silliest thing?
Talk about your tempests in a teacup," she pooh-poohed, clearly pleased.

"Aside from setting the Ritz on its ear, are you enjoying Paris?"

"We've hardly done anything yet. We've gone to some of the big
couture houses and the rue de la Paix. We've drunk Calvados in the
shadow of the Arc de Triomphe like Charles Boyer and Ingrid Bergman,
and tonight we're going to Maxim's for dinner. All very innocent, so far.
Now that Johnny is out of the picture, you really should come over. You
know what the duc de Morny said?"

I smiled at Sara from my side of the Atlantic. "Tell me, Sara," I
said. "What did the duc de Morny say?"

" 'All good Americans, when they die, go to Paris!' "

"Have you been to the Louvre yet or the Eiffel Tower? Or Notre
Dame?"

"Really, Marlena, do you think I came to Paris to ruin my feet at a
museum or to look at an old cathedral?"

I laughed. At least *Sara* never changed.

"I'd better go now. God knows what this call has cost me. Write to
me, please, Sara."

"I will, Marlena precious. And I'll send you something utterly
gorgeous. And don't worry about that Johnny Grey. When we get back,
I'm going to think of something really rotten to do to him."

I hung up with a lump in my throat. Sara *had* made me feel better
but, still, she was so far away.

2.

They arrived at Maxim's in three different hues of the same, starkly simple, body-clinging, one-shouldered, satin gown, and the majordomo led them to a table.

"Table sixteen!" Sara enthused. "Do you know what that means?"

"No. But I know you'll tell us." Chrissy leaned forward with mock anticipation.

"I just called for a simple reservation. I did not ask for a specific table. And they have given us the table they reserve for Maurice Chevalier, the Aga Khan, and Greta Garbo! It has terrific significance."

"And what is this terrific significance?"

Sara adjusted the row of diamond bracelets on her left arm. "Really, Chrissy. They obviously think we are *celebrities*."

"Everyone is staring at us," Maeve whispered.

"Maybe it's just that they don't like the cut of our American jib," Chrissy said.

Sara waved an irritated hand at her as the maître d' came over with the wine steward at his heels, followed by a waiter bearing a great silver cooler and another bearing a magnum of wine. The maître d' whispered to Sara and Sara nodded solemnly. The wine steward took the bottle of wine from the waiter and held its label up to Sara. A 1928 Château Lafite Rothschild. She nodded again and he placed the bottle in the wine bucket and set it in motion chafing it between his hands. Sara turned toward a table in the corner and smiled sweetly, inclining her head to the occupants.

"Smile, girls," she instructed Maeve and Chrissy. "Count André de Roebech is our benefactor."

"Which one is he?" Chrissy asked. "The cute one with the mustache?"

"*Who* is he?" Maeve wanted to know, "And what does he want?"

"Just somebody who wants to be friends, I guess," Sara said. "That's what I meant. We're celebrities and everyone wants to be our friend."

Sara hung up the phone. "The Vicomtesse de Ramboullet is coming over this afternoon to take us to Madame Madelaine Amodio's who, the Vicomtesse says, runs one of the smartest *salonnières* in town."

Chrissy was sprawled unceremoniously over the Louis XVI rose sofa in the *fin de siècle* drawing room of their suite. "And who is the Vicomtesse de Ramboullet, pray tell, and what is she to us?" She rubbed at a tiny brown-edged hole in the satin upholstery and idly wondered if it had been she who had burned it with a cigarette.

Sara giggled. "The Vicomtesse is old Pushface Pusher from New York. Caroline Pushface Pusher to be more explicit. We went to school together at . . . I don't remember which one it was anymore. We called her Pushface because of her last name. She's a terrible bitch but she can be loads of fun."

Sara embraced the Vicomtesse de Ramboullet as if she were a long-lost relative, and ushered her into the flower-filled drawing room. The tiny Vicomtesse sniffed, "It smells like a funeral home in here."

"Yes," Chrissy agreed. "Half of Paris has sent flowers it seems. All people we don't even know."

"And the telephone hasn't stopped ringing," Maeve added.

"Look at this." Sara laughed with delight, pointing to a silver salver overflowing with engraved calling cards and invitations.

"Of course." Caroline sat down, carefully arranging her full-pleated black and white silk skirt around her. "Expect to be the toast of Paris. We filthy-rich Americans are the new royalty of Europe. It's our money they want. Expect to be proposed to at least once a day by some penniless prince or duc. They have to recover from the war one way or another."

"And your viscount?" Sara asked.

"Henri? He's no longer penniless. I've set him up in an interior decorating business and he's doing fabulously. All the hotels are redecorating."

"You knew he was penniless when you married him?"

"Of course!" Caroline chuckled. "It was an arrangement. The French are marvelous at that sort of thing. I wanted a title—he wanted money. The man was desperate! But when I get bored with being the Vicomtesse, or if I find a better bet, we'll part friends. Henri is as queer as a fifteen-dollar bill."

Maeve looked at the Vicomtesse as if she found her strange. She was the same age as the three of them but she talked like a woman twenty years their senior. Even Sara was not as sophisticated nor Chrissy as cynical.

Now the Vicomtesse looked around the exquisitely appointed room and sniffed again. "I don't know what possessed you to move into the Ritz, Sara. It's so stuffy here. Do you know they won't even accept American movie people?"

"That's their problem," Sara answered. "I think it's just perfect here. The Place Vendome is a wonderful location and we love dining here, and we love the gardens and the terraces, don't we, girls?"

"Oh, yes, we adore everything," Maeve said firmly.

"The Hotel Lancaster has better telephone service. But if you were really clever, you'd stay at the Bristol, which is right next door to the best hair salon in the city."

"I think we'll manage fine right here at the Ritz."

"Oh, well, stay here if you must, but at least get yourselves a chauffeured car. And remember, there are three rules for Americans in Paris. One, never be late for an important dinner—it is considered unforgivable. Second, when you arrive, it is *très* imperative to be *drôle* and *amusante*. Third, do not overdress—that's a frightful sin. And one more thing— stay away from German barons. A ruthless, cold-blooded lot. Sadistic fags, every one."

Yes, Chrissy thought. One had married and shot her mother. But Chrissy thought she knew why they had called Caroline Pusher "Pushface." One's hand actually ached to push in her arrogant face.

Chrissy's heart started to pound when she picked up the heavy gray notepaper and saw the crest of the House of Windsor, the violet ink.

My dear Christina,

David and I have just returned to Paris and there is news of you everywhere. All our friends talk of the beautiful Chrissy Marlowe and we cannot rest until we see this daughter of our old and dear friend.

We can talk about your mother if you would like—if the memories are not too painful, for any of us. It was an unhappy time for the three of us in many ways, but also a time of many pleasant memories.

Do come to our home in the Bois de Boulogne for tea on the fourteenth, at four o'clock, and I will try to collect some of your mother's old friends from the London days. We so look forward to seeing you.

Chrissy was so stunned she let the note flutter to the floor. Sara picked it up and quickly scanned it.

"Good gracious, an invitation from the duchess herself. How mean of her not to include Maeve and me."

"Why don't you go instead of me?" Chrissy asked with a tartness to her voice.

Sara looked at her quickly. "Don't you want to go? The duke and the duchess are the *crème de la crème*."

"She stole the duke away from my mother when Mother came to fight for me in New York."

Sara smiled at Chrissy, "Look at it this way, a hell of a git she got."

266

"I think you should go," Maeve said. "It will help exorcise all the murky past from your system."

Chrissy stared off into space. "Do you really think it will help? Is that what you've been doing?"

"Me?" Maeve paled. "What do you mean?"

"All those little excursions you've been taking by yourself? Haven't they been your odyssey into the past?"

Odyssey? Yes, she's right. She's used the right word.

Maeve did not know herself for sure what she had been looking for when she walked along the Seine gazing into the faces of fishermen; went to the café at the Place St. Michel and ordered a rum St. James as she knew the young and then romantic Padraic had. She searched in vain for the Café des Amateurs, and found the bookstore of Sylvia Beach, places of which her father had spoken one gray day in Truro when they walked the beach and climbed the dunes together.

She supposed she *was* on a spiritual search for the young Padraic who had come to Paris, the young man she had never known. She looked for him in Montmartre and on the rue de Fleurus where Gertrude Stein and her friend Alice had lived and had a salon, where he and other young writers of the day had sipped colorless fruity liquors and eaten little cakes and looked at the wonderful collection of paintings hanging on the walls. He had told her that Miss Stein had paid almost no attention to him at all until the day she read the first piece of work he had finished since coming to Paris, and then she had declared him part of what she called the "generation perdue."

Oh, how her father had laughed then, sitting on the wet sand with Maeve, relating the little story and saying that Gertrude Stein had been as lost as any of them. Not as lost as Scotty Fitzgerald and certainly not as lost as Zelda, but more so than Hemingway, less than Ezra Pound, but far more than Joyce certainly, whom Gertrude had not liked at all. Then they had gone home and her father had gone to the room where he went when he drank.

All the names he had mentioned that day had been foreign to her then, but she remembered being envious of them because they had been lucky enough to know her father when he was younger and gayer and maybe, oh just maybe, more joyful.

So that was her quest, to find that Padraic. And she searched through the streets of the Quarter and outside the Quarter, looking up and down narrow alleys, sitting at countless marble tables in a stream of cafés, in tough bars, in restaurants on the rue des Saints-Pères, the rue Notre-Dame-des-Champs, the avenue de l'Opera, on the Champs Elysées, all the places he had mentioned only once. She even gazed at the Manets in the Musée du Luxembourg because Padraic had been there, had gazed at the same Manets.

But she did not find him. The void was not filled; the ache was still present; Paris did not reveal the Padraic it had known to her. Perhaps, he had never existed at all.

3.

Chrissy felt a complete hypocrite. For all her show of reluctance, she had known from the beginning that nothing could keep her away from the Windsors. She was not at all surprised to find their home in the Bois de Boulogne exquisite—she knew that the divorcée from Baltimore was almost as famous for her taste as she was for causing the abdication of the throne. Of course, Sara said that it had taken the city of Paris to refine the duchess's talent for elegance into a synonym for international chic, but Sara always said things like that.

Chrissy was welcomed into the roomful of strangers with a kind of reticence that was bewildering. The duchess's invitation had been so warm, but now the duchess was restrained, nearly to the point of coldness, and the duke was detached, almost blank. The other guests made a small fuss over her then commented as if she were not there.

"But she is not at all like her mother!"

"Oh, I think she is. The hair, of course, is different—"

"Yes. Christina's was the same very dark color, but a cloud. The daughter's is slick, sleek. . . ."

"And the nose. The nose is different, *n'est-ce pas?* Christina's nose was so patrician, longer and more elegant."

"Well, the Americans *like* these short noses, the buttons. . . ."

Laughter.

Chrissy wanted to say that her nose could hardly be described as a button, but why bother? She felt a small anger that these people, so foolish, so past their prime, had been her mother's friends. Even the duchess, whom she had believed so clever. Perfectly dressed in an embroidered Chinese satin tea gown, her hair in a classic knot, she looked more the emaciated corpse than a breathing person. It was said she barely ate at all.

A Lady Houghton asked if she, like her mother, had bought the lingerie handmade at the convents. Chrissy acknowledged that she had bought the underpants embroidered by the nuns, and smiled to herself. It was Sara who had insisted on it. "When in Paris, do as the Parisians do," Sara had said.

Chrissy couldn't help staring at the duke. He was deep in conversation with a doll-like marquesa about a needlepoint he was currently working on. She could not believe that this tiny, waspish, watery-eyed man had been her mother's love. Had he whispered into her hot breasts in the small hours of the night? Had he kissed tender, hidden spots and cried with fire that he could not live without his beautiful Christina? Chrissy turned away. It was a vision she could not contemplate.

It was then she noticed the swarthy man standing in a corner with his eyes fixed upon her. He smiled at her across the room and the power of his smile was such that it reached her, brilliantly, past the velvet and satin upholstery, the tapestries on the wall, past all the insipid, chattering puppetlike creatures in the room. The smile warmed her and she smiled back, her own individual grin that lit up her face.

"Your mother and I were friends, the best of friends," Aly Khan told Chrissy.

He was not particularly physically prepossessing: the hairline receding, his stature short and almost squat. But his eyes were dark and sad. Or were they dark and laughing? It was almost impossible to say for sure.

His smile was contagious. The voice caressed; it cared. Chrissy was suddenly glad she had worn the bright red taffeta with the cascade of ruffles at the neckline that flattered her long, swanlike throat.

Aly Khan drew her down to a love seat of flowered petit point and she relaxed in the magnetism of his personality. She wondered how much of the legend was true? Was he going to marry the film actress, Rita Hayworth? Were there really *that* many women in his life? Was he the extraordinary lover he was purported to be? Had he loved her mother, and in what manner of ways?

"Christina . . ." He closed his eyes. "Christina was so beautiful you felt she could not be true. I remember the first time I saw her—it was at a Court ball for the Queen of Rumania. I was only nineteen or twenty, Christina was a bit older—she must have already had you, lovely child— and I thought that surely she must be a princess from some faraway fairy kingdom. Her hair was a mist about her face, her eyes—velvety black cherries—those sweet, dark, delicious ones that are bathed in cognac and flamed—her skin . . . translucent . . . like rare thin cream." He seemed lost for a moment in his own reverie. "But it was not the looks alone . . . it was the spirit, the insatiable appetite for life." His eyes fastened on Chrissy again. "And you, why, you're a reincarnation! I can't believe it . . . it is too much to know the two of you in one lifetime!"

Chrissy listened avidly, her mouth slightly open, wet.

"It didn't happen here, you know, in the City of Light." Again he closed his eyes. "It was in London and what a time it was then. Did you ever read Evelyn Waugh?" Aly asked. "He described it perfectly when he wrote of masked parties, savage parties, Victorian parties, Greek parties, Wild West parties, circus parties, and almost-naked parties in St. John's Wood. Yes, there were parties in flats and studios and houses and ships and hotels and nightclubs and in windmills and"—he laughed —"of course, swimming baths." Aly Khan's face twisted as if in pain for a second. "Yes, those were the best of days."

Chrissy shook her head. "You were almost the same age as I am now."

"Are these the best of days for you too?"

"Oh, I hope not," Chrissy breathed. "I hope the best days are yet to come." Then, shyly, "There must be best of days for you too, yet to come."

He shook his head. "Those days with Christina . . . they can never be again." He had been slouching on the needlepoint sofa. Suddenly, he sat up erect. "Or maybe they can be again . . . for a little while." He jumped up. "Ask for your wrap, quickly."

"Where are we going?"

"You'll find out when we get there."

She rose. "But what about the duke and duchess?"

"Screw the duke and duchess."

Chrissy grinned. "Have you?"

Aly Khan roared with laughter. "You are a wit, like Christina." He touched her chin with his fingers. "So much like her. I must make a call. Get your wrap and I'll meet you outside."

Chrissy headed for the front door as unobtrusively as possible. But there was a woman watching, a lady dressed in the so-Parisian black and white. "You're going off with Aly. Be careful, child." Chrissy raised an eyebrow. The woman put a restraining hand on her arm. She was fastidiously made up, her blond hair perfectly coiffed in a French knot, but time had placed slight wrinkles around her eyes. "Do not let Aly break your heart."

"You presume too much, Madame," Chrissy said coolly, arching her neck.

"But he has broken older, more sophisticated hearts than yours, my dear. I knew you when you were a little girl. You used to recite little poems in Christina's Mayfair drawing room. I knew Aly too when he first came to London. I made my debut that year. It was May, 1930, and we were being presented at Court. Aly was there in a white Indian tunic with a high collar, and he wore a white turban with an emerald the size of a child's fist. I cannot tell you the impression he made upon me. I made up my mind that night that I would make him fall in love with me."

"And did you?"

She laughed briefly, quietly. "A little. For a little time. One never could be sure with Aly. One never could be sure how much love existed or for how long. Enjoy Aly, little one. He's a man to enjoy. But don't love him too well."

"Where are we going?" Chrissy asked as they sped along in the Mercedes convertible, so fast she was forced to suck in her breath.

"To the best of days, Christina," he shouted above the rush of the wind.

He pulled into a small airdome. His plane, *The Avenger,* was ready and waiting, and in ten minutes they were in the air.

At the airfield in London, a chauffeured Rolls was waiting.

"There are those who will tell you that Paris or Rome or somewhere in the Mediterranean—I love the Riviera myself—is the best place to be but don't believe them. There is no place in the world like London. I've gone everywhere and in the end I always come back here."

He showed Chrissy the house he had owned in his early days in London, in Mayfair, on Aldford Street. One might have thought he still owned it the imperious way he rang the bell. When a butler answered, Aly said, "We will take a quick look around, Charles," and took Chrissy's arm and led her in.

She saw a drawing room done in oak with a large medieval fireplace, a dining room that resembled a scaled-down banquet hall belonging in a castle. "My idea was to reproduce an old English castle in Mayfair," he told Chrissy. "Christina loved it." He touched a paneled wall, stroked it. "We dined here frequently. But we went everywhere . . . all the places there were to go. To the garden parties at the Palace and to the racing events at Ascot. . . . Christina wore a large picture hat at Ascot, I remember, and I, of course, wore a top hat and a cutaway. . . . We went everywhere that was fun. . . ."

Chrissy and Aly dined at the Savoy and he held her hand across the table while the other diners looked on and wondered. People waved, stopped at their table, exchanged pleasantries, but all the while Aly seemed oblivious to everyone except Chrissy.

He acts as if he's in love with me, she thought with a shiver. And she herself? She was already there too, in that magical land of intoxication.

"We used to go to the Embassy Club on Bond Street often. Christina used to say that the red velvet banquettes and the mirror-lined walls were a good backdrop for her, that they accented her coloring." Aly laughed as if that were a terribly clever thing for Christina to have said.

"But we used to go to the Café de Paris a lot, too. Bea Lillie used to sing and the entrance was a curved staircase and when Christina entered, coming down those stairs, the orchestra played, 'A Pretty Girl Is Like A Melody' for her. . . ."

"Couldn't we go there too?" Chrissy asked. She wanted to walk down those stairs and perhaps the orchestra would play "A Pretty Girl Is Like A Melody" for her too. But from the Savoy they went on to the Clermont where they played *chemin-de-fer* for a while. Chrissy guessed that Aly and Christina had done that too, but by now she was eager to experience that which Christina and Aly must have done best. She knew that moment was coming closer and closer—she felt his hands on her shoulders, her arms, around her waist leaving indelible prints, she was sure.

In the car, with Aly's arms around her, his lips on her lips, her neck, her shoulders, inside the neckline of her dress, she wanted him. For the first time in her lifetime, she *really* wanted a man. Her eyes tightly closed but her mouth open, sucking for breath, she felt the shaky, enveloping circles of desire.

"Christina . . ." he murmured.

She lay in the old-fashioned brass bed in Aly's suite at the London Ritz, marveling at what had occurred. Never before had she been made love to all night long, never had she felt so thoroughly, so magnificently, so splendidly loved.

An immaculately dressed Aly appeared in the doorway; he smiled at her caressingly. "Christina, you must dress now."

"Are we leaving?"

"Yes."

"Where are we going?"

"To the magical land of the Côte d'Azur."

"But my friends. They'll be wondering where I've disappeared to— they'll think I've eloped."

Was her choice of that word wishful thinking? Would he think that she was being aggressive, hinting? She was willing to bet that the world was littered with women who had wanted to marry him. Was her mother among them? He had been not much more than a boy then and her mother had already been a widow.

"Don't worry about your friends. We'll be back tonight."

They made love on the way to the plane in the *tonneau* of the Rolls, he murmuring her name over and over, ". . . Christina . . ."

She wanted to ask him if he had made love to her mother in a Rolls too.

Their bodies entwined again in the cabin of *The Avenger* as it approached the blue green of the Mediterranean. She wondered if Aly had had a plane when he knew her mother. Had they gone to the Riviera together?

"This is the place I call home," Aly told Chrissy. Unlike the other villas in Cannes, the Chateau de l'Horizon was surprisingly modern in architecture and quite splendid, with gardens, terraces, a magnificent pool with a chute that could empty one into the sea below.

Their day went by so quickly, too incredibly fast—swimming, sunning, lunching on the terrace, drinking champagne, *making love*. Was it possible, Chrissy wondered, that she could go on feeling this degree of desire, this intensity of passion. Would it last? *Could* it last?

Then they were back on the plane.

"What happened between you and my mother?" Chrissy finally asked the question. "What parted you? Was it the duke?"

Aly had been kissing the soft flesh of the inner crook of her arm and he raised his head now to look at her, almost as if he had forgotten who she was.

He blinked and pulled away from her. Sorrowfully, Chrissy realized that so quickly the spell was broken, the word *mother* had shattered the illusion. But Christina was not the intrusion; she herself was.

Aly looked down on the lights of Paris below. "It was a matter of commitment," he said dully. "Or more to the point, a lack of commitment. Perhaps it was the wrong time for both of us."

He drove her to the Ritz.

"I'm leaving for Ireland in the morning. But I would like you to come to the chateau next weekend. There'll be other people. Bring your friends."

He gave her a friendly kiss in the lobby. "Good night, sweet Chrissy. Christina would have been delighted with you."

In the elevator, Chrissy wiped away the tears with the back of her hand, as she had when she was a little girl.

"One of my very best friends is the biggest bitch I know," Sara said. "I can't believe *she* disappeared into the great big yonder with Aly Khan, *the* world's most fabled lover, without telling us—"

"Did you expect me to call you and let you watch?"

"Well, heavens, how was it? What did he do? How different was it from other men?"

Maeve listened for Chrissy's answer with the same avid interest as Sara.

"Well, for one," Chrissy said with a straight face, "he didn't have a penis, he had a snake. . . ."

Maeve grimaced but Sara laughed. "If you don't tell, I'm going to beat the hell out of you."

Chrissy sobered. "It *was* different," she said guardedly.

"How?"

"Oh, Sara!" Did she tell Sara and Maeve that it was different because it was a coupling that took place almost twenty years ago? They would think she was hallucinating.

"Well, it went on for hours at a time. Repeatedly."

"But of course," Sara said.

"What do you mean, of course?" Chrissy asked indignantly. "How do you know?"

"*Everybody* knows that Aly Khan can and does make love for hours on end because his father had him learn the technique of 'retaining' and 'holding.' It's an East Indian technique called *Imsák*. God, any man that doesn't go soft on you in a matter of minutes—that's a great lover. *You* should know that, Chrissy!"

Chrissy smiled dreamily. "It's more than that, though. It's also a . . . sweetness . . . that I've never known."

"I wish I could go to bed with him," Sara said wistfully.

Maeve looked at Sara with dismay. *With Chrissy's lover?*

"Don't look at me like that, you old pussycat Maeve. In European circles it's considered déclassé *not* to have gone to bed with Aly Khan. I mean, anybody who is anybody would never admit to such a thing. Even women who haven't say they *have*."

Chrissy sighed. "Well, maybe you'll get your chance. He's invited us to his chateau for next weekend."

Sara clapped her hands, ran to Chrissy and hugged her. "Oh, Chrissy, I'll never forget you for this!"

"You mean you're actually going to try and—" Maeve asked horrified. "After he and Chrissy—"

"What are you in such a snit about? If Chrissy doesn't mind, why should you? Do you?" she asked Chrissy.

"No." Chrissy smiled wistfully. "I don't mind." Her love affair had been over many years before. "In fact, Maeve, I can't think of a lovelier man for a girl to begin with."

"Let's do it, Maeve. Both of us," Sara said eagerly.

Maeve was bewildered, confused. Was Aly Khan really a man that was passed around just so women of the international set could say they had been to bed with him?

4.

Aly asked Sara to go with him to pick up Oscar de Martinou at the Nice airport. "We can jump over to the bar at the Hôtel de Paris in Monte Carlo for a quick drink on the way."

Sara was delighted; she had been waiting for the chance to be alone

274

with him. They had arrived at the chateau on Friday afternoon and it was already Saturday afternoon. Twenty-four hours had elapsed without Aly making a move. It had been enough to make her doubt her sex appeal. But a fast drive to Nice at a hundred miles an hour? In the Lancia? No, it would not be this afternoon.

But she was wrong. As they approached the Hôtel de Paris, Aly made a quick reversal of plans and Sara found herself being propelled toward the harbor instead, across the way from the hotel. As they boarded a yacht named *The Tina,* Sara asked, "What are we doing? Whose boat is this?"

"A friend's. It will be more pleasant and private to have a drink here."

The yacht's personnel welcomed Aly warmly, and in minutes Sara was whisked from a red and gold barroom to a blue and gold stateroom, and, martini glass in hand, to a blue and gold curtained bed. Two hours later, Sara said, "That was lovely." Aly reaffirmed that it had been, indeed.

"But what about your friend, Oscar de Martinou?" she giggled. "Do you think he's still waiting at the airport?"

Aly shrugged. "I doubt it. Right this minute he is probably in the pool at l'Chateau with a cold drink in his hand."

"That's good. I'm so glad."

"Shall we have ourselves a sun on the deck?"

"That will be nice. It's been so cold in Paris even though it's almost spring, and that's definitely wrong. It should always be warm in Paris."

"You should always be warm, Sara, wherever you are. You are a hothouse flower, special and exquisite."

Sara sighed. What a delight this man was.

She found a bathing suit bottom in the stateroom's closet and slipped it on. She cupped her breasts with her hands, looking into the mirror. She had never sunned topless in public before. She smiled at her reflection. "When on the Riviera, Sara, do as the Rivierians do." She was only grateful that her breasts were good, high and firm as was proper.

They drank champagne, and Sara asked idly, "Are you going to marry Rita Hayworth?"

"What do you know about it?" Aly asked and looked out at the sea so incredibly calm.

"I read the gossip columns. After all, you've been halfway around the world with her. You're a terrible scandal," Sara teased.

Aly's face darkened. "My father thinks I should marry Rita . . . because . . . he practically insists." Aly laughed but it was an ironic laugh.

"Because of the gossip? Aren't you your own man?" she chided.

Aly forced a smile. His hand caressed her thigh. "What do you think?" he whispered. "Am I not a man?" Their mouths met, their tongues entwined and then their legs.

But afterwards, Sara wondered. Did he go around making love to beautiful women for his own pleasure or to impress the Aga Khan with his manhood? The father was, after all, something of a Don Juan himself. And she had read that there was a question of succession. The father would pick his successor, the new *Iman,* leader of the Ismailis, and it would not necessarily be his son, Aly—it could be Aly's brother or even Aly's son, Karim. A lot of pressure there. Enough pressure to put Aly very much under his father's thumb.

Sara chuckled silently. She and this accomplished lover of a Moslem prince had more in common than a shared sexual encounter. They both suffered from a father fixation. She wondered if the prince understood his problem as well or any better than she did hers. But then his lips encircled her pink-nippled breast and Sara stopped thinking altogether.

It was almost dark when they ran out of gas only a half kilometer from l'Chateau, and Sara, in her white crepe de chine pajamas, got out to help Aly push his car the rest of the way.

Sara and Chrissy tried to talk Maeve into going to bed with Aly that weekend, too. "It would be so much fun if all three of us did and then we could compare notes," Sara giggled.

"I think that's disgusting," Maeve said angrily. "And besides, he hasn't even asked me."

Sara laughed. "That's the least of it. I don't think he would need much persuasion. Aly loves redheads."

"Forget it! Right now! I don't even want to discuss it!"

"Okay, spoilsport," Chrissy said. "We only thought Aly would be just the right man for you to start on. You can't be a virgin forever, you know."

"Yes," Sara agreed. "The idea of still being a virgin in your twenties is ridiculous."

"Oh, hush!" Maeve said. "It's you two who are ridiculous and can't even see that you are."

It wasn't that she was not attracted to the prince, for she was, she admitted to herself. It was foolish, she knew, but there was *something* about him that reminded her of— No, it was just too silly to even think about. Aly was shorter and less elegant of figure. Nor nearly as good-looking either, by far. What was it then? Only that darkness, a brooding quality that Aly seemed to assume on occasion, an air of romantic melancholy. That, and the fact that both seemed to court disaster. Her father—in his fashion and Aly—he burned his candle at both ends.

5.

Three weeks later, Maeve sat at a glassed-in sidewalk café on the Avenue des Champs Elysées, refreshing herself with a glass of wine after another fruitless trek through the city. It was a Saturday, and all Paris was out taking a promenade, it seemed. Lovers, of course, and families. Nursemaids pushing baby carriages, old roués and young women, fashionably dressed, on temporary leave from their duties as clerks and shopgirls. It was April and Paris was at last warming up. Most likely, they would be taking down the glass partitions that separated the tables from the street any day now.

"Maeve!" A voice called from behind her, a voice rich with the pleasure of coming upon her. Startled, even frightened, she turned. It was Aly Khan.

"I stopped for a quick drink and you are a lovely dividend. I'm on my way to the airfield. I'm going to Gilltown Stud."

"Gilltown Stud?"

"My farm in County Kildare. One of my racing stables."

"Ireland . . ." she said. "County Kildare? That's near Dublin, isn't it?"

"Yes. Do you know Dublin?"

"No . . . yes . . . I've never been there."

But she knew Dublin well. She had read all about it. Her father had been there, after Paris, and there was much of Dublin in his writings.

"Would you like to go along with me?" His smile was very intimate, his eyes burning with persuasion. "Right now."

"Yes . . . no . . . I don't know."

She wanted to, God knows she wanted to, but she was afraid.

"Anybody named Maeve O'Connor with flaming red hair should go to Ireland at least once. Come." He held out his hand. "My car's parked right out front." Maeve took his hand.

They drove through an iron gate manned by two golden lion heads and up a driveway to a beige and green house. Keeping guard were two cast-iron jockeys painted red and green. "Those are my racing colors," Aly told her. "Would you like to see the house first or the horses?"

"Oh, the horses I think." She was not eager to be alone in the house with him. Not yet.

"Do you ride?"

277

"Yes, of course . . . that is not well . . . fair, I suppose." She seemed incapable of a straight answer.

One of the cheerful Irish girls on the household staff found her a riding habit and they went out to the stables. They rode and later, when they returned to the house, Maeve was exhausted but she didn't know if it was from the riding or her own mounting tension. Aly was excited too, she could tell, and not at all tired. They sipped brandy in the library, silently, still in their riding clothes, their eyes meeting, the air around them charged with electricity.

"I'd like to see Dublin," she blurted out.

Aly laughed. "This minute? Right now? It's getting late. Wouldn't you rather wait until tomorrow?"

"No. Please. Can't we go now?"

He had been in Dublin much longer than in Paris. He had made a home for himself here. Maybe, if she walked the same streets, looked at the same things he had looked at, she could find a bit of him. She wondered, at the same time, where he was. She had no idea.

The road to Dublin was winding and narrow and Aly raced along. At one point, they had to pull over to allow some woolly sheep to pass. Maeve could sense the impatience in Aly's body. He was not a man accustomed to waiting. In direct contrast, Maeve watched the peat smoke wander lazily up from chimneys perched on thatched-roof cottages into the misty "soft weather" air, in no hurry at all. The Irish countryside, she thought, was a place for lazy dreams. She had a dream herself, but Aly was a man who lived only for the present.

"What would you like to see first?" Aly asked. "Some of the shops?"

Maeve had not come to shop. "First, I would like to see the Book of Kells."

He looked bewildered.

"It's kept in the library of Trinity College," she explained. No, Aly had never been to see the eighth-century Bible, but Padraic must have, because Joyce had described it as "the fountainhead of Irish inspiration," and Padraic O'Connor had known and admired James Joyce.

They left Trinity and Maeve said she would like to see the house where Oscar Wilde was born; she knew it was nearby. Aly seemed amused. "Oscar Wilde called the Irish the greatest talkers since the Greeks."

Aly laughed and said that he knew the Irish were great talkers but he hadn't known about the Greeks. Maeve worried that he was laughing at her.

"Are you interested in literature in general?" he asked. "Or are you just interested in Irish writers because you're of Irish ancestry?"

Maeve smiled, didn't answer. What could she say? That she was

278

interested in an American writer who went to Ireland to live? "Can we just walk around?" she asked.

They wandered into the bookshops and drank Irish whiskey at Mooney's Pub. They stood in front of the Abbey Theater and wandered around the dark back streets of North Dublin. But in the end it all meant nothing to her. She did not find what she was searching for there and not in O'Casey's Dublin either, in his "city's hidden splendor."

"What *is* it you are looking for, Maeve?" Aly asked. "Maybe I can help."

She could not answer. She was sure he could not help her. She was sure he had never read Padraic O'Connor—he was not a man who looked for life between the pages of books. Tears welled up in her eyes. She smiled at him through her tears, and shook her head wordlessly.

"Oh, my poor darling!" he said, and hugged her close.

She remembered then what Shaw had written of Dublin, after he had gone to live in England: ". . . To me it is all hideously real . . ." But she, herself, had found no reality in Dublin, not at all. Oh somewhere, somewhere, there must be somebody who resembled that Padraic who had made her feel so alive. . . .

Aly's arms were around her. She found them strong and comforting. She looked up into his face. *He* was real. Very much so. His arms were real, his body. Gradually the feeling grew from her loins upward and outward until her body was consumed with a physical lust, her blood infused with heat. Only the face bent down to hers was unclear, a haze.

They found a hotel nearby, a shabby hotel above a pub, and almost raced up the wooden stairs. The prince was not a man for waiting and she had waited long enough.

But once in bed, there was no haste, time was timeless. Their bodies in tandem . . . flesh against flesh. . . . He made love to her mouth . . . rocked and moaned . . . bathed her nipples with his tongue . . . sweetly sucked . . . drew of her into his mouth. . . . Together they searched . . . sensed . . . probed . . . penetrated. . . . She moved on top of him and he on her . . . expanding . . . throbbing . . . tender touching . . . the tearing of flesh with frantic fingertips. She found herself climbing that mountaintop of bliss that could not distinguish carnal from mystical, real from unreal, flesh from spiritual. She cried out his name. . . .

She opened her eyes to see him staring at her with hurt in his eyes, smiling sadly, even reproachfully. "You called me 'Daddy.' . . ."

Her eyes were wide. She broke out in a nervous perspiration. "You are mistaken. You must have heard wrong . . . I called 'Aly.' They must sound alike."

Aly smoothed the hair that covered the pillow in a wild disarray. "Of course," he said with commiseration.

6.

"Miss Rita Hayworth and Prince Aly Khan invite you to their wedding . . ." Each of them received an invitation to the wedding on May 27.

"Shall we go, do you think?" Chrissy asked.

Sara gasped, "Of course! I wouldn't miss it for the world."

Maeve felt too embarrassed not to go if Sara and Chrissy did.

The civil ceremony was held in the town hall of Vallauris, the community in which l'Chateau lay. First, Aly arrived in a gray Alfa-Romeo, in black coat and gray striped trousers. Then the Aga Khan and the Begum came in a green Rolls—the Begum wore a blue sari, the Aga, a cream-colored suit and dark glasses. Finally, the bride arrived in a white Cadillac and wearing a blue hat and dress.

At the reception at the chateau, a cocktail invented especially in the couple's honor was served. The Ritaly cocktail consisted of two-thirds Canadian Club, one-third sweet vermouth, two drops of bitters, and, of course, a cherry. There were literally thousands of flowers and the swimming pool boasted two hundred gallons of eau de cologne. The guests ate lobster, cold meats and caviar, and were impressed with a one-hundred-and-twenty-pound wedding cake.

One guest, a Society woman turned cabaret singer, told the friends, "The question is not, 'Did you sleep with Aly?' but rather 'Did *he* with you?' Of course, now everyone claims *she's* the one who made Aly come."

The girls looked at one another with the question in their eyes, and then they laughed so hard they almost cried.

7.

In June they held their reunion in the dining room at the Ritz and toasted Marlena, still back in Cambridge. They had expected her to join them now that she was graduated, but Marlena had surprised them. She had recovered from Johnny Grey's defection and had found herself a new lover, a young man at Harvard Law, and, in the fall, she would enter law school herself.

Peter, Marlena had written, was the nicest, sweetest, dearest human being she had ever met. She had added, "with the exception of three sweet young things whose return I yearn for. . . . Peter may not be as handsome as a certain party who shall go nameless, but as my mother would say, 'handsome is as handsome does,' and to that I say, 'Amen!' "

"I'm so proud of her I could die," Sara declared. She didn't know if she were prouder that Marlena was in law school or that she had emerged from the Johnny Grey debacle so well.

"But I'm *so* disappointed about Mama not coming to Paris."

"Why isn't she coming?" Chrissy asked. "She's well, isn't she? She's not . . . ?"

"Drinking?" Sara finished for her. "No, she's not. It's just that she hasn't enough confidence, I guess, to leave Charleston as yet. I guess it's hard to leave the place where one has put one's faith."

She was still looking for such a place herself. And when she found it, she would take her mother to live with her. That was her ultimate goal.

"As long as she's happy. She is, isn't she?" Maeve asked.

"Yes, I think so. She and Aunt Martha get along beautifully. They do everything together, garden, cook, go to all the socials and church doings. But, of course, what I would like to see happen is for Mama to get a beau. Maybe when I get settled someplace and Mama comes to live with me *I* can do something about that."

"I'll drink to that!" Chrissy raised her glass. "In fact I'll drink to us all getting a beau!"

"Sara said her mother was in a place she had faith in. I'd like to drink to us all finding a place like that," Maeve said.

Chrissy laughed. "I take it then that you don't think Paris is that place?"

No, Sara thought, Paris is more a place to have a damn good time. But still, she had to find something for herself to do. Especially since Chrissy seemed to have found herself and was studying art at the Sorbonne and Maeve was so busy writing, all day and night, after all the years of swearing that she would never take pen to paper. Golly, Sara thought, she was like a woman possessed.

"Now I want to drink to Chrissy's art and to Maeve's writing," Sara said. "And I want to say that I am proud to be their friend. . . ."

Chrissy laughed and Maeve cried.

Sara found Maeve's hidden manuscript, read it through, and told Chrissy about it. Then Chrissy read it and confirmed Sara's opinion— Maeve was a genius, just like her father.

"We have to do something about this," Sara said.

"What do you mean? What do we have to do?"

"Submit it to somebody for publication. Maeve's already working on something else and has relegated this amazing piece of work to her steamer trunk."

"You mean, submit it for publication behind her back?"

"Exactly."

"No, Sara, we can't do that. Maeve would be furious. She'll be mad that we even found her manuscript and read it. You know what a stickler for privacy she is."

Sara laughed. "Don't be ridiculous. If she's our friend she can't be a stickler for privacy. She has to share."

"*You* tell her that, Sara. And while you're at it, tell her we've read her fucking book too and think she should be published. But, please, do me a favor and do it when I'm not here. Maeve doesn't get angry often but when she does I'd rather not be around."

Chrissy was right. Maeve *was* furious when she discovered that the two had read her book. "I've a good mind to move out and get an apartment by myself. That's the only way I'm going to get any privacy. How *dare* you read something I haven't given you permission to read? Don't you have any integrity at all?" she asked them both but looked at Sara.

"The only reason you're so angry, dear Maeve, is that you know we're right. That your novel *has* to be published. And that's the only real integrity at stake here."

"Look, Sara, why don't you get some project of your own? You're full of competitiveness, ambition; you love recognition and approbation. Why don't you go find these things for yourself and leave me alone. Go work your aggressions out by yourself."

"Fine, I will. But whatever I do, *you* still have to publish your book. What are you afraid of? You're acting like a terrible coward. She *is* acting like a coward, isn't she, Chrissy?"

But Chrissy wouldn't answer. She believed that a person's fears, her own particular demons, were personal property. When Sara pressed her, she shook her head. "It's Maeve's book and it's Maeve's life. Sometimes we think we own each other. In the end, we can only own ourselves. Leave Maeve alone, Sara."

"No!"

Maeve and Chrissy looked at one another in astonishment. Sara was really incredible!

In the end, as usual, Sara won out. She herself took Maeve's book to a French publisher whom she had met on her social rounds. "He adores it, Maeve! He says that one day you may be as fine a writer as your father."

Maeve, already sorry that she had acceded to Sara's nagging, prayed that wouldn't be so. It was enough that William Faulkner had won the Nobel for '49 and that Padraic had been passed over again. How would he react to the publication of *her* book? Especially if people were going to say that she was as good as he was? Was she deliberately provoking him out of hiding with her own book? Had she tempted fate? Laughed in the face of the gods who meted out punishment?

"I've let you talk me into this, Sara. And I hope we all won't be sorry. But, please, in the future, let me make my own decisions. And do something on your own. You've got too much creative energy to just run around, spreading your peacock feathers for silly people at silly parties."

"But I am doing something. I'm studying with Jean Doucet of the Comédie Francaise. That's doing something, *n'est-ce pas?* And there are my voice lessons. Let me demonstrate." She dangled her head forward, closed her eyes, and counted to six. "That's good if one is nasal. And to counter stridency, one has to relax the neck muscles so—inhale, exhale, count to four slowly for each inhalation and exhalation. And yawning is very good. You do it"—she opened her mouth and made a long yawning sound—"thus!"

Maeve laughed.

"And I'm taking a course in self-rejuvenation of the skin. Everyone should take it."

"At twenty-one, Sara?"

Maeve waited for the months of prepublication to pass, nervous that her book wouldn't be well received, terrified that it would. Would her father get in touch with her? Would he read her book? Perhaps her book would come out and go away unnoticed, unheralded, and no one would even know that she had written a book at all.

But the French critiques, and then the reviews of the English version from the United States, were so good that they were almost overwhelming to Maeve. All the reviewers wrote about a literary discovery . . . a near genius. . . . One said that she wrote with a beauty of language that was completely absent from the writings of her contemporaries. Many compared her with her father, which was inevitable since they were father and daughter and *both* were now considered extraordinary writing talents.

"But it's so ridiculous to compare us," Maeve cried. "We write so differently . . . about such different subjects. It's like night and day."

A few critics actually insinuated that her talent was greater.

"What does this mean exactly?" Chrissy asked, reading from a review: " 'Maeve O'Connor's talent, at twenty-two, begins where her distinguished father's leaves off—it will be interesting to see at what point Padraic O'Connor's next novel takes off on this scale of comparison. . . .' "

"I think it says that Maeve is already better than her father," Sara said with pride.

"Don't be ridiculous!" Maeve snapped. "I'm just a beginner. I could be just a flash in the pan—"

"Let's have no more false modesty, please," Sara said complacently. "Don't fight it, honey chile. Face it! You're the greatest! Maeve, you're a star!"

Maeve made a decision. *Sojourn in Paris* would be her last published book. If she wrote again, it would be just for herself. There could be no more comparisons.

"How's the book you're working on now coming along?" Sara asked. "I think you shouldn't wait too long to publish the next one."

"Sara, I'm firing you as my manager right now," Maeve said. "Work on your own career."

"Well, shame on you, Maeve O'Connor. I would think you'd care to show a little graciousness. Not that I want any appreciation, but it would be nice if once in a while you could be properly happy about something! As for my career, it's doing very nicely, thank you. I was keeping my news as a surprise but this seems to be the time to reveal it. I've a part in a Jean Gabin movie. It's a tiny little part, but it's very exciting. And you wouldn't believe the sex appeal of that man!"

"Oh, that's wonderful news, Sara! I'm so thrilled for you." Maeve hugged Sara. Perhaps now Sara would leave *her* alone.

"Gosh, that is super!" Chrissy cried. "Let's go out and celebrate. And when do you think we can meet Jean? I'd adore going to bed with the man Marlene Dietrich slept with!"

"I saw him first," Sara said. "But I'll let you have seconds." Then, as an afterthought, "But only if you let me arrange a show for you first. A one-man show. I know Freddy Allerton—you know, the gallery on—"

"Oh, Lordy!" Chrissy pretended to collapse. "Maeve, save me from her!"

"Artists who don't show are afraid of failure," Sara pronounced. "It's easier not to show than to risk ridicule and rejection."

"I am not afraid of failure, Sara. I don't have to prove anything to anybody."

"Don't you?"

"Oh, Lord, protect us from amateur psychiatrists. Sara, I'm just not ready. I have to perfect my craft first. When I'm ready, you'll be the first to know. And you can be in charge, you can make all the arrangements, I swear!"

Maeve began to feel her father's presence again but now it was a very much in-the-present presence—a wrathful, angry presence, eager to exert penance for past rebuffs and for the new success that was hers. Again she craned her neck looking for shadows in doorways, afraid to turn around at parties, terrified that the person who bumped into her in a bookstall would be he. Again she heard footsteps echoing every footstep of her own.

More and more she remained indoors, going out less and less until she was almost a recluse, a prisoner of her own making. Nothing Sara or Chrissy did or said impressed her. "You want me to work on my next book, don't you, Sara?" she joked, although she did not feel at all comical. "Then let me be—I need solitude."

But as the days passed, she grew ever more certain that he would reach in, into her isolation, and find her.

8.

Sara wouldn't have missed the party the British gave at their embassy in June for the world—the British Embassy was one of the most elegant in Paris. But she had to go alone. Maeve wouldn't leave their rooms at the Ritz and Chrissy had gone to the Lido with some friends visiting from the States—newly arrived visitors always wanted to go to the Lido thinking it so characteristically French.

Nancy Chartres came looking for Sara in a gold and black powder room at the Embassy. "I have someone who wants to meet you, Sara."

Sara, brushing fiercely at her new Italian cut to give it a wilder, windtossed look, demanded to know who it was. "I don't want to waste my time just meeting *anyone*—that's such a bore. Is it a *he?* Is he famous or at least, handsome? Is it a movie star? Is it Cary Grant? I heard he was in town."

Nancy Chartres laughed. "It is a *he,* he is both famous and handsome, he is decidedly not Cary Grant and he is not a movie star. But *he* is very determined to meet you."

Sara smiled at her reflection, pleased at last with her hair. "Why is he determined to meet me? Was he struck with my world-famed beauty?"

Nancy reflected, taking Sara's last question seriously. "Nooooo, I don't think so. He *knew* exactly who you were and everything about you. All about your friends and that you live at the Ritz." She gave a little laugh. "It was almost as if he had *researched* you and came here tonight with the intent of meeting you—"

"Well," Sara said, intrigued, "lead on, by all means! Let us not keep my fan waiting."

Sara recognized him at once although she had only seen photographs of him. Not for a moment did she dream it would be Padraic O'Connor, her own darling Maeve's long absent father!

"Maeve will faint!" were the first words out of her mouth.

Sara thought she might faint herself. Never, but never, had she seen a man so handsome, so *distingué* in his black cutaway. He didn't look like anyone's father. Ageless, she decided, the face so smooth, so perfectly poetically pale. Those eyes—they were so blackish blue they made a girl's heart go pit-a-pat. He *could* be a movie star, she thought. He absolutely exuded raw animal magnetism. One of those very rare men whose very proximity made a woman's body tingle. And besides all that, that brilliant mind!

How could Maeve have gone all these long years without seeing him?

"I'm almost afraid to take you home," she said, as he bent his head to catch her breathless words, as his hand held hers long after Nancy Chartres had made the introduction and drifted off. "The shock of seeing you might be too much for Maeve."

He acknowledged this possibility with the suggestion they keep his presence in Paris a secret from her for a while. Sara would help him break that news to her gently, wouldn't she? And Sara—Sara was thrilled to share a secret with him, to plan this surprise for Maeve. He explained the problem with his daughter. His own sister, Maggie, childless herself, had wanted Maeve for her very own and had poisoned sweet, trusting Maeve against him. Sara was shocked to learn this—Maggie had seemed like such a wonderful, wise woman—but Sara knew and understood what strange things love and the desire of one human being to possess another could do to people. And, of course, she wanted to help him regain the love of his daughter and be instrumental in their reconciliation.

"She needs you," Sara told Padraic. "Poor Maeve, it is so hard for her to find happiness. How terrible that her Aunt Maggie did this to her in the name of love! She has made Maeve so neurotic. We, Chrissy and I, have tried to make Maeve have fun, to make her laugh and enjoy herself but—" She shook her head helplessly.

He smiled into Sara's eyes, his mouth bare inches from hers. "Together we'll do it, won't we, Sara? Exquisite little Sara. . . ."

They walked through the streets of Paris together, hand in hand, exploring the night, each other. Sara had so many questions. Had he come to Paris just to find Maeve and to reconcile with her? Was he writing a new book? Did Paris figure in the book? Had he read Maeve's book, *Sojourn in Paris*? What did she think of it? She just knew that he was *so* proud of her, wasn't he? How did he know that Maeve was in Paris? What was his new book about? Did he think that he and Maeve wrote in the same style?

Sara was so busy asking questions she hardly noticed that Padraic didn't really answer most of them. She was so preoccupied with studying his profile as they walked that she barely noticed that his answers were hardly to the point, so entranced with the *sound* of his voice that she almost didn't hear the words.

By the time dawn came to the Paris streets, Sara was exhausted with the extremity of her emotional response to the father of her friend. She knew almost nothing more than she knew at the beginning of the evening. Yes, he had come to Paris to reconcile with Maeve and it certainly had not been difficult to find her—she and her friends had enough publicity for that. And no, he did not think Maeve's and his own writings were in any way comparable. *His* were experiments in the ex- ploration of the human psyche. Sara did not stop to even ponder what that meant. Even if she had, her sensibilities were too confused to make sense of anything. And it never occurred to her to take anything he said at less than face value.

They stopped for breakfast at a workingman's café. He stared into her eyes, magnetizing her. Would she come back to his hotel with him? She had so bewitched him, he said, that even Maeve and his reconciliation would wait another day. Now, he said, for him there was only Sara. . . .

Sara had sensed the fatal attraction from the moment they had been introduced, had felt the pressing compulsion. Go with him? Oh God! Yes! At this particular moment she was willing to forget for a little while . . . Maeve . . . her own father, everything and everybody . . . for a little while anyway.

Sara didn't come back to the Ritz for three days. Aly might have been the world's greatest lover but he was only a man. Padraic O'Connor was a god. She lay in bed in his room in the little hotel on the Left Bank for all of the three days, getting up only to shower or to eat and drink or sit at the small table in Padraic's dressing gown. She didn't leave the room, not even when he went off for a few hours on his own.

She knew that she had to go back and speak to Maeve; to convince her how wrong Aunt Maggie had been; to tell her that she was the luckiest girl in the world to have such a father. But the truth was that she wasn't ready to share him with Maeve just yet or to think of him as anyone's father. She only wanted to savor him, to stay there and have Padraic come to her, make love to her, kiss her feet, toe by toe, run his lips up her legs, one leg then the other, move his tongue between her thighs, glide it over her belly and into her navel, feel his mouth on her

287

mouth and then on her breasts, up the sides to her armpits, feel that mouth on every inch of skin until she quivered and shook convulsively and couldn't bear it until he inched his organ into her, slowly, oh so languorously, an eighth of an inch at a time, until she screamed and screamed for more . . . screamed for his tongue in her mouth, infinitesimal fractions of inches at a time, and then, oh dear God, yes, in the mouth of her sexual opening, slowly, so slowly that she clawed at him for more. Always, she wanted more. And when she was almost incoherent with the exquisite agony of it, with the ecstacy of it, he would turn her over and start again, beginning at the nape of her neck and working down, tracing her spine delicately with his lover's tongue, over the hills of her buttocks and the delicate flesh that lay beneath her anal orifice, until she begged him to enter there. He transformed her into a wild creature of some far-off plain, shrieking, craving, unbridled, a Circean wanton. When spent, she joyfully cleansed all parts of him with her own lips and tongue, in tribute to his beneficent gifts.

Sara was ready to leave that room only after Padraic told her he wanted to wed her and take her away like a princess to his castle in Ireland on the isle of Aran, where the land and the sea were as wild and unyielding as their love. She buried her face in his chest. Oh, yes, she wanted that. But, of course, they had to see Maeve first. Immediately. And after she and Padraic had convinced Maeve how wrong she had been about her father, after Padraic and Maeve were reunited as father and daughter, how delighted Maeve would be that she, Sara, her beloved friend, and her beloved father had found each other. They must go to Maeve at once!

Since Sara had come to Padraic's hotel room in her ballgown, he went out to buy her something more suitable to wear. In the meantime, Sara showered, brushed her hair, made up her face with the cosmetics she carried in her evening bag. Facing herself in the mirror, she was deluged for a few moments with doubt. She had married Rick Green in haste and what a disaster that had been! But, of course, she had not been intimate with Rick before the marriage, she reassured herself. She could not possibly have known Rick then as she knew Padraic this moment! But what would Maeve say? Would she really be happy to have her marry her father? It *was* really incongruous—she would be Maeve's stepmother. . . . Sara laughed. It was amusing, to be sure. They would all be amused— Maeve, Chrissy, Marlena. Maybe Maeve would even come to stay with them in Ireland. And her mother. Bettina would surely love Ireland. Everybody said how beautiful it was. Green and lovely and full of flowers. They could all be happy together. . . .

She applied mascara to her lashes. She looked a fright without her mascara—her lashes were so light she looked almost lashless. All of a sudden, just for a second, she wondered why a man like Padraic would want *her*? God knows, she laughed, she was no brain and *he* was brilliant! Rick had wanted her money but Padraic was rich, he had oodles of money of his own. Of course she *was* pretty—many people said she was beautiful. But a lot of women were beautiful. What did he see in her, she wondered, that was extra special? But then she sprayed herself with a whiff of perfume. She *was* Sara Gold, *the* Sara Gold, known for her wit and terrific personality, for her style and élan, for that elusive, special *je ne sais quoi*. . . . And why look a gift horse in the mouth?

Padraic came back with a severely plain black dress. What an odd selection for a soon-to-be-bride, Sara thought. He should have bought her a dress wild with color, splashed with glorious flowers—that's how she felt!

"Heavens," she said. "I look like I'm going to a funeral instead of a wonderful reunion!"

On their way to the Ritz, Padraic again warned Sara how set against him Maeve would be, how thorough a job Maggie had done on her until she had really believed him a monster. And he warned her how upset Maeve would be at first to hear that he and Sara were to marry. Sara had to realize that a great part of Maeve's displeasure with him, a great part of her neurotic unhappiness, was caused by an underlying Electra complex that poor sweet Maeve could not even acknowledge to herself.

"Oh," Sara cried. "My poor, darling Maeve. But of course!" It was not surprising at all if she stopped to think about it. The beautiful, glamorous father; the closeness and isolation from the world they had shared; no mother—naturally Maeve had idolized and idealized her father into a lover figure. And not even realizing the full implication of her obsession, she *would* feel guilty and transfer that guilt into anger against the man who had triggered the unnatural feelings within her.

Good heavens, how Maeve must have suffered! No wonder she was afraid of men, afraid of her own sexual feelings. But they, she and Padraic together, would help Maeve. And maybe she really *would* come to Ireland with them. They would be friends, the three of them. Special friends. How wonderful to have her friends and this . . . this magnificent love, too. Who would ever have thought she could be so blessed?

They decided to phone Chrissy to come downstairs to the lobby first, to explain to her what was happening so she would be able to help break the news to Maeve. Chrissy, in a state after having worried about the missing Sara for three days—they had been ready to call the *gendarmes*, for God's sake—came bursting out of the elevator ready to tear into Sara for being so selfish, for letting her friends worry themselves sick about her. She moved toward Sara quickly, until she realized that Sara was waiting with a tall, black-suited, imposing man. And Sara herself was in black. Walking more slowly now, it struck Chrissy how odd they looked together, both in black in the month of June. Vaguely disturbing.

289

As she came closer, Chrissy recognized the man beside Sara and she shivered with some unholy premonition.

He kissed Chrissy's hand and she felt her legs go wobbly under her. So this was Maeve's father, she thought, sitting down because she did not trust her legs to support her. Then Sara and Padraic sat down too. It was all Chrissy could do to look at him. She had always pictured him as some wild Irishman, but he was dressed in an almost Edwardian-cut suit—he appeared so polished and aristocratic and underneath it all he reeked of sexuality. And while her own, poor, weak body could not help but respond, her head nervously recorded that the aura was dangerous, threatening. Now she knew without being told where Sara had been for three days and what she had been doing.

Sara and Padraic repeated their story for Chrissy, told her what had to be done about Maeve and asked for her help. Chrissy was not even surprised to learn that they planned to marry immediately, it was almost a feeling of déjà vu. She looked around at the tableau they presented— the nineteenth-century furnishings of the Ritz's public room, she in her red mandarin lounging gown, Sara in her plain black dress, Padraic in his black suit with the air of the nineteenth century about him.

Padraic gave her his hand to help her rise and Chrissy forced herself to take it. There was *something*—she couldn't put her finger on it— something that attracted and repelled her at the same time. A line from Shakespeare shot through her head, a line she remembered from a literature class. "The devil hath power to assume a pleasing shape." Oh, dear God, she thought, what are we all to do?

Padraic said he would wait in the lobby while Sara and Chrissy went upstairs to Maeve. They would call him after Maeve had been told the news about Sara's and his prospective marriage, after Maeve recognized and accepted that the bad feelings between them had been a misunderstanding, a misunderstanding activated and perpetuated by Maggie.

Padraic went to the men's room to drink from his silver flask. No, he did not have to see Maeve. Everything was proceeding as planned. He had laid out the plot and his characters would fall into line. He closed the flask. There were *so* many ways to skin a cat. He returned to the lobby to wait for Sara to come down again alone.

Chrissy went into Maeve's room while Sara waited in the sitting room of the suite. Chrissy decided she would proceed step by step in order to soften the shock. First she told Maeve that Sara had met Padraic. A cry of anguish escaped Maeve's lips. Then Chrissy told her how Padraic had explained the quarrel between Maeve and him, that it had been manipulated by Aunt Maggie.

"Quarrel?" Maeve gasped. "What kind of a foolish, inadequate word is that?" She closed her eyes in agony. "Oh, Chrissy, you don't know what you're talking about—you just don't know."

"I'm only repeating what Sara has told me. She wants you and your father to make up—"

"Make up?" Maeve whispered. "That is so incongruous— I can't even begin to tell you how— Where is Sara?"

"In the sitting room."

"Tell her to come in here!"

"Try to calm down, Maeve. Please! Before Sara comes in though, there's something else you should know."

Maeve sat on her bed, eyes tightly closed, rocking back and forth, waiting to hear what else Chrissy had to say.

"Sara is going to marry your father."

"Ohhhhh, noooo! No!" Maeve howled like a small creature caught with its foot in a trap. She collapsed on the bed sobbing piteously. She held out an arm for Chrissy. Chrissy ran to the bed and Maeve grabbed her hand and wrung it, tugged on it. "Chrissy, she can't. Chrissy, he's not like other men! Chrissy, I think he's mad!"

Chrissy was surprised to realize she was not even shocked to hear Maeve's words. For whatever reason, she believed Maeve, accepted what she said as fact. Something had to be done. *God, help us, what is there to do?*

"Maeve, whatever you think of him, I think you have to talk to him and to Sara."

"No. I won't! I won't talk to him! He mustn't come here. Chrissy, he mustn't!" Maeve cowered like a craven animal.

Oh, dear Lord, Chrissy thought, anxious now that Maeve would really break down.

"No, Maeve, he won't come in here, I promise. But why don't you talk to Sara alone, without me? You'll be able to talk more openly that way—"

"No, you stay with me. Anything I say to Sara you can hear. Promise me you won't leave."

"I promise." Chrissy wanted to cry. She's even afraid to be alone with Sara, as if Sara's already tainted, as if Sara's already part of him, and both of them are her demonkinds. *Poor Maeve! Poor Sara!* The tears rolled down her cheeks. She couldn't help either of them.

But when Sara came in, ran to the bed, wrapped her arms around Maeve, Chrissy was relieved to see that Maeve did not draw back. They rocked together a few moments and oddly enough, Maeve grew calmer, smoothed Sara's hair, wiped the wet from Sara's cheeks with a corner of the bedsheet and spoke to her quietly.

For Maeve, it was the same conversation all over again, the same one she and her Aunt Maggie had already shared. Maeve listed all of

Padraic's transgressions, one by one, excepting the one that had involved her as well. But it was Sara who played the devil's advocate this time, refuting each transgression as Maeve had once done herself.

"My darling Maeve, can't you see how all these things can be reasonably explained? Aunt Maggie was just sick, sick with jealousy. Padraic understands that. He forgives her."

"He forgives *her?"* Maeve shook her head. "Sara, I cannot tell you how terrible it is for me to sit here and say this about . . . about him. I love him but it is he who is sick. I don't know why or what . . . I don't know if he was born this way or if it's the alcohol or something else that has done this to him, but he is just not right." She couldn't bring herself to say that he was evil. She still didn't know for sure what he was. She just knew that she was frightened of what he could or would do.

"Sara, he's not like any other man you have ever known, not like any other mortal man."

Chrissy watched now, as if in a dream. Both women sat, impossibly calm and said the most unusual things in the most ordinary of voices.

"No, he is not like anybody I have ever known," Sara said. "No one in the world could possibly be on the same plane as Padraic—he is so extraordinary that it is no wonder everyone misunderstands him . . . his sister . . . you . . . his mother."

"His mother?" Maeve said. "He led *her* to her destruction. Haven't you listened to anything I've said? Is the web he's spun around you so thick you can't hear? Isn't it enough that he's blinded you?"

"That's *Maggie's* story . . . that he led his mother to her destruction, darling."

"Aunt Maggie was already dead when he took his mother down to the depot and pushed her, or made her jump, on the tracks—"

"Maeve," Sara said reasonably, "you don't know that. Can't you see that it's all in your head, that you had been preconditioned to believe that—that you've deliberately *let* yourself believe it?"

It was no use. Maeve looked helplessly at Chrissy and Chrissy looked back just as helplessly. Maeve turned her back to Sara. She had to steel herself to tell Sara the final truth, the truth that could set her free. This— the final sacrifice for her friend, the last act of betrayal against *him.*

Chrissy listened in wonder to the incredibly low melodious voice, speaking the incredible words.

"Sara, I had not yet met Aunt Maggie when *he fornicated with me."* She had to use those words to make an impression on Sara. "I was ten years old and he took me and fucked me day after day and I didn't know it was wrong and I loved it and I loved him and he fucked me and fucked me until I was twelve years old and pregnant. . . ."

When the low, incredible words stopped, it was Sara not Maeve who cried, her sobs reaching all the corners of the bedroom.

Finally, Sara choked out words: "My poor darling Maeve, you're so

292

sick with jealousy you don't realize what you're saying. Aunt Maggie's perverted your thinking, and your own sick desire for your father has warped your mind. Maeve, oh Maeve, you cannot have your own father in that way! Don't you know that?"

"You still don't believe me," Maeve said finally, flatly. "Do *you* believe me, Chrissy?"

Speak, goddamn you! Chrissy said to herself, but she could not speak. She was thinking of all the terrible moments in her own life. When they tore her away from her mother in that courtroom. When she learned that her mother was dead and that she would never see her again. When she lay sick in mind and body in her own vomit in the chapel of the school in Montreal and learned that Jacqueline Payot was dead. When they cut her baby out of her in the lotus land of Hollywood. And this moment, in this surrealistic dream of horror, this moment would live on as one of the highlights of all the terrible moments. . . .

Maeve smiled feebly, sickeningly. "I wish I had the baby here—then you'd believe me, wouldn't you? But they had to give my baby away. . . ."

Chrissy ran into the bathroom and retched into the bowl. She tried to hurry it, to get it over with, so she could return to the bedroom; she was afraid of what might happen yet.

Maeve was whispering hoarsely, "I beg you, Sara, don't do this. He is just using you to *revenge himself on me* because I turned away from him!"

Chrissy wiped her mouth. She had to find her voice. For both their sakes. She could not just stand by and let this tragedy happen. "Sara, don't do it! It's wrong. You love Maeve! You have to believe her! If you don't, your marriage will be born of evil!"

Sara looked from Maeve to Chrissy, "I don't believe what I'm hearing: *born of evil!* What incredible shit! I can't believe this whole scene is happening. I find the great love I've been searching for my whole life and you both want to take it from me. I forgive *you*, Maeve. I know how tormented you are and how ill, with this perverted desire for your own father. And we, Padraic and I, want to help you. But *you*, Chrissy? Instead of trying to help poor Maeve with this terrible problem of wanting to fuck her own father, instead of trying to be happy for me, you recite some garbage of your own. How can you believe all the insane drivel that's been spouted here this afternoon? *Do* you believe it? Or are you just jealous too?"

Chrissy said, "I'm not sure what I believe. I *think*, knowing Maeve, I have to believe what she says. All I *know* is that I do have this terrible feeling—call it a premonition—that something terrible will happen if you marry him!"

"I've heard enough," Sara said, weary with anger. "I'm not going to listen to any more of this rot. But I hope you both think about what you said today and I can only hope you think better of it—"

293

She walked out and Chrissy ran after her.

"Sara, what are you going to do?"

"I'm going downstairs and tell Padraic that I've failed. I have not been able to reconcile him with his daughter. He'll be distraught, of course. I'm leaving now. I'll send for my things—" Then she said forlornly, piteously, "I don't even have anybody to stand up for me when we marry. . . ."

"Oh, Sara . . . I will," Chrissy said, feeling terrible for her, feeling terrible for all of them.

Sara tried to be haughty. "Under the circumstances, I don't know if I should let you. And I don't know why you would want to considering—"

Want to? Chrissy tried to grin, to make a final joke. "What are best friends for?"

Chrissy went back into Maeve's room. She was kneeling by the bed, her hands holding a silver rosary, her Aunt Maggie's rosary, intoning in such a low voice that Chrissy could not make out the words. She wondered for whose soul Maeve was praying.

———

At Orly, Maeve and Chrissy had a final drink. "I guess this is the annual reunion," Chrissy said with irony. "Do we drink to our absent members?"

"Chrissy, stand by her. I can't, but perhaps you can."

"I'll stand up for her, as I said I would but . . ." She shook her head. "What will you do, Maeve?"

"I have lots of work to do. It's quiet in Louisburg Square and people don't talk about their emotions."

"But you've left all your papers, your writings. . . ."

"Burn them. That's not the work I was talking about."

Chrissy wanted to object but this wasn't the time.

Chrissy didn't leave until Maeve's plane was a speck in the sky. She thought about the day they had arrived in Paris, laughing and excited, thinking they owned the world. *Yeah, our hearts were young and gay.* Today, she felt a hundred years old. And it wasn't over yet. She still had to watch Sara be married. And she had never gotten up the courage to ask Maeve what she so desperately wanted to know. What had happened to Maeve's baby? Where was it?

———

The wedding was a civil one. The bride wore beige silk, the matron of honor, yellow silk, the groom, black. There were no other guests. They had lunch at the Tour d'Argent overlooking the Seine and Notre

294

Dame. The bride ordered *poulet farci Parisienne* and ate nothing. The matron of honor ordered *l'estouffat de boeuf* and ate two bites. The groom ordered only a pear with *bleu de Bresse* and *velours au chocolat* and ate it all.

He drank one glass of cognac and no more, spoke only a few words, smiled agreeably with a degree of cool detachment. But when Sara urged Chrissy to come with them for a little while, at least, to Ireland, he joined in the invitation warmly. He refilled Chrissy's glass with the champagne he had ordered and not drunk and focused his eyes upon her compellingly. She forced herself to tear her eyes away from his and back to her glass, which she held with a trembling hand. No, much as she would have wanted to go along just to keep watch over Sara, she could not. She could not trust herself.

Between them, Chrissy and Sara drank two bottles of champagne. When Sara became sick, Chrissy escorted her to the powder room and, sitting on the tiled floor in their wedding finery, Chrissy held Sara's head as she emptied herself into the bidet. They thought this was very funny, even as Sara retched. They were quite drunk.

"Hey, Sara, I thought you were going to marry only Jewish cocks."

"I did that once. Look at what it got me—a knife in the belly." And they laughed some more.

"Oh, Chrissy, do come with us to Aran. Please."

Chrissy stopped laughing. "I can't do that. There's something . . . there's somewhere else I have to go. Oh yes, I remember. I have to go home."

Sara was finished. She wiped daintily at her mouth with her lace wedding handkerchief. "Where is that, Chrissy. Where is home?" she asked, cocking her head.

"You once told me, Sara. You told me home is where the heart is."

IRELAND/BOSTON/NEW YORK
1950-1951

1.

They spent two days in Galway and the surrounding countryside waiting for one of the *currachs,* the wicker-worked and tarred canvas boats, to take them to their home on Inishmore, one of the islands of Aran. Being Sara, she had found Galway and Donegal and the stone-walled roads of Connaught primitive but charming nevertheless—the rose-covered, moss-thatched cottages, the donkey carts on the roads, the old women wrapped in black shawls, a picturesque band of wandering tinkers in their horse-drawn caravan wagon. The glimpses of wonderful ancient castles filled her heart with romantic anticipation—hers, she fantasized, must be even more magnificent. She tripped about on her high heels in a white silk shirtwaist dress and breathed the soft, moist, wonderful Irish air; gazed at the evening sky dressed in the loveliest shades of red, pink, and yellow; wondered at Padraic's profile so clean and sharp and inspiringly heroic, and felt as if she were in Wonderland and her name was Alice.

In Galway's central square, she saw the statue of the famous Gaelic storyteller, Padraic O Conaire. "Why, that's your name! Isn't it wonderful? It has to be you! Of course it's you!" Padraic looked at the little leprechaun figure sitting on his pile of rocks and laughed. "Is that the way you see me?"

Since they had first met, Sara had seen Padraic drink very little and she presumed that the drinking Maeve had spoken of was just one more malevolent lie they told about him. But once they had left Paris, she saw the first signs of dedicated drinking, unobtrusive to be sure, from a silver flask he carried in an inner pocket. *When* he managed to refill it, she didn't know, but refill it he must have. She smiled at him as their eyes met over his flask at one point and she didn't speak, but a little pinpoint of worry flashed through her brain. She had seen what liquor could do to a person and, besides, *his* eyes were no longer smiling when they met hers—they had darkened like the Irish sky had. It had been bright and sunlit one moment, brooding the next.

She managed to get into the *currach* unaided since neither Padraic nor the boatman came to her aid. The boatman, in a dirty white sweater of undyed wool with a strange design woven into it, was sullen. He spoke a few words in Gaelic to Padraic, who answered him in kind. Padraic seemed to have forgotten she was there. He stared out to sea, which had turned gray and then black.

It started to rain again, that peculiar Irish rain that came and went. Out at sea, it was a cold rain, even though it was summer. "Where is our luggage?" Sara asked suddenly, hugging herself. "I need something, a sweater, a coat."

"Here." Padraic picked up a black shawl lying on the bottom of the boat and tossed it to her. "I wouldn't worry about your luggage, it will come . . . piecemeal." He laughed. "But you won't be needing too much of it, so I wouldn't be disturbed."

Sara wrapped herself in the smelly black cloth, grimacing. Of course she would need her wardrobe. Wouldn't they be entertaining in their castle? What wonderful parties they could have, transporting guests from the charming Galway harbor over to their island in these cunning little boats? She tried to overcome her nausea from the stench of the shawl and the motion of the dipping boat, smiled brightly at the sour-faced dour fisherman. "Your sweater is so beautiful. I know it is handmade. Does the design have any special significance?"

"*Ni thuigim,*" was the curt reply.

Sara looked bewildered.

"He speaks only the Irish," Padraic said, smiling a bit at Sara's discomfiture. "He said, 'I don't understand.' As for the sweater, it serves two purposes. One, obviously, is to keep him warm. It is made of the Aran unbleached wool, *bainin,* impregnated with oils to make it warmer, weather-repellant to withstand the wind, the driving rain and the cold. Life here is hard and the seas are violent, vicious, shark-infested, and the *currach* is small, as you can see, and fragile and"—Padraic laughed— "these men do not know how to swim. The design worked into the wool is the sweater's second purpose. It stands for his family name, making the identification of his body easier. . . ."

Neither did she know how to swim. The wind blew and the rain came down even harder, driving, as Padraic had just said. The sky was as dark as the cloak Padraic had placed about his shoulders, blowing about him, as he stood tall, facing the swirling waters. Despite the shawl, a cold chill ran through Sara's body.

Sara would never forget her first view of the bleak rocks of the island that would be her home. The great walls of stone rising out of the water;

the rocky, windswept terrain; the sky, so blue on the mainland and now sullenly gray; the waves breaking so pitilessly against the inhospitable shore. So bleak, so bare, so terribly bare.

Where were the Irish roses? Where was all the beautiful green Ireland was so famous for?

"Where has all the green gone?" she asked, stricken.

Padraic drank from the silver flask, and this time wiped his mouth inelegantly with the back of his hand. He sang in a sweet Irish tenor:

"Oh, Sara dear, and did ye hear the news that's going round?
The shamrock is by law forbid to grow on Irish ground.
No more Saint Padraic's Day we'll keep, his color can't be seen
For there's a cruel law ag'in the Wearin' o the Green . . ."

Sara had no realization at that moment that the street song that had become an anthem was a political song, and not a comment on the land of Aran.

She looked down at her useless high-heeled summer sandals. How would she walk over those sharp rocks with them? Black, mascaraed tears ran down her pink cheeks. Why hadn't Padraic told her that she would need other shoes?

"Where is the castle? Is it very far?"

She was tired and dispirited—what she needed was to take off her shoes and her ruined silk dress, to soak in a lovely hot bath brimming with scented bubbles, to sip at a martini with two olives, very dry and very cold, to eat a delicious supper sitting across from her lover-husband, who obviously needed a hot bath and a cold martini too, to restore his mood.

Padraic smiled. "Oh, it's not that far at all. Up the cliff there."

Sara looked up and saw only a wrecked ruin of what appeared to be some ancient fort. Down below, around them, were low cottages that appeared to be no more than two rooms at best, really no better than huts.

"All I see up here is that stone ruin."

"That's a prehistoric fort. Our castle is behind the fort. You can't see it from here." He extended his hand. "Come, my pretty, let me help you."

Gratefully, Sara took his hand, smiled up into his face. Really, she must try to be a good sport and not ruin everything with her whining. It was Maeve who said she was forever whining.

It had stopped raining and as Sara made her way, tripping and stumbling on the stony earth, Padraic impatiently pulling on her arm, she saw the inhabitants of the island busy with their daily routine—a few children walking with a little cart piled with peat, men cleaning fish, black-shawl-wrapped women knitting outside their limestone cottages. Though it was late evening, there was still light, a strange unearthly light here in the summer of Aran. She saw a whitewashed building, larger than the other houses, saw the cross.

Suddenly, a terrible thought came to Sara. Where were the telephone poles? And the wires for electricity? All she saw was a bareness. Afraid to ask Padraic, afraid to hear his answer, she thought despairingly of her hair dryer, her phonograph, her radio, her darling, brand-new custom-made television set. All throughout America people were watching Ed Sullivan and *she,* who had practically been an intimate of Ed and Sylvia's, *she* was here on some godforsaken island amongst a band of half-savages.

But then she looked at Padraic silhouetted against the mountainside and comforted herself. Who would have time for Ed Sullivan, anyway? They, she and her beautiful new husband, had better, lovelier things to do.

They had finally reached the top of the cliff that overlooked the sea. Now all that remained was to circle the fort. Sara tried to hurry, impatient to catch a glimpse of their home, to get inside and take her bath, to lie down. She was physically and emotionally spent and she hoped that Padraic had a competent housekeeper who would have everything ready —a fire going in all the fireplaces, and whatever they used for illumination in this wilderness lit. Candles, probably. Candles would be nice. How romantic! she sighed.

"Look down." Padraic held her shoulders fast. "Did you ever see such a sight in your sightless life?"

"What are you talking about? What sightless life?"

He smiled enigmatically. "I meant—did you ever see such a sea?"

Sara pulled back. It just struck her. She had seen only children here, and weatherbeaten old men and worn-out old women gnarled with time. Where were the young and the lovely romantics? The young women and men? Where, for that matter, were the middle-aged?

Where was the castle? Sara wondered. Had it disappeared along with the green grass and the pink roses? Having circled the fort, all Sara saw were more heaps of stone and piles of rocks, and one hut standing in the shadow of the ruin. She turned to Padraic, the question almost on her lips, her nose twitching with emotion, and more tears welling in her eyes.

"Welcome to O'Connor Castle, me darling," Padraic laughed. And laughed and laughed.

"All right," Sara said, gazing at the dismal hut. "Where is the goddamn castle?"

What kind of a rotten joke was this? Didn't he realize she was too tired for jokes?

"You've had your laugh, but where are we going to spend the night?

If you tell me I have to turn around, walk back down that cliff, and make my way through that village; and then take another ride in that miserable little boat, I'm going to spit in your eye." She forced a smile. God knows she didn't want anyone to think she wasn't a good sport, especially her new husband.

Padraic seemed hurt. "I'd be hoping you'd be pretending it was a castle for the few days we're going to be here. This is our honeymoon cottage, Sara, me love. I can't be believing that you don't want to spend a few days here—here in this splendid isolation. With no one around but the natives who don't, *or won't*"—he laughed—"speak the King's English. I would have thought for sure you'd be welcoming this chance for us to be completely alone with no one about to spoil our lovemaking."

Sara was embarrassed . . . ashamed to be found so wanting in romantic spirit. *Of course* she wanted to be alone with him! She threw her arms around him. She assured him she was thrilled to be here on this fascinating island with him. It was just that . . . well . . . she *had* been expecting a castle, charmingly old but with hot and cold running water and all the amenities.

They went inside the two-room cottage that had only an earthen floor. Sara was still puzzled. "Do you . . . have you lived here?"

"Yes."

"And the castle you spoke of?"

"It exists."

"Where?" Sara persisted.

"In the mountain country outside of Dublin."

"And you really live there? And only come here occasionally?"

"Something like that."

"Where do you really make your home?"

"Wherever I hang my hat." He went to a shelf and removed a bottle of whiskey. "Do you plan to be asking questions or are you going to be having a drink with your husband?"

Sara laughed shortly. "I *was* planning on having a bath but I guess I'll be having a drink with my husband."

"That's better thinking, me love."

He toasted her and they drank. She thought that the brogue Padraic had assumed since they had arrived in Ireland was very cute, but she hoped that he wouldn't keep it up for too long. She could foresee that it might become tiresome. Padraic poured her another and she drank that too. Actually, she was thinking more of food than of whiskey, but she did not want to say anything to spoil the mood. After they drank they made love and then Sara did not think of anything except the loving itself.

She awoke in the middle of the night to find the place next to her in the bed, empty. She went into the room that served as a combination kitchen and living room and found Padraic staring into the peat fire. He turned and looked at her naked form and said, "Why is your hair the color of buttercups?"

Another joke? Sara laughed uneasily, seeing the bottle at his side. "What color would you want it?"

"The hue of the setting sun when for a few rare minutes it breaks into flame."

Sara stared at him for a few seconds then went back to bed.

She got up the next morning to find the room flooded with sunlight. And she heard whistling from the other room, a soft melodic tune. Oh, today was a summer day after all. She jumped out of bed and ran to the doorway. Padraic, dressed like an Aranian fisherman himself, was pouring water from a huge kettle into an oversized washtub. He looked up and smiled at her, a huge smile as sunny as the day itself. "Is it a **bath** you'll be taking, my bonny bride? Here it is, all ready for you to be gracing it."

He had heated the water himself! Now, he soaped and washed her and kissed her every inch. Then, wrapping her in a large sheet of toweling, he carried her back to bed. How could she have doubted him? Not that she had really doubted him exactly, but yesterday had held a few bad moments for her. But they were gone, past now . . . now, was only love.

He gave her a handwoven dress to wear and the island-made moccasins of leather tanned by the natives themselves, and sat her down to the breakfast of fish he had cooked himself in the open fireplace. The bread, he confessed, had been baked by one of the village women.

"Now what will you be thinking of your honeymoon?" he asked, clearing away the dishes as she sat and watched him.

"A honeymoon fit for a princess," Sara sighed with satisfaction.

2.

Maeve called me as soon as she arrived in Boston. I could tell from the tone of her voice over the telephone that she had bad news to tell me. I already knew, of course, that Sara was married. Sara had called me from Paris to say that she was getting married and had called her mother, too. But that's all Sara had said. That she was very happy and that Maeve's father, Padraic, was just *too-too* to even describe over the trans-Atlantic wires. Of course, I had noticed that Sara did not bubble as much as one would expect from Sara, considering she was getting married. She had not talked about Maeve or Chrissy, only said they would be coming home. And it was only after she had hung up that I realized that she hadn't asked me about Peter or my law school, which really wasn't like Sara at all. But I put that down to premarriage excitement and figured that I would be hearing from her again soon.

"So now you know everything, Marlena," Maeve said. "Or as much as I know, anyhow. I guess Chrissy will be arriving in New York in a few days and she'll have a little more to tell us. About the wedding, anyway."

I was speechless. I had cried through Maeve's terrible story but now I was dry-eyed, voiceless, and more worried than I had ever been in my life.

"There's nothing we can do," Maeve said. "Just hope that Sara sees that she's made this awful mistake before it's too late."

Before it's too late. . . . God, that had an ominous sound!

"And I wouldn't say anything to Sara's mother about what I've told you. There's just no sense in worrying her before she guesses something is terribly wrong. . . ." And Maeve burst out crying now. I tried to console her and we hugged each other. I had been thinking only of Sara. Now I first realized how terrible all this was for Maeve. My God! Poor Maeve! How *she* had suffered! I promised I would say nothing to Aunt Bettina. And not only for Aunt Bettina's sake, for Maeve's too. She had bared her soul and the whole world didn't have to know her secrets.

It was hard for me to leave Maeve alone in that house on Louisburg Square. She seemed so alone now. I promised I would come back soon.

"And make sure you bring Peter with you," Maeve said. "I'm just dying to meet him!" She smiled at me through her tears.

I went off to see Peter. I had to tell him everything. I knew he would offer me comfort. Poor Maeve, I thought again. Who would offer her comfort? God, she was valiant!

Maeve took charge of the Abbott and O'Connor philanthropies. The administration of the museum, although she appreciated its beauty and obvious worth, did not really interest her. It was well supervised and getting along quite well without her. It was the children's hospital and the two homes, the one for the aged and the one for young girls, that needed attention and loving care to function at their best. Those were the places to which families in despair turned for the basic requirements of life. But as she went about these institutions, she saw a need that wasn't being answered. There were not enough facilities to help those in need of guidance in the area of mental health, the one field that interested her most. She could set up a mental health clinic, a family-oriented

302

facility where all the members of a troubled family could get the help they needed.

Was it too vast an undertaking for her? she wondered. Was she too young? Too inexperienced? She had never finished her nurse's training. Even if she had, it still would have been inadequate and irrelevant to heading a project of such scope. But still, she *could* get all the help she needed: experts, psychologists, sociologists, administrative people. Money was really all it took. Money and the desire. She had the money, so much more money than she needed or could ever need. The poor people of Boston needed this kind of facility, and she—she needed such a project of her own. She had to do something really worthwhile and she had to busy herself so that she wouldn't think of Sara—Sara, so pretty and clever and giving, always ready with an answer to everyone's little problems, laughing all the way. Maeve hoped that Sara had finally learned to swim—she was so far out of her depth in deep, murky water.

———

Chrissy moved back into Sara's house, staffed it, set up a studio and tried to settle down to work. Work was what she needed—she had had enough of the social life, enough of men to last her a lifetime. That's how she felt at the moment, anyway. But she found it difficult to relax, to work in Sara's house. The house did not feel like a home. Perhaps she should redecorate? Was it the ghosts that haunted the house that made her restless? Bettina and Maurice Gold? Rick Green and the debacle of his and Sara's marriage? Those three young, innocent debs? Had they ever been young? Only in their early twenties and, God, the things they had lived through! Had any one of them ever been really innocent?

But she couldn't redecorate the house without Sara's permission. Maybe Sara preferred everything as it was—a reminder of the days when she and her parents had been together, before her mother had been sick. She would write to Sara. She would have loved to call her—it would really be super to talk to Sara, see how she was doing, but there were no phones at O'Connor Castle.

She had gotten that one letter from Sara, that very formal letter that did not sound at all like Sara. And it was typed. Who had typed it? A secretary? Padraic? Chrissy knew that it wasn't Sara because Sara did not know how to type and this typing was too even, too perfect. Maeve had also received a letter from Sara, perfectly typed as well, but hardly formal in tone.

Maeve had called Chrissy the day she received it, terribly upset, and no wonder. It had been almost a dissertation in pornography, so vividly and graphically had Sara described the O'Connors' lovemaking. Chrissy had not even heard some of the words before. Some words Maeve knew because she was somewhat familiar with Middle English, but that was strange in itself—Sara who had written them, wouldn't have been. But most of the words were the four- and five-letter ones known the world over, and a host of others of all lengths, grotesqueries that made one's skin crawl.

"The thing is," Maeve said, "Sara never talked like that. She never used such words. Oh, once in a while, maybe, a dirty word, deliberately just to shock me—but *this!*"

"I think we have to accept the fact that Sara didn't write the letter," Chrissy said.

"No, I don't think she did," Maeve said.

No, she didn't. He did. To torture me.

Chrissy never wrote the letter asking permission to redecorate Sara's house. Under the circumstances it seemed rather ridiculous. Anyhow, it was time she had a place of her own, she decided. A new place without ghosts. There was no reason she shouldn't have her own home. The newspapers called her one of the richest girls in America, which was really amusing. Sara and Maeve had far more money than she, only, of course, less publicity.

She bought a co-op on Park Avenue in a newly built house, not far from the Marlowe Museum of Art, which had been Grandmother Marlowe's great house. Well, she thought, the apple doesn't fall far from the tree. Thinking herself very witty, she only wished she could have said it to Maeve or Sara. It was no fun making funny comments to oneself.

She settled down to work in earnest. Fresh from Paris, she was very much enamored of the Impressionists and of Manet in particular.

3.

The first few weeks passed for Sara in a confusing, ever-changing pattern of idyllic lovemaking and bewildering rejection, of an entertaining Padraic and the moody poet. But each time she began to resent the moody poet, the curt words, the abysmal silences, the drink-inspired harsh words, the charming Padraic seemed to sense it and managed to emerge, making love to her, beguiling her with fancy words. It did seem strange that he had so many faces. In Paris he had been elegant and eloquent, with Continental manners. Here in Ireland, he was alternately blarney-country Irish complete with brogue, or the dour Celt with nothing save bitter words. But fresh from her bed of love, Sara supposed that this was what made her husband so fascinating, for fascinating he was. Some days even passed that she didn't ask Padraic when were they leaving the island where the weather changed as often as Padraic's mood.

4.

Once Maeve decided to go through with establishing her O'Connor Mental Health Clinic, she thought of nothing else. She had to find the right piece of property, build the plant, and then search out the right people to staff it. But first, came the funding. One didn't have to be an expert to figure that out.

She consulted her attorneys, her advisers.

"But hardly anyone funds an enormous undertaking of this sort by oneself. The thing to do is start out with your own contribution then seek out other money. We would have some names for you. And there's your family—the Abbotts, other members of the Boston community. You have to talk to people, they'll contribute and send you to other people who will contribute."

"No, that could drag out forever. I want to move on this quickly. I'm prepared to give all the money needed to get this going by myself."

"Have you talked with your uncles about this, Miss O'Connor?"

"My granduncles," she corrected. "No, and I don't have to. The money is mine and I don't have to consult anyone. Just tell me what has to be done and help me do it."

Respectable and respectful gentlemen all, the lawyers saw no further reason to argue with this young lady of such obvious will and determination.

"Very well. There are two initial steps. First, you will need to establish a fund for the immediate implementation of the clinic. Then you will have to set up a foundation to maintain its support. As for the foundation, there are two ways to do that. We can include your mental health clinic in the existing foundation that supports the O'Connor Hospital for Children, the O'Connor Home for Girls, and the Abbott Home for the Aged. Or, we can set up an independent foundation for the clinic alone, as your aunt did for the Home for Special Children in New York."

"The Home for Special Children in New York? I'm not familiar with—"

The men smiled speciously. Miss O'Connor was obviously not as well-informed as she pretended. She had not done her homework properly.

305

"You've had all the documents on that particular philanthropy of your aunt's, Miss O'Connor, along with the documents on the other homes and the hospital and the museum. You've had the budget for the home submitted to you along with the other budgets. Granted, your aunt did not wish to associate her name with the home, indeed her uncles and her cousins are in complete ignorance of its existence, but we have not withheld any information from you, its trustee," Mr. Carraway was pleased to inform her.

She was guilty and they had found her out. She had not read through the small mountain of papers they had continually sent her. She could not fault Carraway, Carraway and Stans in any way.

Why had her aunt set up a Home for Special Children in New York? Why had she kept its existence secret from the general public and from the Abbotts? From her niece to whom she had entrusted the welfare of all the other institutions? It was all becoming too clear and her heart beat rapidly, as fast as the thoughts churned through her head.

"When did my aunt establish the Home for Special Children?"

"In the fall of 1940."

Of course. Only, Aunt Maggie had overlooked one detail. She had failed to realize that once she died and Maeve took over, she, Maeve, would learn of the home's existence.

Maeve's body was completely drenched with perspiration. She put her hands to her head, smoothing her hair, at the same time trying to smooth out the thoughts that whirled within her brain crazily.

"Excuse me, gentlemen. We'll discuss this further next time. I'd like to study up on the home in New York before we proceed. I want to thank you all, you've been most . . . helpful . . . cooperative."

She searched for her car on the street. She had forgotten where she had parked it. She ran up and down Beacon, then remembered that she had parked it on a side street. Finally, she sighted the red Thunderbird, a product of Detroit. Aunt Maggie, who always worried about the mills of Massachusetts and the employment of its workers, as well as all American laborers, had always said it was important to buy American, and, when feasible, Massachusetts-made products.

And babies, Aunt Maggie? What do we do with our unwanted Massachusetts-born babies? Do we export them out of the state?

It was a house in the Gramercy Park section of New York, a neat, red-brick building, with two small trees planted in front, a nice, respectable town house of which no one had to be ashamed. Only a small discreet brass plate carried the words—the New York Home for Special Children. Not for children who were especially bright, especially gifted, or especially talented. A home for children who had special needs generated by special problems, problems visited upon them by a malevolent society, or a wrathful God.

306

Maeve had been so sure that her baby was here she had not even gone home to change her clothes. She had just gotten into the Thunderbird and started driving, stopping only once for gas and to call the home that they should expect her that afternoon, that the benefactor was coming to visit the benefited.

She had thought about nothing else driving down from Boston. How blind she had been not to realize that her baby had probably not been placed out for adoption—that it was almost a foregone conclusion that her child had not been born normal. She could not even plead ignorance. Yes, when she had first given birth, she had been a disturbed child herself. But afterwards, when she grew more knowledgeable, when she was in nurse's training—how could she have not discerned the truth? All those years. . . . But Aunt Maggie knew that the baby would have little chance of being born normal. She had been efficient—setting up the home. And she must have reasoned that if, by some special dispensation from the Lord, little Sally turned out to be an ordinary little girl, other arrangements would be possible later on.

Maeve understood that if it had turned out that way . . . if Sally had turned out perfect in every way . . . if by some miracle, she had been unscathed by the misfortune of her conception, she would *not* be beyond that neat, shiny black door with the shiny polished knocker.

Maeve forced herself to walk up the three short steps, to rap the knocker three times. A woman wearing wire-rimmed spectacles, a brown sweater and a long tweed skirt, answered the door, looking askance at the disheveled young woman with a mass of red hair that obviously had been wind-tossed for hours.

Maeve introduced herself and shook the woman's limp hand briskly. It took all the control in the world not to yell, "Show me your files! Show me your children!" as she politely requested the records. They went into the office and Miss Whittaker asked, "Are you sure you wouldn't rather look around first? See the children? Speak to some of our therapists?"

"Subsequently, Miss Whittaker, subsequently."

Maeve traced her finger down the list of children who were in residence at the home at present. There was no Sally anything! She closed her eyes. She didn't know if the weakness she felt was relief or disappointment. Was she so terrible a mother that she'd rather see her child deformed in some fashion than not see her at all?

Miss Whittaker, taking further note of Maeve O'Connor's distraught state, asked if she would like a cup of tea.

"No, thank you. I'm fine. Now I would like to see the list of the children that were here in the home but left, for whatever reason."

"Certainly. There are *always* children who return to their real home.

That is our purpose, after all, to help these children lead normal lives, as much as possible—"

"Of course, I understand that. And there *are* children who leave here to be placed in adoptive homes, are there not?" Maeve asked.

"In certain cases, yes. We place children in foster homes if their natural home is not considered beneficial, or if the natural parents are reluctant to have them back." She smiled. "There are many adoptive or foster parents who will take children who are not completely . . . adjusted. Many of our children, while not exactly what the lay person would consider normal, are very sweet and loving."

"I'm sure, Miss Whittaker." She took the second list Miss Whittaker finally handed her. "What particularly interests me"—Maeve strove to choose her words carefully—"is the child placed here, say as an infant, who is presumed . . . abnormal in some way . . . and then turns out to be perfectly normal. What happens to that child?"

"In my particular experience that particular problem hasn't arisen. Of course, I myself have not been here at the home that long."

"I see." Maeve scanned the list of the children who had left, for whatever reason, looking for the name Sally. Maeve could not even guess at what last name had been given her daughter, though she doubted very much if Aunt Maggie had used the O'Connor or Abbott names.

No, she could not find any Sallys. No Sally had come here, been found normal, and then been given out for adoption. Disappointment flooded her body.

She sat down now, trying to pull her thoughts together, to think what to do next, to try to control her shaking legs. All along she had been indulging in a fantasy—Baby Sally had come here, been found to be not only perfectly normal but well above average, had been placed in a perfectly wonderful home and then she, Maeve, visited there on some pretext. She did not reveal herself as the mother but became Sally's fairy godmother who saw her every day and brought her presents, and whom Sally adored.

"Is there some child you're particularly interested in?" Miss Whittaker asked. "Perhaps—"

"There was a child in whom my aunt took a special interest. I have no idea why—but she asked that I check on her from time to time. But I thought my aunt said her name was Sally," Maeve mumbled. "I don't see that name on your lists."

"Perhaps your aunt was wrong . . . about the name. Or you didn't hear her correctly? There *is* a way to check this out properly. If you will allow me. If you had told me before—well, no matter. Do you know the year the child came here?"

"Yes," Maeve muttered. "1940. She was an infant at the time."

"We can only accommodate twenty children at any one time, so it

308

is not too difficult to check out. And half of the children who come to us, stay on . . . so you see, we don't have that much of a turnover."

She pulled out some more files. "Let's see what we have here," she said, and hummed as she read. "A girl child. Infant in 1940. About ten or eleven now—" the woman looked at Maeve speculatively.

She's wondering if it's my child, Maeve thought. But she'll abandon that theory, thinking I'm too young. She'll probably come to the conclusion that the baby I'm looking for was Aunt Maggie's illegitimate child.

"We have three girls here right now who fall into that age group—"

"Let me see them—" Maeve jumped up.

"Please, Miss O'Connor. Let's check the records first. In 1940, we had . . . *four* girl children who were in their first year of life—that's quite a few, considering. . . ."

"Yes . . ."

"Of those four"—Miss Whittaker stopped to adjust her glasses—"one left two years later. The parents moved to Minnesota and they took the child with them. And then another of those original four . . ." She paused again.

"Yes?" Maeve prompted. For God's sake, was this woman deliberately trying to torture her?

". . . was adopted in 1945. That was just before I came here. The child had made remarkable progress while she was here."

"You mean she was cured? Normal? What?"

"It seems she had been physically handicapped and—"

"What was her name?" Maeve demanded.

Miss Whittaker hesitated. She couldn't very well withhold information from this O'Connor woman, although it was highly irregular. "Joanne Watt. Her mother married, it seems, *after* the baby was placed with us and then, later, when the child was ready to be placed in a family situation, the real mother simply didn't want her."

No, Joanne Watt couldn't be her Sally. But Maeve was glad that she had found a home where she was wanted.

"We work with other agencies, you understand, in cases like this. We feel that an important part of our work is to—"

"And the other two?" Maeve cut her off. "The remaining two who came here in 1940? Are they still here? Are they two of the three girls that you said were here now?"

Miss Whittaker studied the records further. Maeve could not control herself any longer. "Are they or aren't they, Miss Whittaker?"

"Yes, they are. But both are listed as having parents unknown so their names would necessarily be made up. Alice Hart and Jane Pearce."

"Red hair . . ." Maeve mumbled.

"I beg your pardon?"

Maeve tried not to scream. "Is one of them red-haired?"

Miss Whittaker glanced at Maeve's own wild hair but Maeve no longer cared. "My aunt said the baby had red hair!"

"No, I'm afraid not," Miss Whittaker said now, almost kindly.

"I want to see them, the two girls."

"Of course." She checked her wristwatch. "It's getting near our dinner hour so this is our quiet playtime. We like the children to settle down before they eat. Will you follow me?"

Maeve walked beside Miss Whittaker, but without hope. In a large, pleasant room a few children of different ages sat at a table with an assortment of playthings laid out. One tall boy, an adolescent, banged on a wall with a stick while a young man spoke to him quietly. One group sat on the floor being read to and another group was listening to a record on a phonograph.

"We try not to categorize the children by—" but Maeve was not listening. Sitting at the table, pushing around colored cut-out letters, unsmiling, was *her child, her daughter, her baby, her beautiful girl.* Maeve raised her hand, speechless. She tried to find her voice but nothing came out. She wanted to run over to the unsmiling child, to snatch her up and run with her, out of the home, away somewhere to some magic place, where everything would be all right, where everything would come out differently.

"Are you all right, Miss O'Connor?" Miss Whittaker asked.

"That little girl, the one with the black curls—she's one of the two you mentioned, isn't she?" Maeve's voice was hoarse with emotion.

"Yes, that's Alice." Miss Whittaker looked at Maeve curiously. "But certainly she isn't the child you were looking for? She doesn't have red hair, after all. . . ."

Oh, I recognize her. There's no mistaking her. She's the picture of her father, you see. It's just that Aunt Maggie lied—lied about the name, lied about the red hair. She must have called her Alice after her grandmother.

"I must . . . I mean I'd like to see Alice . . . please. Alone."

"We call her Ali . . . that's what she calls herself. When she speaks, that is. It is not unusual for these children to refer to themselves in the third person."

"I want to see her alone, Miss Whittaker. Right away!" She heard her own voice. Too loud. Too harsh. Too demanding. But what was she to do with this woman?

She forced herself to smile. Her whole body ached, her arms. She had to take Ali into her arms and hold her close, to rock her and croon to her.

"Very well. We have a visitor's room for those children who have parents who come to see them." She snorted. "You would be surprised how many don't come at all."

310

Maeve would not be surprised at all. Poor baby Ali. She had never had a parent visit before. She had had no one at all. She bit her lips to keep from crying.

"If you'll come with me. And then I'll bring Ali to you. But please, Miss O'Connor, will you remember that we don't *ever* treat our children with an excess of emotionalism. Especially Ali . . ."

"Why especially Ali?"

"While we do not classify Ali as autistic—she does speak . . . a little . . . she is withdrawn—a not uncommon reaction to her . . ." She groped for a word that Maeve would relate to.

Maeve had no more patience. "I understand—"

Finally she was shown into a small sitting room furnished with a couch and two armchairs, and after several minutes, Ali was at last brought in.

"This is Miss O'Connor, Ali. She wants to be your friend. Would you like to shake hands with Miss O'Connor?" Then to Maeve, "Offer your hand."

Maeve desperately wanted to scoop Ali up into her arms. But she restrained herself, stooped down and held out her hand. "Hello, Ali." *Hello, love.* Ali looked at her, unmoving, unsmiling, did not put her hand in Maeve's.

She had to get rid of that woman. "Maybe she'll shake hands later," Maeve said, and waited frantically for Miss Whittaker to leave. Finally, hesitating, she did so.

What does she think I'm up to? Kidnapping?

Oh God! Would that she could!

Slowly, she picked Ali up in her arms. *Oh God!* It was at once the most exquisite moment in her life and the saddest. Little Ali was ten years old but it seemed that she weighed nothing at all. Maeve felt as if she were holding a babe in her arms. She sat down, cuddling Ali, looked into her eyes. Oh yes, his eyes. But yet not his eyes. Blue as the sky, Maeve thought.

"My name is Maeve, Ali. Can you say that?"

Ali looked back at her and Maeve could swear she saw a sad intelligence in those blue eyes.

"Oh, Ali, Ali, I love you."

She rocked her. "Rock-a-bye baby, in the tree top. . . ."

Oh, she had brought no presents with her. She could cry at her oversight. She had never given this child, her child, *anything.* She ground her teeth in agony. Nothing but misfortune and this empty life. Oh, God, you've been cruel! She hunted in her bag for something to give her baby, something that might bring a smile to her solemn face. A shiny coin? No, what would that mean to a child who never left this house or the garden behind it, who didn't know you could buy a candy bar with a

311

silver coin. Maeve took off her pearls. They had been Aunt Maggie's. Maybe they would bring a smile to Ali's face?

Ali didn't smile, but she did dangle the rope of beads.

"Oh, if I could take you home, Ali, I would get you to smile, I just know I would. I would play with you all day long and tell you stories and sing to you. . . ."

"Play," Ali said, "Ali play."

Maeve wanted to scream with joy. There, she had said a word, two words. Oh, if she could only take her home she could teach her . . . love her . . . love could work miracles! But how could she? To what would she be exposing Ali? All anyone had to do was look at her to know whose child she was. She didn't care about herself. Let them all go to blazes! Even Maggie. Maggie had let her give birth to this beautiful, helpless, *sick* baby—knowing that she wouldn't be normal—in the name of her Church! How could she, Maeve, ever forgive that?

Driving down from Boston and thinking all the while, it had not occurred to her to blame Maggie. But now, holding her marked child, she damned her. And him! And herself! What a terrible fool she had been, holding on for dear life to that small piece of him that she had loved and wanted, in spite of everything! Never before had such a bitterness washed through her, the bile of it was in her mouth and she was sick with it!

She hugged the girl to her fiercely and kissed her face, her eyes, her hair. Ali looked at her with *something* in those eyes, Maeve could swear it. Oh, Ali, Ali, Ali! Would that I could take you with me, to hold you and hug you and kiss you every day, every hour. But she couldn't. She couldn't let the world know she existed. If the world knew Padraic would know and come for her.

"I love you, Ali. And now that I have found you, I will never leave you, I promise you!" She pressed the child's cheek with her own and her tears fell on the little girl's face. Ali looked at her and wiped a tear away.

"Maeve loves Ali."

"Love Ali?"

"Yes," Maeve laughed. "Love Ali."

And while I can never really even the score with your father for you, Ali, my love, I'm going to get him, I will, I will!

When Miss Whittaker came back, she found Maeve singing songs to Ali, songs Maeve had thought she had forgotten. Where had she learned them? Who had sung them to her? She had never had a mother.

"It's Ali's dinner time."

"Couldn't I stay and eat dinner with her?"

"I'm sure you wouldn't want to disrupt the dinner hour for the other children, Miss O'Connor," Miss Whittaker gently reproved her.

Maeve was tempted to insist, to push her weight around as patroness. But she resisted, restrained herself when Ali was turned over to a young woman who led her away.

"I'll be back to see you, Ali," she called after her. To Miss Whittaker she said, "Now that I'm living in New York, I'll be here often. My aunt would want that, you understand. And I'm very much interested in the home." Maeve smiled at the woman who looked upset at this information. "I'll be very helpful to you, Miss Whittaker. You'll see," she said cheerfully.

"I didn't know . . . that you had moved to New York."

"Oh, yes . . . in fact, I'll be back tomorrow. I had some presents for Ali and I forgot to bring them. In fact, I have presents for all the children in the home."

Maeve was walking down the front stairs when Miss Whittaker called from the doorway. "You forgot your pearls, Miss O'Connor. I'm sure you didn't intend to leave them with Ali."

"Oh, yes. Please give them back to her. I gave them to her as a present." Seeing the expression on Miss Whittaker's face, she added, "They're not real. They're from the five-and-ten-cent store."

Chrissy threw the door open wide. "Maeve! Why didn't you tell me you were coming?" Then, noting Maeve's disheveled state, "Don't tell me! You flew here on your broom!"

"Thanks a lot. How about a drink?"

"Golly, yes! You look as if you could use one!"

Chrissy went to the bar in the all-white *moderne* living room and pulled out bottles, glasses, ice. "What shall I make you? You name it. I can mix anything. They don't call me Barmaid Marlowe for nothing."

"How about a glass of hemlock?"

"That bad?" Chrissy asked, pouring gin into a tall, narrow, crystal pitcher.

"I don't know. I'm not sure. Right now I'm such a mixture of conflicting emotions, I feel like I'm on a roller coaster and I don't know if I'm enjoying the ride."

Chrissy came over with the cocktail, lit a cigarette, and threw herself down on the overstuffed white cushions. "Tell Chrissy all about it, dear."

"Chrissy, do you have room for a boarder?"

Chrissy clapped her hands. "Do I have room for a boarder? Do I have room? Eight rooms full!"

"But you do work here. Will I interfere?"

"The room next door"—Chrissy gestured with her thumb—"is my studio. That leaves seven rooms. My bedroom leaves six. Kitchen, dining room, living room. That leaves three. You can have a room to sleep in and a room to work in, if that's what you plan to do, and that still leaves an extra room. What do you think we should do with that one? I know—that will be a room to screw in. Just in case we bring home some stray gray cats."

"Oh, Chrissy." Maeve hugged her. "Thank God for you. I don't know what I would have done if I didn't have someplace to go tonight after—"

"Look, Maeve. I'm not Sara and I'm not going to keep after you until you tell me what happened today. But if you want to tell me, I want to hear."

"I saw my baby today, Chrissy!"

Chrissy started to cry even before Maeve did.

5.

When Padraic was cheerful, Sara was reluctant to spoil his mood by asking him when they would be leaving. Maybe in the afternoons when they had their happy hour, after Padraic had only one or two drinks. If she was careful and caught him at the right time, a delicate balance between two and three drinks, she could ask him almost anything.

They had been here at least a couple of months—she had lost track of the time—the end of June . . . July . . . August . . . September. . . . It was almost three months. Her enchantment with the island abode had dissipated after the first two or three weeks. There was *nothing* to do but drink and make love, and she discovered that she required more of life than screwing and she had never been *that* fond of drinking. Sometimes when Padraic was particularly sweet, he would read to her in his lilting voice, talk to her about things she had never even contemplated before, and that was nice. He took her about the different villages on the island and showed her how the islanders grew potatoes in the crevices of the stony ground. "Whatever soil there is here was brought over from the mainland and mixed with the sand and the seaweed."

He showed her the ancient stone dwelling called a *clochan* and he took her to see Teachlach Eine near the village of Killeany, the remains of the monastic settlement from the sixth century and of the nearby ninth-century church founded by St. Brecan. He pointed out the Teampall Bheanain, probably the smallest church in the world. "Fascinating," Sara said, even as she worried about the state of her poor tender feet.

Sara paid only one visit to the ancient fort that shared the top of the three-hundred-foot cliff with their own cottage. With Padraic assisting her, they made their way past the outermost circle of defense, a thirty-foot width of sharp-pointed stones sticking four feet into the air. "It's called a *chevaux de frise,*" Padraic instructed. "Many a warrior must have been cut to ribbons—"

Goosebumps rose on Sara's arms.

"One hopes it will keep tourists away . . ." he said moodily.

"Tourists?"

"There is always talk of starting some kind of steamer service to the islands . . . but the talk evaporates on its own."

And no wonder, Sara thought. Why would anyone in his right mind want to visit this forsaken eerie place?

Then they made their way past a stone wall and then another, twenty feet high, until they were in an inner court. In one corner was a chair and a table with a typewriter and a mess of papers. On the floor were heaped piles of books and a clutter of bottles, some filled, some empty. *So this is where he disappears to when he goes off on his own.*

Sara started toward that corner—she wanted to see what Padraic was working on. But he pulled her back. "You don't want to be going into the corners of the court. All along the walls and *especially* in the corners there are all kinds of bugs and spiders, red big ones, black ugly ones, yellow slithery ones and purple poisonous ones. Some are beautiful. So beautiful you wonder why they are the insects and man is man."

Sara's skin crawled.

Padraic swiped at her arm suddenly, and stamped furiously on the ground. "There, you see." He smiled. "One was crawling on the fair skin of you but I got him. It's you, Sara. You're so lovely even the insects are attracted to you."

Sara wanted to leave the ruin then. It was almost all she could do not to run out by herself. But Padraic wanted to show her the steps on the inner walls leading up to the tower. "From the top you can see the most wondrous view. Come!" He took hold of her hand.

Sara looked up. The narrow stone steps went almost straight up, so high she felt dizzy merely contemplating them. The way down must be even steeper, more difficult to maneuver. A wave of nausea enveloped her.

"No!" She pulled away.

He laughed. "Afraid of getting dizzy way up there on top, are we? All right, then. We wouldn't want you to be taken with a fit of vertigo up there, now, would we? It's a long way up, but it could be a lot shorter of a way coming down."

"Let's go," Sara said. It was cold and damp and musty in the court, with mold growing in the nicks and crannies.

After having finally cleared the fort over the shards of stone, Sara breathed deeply in relief. Even if the day was again hung over with clouds, the air at least was fresh. She was actually glad to get back to the damn cottage. She needed a drink badly.

"Have another," Padraic said after she had downed the first one. "Your nerves seem a bit ragged."

"When are we leaving here, Padraic?"

"In a little bit. As soon as I'm finished with that which I've been working on."

"A novel? Is that what you've been working on in the fort?"

"You might say that."

6.

Maeve returned to Boston to pack her personal belongings. I went over to keep her company as she cleaned out drawers and filled cartons. "I'm going to miss you," I said. "You were here such a short while—"

"Yes. There's a time and place for everything, as they say, and my time in Boston is over."

"I know you have to be close to your little girl. Everything's changed so. . . . Sara gone—"

"You're not going to miss *anybody,* Marlena," Maeve said, teasing me. "Not with Peter around. When are you two planning on getting married, by the way?"

"Well, Peter graduates next June. We've been thinking about a June wedding in Charleston. Right after graduation. I hate to even think about getting married without Sara here. And the way things are I bet she won't even come." I knew the subject of Sara was painful to Maeve and I shouldn't force her to talk about her but I *was* concerned.

"Have you written to her?" Maeve asked me.

"Yes, of course. I had to tell her I was engaged!"

"Did Sara answer your letter?"

"No. I mean—I did get an answer but it was strange. She never said one word about Peter being Jewish, which is really weird considering it's Sara—I thought she'd have at least one funny comment on that . . . you know."

"What *did* she say?"

"She just asked how I was and told me how lovely and quaint Aran was. Maeve . . . I don't think Sara wrote that letter!"

"I don't think so either, Marlena. I'm pretty sure Sara's not even getting our letters. And I think *he's* writing the letters for Sara, without her knowledge. I get *terrible* letters with all kinds of foul language."

I didn't know if I was more worried about Sara, or felt worse for Maeve. "But *why,* Maeve?"

"I don't know why he's not giving our letters to Sara, but I know why he's writing those letters to us in her name. Especially those terrible letters to me. It's to worry us . . . especially me. He doesn't *want* those letters to sound like Sara. What about Bettina? Has she received any letters? Has she said that they seem strange to her?"

"Yes . . . to both questions. She said she can't believe how Sara's changed. That she sounds *so* cold. . . . Poor Aunt Bettina . . . I've told her that it's her imagination. But I don't know how long she'll swallow that. And she's just dying to see Sara. But, Maeve, if he's writing letters for Sara and sends them to us, what about Sara? Why isn't she writing any? Where are the ones she's really written or should have written?"

We looked at each other. The answer was obvious to both of us. They were just not getting mailed. . . .

"What are we going to do about Sara, Maeve?"

"I don't know. Sara's an adult. A married adult. We can't go there and take her away by force. Whatever has to be done for Sara, she has to do for herself."

"I suppose," I said, unconvinced. "But it doesn't stop me from worrying about her just the same."

"We all worry about her. But Sara's smart. And strong. When she's ready, she'll free herself."

"I hope you're right, Maeve."

Maeve tried to smile at me. "I hope so too."

Then I guessed that she wanted to change the conversation because she said, "How is your mother taking your Jewish fiancé?"

"Oh, she's getting used to it," I laughed. "At first I thought she'd have a heart attack—she said that was what came of going to a radical college like Radcliffe. But Peter's been darling with her—she *had* to come around. And Aunt Bettina just loves him. Poor Aunt Bettina . . ." I began again, and then stopped. "What are you going to do with your house here?"

"I'm donating it to the city of Boston. It's going to be a mental health clinic."

"A mental health clinic in Louisburg Square? Oh, my goodness! Won't the other residents here have a fit?"

"I'm leaving that small detail to my lawyers. They're paid enough— let them earn their money!"

I looked at her her tone was so sharp. Maeve *has* changed, I thought. She sounds a bit hard.

"And what about your grandmother's house?"

"That house doesn't belong to me. It's my . . . it's Padraic's house."

No, she was not going back on her plans to give a mental health clinic to the city of Boston, even though she planned never to come back to Boston again. She just would not be personally involved. She didn't ever want to see Aunt Maggie's house again. She knew that someday, when her anger faded, she would be able to forgive Aunt Maggie for allowing her to give birth to Ali—but she would never really understand it.

She was leaving everything behind. The house, the philanthropies, the memories. She was ready to resume her writing career. She was going to meet her father on *his* playing field. If the critics were right—if she had as much talent as they said she had, she was going to do her damnedest to outshine him, best him. She had to do something to get even with him for everything he had done. For Ali. For Sara . . . poor Sara. . . .

Maybe *she* would win the Nobel and then he would see how he could live with that! She locked the door to Aunt Maggie's house and didn't look back.

As Maeve left Boston and headed south, she made an abrupt turnaround. There was just one more place she had to see before she turned her back on the past forever. She would make one last trip to Truro. She crossed the bridge over to the Cape and drove down Route 6. It was not the same Route 6 she remembered, but then again, hardly anything of her memory was the same. But she found an exit for Pamet Road and everything started to look familiar again. There were the marshes and the dunes and the moors, and there was Cranberry Bog Trail and there was the narrow dirt road that led up to the old house that was theirs—high on the sandy cliff overlooking the sea, still standing in solitary isolation. She left her car and walked up the road.

The house was deserted, the windows boarded up. Who owned the house now? It didn't matter. It was very cold and the wind blew fiercely. She wrapped her fur coat around her more tightly and walked to the edge of the cliff to look down at the raging sea. She stood where he had stood that night, that first night. She had gotten out of bed and looked for him, came outside to find him. It had been a moonless night, a windy, rainy night and very dark—as dark as only Truro could be on a moonless night—and in a flash of lightning she had seen him silhouetted, his cape swirling about him, and had thought she had never seen anything quite so beautiful. She had been only ten then, the same age as Ali was now. What did a ten-year-old know of beauty?

She shook with cold as she walked back down to her car. Mark Twain had written of San Francisco that there was no place so cold as San Francisco in the month of August, but then maybe he had never been to Truro in the month of November.

She turned the car around. She was eager to get to New York.

7.

"Can't we go to the mainland for lunch? I'm sick to death of fish, boiled bacon, and cabbage. Please, Padraic, it would make a change. We've been here for months and we haven't been off the island once. Maybe we could go for lunch and stay for dinner and then sleep over in Galway for the night?"

"Why not?" Padraic seemed unusually amenable. "I'll go look up Eamonn. I think he might be persuaded to take us over. The last I saw of him, his boat was ailing. But he must have it patched up by now. Pretty well, anyway."

Pretty well?

"Can't you get somebody else?"

"Everybody else is working on the church, I think. I'll go looking for Eamonn."

"I'm not going out on any boat that isn't safe."

"I didn't say it wasn't."

"But you don't know for sure it is. I'm not going out on those waters without being sure."

"That's right. You don't know how to swim, do you? Well, let me go checking now."

It seemed like he was gone for hours. She didn't have a goddamn clock. And her wristwatch had stopped a long time ago. How could she reset it if she didn't have a telephone to call for the time. Or a radio. Or anything. She started to cry. She could count all the things she didn't have and the list would take until tomorrow. And the only way she would know it was tomorrow would be because it would get dark and then it would get light. She poured herself a drink. Why not? She didn't have anything else to do. She hadn't had anything to do for days, weeks, months. . . . If she didn't get off this island she would go mad. She was sure of it. She poured herself another drink. And if she didn't find somebody to talk to besides Padraic who only talked when it suited him, the bastard, she would go mad twice over. She took another drink. By the time Padraic returned, Sara was incoherent with drink.

The next morning he attacked her. "I finally find Eamonn and check on the condition of his *currach* and return to get you and what do I find? You, drunk, disgusting and revolting!"

"Yes? And when did you return? It was almost night. And how dare *you*, of all people, rake me over the coals for drinking?"

"A man drinking is one thing. A woman sodden with drink is a vile obscenity."

Oh, my God! Was she turning into a drunk? Like her mother had been? No, damn it! She wouldn't drink! She wouldn't be a drunk. And no one was going to turn her into one. Not her goddamn husband or anybody else. But something *was* happening to her. She *was* changing. But was it any wonder? This island—the loneliness. Why had he married her? To bury her here? She, Sara Gold, who used to lead the conga line at El Morocco? If he didn't want her to be herself what did he want of her anyway? She had to get off this island and soon. She had to get away at least for a day—*now!*

"Why can't we go to Galway today? If Eamonn's boat is safe why can't we go now?" she pleaded.

"Who knows what Eamonn is doing today? I refuse to go looking for him again just to come back and find you in a stupor."

"I won't be. I promise!"

"I hope that I can be believing that, Sara."

She watched him walk away in the direction of the fort and knew that he would be gone for hours. Goddamn it! What was she supposed to do in this hellhole by herself for hours on end?

She needed a drink! She didn't give a damn what she promised him. But she had promised *herself*. She began to cry. If she didn't have one drink, what *would* she do? Go crazy! And what about her goddamn friends! Not one letter from anybody. Not even her mother. *Mama, how could you betray me like this?* She knew Maeve was angry with her. But how about Chrissy? Marlena?

She poured some of his precious liquor into a glass. She would fix him! She would finish off the bottle for him! She tasted the liquid. It wasn't gin. It was too bitter to be gin. And it wasn't vodka. Vodka was smoother than this stuff that burned terribly going down. Well, whatever it was, it felt good once it was down.

She didn't need him. And she didn't need Eamonn and his lousy boat, either. It would probably sink anyhow and she would be stuck out there in the fucking waters, with the fucking sharks! She would find somebody else to take her to the mainland and she would never come back. Tomorrow she would do it, look for some fisherman in a seaworthy boat, and as she was sailing away she would laugh in Padraic's handsome, fucking face!

She took the next drink straight from the bottle.

When Padraic returned he took no notice that Sara was again drunk. "Come to bed," he said sweetly and proceeded to make love to her. Numb, Sara lay there until, abruptly, he stopped and got out of the bed.

"What's the matter?" Sara asked. "What's wrong?"

"What's wrong?" He laughed. "You have as much feeling for love as one of those stones out there."

He stormed out.

She had to get out of here, out of this hut and off the island. What had he said? *As much feeling as one of the stones out there?* The killing stones of the *chevaux de frise?* A chill ran through her. *Tomorrow* she would stay sober so she could think clearly about making plans for leaving. But now, in the middle of the night, she needed a drink.

8.

"I was wondering when I would be allowed into this studio," Maeve said, "wondering what you were hiding in here. I thought maybe it was a few dead bodies."

Chrissy giggled. "You might call them dead bodies. Manet. Gauguin. I used them, in a manner of speaking, and then discarded them. There they are over there in the corner—my earlier paintings. . . ."

Maeve took a quick look—Paris street scenes mostly in bright vivid colors.

"I *like* the colors—"

"Please, Madam, no quick judgments. These over here are a later period. Bernard, Kandinsky, Braque."

"Really, Chrissy, why are you making fun of yourself? They're *very* good."

"Please, Madam. You have yet to see the *latest* period. In the manner of the Abstract Expressionists, I present—" She unfurled a covering sheet. *"Voilà!"*

Maeve felt a surge of pride. She marveled at the change in Chrissy. She was self-mocking but she worked hard. She was really serious about her work, and the long line of one-night lovers had stopped, for the time being anyway.

Tears rolled down Maeve's cheeks.

"For gosh sake, I didn't think my work was *that* bad!"

Maeve shook her head. "I was just thinking—if Sara were here, she'd have you in a show tomorrow!"

9.

She would not drink at all today. No, she was going to pull herself together. She just had to figure it all out. Try to figure out how long she had been here. She knew she had been married in June. For the life of her she couldn't remember the year exactly—she had gone to Paris the end of . . . '48 . . . yes, she was pretty sure of that. Had they been married in '49 or '50? . . . Had she missed Christmas? But of which year? It was too much for her . . . she would think about it later. . . . It was that green stuff . . . she suspected that it was— She forgot now what she suspected it was. . . . Well, she would think about that later too. Right now she had to do something to get her mind off not drinking. She could write letters . . . but nobody wrote back. Well, to hell with them, too! They weren't worth much with all their talk of undying love if they had so quickly and easily abandoned her.

She picked up one of Padraic's books. Shakespeare . . . She sighed. It was hard enough to get into Shakespeare without having to concentrate on not drinking. Without having *not* to think about all the dangers that surrounded her. *Him!* The relentless cold. The insects that crawled around inside the fort. The sharp, pointed stones that lay everywhere. The drop of the cliff to the shark-infested waters below. The alien people of the island who spoke not to her but regarded her with sullen suspicion. She opened the volume with trembling hands. *Macbeth.* Oh, God! Just the thing to merrily pass the time of day. God, but her nerves were bad. She wet her lips with her tongue. Her lips were parched, cracked. She would leave this terrible place and then everything would be all right.

When Padraic walked in, he was cheerful as a leprechaun, but she was as wary now of his good cheer as of his black moods, his mean-spirited drinking.

"And what have you been doing with yourself, little wife? Have you been washing the clothes or cooking us our supper?" he mocked her. He knew of course that she hadn't—Fionna came up the mountain every day for a couple of hours to do whatever work needed to be done. Fionna was glad, Sara assumed, to earn a little money for the family to buy supplies with in Galway. She could only assume—not even Fionna spoke to her.

Sara didn't answer him.

He grabbed the book out of her hands. "Oh, it's been reading she has! And what has she been reading? Bless my soul—*Macbeth,* is it?" He went off into gales of laughter. He could barely speak from laughing. "And I was beginning to think you couldn't even read!"

"Shut up, you bastard!"

"You can't cook, you can't heat the water, you don't even keep yourself clean anymore, but you can use your foul mouth, I see. Well, but you'd better be learning how to clean this place up and yourself. Fionna won't be coming up anymore. There's cholera down in the village."

"Cholera!"

"Yes, my lovely. Cholera and it's spreading. You'd better be scrubbing everything down. This place looks like its crawling with the bacteria."

He took a swig from his bottle and sang, "For she's a young child and should never've left her mither."

Damn him, what was he singing? Oh God, she would get cholera and die and never see *her* mother again.

She grabbed the bottle from him and drank.

She wasn't even sure if she should believe him about the plague. She didn't know what to believe anymore.

He took the bottle back from her and deliberately wiped off its mouth before drinking from it again.

"Ye can't be too careful now that the germs are everywhere."

"Oh, you bastard! You . . . rat!" She cried. She cried for that little girl who had once thought rat was the worst thing you could call a person.

10.

Chrissy could barely wait for Maeve to come home from visiting her little girl. When Maeve returned, humming softly to herself, Chrissy had the champagne ready.

"Come right over here, get your glass, and let me tell you my news. Today we're toasting *me*."

"Super. I would love to toast you. Over a low fire until you're a nice golden brown."

"Really, Maeve. For someone who's supposed to be a fine writer you make the lamest jokes."

Maeve giggled. "What's your news?"

"The Kristen Gallery is giving me a one-man show in March."

"Marvelous!—Have you told your Aunt Gwen?"

"Not yet. But I can't wait. She'll absolutely die. You're in a divine mood yourself. Did something good happen today?"

"Yes," Maeve beamed. "Ali smiled."

"Oh, Maeve!" Chrissy's eyes teared. "Let's drink to that!"

11.

"Still warming your curbeens in bed?" Padraic asked. "It's almost noon. You're really turning into quite the slut, aren't you?"

"You son-of-a-bitch! It's all your fault! Keeping me a prisoner on this goddamned island." But she spoke without heat. She was numbed and, at the same time, disoriented, with the alcohol she had already consumed that morning. She felt as if her brain were leaping around in her head.

"You're not a prisoner, Sara my sweet. Well, not so sweet anymore. In fact, you look quite the hag. Life's most bitter truth—there is nothing more sour to the taste than a beautiful woman gone bad. But to get back to my original statement this lovely mornin', no one is keeping you a prisoner. All you have to do is walk down the mountain, make your way to the shoreline and find one of the fishermen to take you across. Of course, it is still winter and it's colder than a dead love out there and the sea is as stormy as I've ever seen it and the sharks are really hungry this time of year. And you better be careful walking—I saw a snake yesterday, just outside the door."

"A snake?" she asked dully. "There aren't any snakes in Ireland. Saint Patrick drove them all off. . . ."

Padraic laughed, practically bent over from the laughing. "Where do you think he drove them off to? To the Isles of Aran."

12.

"Aunt Gwen! How lovely of you to come."

"Really, Chrissy, would I *not* come to my niece's first show?"

"You look pretty nifty, Aunt Gwen." Aunt Gwen was really avant-garde in her three-piece pinstriped trouser suit and her Greta Garbo hat. *My goodness, what next, Aunt Gwen?*

"Why, thank you, Chrissy. You look pretty nifty yourself, if somewhat Bohemian."

"It's my Montmartre look. I thought it would be very appropriate for the opening of an art show entitled, 'April in Paris.' "

Chrissy twirled around for Gwen's benefit, setting the full, ruffled skirt, the large golden rings dangling from her ears, and the long smooth bell of hair in motion.

"Very effective, Chrissy."

Wasn't Aunt Gwen going to say anything about her paintings, Chrissy wondered with amusement.

"Have you had some wine, Aunt Gwen?"

"There's time for that. I'm not leaving yet. There are some people here I want to talk with. You have a good turnout, Chrissy. I see quite a few of the really important people in art here today. I suppose it's the Marlowe name."

Zingo!

"And I see that pretty Irish friend of yours over there, talking to the indomitable Miss Force. What's her name again?"

Zingo!

"Maeve O'Connor, Aunt Gwen. She's kind of famous, you know. Her novel was published last year and she received tremendous acclaim!"

"Oh, yes, I vaguely remember something. But what has she done lately?"

"She's working on another book," Chrissy mumbled.

"And that little Jewish friend of yours? The Gold girl. She married O'Connor's father, didn't she? Very interesting, that. How is she doing? One would think she'd be here today."

And zingo again, Aunt Gwen. Well, she was not about to discuss Sara with her.

"You'll have to excuse me, Aunt Gwen. There are people waiting to talk to me."

"Of course. By the way, Chrissy, I'm very pleased with you."

Oh?

"You have talent. But I'm not at all surprised. You're a Marlowe, after all, and all the Marlowes are talented."

Chrissy sighed.

You should know, Aunt Gwen. Your own photographs of nudes are quite notorious.

Gwen was back the next day.

"Your reviews were quite good, Chrissy. I *am* proud of you."

"Well, the critics were not unkind, let us say," Chrissy said modestly, pleased in spite of herself that her aunt had come back to tell her that.

"Did you sell many paintings?"

"A few. But it was only the first day."

"Of course. I would like you to donate at least two of the paintings to the Marlowe Museum. You are a Marlowe, after all."

Chrissy didn't quite know if that was a zinger or not.

"*Donate*, Aunt Gwen? The Marlowe Museum does have an Acquisition Fund, does it not? The Marlowe Museum will have to *buy* my paintings, if it wants them. I am a Marlowe, after all, and we Marlowes didn't get where we are by giving things away."

Gwen Marlowe smiled thinly. "Of course. I'll be in touch. By the way, did you hear about Gwennie?"

Go ahead, Aunt Gwen. Let's hear it. What wonderful thing has little Gwennie done to diminish my achievement?

"She gave birth to twins just two months ago. That's why she won't be able to come to see your show. The most darling little girls, pretty as a picture."

Double zingo!

"How did the show go today, Chrissy?" Maeve asked when Chrissy came home from the gallery.

"Good. Sold a couple of more paintings. Aunt Gwen was in. Get this—she wanted me to *donate* a couple of the pictures to her Marlowe Museum."

"What did you tell her?"

"To go fry an egg—"

Maeve laughed.

"You know what? I think I'll give Marlena and Peter one of my pictures for a wedding present."

"I think that's a lovely idea."

"What will you give her?"

"I've been thinking about it. Marlena is getting married in June and a June bride should have a wonderful wedding trip. And I don't think their budget can accommodate a very grand honeymoon. So I thought *that* would make a nice wedding present."

"What a super idea. Golly, I wish I had thought of it. Your present will make mine look really tacky. Where are you planning on sending the lucky couple?"

"The British Isles. England, Scotland, and Ireland. To the Isles of Aran."

But of course. Where else?

Chrissy hoped that June would not be too late.

13.

Sara had not been out of the cottage for days. And she tried not to eat. She was convinced that the food was laced with the bacteria that covered the island. And those insects . . . from the fort . . . they were all over too. She tried not to get out of the bed at all. Why had she ever come here? Oh, yes—because she had married Padraic. It was the honeymoon . . . wasn't it? She slept and then wakened, in fits. Why was she here? She couldn't recall. . . . Once she sat up with a surge of terror. *She was here so Padraic could destroy her. . . .*

She had to wash her hair. When had she washed it last? But she didn't have any shampoo. No hot water. A blonde needed to wash her hair often. Somebody had said that once. She tried to think who had said it. It was very important that she remember. The more things she remembered the less she forgot. She laughed, sucking her fingers. It had been Sara Gold who said that.

Underneath the bed was her makeup case. She didn't like to go without her makeup. A girl should *never* go without her makeup. She would put on some lipstick. But she had to pull out the makeup case without looking under the bed. There was a family of snakes living there and she couldn't disturb them. She pulled out the case very carefully, careful, careful, not to make a sound.

She peered into the mirror. Oh, Lordy, whose face was that? Whose hair? Not Sara's. Sara had yellow hair. This lady's hair was dark with dank. Dark, dry cotton candy. When she touched it, it broke off in her hands to become dust. "Who are you?" Sara asked the lady in the mirror, and giggled.

As quickly, she stopped. How long had she been here in this room? She had a calendar, she remembered, in the suitcase over in the corner. She had seen it there, hadn't she? She had to get the suitcase. But it was not easy. She took a drink from the bottle that she kept hidden under the covers and then got out of the bed carefully, and, hopping from one foot to the other to fool the bugs, reached the corner of the room, grabbed the suitcase and hopped back to the bed, stumbled into it.

She pawed through the filmy lingerie, white silk dresses, black thin ones. Such pretty things. Whose were they? She pulled off the dirty sweater she wore, tried to pull on something of rose-colored chiffon but the effort was too much. She wailed, giving up. Then she saw the calendar stuck in a pocket of the suitcase and snatched it out, looked at it blankly. What month was it? How long had she been here? If only somebody would write to her. Why didn't they answer her letters? She had written some, she was pretty sure she had. To—? Her Mama. Where was her Mama? And to her friends. She couldn't think of the names but she thought she had written to them. But they had all forgotten her, even Mama. They had left her here with the stones and the fort, the strangers and the cholera, the spiders and the bugs and the sharks. And the germs everywhere.

She drank some more of the green liquid. She wasn't going to eat today. She knew he was trying to poison her. If she didn't eat, he couldn't poison her. She could drink though. The alcohol killed the poison and it was sweet. Alcohol had sugar in it. Somebody had told her that once. She laughed. Her father had told her that. She was certain of it.

Daddy! She could write to her daddy! He would come for her. She could write the letter when she found a pen. She could write the letter tomorrow and get one of those fishy fishermen to mail it. She giggled. She would give him some money. Where was her money? She had lots of money. Where was her checkbook? A girl should never be without her checkbook. She would have to find her checkbook and then she could mail the letter.

"Sh!" she said to the room. "Don't tell him!"

Padraic came in, found her naked to the waist, chewing her fingernails, what was left of them. They were a bloody mess and he wrestled with her to clean them with antiseptic. He had no intention of letting them get infected. He even washed her body every few days to keep the sores away. She was almost ready to be taken home. A few more weeks, he judged, and she would be ready. And she would be delivered without a scratch showing. He would even wash her hair.

He slopped some food from a pot into a bowl.

"It's dinner time, me love. You'd better be eating—else there'll be nothing left of you and that won't do at all. Now, if you eat this up, you can have a nice drap to wash it down. And if you don't eat you don't get a wee drap."

14.

Chrissy came home from the gallery, found Maeve in her bedroom. "Well, that's the last day of this show. What a relief!" Then she saw that Maeve was packing a flight bag.

"Where are you going?" she asked, surprised.

"I've booked a flight to Shannon for tonight."

Chrissy turned white, sat down on the bed. Deadly quiet, she asked, "You heard something? What's happened?" Then she screamed, "Is she dead?"

"No! No!" Maeve hugged Chrissy. "But I'm going there to bring her home."

"But you said—you said we couldn't do anything . . . that Sara had to do it for herself," Chrissy cried.

"I know I said that, God forgive me. But a couple of weeks ago, I looked at Ali and I realized that sometimes people just *can't, cannot* do for themselves. And I got in touch with some investigators in Shannon and they went to Aran. . . ."

"What did they find?" Chrissy shrieked, not able to bear waiting for the next words.

"Calm yourself, Chrissy, please. She's alive! They didn't see her— they said they couldn't gain access to the cottage where she lives—"

"Then how do you know she's alive?"

"She is. The investigators spoke to the people on the island. They say that she . . . Sara . . . doesn't come out of the cottage anymore but that she *is* there. . . ."

"Maeve . . . you said *cottage*. Is that cottage as they use the word in Newport—the great houses?"

"No. Cottage like in hut. There are no castles there, Maeve, no great houses on Aran. There are only the most primitive dwellings."

Chrissy wrung her hands. *How could Maeve be so calm?*

"Are they sure she's there?"

"Yes. But, Chrissy, from the description they gave, well, she . . . she's not well, Chrissy. Not physically, not mentally. But she's alive so I'm going to get her out . . . before . . ." Her voice broke. ". . . she can't be saved."

"Why didn't the investigators just break in and take her?"

"They couldn't. They don't have the authority and *we* can't give it to them. Not from here, anyway." Maeve sounded so sure and hard.

"But *you* can't go Maeve. I'll go."

"No, I have to. I got her into this—I have to get her out. If it weren't for me, my father would never have picked Sara to do this to—"

"But how can you see him? It's too much for you to have to do that!"

"On the contrary. I'm the only one who can do this. I *know* how to deal with him now."

"Well, then, I'm going with you!"

"Are you sure?"

"Of course I'm sure. Besides, in numbers there's strength. I'm calling for a seat. If there isn't one available I'm going to buy the fucking airline!"

Maeve's fingers were busy with her rosary, her lips moved silently. Chrissy knew that she was praying that it wasn't too late for Sara to be saved. She wanted to pray herself. Hell, she didn't need a rosary—all she needed was a God. She closed her eyes and prayed.

The two Irish inquiry agents met them at the airport in Shannon and drove to Galway where the men had a boat waiting for them in the bay.

"Be prepared," Dermot Leahy warned them. "It's a rough trip over and a rougher trip once we get there."

The weather changed and it started to rain. Chrissy and Maeve held hands tightly, frightened as they had never been before. The sea was black and rough. And the faces of the two men with them were grim and unsmiling, like men must look when they are going off to war.

Chrissy was shocked when they landed on the island of Inishmore. Never had she seen such gray desolation. It was spring all over the world but there was no spring here. Was there ever? How could Sara, little gay flower that she was, ever have survived this, she thought with a sinking heart.

But Inishmore was no shock to Maeve. It was what she had expected.

"We have to go up there," Finley Devereaux told them, pointing, his mouth a straight line. "Up to the cliff to where the fort stands." The women looked up to see the ominous ruin. "The cottage lies behind it— you can't see it from here."

"Oh, she can't be alive," Chrissy moaned.

"Hush! She will be, she will be! We have to be very brave, Chrissy, or we'll never pull this off."

How can Maeve be so unafraid?

Maeve was thinking, this is a test. God is testing me. If I can see *him* and not falter, then Sara will be all right. If I can see him and not falter and save Sara, then *I* will be all right. If I can see him and not falter and save Sara and come through this all right myself, I can save Ali!

"We have to circle the fort—the cottage lies on the other side," Dermot Leahy said.

"Oh, God, Maeve, look at those ugly stones sticking up into the air—if you fell on them I bet they would pierce your heart."

"That's the *chevaux de frise*," Finley Devereaux said. "In ancient days many an invader must have fallen on those rocks," he said with a peculiar satisfaction.

"Don't look at the stones," Maeve said. "Just keep your eyes averted, Chrissy."

She herself looked up to the top of the fortress—to the centuries-old observation tower that reached toward the sky, the highest point on Aran, from where one could survey not only the vast, wild sea, but all the island below. And there, looking down on them, like some ancient warrior of destiny, a *Sinn Feinian* waiting and watching for the invader, *he* stood, a black figure draped in the cape she remembered well, etched against the darkening heavens.

She did not drop her gaze. She would not falter.

Chrissy looked up too, to see what Maeve was staring at.

"Oh, my God!" she whispered, reaching out to encircle Maeve with her arm.

"It's all right, Chrissy. I'm all right. Let's go and get Sara!"

"The door is locked," Dermot Leahy said.

"Knock the damn door down," Chrissy cried. "What the hell do you think you're here for?"

Leahy looked at Devereaux. Still they hesitated.

"Shove! Whichever man knocks the door down first gets a thousand-dollar bonus!" Chrissy yelled furiously.

Both men heaved together and the weak little door caved in.

For a second the women hung back, not daring to look, then rushed in. The first room was empty save for the stove and the few pieces of furniture. But from the other room the keening of centuries could be heard, a wailing as bloodcurdling as anything they had ever heard.

On the bed in the corner a cowering emaciated form now wailed low. Chrissy sobbed as she gazed in horror at the almost unrecognizable Sara; Maeve wept silently.

"Sara, it's us . . . Maeve and Chrissy . . . we've come to take you home, darling Sara."

"Sh! You'll wake the snakes," a failing, rasping voice whispered.

"Oh, Maeve, Maeve, we are too late. . . ."

"No! We can't be! I won't let it be!" To the men: "Pick her up, for God's sake! Carry her out! What are you waiting for?"

It took only one man to carry Sara down. Devereaux held her while Leahy kept his eye on the tower. The crazy bastard could have a rifle as well as not.

Chrissy ran at Devereaux's side, saying over and over, "We love you, Sara, we love you, Sara, we'll take care of you. It's Chrissy, Sara, it's Chrissy . . . and Maeve. . . ." She turned around to look for Maeve to join in this litany. She saw Maeve standing still, looking back toward the ruined fort, looking up.

"Maeve, come on! Maeve! They say he could have a rifle."

But Maeve stood there, her right arm upstretched, her hand a fist, and she was shaking it into the heavens.

SWITZERLAND 1951-1952

1.

It had not been easy taking Sara across the bay—a frenzied creature, alternately violent and craven, terrified of the water and the specter of sharks. It had been a traumatic journey, even for the implacable inquiry agents. But once in Galway, Chrissy swung into motion displaying a talent for executive action that amazed and reassured a grateful Maeve. She found a doctor, talked him into sedating Sara, then arranged for an ambulance with attendants to drive them to Shannon Airport. With Sara stowed away in the ambulance, temporarily safe and mercifully sleeping, Chrissy set herself up in the lobby of The Great Southern Hotel, and after ten or twelve phone calls managed to secure a private plane to meet the ambulance in Shannon—it was inconceivable to transport Sara on a commercial flight—and then served notice on the Clinique Lutece outside of Lausanne to be prepared for the arrival of a new resident.

"Why Switzerland?" Maeve asked. "I thought we were taking Sara home."

"When Sara recovers she will be mortified and humiliated if anyone in New York has seen her the way she is now . . . or if word has leaked down to Charleston about how really bad off she was. . . . And the people at Lutece are known for their discretion as well as for being experts in . . . revitalization."

Revitalization! Had Chrissy hit upon the term haphazardly? Or had Dr. Lutece used it in his conversation with her? Maeve preferred not to know. The word covered such a multitude of meanings, and what a lovely ring it had. . . . "Revitalized" conjured up pictures of a radiant Sara growing stronger every day, more vital each week, a rosy, glowing Sara with once-again luxuriant yellow hair sitting up in bed amidst her lacy pillows in a lacy pink negligee having her nails painted ultra-violet purple, saying in her usual exuberant style, "I had the most wonderful massage today. You must have *Le Homme* give you a massage! If word

332

should get out, heaven forbid, that you haven't had a massage by *Le Homme* while staying in Lausanne, your name will be absolutely mud!" or some other such wonderful Sara-ish nonsense.

Oh, God, let that day come! And if you, Sara, will only recover, I promise you can tell me what to do and nag me about any little old thing you want, and I won't let out a peep. . . .

They sat and watched while Sara slept, crying out now and then in a restless, thrashing sleep.

"At least we're rid of the laughing detectives—Chuckling Dick Tracy and his partner, Smiley Sam Spade," Chrissy said, trying to make Maeve relax a little, and was rewarded with a grateful smile.

Now that Sara was in the hands of the Clinique Lutece, all Maeve and Chrissy had to do was await the evaluation of Sara's condition. They registered at the Lausanne Palace Hotel to do their waiting.

"You call Marlena," Maeve said, "and I'll call Bettina."

"How much do we say?" Chrissy asked nervously.

"You tell Marlena the truth, and that we're waiting for a prognosis—"

"All right." Chrissy took a deep breath. "And Bettina—"

"I'm going to soften it as much as possible. There's no reason to make *her* sick with anxiety."

"Poor Marlena. She's getting married next month and she has to hear this."

"Well, at least there's something positive to know now. Marlena's been sick with worry anyway. Now at least we all know that sick as Sara is, she's out of—"

"Yes."

Every morning for five days they called the clinic to be told that there was no word as yet. The tension was unbearable. They shopped for clothes, having brought practically nothing with them, took the baths, had afternoon tea, sat in the hotel bar listening to American tunes, even went to a white-tie gala to pass the time viewing the haute couture clothes worn by the fashionable international set who were presently "at home" in their chalets. They waited.

Finally, when it seemed that the suspense had become impossible to endure, they were summoned to the clinic, ushered into a darkened, richly furnished room, seated together on a brown velvet-upholstered sofa, and served sherry by a woman dressed in wine red silk who appeared to be more the splendid hostess than an assistant in a clinic for the ill. They were told that Dr. Lutece *himself* would be in presently to talk with them.

333

"Do you think we kneel and kiss his ring when he enters the room?" Chrissy whispered.

"Maybe it will be enough to curtsy."

When Dr. Lutece finally made his appearance in a business suit and not vestal robes, they breathed a sigh of relief. "You have brought your friend to the right place," Dr. Lutece began, and the girls breathed another sigh of relief. It sounded as if the doctor was going to give them a positive prognosis.

"We make use here of therapies the primitive Americans are reluctant to try—for whatever reasons." He shrugged and threw his hands up in disgust. "Cellular rejuvenation is probably the only answer to Sara's physical condition." He lowered his voice to a near whisper and Maeve and Chrissy had to lean forward to hear him. "That and sleep therapy in conjunction with certain other techniques. . . . Fortunately, Sara's alcoholism has a short history so the alcohol has not had time to make extensive inroads. There is vitamin deficiency . . . malnutrition . . . a certain amount of degeneration . . . all not insurmountable."

Not insurmountable! They exchanged looks, their spirits soared.

"Her hair?" Chrissy asked, feeling foolish. But how would Sara make a complete mental recovery if her hair wasn't restored to what it had been.

The doctor reared his head and snorted, as if almost to say: of what consequence *hair?* But he said, "A month . . . two at the most."

Blessed relief.

Then Dr. Lutece turned his back on them, worked the cord on the drawn draperies, opening them to reveal a wall of glass that looked out on the Swiss countryside, a vista of purple mountains and blue sky. "The psyche—that is another story."

The good feeling evaporated, the tension mounted again—they reached out for each other's hand.

Dr. Lutece swung around, "The psyche will take longer."

The friends exhaled. Dr. Lutece had just said "longer," not "never," not even "perhaps."

"How long?" Maeve asked.

The doctor frowned, snapped his fingers. "Impossible to say . . . three months . . . six months . . . twelve. As in the case of the physical, time is on Sara's side. The state of paranoia has not existed long enough to make a full recovery impossible. Had she not been exposed to so many phobias concurrently, the task would be that much easier."

"What do you mean, Doctor, by so many phobias?"

"We have been observing and testing Sara for several days now and we have found present, in varying degrees, an astonishing number of fears." He picked up Sara's file and read to them. "Acrophobia, fear of high places. Aichmophobia, fear of sharp or pointed objects. Aquaphobia, fear of water. Arachnephobia, spiders. Entomophobia, insects. Particularly pronounced. And so forth and so on. I will spare you the entire list.

334

Of course, the greatest phobia we have to contend with here is the fear Sara has for the person who instilled all the other fears. Since it would take countless months to eliminate all the phobias, one by one, it seems more expedient at this time to work on the last fear I mentioned and hope that this will make the other phobias easier to deal with. Yes, we can help your friend Sara. I think the person who would be impossible to help is that person who has almost destroyed her psyche. Ironically enough, what he has managed to do in a year's time is astounding. He himself would have made a brilliant doctor of the mind. . . . I regret that it is not possible to study his case. . . . Fascinating. . . ." His voice became nearly inaudible as he pondered the possibilities of Padraic O'Connor as subject.

"I think I should say something else here so that you can better understand Sara's problem. The normally neurotic person *can* function quite well with one or two, even three of these fears. You both must know people who are in deadly fear of say . . . bees . . . or cannot, for the life of them, climb a ladder. But in Sara's case we already have found fourteen phobias, and there may be more. These phobias, in conjunction with the alcoholism and the extreme isolation. . . ." He spread his hands. Then adjusting the pince-nez on the tip of a pointed nose, he added:

"There is one other thing—Sara is pregnant. Three months pregnant."

Chrissy gasped and Maeve cried, "Abort her!"

Chrissy gasped again and Maeve said to her, quite as if the doctor were not in the room, "Would you really want Sara to give birth to this baby? With the bad, mad blood of the O'Connors?"

"Oh, Maeve!" Chrissy moaned. "Don't say that!"

"It's true!"

"Ladies, please," the doctor said, impatient with irritation. "This discussion is academic. I was simply giving you a point of information. That is all. I was not throwing the question out on the floor for debate." He consulted a thin gold wristwatch. "Sara is being prepared for therapeutic abortion at this very moment. We could not possibly allow this pregnancy to impede our treatment or retard our progress. Now it is time for you two to go home and let us do our work." Dr. Lutece dismissed them.

Go home? Leave Sara here alone, again among strangers? Without a familiar face to lend her support?

The doctor read the questions on their faces.

"You can't help her. We can. To be frank, your presence would be a nuisance." He consulted a calendar in front of him. "You may see her . . . in two months. I will expect to see you here . . . August the first. She will not be ready for you to take her home at that date, but she will be ready to see you. Good day, ladies."

He held out his hand and, in turn, Maeve and Chrissy shook it. He

335

walked out leaving them staring at each other helplessly. It was inconceivable that one would argue with the doctor, even if he had given them the chance.

They accepted drinks from the stewardess, refused food, not speaking, busy with their thoughts, both thinking of Sara, her body now barren.

"I guess it would have been traumatic for Sara to come out of this and find herself with a baby who would keep this whole thing fresh in her mind forever," Chrissy said, thinking out loud more than anything. Then realizing what she had said, to Maeve of all people, she covered her mouth with her hand. *God, I'm an ass!*

"Forgive me, Maeve. I'm really a horse's ass."

"It's all right, Chrissy. When I first saw little Ali, I cursed Aunt Maggie for allowing me to give birth to her. But now, even though I still can't look at her without my heart breaking, I cannot say I'm sorry she's alive. She is so sweet and I love her more than life itself. But that's from my viewpoint. How about Ali? If she had been given a choice, would she have chosen this half-life she's forced to live? I can tell you one thing—I'll never have to ponder that question again."

"What do you mean?"

"Do you think I would ever give birth to another child?"

"But Ali was the product of . . . you know. . . . That doesn't mean . . . that another child of yours would—"

"What I said in Dr. Lutece's office . . . about the O'Connor blood, I meant it. I just wouldn't take that chance."

What could she say in answer to that? Chrissy wondered. "I . . . I want a baby more than anything else—"

"I know." Maeve took her hand. "And you will have one."

"I don't know about that. I threw two chances away. Maybe God will punish me and never give me another chance."

"He will. God is good."

"I wish I had your faith, Maeve. After all you've gone through—"

"It's not a matter of faith, Chrissy. What are our choices? What if we don't believe? How do we go on?"

Over the speaker came the captain's announcement that they would be landing in about ten minutes and that the weather was fair.

"Golly, when Sara finds out that she's missed Marlena's wedding, she'll feel terrible," Chrissy said, lighting up a cigarette to get it in before the No Smoking sign went on for the descent to land.

Maeve rolled her eyes. "Good Lord, how quick they forget. Just listen to what you're saying. If Sara *can* feel terrible about missing the wedding, what a lovely thing that will be!"

"That's true, isn't it?" Chrissy grinned. "I hope she's absolutely miserable about missing the wedding. Are you still going to send Peter and Marlena to Ireland for their wedding present?"

"I think not! What I think I'll do is ask them to extend their honeymoon a bit. And then have them go to London and Paris and end up in Switzerland right about the first of August. What do you think?"

"I think that's a divine idea. And you know what—I think Marlena will think it's divine too."

2.

Chrissy went back to her painting and Maeve to her writing. Her second book was almost finished; she had promised to deliver it in early fall. The first few days that they were back from Europe, Chrissy said nothing. But after two weeks had passed and still Maeve had not gone to see her daughter, Chrissy didn't know what to make of it. Was it possible that Maeve just couldn't bear to look at the child that looked so much like her father? Finally, she couldn't hold back the words any longer.

"I don't understand what's going on with you, Maeve. Are you *so* busy with your book that you can't spare an afternoon to spend with Ali, or what?"

"I thought you knew," Maeve said expressionlessly. "I can't go to see Ali. Not for a while, anyway."

Chrissy was stricken. "Why can't you? Golly, do you realize what this will do to her? First you see her constantly, pay all kinds of attention to her, shower her with love until she actually responds . . . she smiles . . . she talks . . . and then you pull the rug out from under her. Stop seeing her? This could be a terrible setback. . . ." Chrissy's voice trailed off. She had said too much, as usual.

"Don't you think I know all that?" Maeve's voice was tortured. "I can't sleep nights thinking about it! Why do you think I don't go see her? Because I can't risk *him* finding out where she is. When I knew where he was—in Aran with Sara—I could see her. But now—where is he? He might be here . . . in New York . . . spying on me. How long do you think it would take him to make the connection between me and the home? And don't forget that I told Sara I had had a baby, Padraic's baby. We don't know if she repeated that to Padraic. If she did—anything's possible. Don't you see that? No matter how far-fetched my thinking might be, I just can't take the chance."

"Oh, Maeve! How terrible for you not to be able to see Ali! And terrible for her! What will you do?"

"Just write my books and send presents over to the home. That's all I can do."

"How about Aunt Chrissy taking over? And telling Ali that her Maeve

337

has not forgotten her. I could go on a regular basis. Maybe I could work with the children too. You know—drawing and whatever—"

Maeve hugged her. "I think that would be lovely, Aunt Chrissy." She laughed. "But I don't know how lovely Miss Whittaker will think it is. She's an awfully hard nut."

In a year or so Sara might be free of *him,* Chrissy thought. But when would Maeve?

3.

A week before the wedding, I told my mother that I had invited Uncle Maurice.

"Are you out of your mind?" Mother asked, arranging roses. She did not even bother raising her voice—the idea was clearly such a preposterous one to her, she would not waste her breath.

"Mother, I don't think you heard me correctly. I didn't say I was thinking of inviting Uncle Maurice. I said that I *had.*"

She put down the Crimson Beauty she was about to place in the milk glass vase. "How could you do such a thing?"

"I thought it was the right thing to do. Uncle Maurice has been very good to me, Mother. He even paid my college tuition. . . ."

"We didn't ask him to, did we?"

"I think that's beside the point, Mother. He *did.* And he's so worried about Sara. It's harder to worry about someone when you're all alone and have nobody to share your worry with."

"It's hardly our fault or our concern that he's all alone. Did we tell him to marry that English woman? Is it our fault that she left him and went back to England?"

"Oh, Mother . . . try and have a little compassion. I bet if Sara were here, she wouldn't want her father to be alone, she would relent . . . a little, anyway."

"That's all good and fine for you. And Sara. If she were here and well. But I'm thinking of Bettina. She's going to think you're a mighty unfeeling niece and she'll be right. She'll probably refuse to attend the wedding altogether and I for one wouldn't blame her!"

Aunt Bettina, in the hall off the dining room, overheard our conversation. She came in and said, "It's all right, Martha. I appreciate you trying to spare my feelings, but Marlena's right. Maurice has been good to her. And he is alone. In the end, he hasn't been as fortunate as I. After all, I have you and Howard and Marlena . . . as well as my Sara, who, God willing, will be well soon and as sweet as ever. And Marlena's right, I think, about how Sara would feel about Maurice. I think she would want us all to welcome him into our family circle on Marlena's happy day, under the circumstances. And I'm strong now, Martha, thanks to you. . . ." She went over and kissed her sister, who cleared her throat. "I can stand seeing Maurice. I can even forgive him. I can wish him well."

Mother wiped her hands together. "Very well, so be it. It's your wedding, after all, Marlena, and as for you, Bettina, you always were an old softie."

Since Sara had first left for Paris, I must have said to myself a thousand times, "Golly, I wish Sara were here to see this . . . or hear that. . . ." And I knew I would certainly say it or think it on my wedding day. But right now how I wished she could be here to see her mother, hear what she had just said. Oh, she would be so proud. I thought of how Aunt Bettina had behaved that night of the terrible dinner party ten years ago and how she appeared tonight. Still lovely and so dignified and so fine—a real fine Southern lady.

––––––––

The church wedding followed a private Jewish ceremony, and the reception was held in the garden of the old Leeds house. The bride wore a wedding gown of Brussels lace that her mother had worn before her and the two maids of honor wore matching pale pink dresses of bouffant organdy and leghorn hats trimmed with deep pink velvet ribbons. Pink champagne flowed and the tables were draped in pink organdy with deep pink napkins and deep pink roses, and the air was aromatic with the scent of many flowers.

"What a heavenly day!" Chrissy breathed. "May this marriage be made in heaven and last, for God's sake!"

"I agree," Maeve said. "But just don't get in my way when I grab for the bride's bouquet or I'll mow you down."

"Just you try. I've been single for years now. How long do you think this situation can go on?"

Maurice had sat in the very last pew of the church, then hovered at the edges of the party until Bettina found him drinking champagne by himself.

"Maurice!"

She held out both hands to him but he kissed her on the cheek before taking them. She could feel the wetness of his tears. "Bettina . . ." He could hardly speak. "I'm making a fool of myself. Forgive me." He wiped at his eyes with an initialed handkerchief. "I can't believe how lovely you look. Your eyes—why, they're as blue as the first day I saw you. And your skin, it's the skin of a young girl. You put the bride to shame." He smiled almost shyly at his own words.

Bettina was beguiled. Maurice sounded for all the world like a different person from the man she had lived with.

"You look well yourself, Maurice," she lied.

He shook his head. "I'm feeling my age, Bettina. I'm almost sixty. I have almost fifteen years on you and I'm feeling each and every one. It's damn decent of you to even talk to me, Bettina. When Marlena invited me I thought, God, they're going to raise holy hell with her for that. But then she called me again . . . she's a sweet girl . . . and re-affirmed her invitation. She said that both her mother and you wanted me to come. I really don't deserve your forgiveness or your sister's charity."

Bettina could not bear Maurice so humble.

"This is a wedding day, Maurice. Let's not talk about past hurts. You have some champagne and I'll have fruit punch and we'll drink to Marlena and then we'll drink to our Sara, just you and I."

"Oh, Bettina, our Sara. . . ." He broke down and sobbed.

Bettina put her arms around the man she had loved and lost and now forgiven, and comforted him. "She's going to be all right, Maurice. Maeve and Chrissy—they've been so wonderful—they've sworn to me that the doctor said Sara would be as good as new . . . soon! Soon, Maurice! We'll both see her soon."

But he didn't seem able to stop crying.

"I don't know how I'll ever thank you enough for your wonderful wedding present, Maeve. And if it weren't for ending up in Switzerland and seeing Sara . . ." My voice broke. "I don't know if I . . . Peter and I, could have accepted such a generous gift."

"Oh, hush, you just have a divine time . . . for all of us. And if you really want to thank me, just throw the bouquet in my direction," Maeve said with a glint of mischief in the laughing green eyes. "It will just kill Chrissy if I catch the bouquet instead of her."

"All right, I'll try. You just be in the right spot. I'm not known for accuracy."

"What's going on here?" Chrissy came over. "Do I smell a conspiracy? I thought before you leave, Marlena, and throw your bouquet in my direction, we three should have our annual toast and drink to our absent friend who will be with us next year at this time."

"To Sara!"

"To next year and the four of us together!"

"And Peter too!" I added.

Chrissy and Maeve were so busy jockeying and squealing for the best position, elbowing each other out of the way, that when I finally made my toss, a Charleston girl, a Williams cousin twice removed and only seventeen, managed to catch my bouquet of pink sweetheart roses and baby's breath.

4.

On the very first day of August, Chrissy and Maeve presented themselves at the clinic and were shown to Sara's suite. "Go right in," they were told and for some reason they tiptoed in, fearful, not knowing quite what to expect. Sara was propped up in bed, surrounded by a small mountain of pillows, reading the latest copy of *Vogue*. They gave small cries of exultation! It was their old Sara. A beautiful, glamorous Sara! The hair they had so worried about was piled on top of her head in a cluster of curls—the pale yellow of butter churned in winter. She was wrapped in shocking pink, maribou trimmed, and the hands that held the magazine flashed incredibly long nails, exquisitely manicured and painted the same shade as her negligee. And she was completely made up, even to a penciled-in beauty mark.

But Sara didn't even look up! It was as if she had not heard them come in, had not heard their sounds of joyful surprise. They approached the bed and still she ignored them.

"Sara?" Maeve said tentatively.

"Sara?" Chrissy asked, anxiously.

Sara turned a page of the magazine, sipped from a glass of water that stood on the nightstand.

"Sara . . ."

"Sara, it's Maeve and Chrissy, dear."

Still, Sara did not look up.

Maeve took her hand and kissed it. Chrissy kissed her cheek. Sara turned another page. The friends exchanged disheartened looks of disappointment—they *had been* led to believe . . .

All of a sudden, Sara threw the magazine across the room and looked at them directly, "Well, it's about time you two bitches showed up!"

They stared at her with incredulous eyes and gaping mouths, until Sara burst out laughing.

Maeve clutched her heart. "Oh, Sara! Oh, Sara! How could you? How mean!"

Chrissy started to cry. "What a lousy joke! What a lousy stinking joke!"

Sara held out her arms to them. They threw themselves on the bed and the three hugged and kissed and wept.

"I really can't talk about any of it yet. But there's something I have

341

to say," Sara whispered. "Thank you. Thank you for what you did for me—thank you for loving me when I didn't deserve to have you love me."

"Oh, shit!" Chrissy said.

A woman in nurse's white came in and said that Dr. Lutece suggested Sara get dressed and go out for a walk on the grounds with her friends. Sara's face hardened. "I'm not getting dressed and you can tell Dr. Lutece for me that I'm not going for any walk."

"But your friends would like to go for a walk in the garden, I'm sure."

"Don't be sure." Sara turned to Maeve and Chrissy. "Tell her you don't want to go for any walk in any garden!"

"Sara looks just wonderful, Dr. Lutece. How can we ever thank you?"

Dr. Lutece ignored the offer of thanks as if not worthy of his notice. "Do not be deceived by Sara's appearance. The sleep therapy has accomplished most of that. She is not as well as she appears. As I told you, the physical was the easy part. Sara has yet to go outside the Clinique. She will not be well until she can face the terrors of the world and, believe me, the world can be a terrifying place."

Even I know that, Doctor, and I'm not as smart as you. "Sara's cousin and her husband will probably be here tomorrow, Doctor," Maeve said. "Can they see her?"

"Is her cousin a trusted friend?"

"Yes."

"Good. Sara must know that her friends are ready to support her."

"Sara! Oh, Sara!" I cried.

"Is that all anyone is going to do around me? Cry?" Sara said with feigned exasperation.

"My husband is with me, Sara."

"Yes, I know. So you went and got married without me, did you? Without my stamp of approval?" Sara teased. "Is he excruciatingly hand-some?"

Oh, it *was* the old Sara.

"Not exactly excruciatingly. But he *is* always sweet. May I bring him in?" I had been instructed to ask Sara first as Sara was wary of strangers.

"No. I'm too thin. I'd rather not meet anybody . . . new . . . until I've gained some weight."

"Come on, Sara. Peter's come all this way to meet my famous cousin."

"Famous for what?" Sara asked with bitterness.

342

"Anyhow, Sara, it was you who told me a girl could never be too thin or too rich."

"That old chestnut! I was just repeating somebody else. And it's not true. I am *too* thin. All my titties are gone," Sara wailed. "Where have my titties gone?"

Dr. Lutece apparently approved of the exchange between Sara and me. It was good, he said, that Sara bewailed the loss of her chest measurement. It was a form of awareness; hopefully, she would strive to improve her figure. The will had to be there. That she had refused to see Peter was not unexpected. I was to come back each day and urge Sara to meet my husband. Perhaps by the end of our stay there would be some progress.

"Tell me all about the wedding. I want to hear all about everything."

We were in the sitting room of Sara's suite, Maeve sitting crosslegged on the floor, Chrissy sprawled on the sofa as she always did, I sitting across from Sara.

"The color scheme was pale pink with darker pink accents. Maeve and Chrissy wore pale pink organdy and the tablecloths were organdy. And we used mostly roses, pink and crimson. And we even had pink champagne."

"Pink champagne! If I had been there I never would have allowed pink champagne. Absolutely—" She was about to say tacky, and we all knew it and laughed. This was our old Sara.

"No, I take that back. Considering the color scheme, pink champagne was really the only way to go," she amended. "Lovely . . . And who was there? I want to hear the whole guest list."

I looked at Maeve and Chrissy for guidance. Should we mention Sara's father? Maeve and Chrissy nodded yes, but none of us was at all sure that this was the proper move. We should have asked the doctor.

I went through the list, mentioning all the relatives and friends whom Sara knew and then, last of all, "And your father came, Sara."

I paused, waiting for some comment from Sara. When there was none, I continued: "As you know, Sara, he was always good to me and it was all right with your mother. You see, his wife left him. She took her children and went back to England and Aunt Bettina felt sorry for him. She was very kind to him—she forgave him and they spoke at the wedding like old friends."

We all held our breath. But Sara buffed her nails and said nothing. Hadn't any of it registered at all?

Sara was tearful now that I was leaving, going home.

"Tell Mama that I love her and that I'll be seeing her soon."

"Are you sure you don't want her to come see you here?"

"Here? In this place? No. I couldn't do that to her. You make sure she *doesn't* come, you hear? I never want her to come near such a place again."

"It's not bad here at all, Sara. It's more like a . . . spa than a clinic. If it weren't, you wouldn't be looking so good."

"Haven't I taught you anything? Never judge by appearances," Sara said darkly. "And tell your Peter I said hello. And to take care of you because you're mighty precious, Precious."

"Oh, Sara, please, just say hello to him yourself. After all, I went and married a Jew only to please you."

Sara laughed. "That's pretty funny, all right."

"Please, Sara."

"No, I can't. I'd like to, but I just don't think that I can."

But I thought I detected signs of weakening.

"Please, Sara, for your favorite cousin. You once said you wouldn't refuse me anything."

"I never said that. You're making that up!"

"Oh, Sara, you're a terrible liar. You said it and now you're refusing me the very thing that would send me home happy!"

"Oh, all right! I'll see him if it means that much to you. But I'm sure I don't know why it does."

"It does, it does, Sara. I need the Sara Gold stamp of approval."

When Peter went in, followed by me, I could see that Sara looked at him suspiciously as if thinking: *And what is he after?* But she forced herself to smile. I could see that the smile was forced as if she were smiling for my sake.

"Hi, Cousin Sara," Peter said. "I'm awfully glad you're just as pretty as Marlena said because I'd hate to be married to a liar."

Sara tossed her head and said, "Welcome to the family of the Charleston Leedses, Peter Wiener. Did you all know that our ancestor, Marlena's and mine, fired that first shot at Sumter that was heard 'round the world?"

Peter laughed and so did I—with relief.

"For goodness' sake, Sara Leeds Gold, are you still telling that story? I've told you a zillion times—that shot heard 'round the world was the Revolution and not the War Between the States!"

Sara shrugged. "Do tell, Marlena! Petey Wieney, you'll just have to do something about that girl. She *is* officious, or haven't you noticed?"

Again, Maeve and Chrissy waited for Dr. Lutece to come to them in the teak-paneled room with the view of Mont Blanc, and again they were nervous. This was evaluation time again. Perhaps this was the time he would tell them how much more time Sara needed. He entered the room and began right in without a pause for the amenities.

"I am prepared to take a step that is without precedence at the Clinique. At this time, I think Sara needs the reassurance that she is loved and valued. I have discussed with Sara having her mother come to visit her but it seems very important to Sara that her mother does not see her ill. In the past, she has been the person her mother has leaned on and Sara cannot have that image taken away. And she rejects her father as a supportive person. To the contrary, she still insists on seeing her father as the root of her problems. In the absence of an adequate husband or parent figure, Sara sees her friends in the role of surrogate parents, the only people she can count on to love her no matter what. Usually, I would discourage this kind of attachment—I would prefer for the patient to make independent strides. But I think Sara needs a sense of her past now, needs your support. I believe your presence here will actually speed her recovery. This past week spent with the two of you and her cousin seems to have done Sara immeasurable good," he said with as much enthusiasm as the girls believed him capable of showing. "I cannot deny that I see an improvement. And that she finally agreed to meet her cousin's new husband and that she made an effort to be gracious, I find encouraging. Therefore, I am inviting one of you to stay here with Sara at the Clinique. In fact, you may alternate, a few weeks or a month at a time." It sounded as if he were offering them a gift. Even if they hadn't wanted to stay, which was not the case, neither one would have had the temerity to refuse this gift.

Maeve insisted that she would stay and that Chrissy go back to New York. "I'm still too afraid to go near Ali. And I haven't asked Sara yet if she mentioned my baby to. . . . It's just too dangerous for me to take the risk. I can finish my book here just as well as in New York and this way, you, at least, can continue visiting Ali. To speak in Dr. Lutece's terms, you be surrogate mother to my daughter and I'll do the same for Sara."

"I hope he's worth it," Sara said.

Maeve looked up from her work.

"Who is 'he,' Sara?"

"Peter Wiener. Petey Wieney. Marlena's not finishing law school and she only had a year to go. And now she's going to live in New Jersey. Saddle River, New Jersey. That's where his family is."

"Well, that's where Peter's going to practice law. I guess she has to go with him, doesn't she?"

"Like Ruth in the Bible."

345

"I suppose."

"I once read something else from the Bible, something like 'He shall leave his father and mother and shall cleave unto his wife.' "

"The important thing is that they cleave unto each other."

"Yes. If he's worth it."

"You liked him, Sara. Didn't you?"

"Yes. But me! What do I know about men?"

Maeve smiled wistfully, "I'd say as much as any of us do."

"Today, Sara, my love, we *are* taking that walk in the garden."

"Why can't everybody just leave me alone?" Sara asked sullenly.

"That's not why I'm here, Sara, and don't you forget that," Maeve said spiritedly.

"Forgive me." Sara rushed over and grabbed her hand, put it to her cheek. "I *am* horrid. Forgive me for everything! I've never begged your pardon for doubting you that day in Paris. . . . For the awful things I said to you."

"Oh, Sara. It has never been a question of forgiving. We are all victims."

"Sara, you don't need that heavy coat. Or that scarf on your head. It's warm outside. Beautifully warm."

"I do so need them. There are so many frightening things out there."

"I know, I know. But you've always been so brave, Sara. And I'll be with you. Every step of the way."

"I'm going to town to mail my manuscript, Sara. Won't you come with me?"

"For God's sake, I've gone outside with you every day. In the garden and out on the trails. Even up that goddamn mountain. Is nothing enough?" Then, already regretful of her tone, "Honestly, you give some people an inch and they want a foot."

"You're wrong. I want the whole leg. And you have some shopping to do."

"I don't need anything."

"You do. You need sweaters and slacks. And shoes. You only have the one pair. And what is Sara Leeds Gold doing with one pair of shoes?"

"But I'm not Sara Leeds Gold anymore."

"You could have fooled me."

"Aren't I Sara O'Connor?"

The name hung heavy between them.

"No, *I'm* O'Connor. You're Gold."

Maeve sighed. She might as well go all the way and tell Sara what they had done.

"Chrissy's arranging a divorce."

346

Anxiety coursed across Sara's face, starting with her eyes and running down to her mouth. "But how can she? I'm here and she's there."

"Chrissy's hired lawyers. When the time comes, you'll get the papers here to sign." Then Maeve laughed. "If Chrissy doesn't sign the papers for you. Remember at Chalmer's? Chrissy was the official forger in residence. She signed notes for everybody—from parents to the office, from the office to the parents, from teachers to the office. . . . Remember that time she signed a note for Lulu Jenson from a Dr. Ludwig Von Hefferman and Miss Chalmer's secretary was suspicious and spent a whole day trying to locate him?"

They laughed together and the bad moment passed. They started remembering other funny things that happened at school. But suddenly, Sara's brow wrinkled again. "What about my money? Who is looking after my money?"

"It's all being taken care of, Sara."

"But somebody has to check up on my father to see that he doesn't cheat me."

"Oh, he's not about to do *that*. You *never* thought that. Not *ever*. You always said, even when you were your angriest at him, that you knew he loved you. You always said that maybe he hadn't loved your mother but that he did love you."

"You're wrong, Maeve. What I always said was that I knew he loved me, but that he just didn't love me enough."

"Oh, Sara, there is such a thing as loving someone *too* much. Who can say how much love is enough?"

They came back from the village. Sara's cheeks were flushed with success, her arms filled with packages. "Next time, I'll get some skiing things. Just to wear, of course, if we go to Gstaad. No one is actually going to get me on a pair of skis."

"Why not?"

"Just you hold on, Maeve O'Connor. I know that when I leave here I'm supposed to be as free of fear as I used to be, and able to do anything, but that doesn't mean I'm going to do something I never wanted to do before I came here, either. And that includes sliding down a pile of snow on my ass! Après-ski is still more my style!"

"Vive la style Sara!"

"Oh, my God!" Sara exclaimed, reading the letter that had just arrived from Marlena.

"Is something wrong?"

"Nothing is wrong. Everything, it seems, is divine in Saddle River, New Jersey. Marlena is pregnant! She says she's suffering from morning sickness but she doesn't give a damn! She's happy as a lark. And Peter's happy as a lark. And they're buying a house and they're happy as two larks in a tree. And I'm happy for them! Isn't it wonderful news? But can you imagine Marlena with a baby?" Sara asked.

"Of course I can. Why not?"

"I don't know. It just seems funny to think of one of us with a baby, that's all." She clapped her hand over her mouth. "Oh, Maeve. I *am* stupid. Forgive me."

"Would you please stop saying that—'Forgive me'? It's not necessary and it's annoying."

"Oh, you are mad at me! I am sorry!"

Could she ask Sara now, Maeve wondered, if she had told Padraic about Ali? She had to know. But no, she couldn't ask her yet. It was still too soon.

"Oh, for God's sake. Stop saying you're sorry, too."

"All right, I will. Can't Sara-Wara make it up to Maevey-Wavy?" Sara got down on her hands and knees.

"Oh, hell's bells," Maeve laughed with exasperation. "Will you get up? There's nothing to make up for. Wait a minute, there is something you can do for me."

"Anything."

"There's that party I'm invited to at Noel Coward's villa. I want you to go with me."

Immediately, Sara's mood changed. "You never wanted to go to parties before. How come you're so hot to go to this one?" she asked suspiciously.

"Well, Noel Coward *is* a very brilliant man—famous for his wit. I'd love to meet him."

"Why did he invite you to his party if you've never met?"

"How do I know? Maybe he heard *I* was witty and brilliant and he wanted to meet me. I am a famous author, you know," Maeve teased.

"How did he know you were here?"

"What is this—an inquisition? You know how these things work. When you're a New Yorker, New York is a small town. When you live in Paris, Paris becomes a small town. Everybody always ends up knowing who's in town and who is sleeping with whom. When we went to the Eagle in Gstaad—the night they were throwing the food at each other—I ran into Nancy Constantin and she knows everybody. So it's not hard to figure out how we received the invitation."

"Oh. Now it's *we* who received the invitation. Before it was only *you.*"

"I'm not sure what the goddamn invitation said anymore. You said you would do something for me and that's it. You're going."

"Oh," Sara wailed. "I can't believe how things have turned around. It used to be that I urged you to go to parties and now, you're *forcing* me. Well, I don't have anything to wear."

"Last time I heard, they hadn't closed the stores. Neither here in Lausanne nor in Gstaad."

"Really, Maeve, you never were so . . . relentless."

"I'm tired of fighting with you, Sara. You're going with me to the party or I'm going home to New York and you can stay here in this place alone."

Sara shook her head. "Relentless . . . no one will believe this . . . no one!"

"What do you think everyone will be wearing? Après-ski or silk?"

"The Sara I knew didn't give two cents for what anyone wore—she set her own style. And that's exactly what you're going to do. What do you *feel* like wearing?"

"I don't know. I don't even want to go."

Maeve instructed the saleswoman to bring out whatever she had, one creation after the other. Finally Sara said, "That one. I'll try that one on."

She came out in the short black silk satin organza with a halter top and ruffled skirt. "That's my Sara," Maeve said in complete approval.

"What shall I do with my hair?"

"Just let it flow. It looks wonderful just the way it is now, like the mane of a wild lion. Sara, you look magnificent!"

"Why not?" Sara complained. "Look at what they've done to me. I've been put to sleep for weeks, injected with sheep serum, monkey gland serum, serum made from bulls' testicles."

"Really, Sara! You're exaggerating," Maeve objected, wrinkling her nose.

"They've shot wax under my skin and they've peeled me, vacuumed me and hosed me down with some kind of smelly water and almost drowned me in radioactive mudbaths. They've even fed me gardenia petals. . . . They've oiled me and pounded me and made me jump up and down and slipped me seventy-six kinds of vitamins. There's absolutely nothing they *haven't* done to me. Between you and me, Dr. Lutece is a charlatan. What they're really running at Lutece is a high-class beauty parlor under the guise of medicine."

"Only you could complain about looking well."

"But I'm still too thin and you're making me expose myself in public."

"Yes, I am," Maeve complacently agreed, choosing a dress for herself—a long brown wool.

"You know who you look like in that dress?" Sara asked testily.

"I'll bite. Who?"

"Your Aunt Maggie."

"What does that mean?"

"It means that, as usual, you're trying to hide your light under a bushel of corn and you look like somebody's maiden aunt. In this case— your own."

"The expression, Sara, is a bushel. Just a bushel. No corn. And thank you for the kind words."

"Look, you're making me go to this party. The least you can do is let me pick out something for you that will show the world you're not afraid to be your most attractive."

"Very well."

"Whatever I choose, you'll wear?"

"Yes."

Sara instructed the saleswoman to bring back a bronze kid evening gown they had looked at. It had a tight skirt and slits up either side.

"Isn't it kind of extreme? . . ." Maeve asked, already sorry she had promised to wear it.

"Try it on," Sara said imperiously.

The Lutece Rolls, white and discreetly unmarked in any manner, took them up a road lined with pots of pink and white petunias to Noel Coward's pink and white chalet high in the hills.

"I think I'm going to be sick," Sara said.

"How do you think I feel in this bizarre get-up you chose for me?" Then, taking pity on Sara, Maeve said: "You don't have to circulate— you can just sit and speak only when you're spoken to."

Maeve quickly scanned the celebrity-filled room. Noel Coward sat in a purple smoking jacket on a purple sofa, reclining against a mass of needlepoint pillows, with several of his guests seated at his yellow-velvet-slippered feet. David Niven, for one . . . and yes, it *was* Gary Cooper!

"Look, Sara, Gary Cooper. . . ."

"Big deal! I want to sit down."

Maeve found a sofa placed to one side of the room strategically out of the mainstream. "Probably no one will even pay attention to us. The room is full of important people. None so beautiful as we, of course, but slightly more illustrious, shall we say? See, there's Charlie Chaplin over there chatting with Somerset Maugham."

"God, Maugham's ugly! And Chaplin's no beauty, either."

"Sh! For heaven's sake, Sara! Sit!"

"Can you move that potted palm from over there and place it in front of this sofa?"

"If you like, I'll put it in your lap and you can hold it in front of your face," Maeve said.

"You *are* mean. Dr. Lutece said I could have one glass of wine. Do you think you could manage to call that waiter over? Oh dear, there's one of the Rothschilds headed over here. Isn't her name Marie? What will I say to her?" Sara panicked.

"Say 'How are you, darling? You look simply marvelous!' "

"Sara Gold! Haven't seen you since Paris. At the do Laurette Giroux gave at Versailles, wasn't it? How are you, darling? You look simply marvelous!"

Sara looked at Maeve helplessly.

Maeve stuck out her hand. "Hi! We haven't met, have we? I'm Maeve O'Connor. Terrific party, isn't it? Sara has a bit of a cold, laryngitis actually, so we've been kind of keeping to ourselves. Haven't even been on a pair of skis yet. But I've heard the trails are really good this year . . . really . . . powdery. . . ." She hoped that this was the right word.

Finally, the Rothschild woman moved on. They didn't discover her first name.

"That wasn't so difficult, was it? I can't seem to get the butler's attention. Can you stay here for a few minutes while I go get your glass of wine and just say a few words to our host?"

"Are you trying to get away from me? Why must you speak to that skinny piece of—?"

"Sara!"

"Well, I'm sorry, but I don't even see why everyone makes such a fuss over him. Those dumb little songs of his. What passes for wit is beyond me."

"I'll just be gone a minute. Sara. Oh, look, that's Orson Welles over there by the piano with Harry Hartman."

"I really don't give a shit for Harry Hartman. As for Orson Welles, the 'boy genius' is over the hill. Oh, Lordy, look who's coming over now! *Your* friend, Nancy Constantin. . . . Nancy! How are you, darling? You look simply marvelous!"

"It's you who looks simply marvelous, Sara. Doesn't she, Maeve? You're glowing! I've heard that you were a bit under the weather but you certainly don't look it. It must be this wonderful Swiss air. And those doctors don't hurt, either. I always say Switzerland is the best of places. Between the banks, the doctors, the slopes, the wonderful cuisine and the tax situation, what else does one really need? Have you been out yet? I mean on the slopes. The talk is that the Aga Khan is going to sell his villa here and take up residence around St. Moritz. Have you heard anything? What I don't like about St. Moritz is the overdressing that goes on there. One would think it was Paris instead of just ski country."

"I couldn't agree with you more," Sara said. "It *is* more casual in Gstaad and, goodness gracious, if one can't be casual when one's skiing or relaxing *après de,* when can one?"

Maeve slipped away. She would get Sara's wine and then she would introduce herself to her host—he had invited her, after all.

She picked up a glass of white wine from the butler's tray and looked to see if Noel was reasonably uninvolved at the moment.

"You're Maeve O'Connor, aren't you?"

Maeve swung around. It was Harry Hartman. She had never seen any of his movies when she was growing up—she hadn't seen more than three or four movies at all in those years—but not to know who Harry Hartman was, or not to recognize the pixie face, was practically un-American. Harry Hartman was, after all, an Institution.

Maeve took a fast gulp of Sara's wine. "I recognize you, but how do you know who I am?"

"From the pictures of you in the papers and magazines when you were Debutante of the Year. Though it was the Twin Debs of the Year, wasn't it?"

"You have an excellent memory, Mr. Hartman." She sat down since Harry Hartman was a couple of inches shorter than she. He sat down next to her. "That was a long time ago."

He laughed heartily. "You're all of what—twenty-three? Twenty-four?—and that was a long time ago? In that case, what can *I* say?"

Maeve guessed that Harry Hartman must be close to fifty.

"But even if I hadn't remembered your pictures from the papers then, I would still have recognized you from the photo on the cover of *Sojourn in Paris*. A wonderful book! Both the book and its author are unforgettable."

"You're very nice to say that. I wish I could say something equally nice to you, but I must confess I've never seen one of your pictures. Though I would certainly love to. It's just that I've never gone to the movies very much."

"Perhaps that's been one of your wiser decisions."

"Well, it hasn't really been a conscious decision. I will make sure that I see your very next picture."

His merry dark eyes smiled at her. "I'll have to make sure that you do. If I send you a very special invitation to the premiere, do you promise to attend it with me?"

"I might," she said. "If I can."

She liked him. She could see why he was a star; his friendliness must come across on the screen. He made you feel good. He was a nice man. But she did have to get back to Sara.

She held up the glass of wine. "You must excuse me. I have to take this over to my friend—"

"Sara Gold O'Connor . . . She's married to your father, isn't she?"

"You are certainly well-informed, Mr. Hartman. I would think that a man of your stature—writer, actor, director—would be too busy to keep a record of who's married to whom." She rose, and said coldly, "You will excuse me."

He got up from his chair too. "I've offended you."

"Really, Mr. Hartman. You presume, and I don't even know you."

"Call me Harry. And we *do* know each other now. And why bother your friend? She seems to be getting along very well."

Maeve looked over at Sara. She couldn't believe her eyes. Sara was talking animatedly with a suave-looking young man of athletic figure who reminded Maeve vaguely of Gaetano Rebucci. Sara was actually doing more than talking—she was *flirting!* The signs were unmistakable.

"*Who* is that man?" Maeve asked Harry.

"André Pulowsky. He's a ski instructor who's very fashionable at the moment. He's a graduate of Le Rosey so his qualifications are impeccable. He's Gstaad's current rage. The ladies are lining up to take lessons—even those who have been skiing for years. Why don't you let her be? He's probably good for her."

Maeve glanced sharply at Harry Hartman. What did he know about what was good for Sara? Or more to the point, what had he heard about Sara? About Sara and Padraic and herself? "Why don't you concern yourself with what's good for you, Mr. Hartman?"

Harry threw back his gray head and laughed.

"I didn't intend to be amusing, Mr. Hartman."

"I know you didn't and I apologize."

"I am so bored with apologies. Why do people always say and do things they have to apologize for? Wouldn't it be far easier *not* to say or do things in the first place?"

He was still amused. She could tell.

"Perhaps we all are not as sure or as perfect as you, Maeve O'Connor. So we make mistakes and then have to apologize for them."

"Oh dear." Maeve blushed. "Did I sound like a pompous ass? If so, I apologize," and they both laughed.

"Never a pompous ass. I think you're charming and refreshing."

Maeve finished Sara's glass of wine and picked up another from the passing tray.

"I really do have to go over to Mr. Coward and introduce myself. He was kind enough to invite me to his party and I don't even know him."

"Why bother? Noel's main topic of conversation tonight is the delicious little raspberries he has flown in from Israel. He's urging everyone to try 'the delightful little things with oodles of heavenly cream and just a dipping of sugar, darling.' "

Maeve had to laugh at Harry's imitation of the inimitable Noel Coward being precious, even though her cheeks flushed with embarrassment. He *was* their host.

Just then Noel Coward's voice, in perfect imitation of Harry's, carried across the room. "Harry, you naughty little short man, monopolizing my gorgeous guest. Bring that delightful redhead over here this very minute."

The Lutece car came for Maeve and Sara on the dot of twelve. Sara, who was reluctant to leave, wailed, "Who are we? Cinderella? That Lutece is a tyrant!"

353

Maeve couldn't have agreed more.

But Sara was tired. She leaned back against the rich-smelling upholstery. "You're about to get one of your fondest wishes, dear Maeve. I'm actually going to put on skis. André has a waiting list a mile long for his personal ministrations but he's putting me at the top."

Maeve smiled to herself. Sara was certainly getting over her fear of heights quickly. *And after she complained so when I first took her walking up the mountainside.*

"We have to go shopping in Craon su Sierre Monday," Sara said.

"Why must we shop there? That's pretty far."

"Because, sweetie, Bubisport and Alex are the two very best ski shops and they are both in Craon su Sierre. You must remember that in St. Moritz the crowd is more concerned with their partying clothes, but in Gstaad the emphasis is much more on one's ski apparel."

"Well, it's good that I learned that before I left Switzerland. I might have gone home in abysmal ignorance."

Sara sat up straight. "Why do you say that? You're not thinking of going home yet, are you?"

"No, of course I'm not. I'm not going home until you do."

Sara settled back against the seat again with a sigh of relief. "Whew! I thought perhaps you had fallen madly in love with Harry Hartman and you were going to follow him home to California."

"No, Sara, I didn't fall madly in love with him, and no, I am not prepared to follow him whither he goest. But I *am* going to have dinner with him tomorrow night."

"Then you did fall for him?"

"Just because I agreed to have dinner with him?"

"I know you, Maeve. You don't have dinner with a man lightly."

"Really, Sara. It's only a dinner," Maeve protested. But she *was* looking forward to their dinner date already and she had just left him.

"Maeve?"

"Yes, Sara?"

"What do you think Dr. Lutece will say about the patient having a little diddle of sex?"

"Mmmm. Well, there's the Italian-Swiss, the Austrian-Swiss, the German-Swiss and the French-Swiss. Since Dr. Lutece is French-Swiss he'll probably say, 'Oo la la!' "

"Are you going to Harry Hartman's chalet for dinner *à deux* again? That's seven nights running, not to mention several luncheons."

"Do you mind? You have your ski lessons. Anyhow, Harry is going back to California in a couple of days. He's starting work on a picture."

"I wish I could see what you see in him. He's old enough to be your— Oops, that *is* a no-no, isn't it?"

"Under the circumstances, Sara, I would *certainly* say so."

"All I meant is he's not terribly attractive. He's short and that gray crew cut and that silly little nose. I know there's been a lot of women ga-ga over him, but I can't imagine why."

"For one thing, he's a *nice* man. And he's a decent man. And for another, he's a fascinating, exciting man to talk to and *some* of us girls do like to talk. He's one of the giants of the movie industry. He writes and directs as well as acts. *He's* not just another pretty face."

"You can say that again. And I bet he says he wants to make a movie out of your book, right?"

Maeve only laughed.

"But the big question is—how is he in bed? Does he have a big one?"

Sara woke up crying.

"What is it, Sara? Did you have a bad dream?"

"I dreamed about my father. He was crying! I never saw him cry. . . . He was all alone in the dream and he was frightened. It was terrible! And he said that his wife, Violet, had left him—had gone back to England. In the dream I felt so sorry for him that I started to cry too."

Maeve smoothed Sara's hair back from her forehead. It was coated with perspiration.

"What do you think the dream meant? Do you think it's true?"

"You'll have to discuss the dream's meaning with Dr. Lutece. But you *know* it's true. When Marlena was here she told you your father had come to her wedding, that she had invited him because she felt sorry for him—that he was lonely, that Violet had gone back to England. You just couldn't accept it at the time, I guess."

"But what about Mama?" Sara whispered. "What did she do when Papa came to the wedding?"

"Marlena told you that too. Your mother was very nice to him. She forgave him. They spoke together like old friends."

"Really? Is that true?" She let out a huge sigh. "Mama is a great lady, isn't she?" She gave another sigh. "I would like to be a great lady too. Like Mama."

Why the great sigh? Maeve wondered. Was it because that if Bettina forgave Maurice Gold then Sara herself could, too? Then, she would not be betraying Bettina by loving Maurice.

Perhaps she had better discuss this with Dr. Lutece herself.

With Dr. Lutece it was difficult to be sure, but Maeve thought he was pleased.

"Well, Miss O'Connor, it appears that we've done it, haven't we?"

"I don't know, Doctor. Have we? Is it over?"

"Almost, Miss O'Connor. Almost but not quite. There's one more scene before the curtain comes down."

The clinic sent its limousine with Maeve along to meet Maurice Gold. She felt so sorry for the weary Maurice, he was so nervous his hands shook. If he were not careful, Maeve thought, Dr. Lutece would snatch him up and start shooting him up with some of his bulls' testicles serum.

"Please, Mr. Gold, calm yourself. Dr. Lutece assured me it would be all right."

"How can he be sure?"

"If he weren't, he wouldn't have sent for you."

"That simple?"

"It wasn't simple at all."

"How can I ever thank you, Maeve?"

"Oh, it's not I who's responsible for Sara having come this far. I'd like to think I helped, but it's Dr. Lutece. And Marlena."

"Marlena? But she was only here for a few days."

"Yes, but if she hadn't invited you to her wedding, and if Sara's mother hadn't made up with you—"

Maurice Gold rocked back and forth in his anxiety, rubbed his hands together again and again. "Little did I know what would be when we invited Marlena to come to our house, to go to school with Sara. It's turned out that it was bread cast upon the waters. . . ." He was talking to himself, rather than to Maeve. Then, as if remembering she was there, he said, "All this must have been extremely difficult for you, Maeve. Terrible."

Maeve thought of Harry Hartman and what he had told her about making a successful movie. "You have to bring the audience way down low before you take them up, up there to the stars."

Maeve hoped that Dr. Lutece was right. The man was a machine— he dealt in emotions, but he was above them. She, herself, knew Sara better than Dr. Lutece and she had her doubts. Maybe Sara wasn't ready to see her father, maybe she wasn't ready to forgive him, to accept him back into her heart. Maybe she didn't *need* to love him. Maybe that love, like her own, was too cold, too long dead, too decomposed from bitterness and hate. Maybe seeing Maurice Gold would backfire!

And what of Maurice Gold himself? He was already a beaten man, white-haired, prematurely aged. Rejection now by Sara would destroy him. And Dr. Lutece wouldn't even care except to pick up his horse-size injection needle or tell the assistant to prepare the psychiatric couch.

Dr. Lutece wanted Maurice Gold to just walk in—an icy blast of shock. But Maeve could not allow that. For both their sakes, Maurice's

356

and Sara's, there had to be a minimum of preparation, a word or two of warning.

"Where did you go off to?" Sara asked Maeve when she came into the suite, leaving Maurice Gold, already exhausted with nerves, out in the hall. "There's a letter from Chrissy. I'm so mad at her I could scream! She has a new beau and it's Max Kozlo the composer! How old do you think he is? He must be at least sixty. What is she thinking of? Somebody has to talk to her. I think I'll call her up right now. What time is it in New York? I can never remember. . . ."

"Sara, there's somebody here from New York right now . . . outside. . . ."

Sara stared at Maeve for a few seconds without seeing her at all. She knew who it had to be—he was the only one left. . . . Sara walked to the door and flung it open.

"Sara! Sara baby!"

"Papa! Oh, Papa!" Sara held out her arms. "Oh, Papa! I've missed you so! I thought you'd never come!"

Maurice held Sara in his arms for what seemed to Maeve an eternity, both sobbing. She herself couldn't help but weep. She tiptoed out of the room, leaving them alone. She went outside onto the terrace. There were flowers everywhere. She looked down at the village below. It was a scene straight out of a Walt Disney movie. And Sara was its star! Free of sickness, free of Padraic, free to love her father, free to go home. Free!

And she herself? She looked way up. It was a cloudless, blue-green sky. It was far, far too early in the day for a star to appear.

NEW YORK/HOLLYWOOD
1952-1956

1.

"Chrissy Marlowe, you're crazy! What do you think you're doing with Max Kozlo, anyway? I can understand you think you need an *older* man, but isn't thirty years kind of overdoing it?"

Chrissy giggled. "He's *forty* years older than I am and I adore him. He's really very cute. You can't imagine how secure it makes me feel to have this big cuddly bear of a man call me 'Schatzi' and tell me to put on my slippers because my sweet little feet will get cold."

"Hungarians! My mother told me never to trust a Hungarian!"

"Sara, your mother probably never met a Hungarian in her life! Why do you tell such stories?"

But then she became serious. "Sara, I've been *there*—with the young men. I've had the beach-beautiful body and the sexy eyes . . . more than once. . . . And it doesn't mean a thing. Max is a genius, a dignified older man of stature . . . *he's* somebody. . . . And Sara, those boys on the beach with the beautiful bodies . . . they'll *always* be there."

Sara had come up north, along with Martha, Howard, and Bettina, to see Marlena's and Peter's new baby, and had decided to stay on for a while. Life in Charleston had a nice, slow rhythm to it and it had been lovely spending time with Bettina but, loathe as she was to admit it, she had been getting the tiniest bit restless.

She had moved in with Chrissy and Maeve. "You do have the extra room," she told Chrissy, "and I'm not really in the mood to open up my house."

"There's no reason you should live there alone," Maeve told her.

"You ought to get rid of that house," Chrissy said. "It's just eating up money, and what do you need it for?"

"I'll think about it. Maybe I'll give it back to my father. He's been staying at the Pierre."

"Who knows if he'll want it back? Nobody seems to want those really big houses anymore."

"I know," Sara agreed. "Everything keeps changing—doesn't it? Look at Maeve here. Who would ever think that she'd be flying back and forth to the West Coast at the beck and call of a man five-foot-two?"

"Sara, did you ever get your face pushed in?" Maeve demanded. "Besides, he's five-foot-seven."

"Convince him, not me."

Sometimes when Maeve thought about it she couldn't believe it herself, that every couple of weeks or so she was actually flying across a continent just to see a man, talk with him, laugh with him, lie contentedly in his arms. She couldn't believe that she had so easily slipped into this role, or into Harry's bed, for that matter. She, who had thought that she would never love or be loved again. She, who had thought that she would never experience this easy, romantic, but sexually exciting, laughing kind of life and love.

Somehow, in his own low-keyed, smilingly steadfast fashion, Harry had communicated his caring, had made her respond despite her instinctive resistance. She had missed him the minute he had left Switzerland. But he had been constant, had called every day reminding her that theirs was a rendezvous to be kept. Sometimes she wondered how she had managed to become so quickly spellbound. Certainly, as Sara had often stated, his looks were not inspiring. In fact, physically he was the inverse of the other man she had loved. Unpretty for handsome, short for tall, sparkling dark eyes for somber blue ones, hair—short and gray instead of a dark, waving mane. Could it be that this very inversion was the physical attraction? Was her sexuality all that simple, that transparent? No, she decided, it couldn't be. She loved his body making love to hers because—first—she had loved *what* he was, what he stood for, his funny ways that turned tears into smiles, that eloquent personality, his wonderful thinking, the way he looked at things, all the things he believed in, all the underdogs he befriended, all the lost causes he upheld. Maeve found even his stand on not acquiring American citizenship very brave in the face of criticism from so many sides. Harry, Swiss-born, demanded that he be accepted as a citizen of the world because he wanted his movies—the movies that made people laugh in the face of adversity—to be universal. He wanted his acts of benevolence, the causes he believed in and fought for, to benefit not only Americans but all the unfortunates of God's earth.

He was the truest, most unhypocritical altruist she had ever known.

359

She felt honored to be the recipient of his love, and humble in offering him her own. And it was deplorable that a man of his caliber was being subject to all the ugliness that was going on in Hollywood—the inquisitions of the House UnAmerican Activities Committee, the denouncements, the suspicions, the blacklistings in this Communist witchhunt. So far, Harry was too big for them—larger than life. They had not been able to keep him from making pictures. But being Harry, he could not help but suffer for the indignities his friends endured.

Fortunately, Harry was of an indomitable nature. Nothing could spoil his relish for life. And he managed to implant some of that attitude in her. Never before had she herself taken such pleasure in life. If only Harry could accept their relationship as it was. If only he would stop pushing for marriage. He knew her reasons for not marrying him, he even understood some of them. He could not accept any of it.

"I don't feel the need to have children, Maeve. I'm fifty-one and I have a son twenty-four. I don't need any more children to feel complete. All I need is you. If you feel you can't have children—fine. That's no problem."

And Harry understood about Maeve's problem with Ali—that she wanted to be near her daughter even though it was not possible for her to go see her. He even agreed that it might be dangerous for Ali to be visited. Especially after Sara had tearfully confessed that, yes, she had told Padraic about Ali's existence. But Harry thought he had a solution to the problem. "We simply transfer her to a home near us in Southern California. I've investigated and there's a wonderful children's home near Palm Springs. You don't see her now because you're afraid to, but there, you could. I have it all worked out so that you can see her without a chance of her being discovered. I can go to entertain in that children's home without anyone lifting an eyebrow. Now, I go to the veterans' home once a month, and to other hospitals as often as I can. To anybody taking notice, the children's home would be just another stop on my schedule. And when I went, you could accompany me. You could see Ali, my darling, at least once a month. You could have both Ali and Happy Harry Hartman." He did a fancy time-step for her and landed on one knee, arms flung out.

Maeve laughed but that didn't make the very real fear go away. Oh, yes, Harry understood that she feared her father finding Ali. But now Maeve feared for Harry too, because by loving Harry, she had made him vulnerable. What Harry had no comprehension of was the poisoned, driving, obsessive omnipotence of Padraic O'Connor. Only Aunt Maggie had understood that, and she herself, and then Sara. You had to *live* with Padraic to understand.

She had to make sure that Harry never really understood. She had to protect Harry as well as Ali. Especially so now that her second book, *Of Desire Possessed,* had received such widespread acceptance. Her success had been accentuated because the *New York Times* Sunday book section had printed one of those split front pages reviewing two relevant books—hers and Padraic O'Connor's new novel, and the inevitable comparison had been disastrous for *Celtic Idyll*. The *Times* critic had flatly stated that the Padraic O'Connor talent had apparently gone the way of some other great writing talents, down the drain. "What a pity," the critique had read, "that it wasn't the alcohol that trickled away instead. But fortunately for us, there is still an O'Connor to raise the standard from where it has fallen and to carry it forth with superb skill."

Yes, she had defeated him with the written word as she had deliberately set out to do, and there was some measure of satisfaction in that. But she had won only one battle and she could win the war only if she protected those she loved.

2.

"Guess what?" Sara came bursting into the living room. "Marlena's pregnant again."

"But little Joshua isn't even a year old," Maeve protested.

"They don't care. They're thrilled to death. It just means they won't be taking the trip they planned next summer."

"How will Marlena manage with two babies? Joshua won't even be two years old when the baby is born."

"I don't know. They're crazy. Every time they discuss some problem, they laugh."

"Sounds great." Maeve laughed herself.

"I offered to pay for a maid for a year. I said it would be my present for the new baby, but they wouldn't hear of it."

"It's to Peter's credit if he wants to do for his family himself," Chrissy observed. "Peter is doing all right with that law firm, isn't he?"

"I suppose. But I told him, anytime he wanted to strike out on his own, I would help him."

Maeve smiled. "Did you only say that you would help him or did you *urge* him to start his own practice?"

Sara shrugged. "I'm just trying to help, that's all."

"Is that why you're always running to Saddle River?" Chrissy asked.

"I just adore little Joshua. He *is* my godchild. And I do have to keep busy, don't I? Maeve's either writing or flying to Hollywood, and you're visiting Ali or painting or running around with that crazy old Kozlo—"

"How dare you say that about my darling Max?" Chrissy said indignantly. "He might be old, but he's not crazy. Why do you resent him so?"

"Because he's not right for you. Believe me, you're interested in him for all the wrong reasons."

"It's not for you to judge," Chrissy said coldly. "You need something to do, Sara. That's what's wrong. Why don't you get back into acting?"

"Yes," Maeve jumped in. "You do need some kind of work—some activity."

"Forget it. I never really enjoyed acting. It was just something to do. What I really want to do is nothing, except have some fun. Why can't everybody just accept that? The trouble with you two is that you don't have time for fooling around anymore."

3.

Maeve went to Washington when Harry was subpoenaed by the HUAC to testify as to what he knew about Communist activity in Hollywood. Harry asked her not to go and Sara commanded her not to attend the hearings.

"You'll only draw a lot of notoriety to yourself," Sara said. "This is a witchhunt for Communists, and if you publicly support Harry, you'll be branded a fellow traveler yourself."

"Harry is not a Communist. All he has done is befriend many kinds of people because he doesn't know how *not* to be a good friend. He is a courageous man and if I didn't go and lend him my support I would be less than courageous myself. Would you really want that for me? Do you want me to be that kind of a person?"

"Of course not," Sara agonized. "It's just that I'm afraid for you."

"Please, Sara. Don't *you* give in to the climate of fear."

"I'm just afraid of the publicity—it will draw so much attention to you. . . ."

"I'm so tired of living with fear. I've done it almost my whole life. I know what I'm doing is right and I *will* stand up for Harry. This time I *will* be counted."

"Well then—I'm going with you."

"What for?"

"You're going along to show support for Harry. I'm going along to show support for you. And my support means something too! *I'm* one of those capitalists that Harry or his friends are supposed to be undermining."

"Me too," Chrissy said. "I'm going along. I'm a capitalist too."

"God!" Maeve laughed through her tears. "What a circus this is turning into!"

362

The papers had a field day with pictures of Harry Hartman entering the House to give testimony, flanked not only by his lawyers, but by the three glamorous debutantes of '46. One newspaper dubbed the three "the rich girls." Artist Chrissy Marlowe, famed for the custody suit of her youth, gave out this statement for the press: "I can't think of anyone I would rather have portray or protect my way of life than Harry Hartman."

Sara Leeds Gold, not to be outdone, added: "Oh, yes, my good friend, Harry, adores the capitalistic way of life. He's such a good American."

Reading the papers the next day, Maeve wriggled with embarrassment. "Oh my God! Those two statements are enough to turn all America pink."

But Harry laughed so! "I love it! I think the girls are just the greatest I hope my friends all stand by me the way yours stand by you."

"We've always done that for each other. But the important thing now, Harry, is the way *you* stood up for your friends."

She had been so proud of Harry. He had simply said he wasn't a Communist; he had refused to give the committee any names as so many show-business people had in order to save their own necks, and he had denounced those who gave lip service to the American way of life and waved the flag while trying to deny freedom of choice and thought to all men.

"You do understand, Maeve, that this isn't the end of it. What they're after is public humiliation and atonement. I have not atoned for anything since I have not admitted to anything and I refuse to be humiliated. There are still hard times ahead."

"Are you trying to scare me off, Harry Hartman?"

"No. Just prepare you for the worst. As a matter of fact, I'd still like to make you legal. Now that you have become notorious by your association with this pariah, you might as well marry me."

No. The publicity connected with accompanying Harry to Washington was one thing. The actual act of marriage would be more of a psychological trigger stirring Padraic into action against Harry, and Harry had problems enough.

4.

In September of 1953 the women went to Newport to attend Jackie Bouvier's wedding to Jack Kennedy and they stayed in Maeve's house. Although there were sad memories for Maeve there, she had resolved once and for all not to let the past intrude on the present.

There were six hundred guests at the ceremony in St. Mary's Church. It was a splendid tableau—ten bridesmaids in pink; the matron of honor, the Princess Radziwill, in a big garden hat; fourteen ushers, and Jackie's little half-sister as a flower girl and her little half-brother as ringbearer; Archbishop Cushing in his majestic robes; the groom, looking so happy, standing with his younger brother, Bobby. Then the bride came down the aisle on the arm of her stepfather, Hugh Auchincloss, looking positively heavenly in the satin gown with the bouffant skirt, the rose-point lace veil, the circle of orange blossoms in her dark hair.

The three friends, Sara and Maeve and Chrissy, all thought about the father who wasn't there to give his daughter away. They had heard the rumors, as everybody present had. Jackie's father, the handsome Jack Bouvier, had arrived in Newport the day before, but apparently had been either nervous or sad or both because it was Hugh Auchincloss who was making this wedding for his Jackie, and had gone into some kind of a funk, probably alcoholic, and had telephoned his regrets.

Poor Jackie! She adored her father so. Had she shed a few tears when she had to take her stepfather's arm? Maeve wondered.

Poor Jack Bouvier! Sara looked down at her manicure and thought of Jackie's father sitting in his hotel room, unable, spiritually or physically, to make it to the wedding.

Chrissy sighed. Fathers! At least that was one problem she had never had. Or had she? If she were to believe Sara, then she must believe that she did. Oh, shit! It was all too much to think about.

Is Jackie heartbroken about her father? Maeve speculated. You couldn't tell from looking at her. She seemed radiant.

Jackie looks so happy to be marrying Jack—she isn't even thinking about her poor father, Sara thought.

Chrissy's heart filled with envy. Jackie's mother was so proud of her! And Jackie looked so innocent, so full of high expectation, her love was so fresh, so untarnished!

There were twelve hundred guests at the reception at Hammersmith Farms. There were people from New York, people from Washington— Kennedy people and Bouviers and Auchinclosses and Lees—and the international set from everywhere. It was a perfect day for an outdoor wedding. "Even the weather wouldn't dare doublecross Jackie Bouvier," said Sara.

"It looks that way," Maeve agreed. It did seem that destiny had kissed this bride. And the air was so wonderful, half-summery, half-fall-like; it smelled of the sun and the bay and of greenery turning yellow.

"It's a super *looking* wedding," Chrissy said. She liked the huge striped tent and the guests dancing dreamily to the fifteen-piece orchestra. Last time, she had eloped and missed all this. This time, she would do it properly.

"Sara, how would you like to have my wedding to Max at your

house in Southampton? If we hurry, we can still make it an outdoor reception."

Sara almost choked on her champagne. "Did I hear you right?"

"Yes, dear."

"Maeve, did you hear her? She really plans on *marrying* Max Kozlo."

"I heard her."

"But why are you marrying him? Besides all that crap about looking for a father. He doesn't look like he has a good fuck left in him!"

"But he does." Chrissy grinned. "I'm already pregnant!"

Maeve kissed her. "I'm so happy for you!"

"So, outdoor wedding or not, it appears that we still have to hurry with the wedding plans, doesn't it?" Sara said matter-of-factly.

"It would be nice if you congratulated me, Sara."

"I would, Chrissy, if I were sure *why* I was congratulating you. For marrying Max? For having a baby? Or for marrying Max because you're pregnant and you *so* want a baby?"

Sara and Maeve were discussing whether they should buy an apartment, since Chrissy and Max would probably be living in Chrissy's apartment, or whether they should move back into Sara's house on Fifth.

"It would be easier," Maeve said about Sara's house. "It's already there, waiting, and it is a good location. The only problem is getting a staff together. These days, it isn't easy."

"Well, we can move into the house while we look for an apartment anyway. The wedding is only two weeks away and we do have to get out. Max's son is going to be living with them too, don't forget. Can you imagine Chrissy with a twenty-year-old stepson?"

"Not really." Maeve smiled. "But they'll be a real family, what with a grown son and a small baby."

But then a few days later, Chrissy announced that Chrissy and Sara didn't have to bother moving. She and Max and Max's son, Sasha, were going to the West Coast. "So you two can just stay on here in the apartment if you like."

"But what's happened?" Maeve was shocked, thinking of Ali who would lose her only visitor.

"Max has signed a contract to write music for the movies. He says it's a new challenge for him, a change. And it will be nice for the baby to start out life in sunny California, don't you think?"

"But we'll be separated," Sara said dully.

"We'll still see each other. All the time," Chrissy said. "It's only hours away, after all."

Maeve still said nothing.

"I know what you're thinking, Maeve. And if you're willing, I have a plan. We'll move Ali to the West Coast too, place her in a home nearby. Then I'll still be able to go see her all the time and you can even sneak in a visit too when you're out West visiting Harry and me and my darling baby."

"Wait a minute, Chrissy. The only reason I've stayed in New York at all was to see Ali the few times I've managed and to be near her even when I haven't been able to see her. But if you're going to be out in California, and Ali has to be there too, and Harry is there, what will *I* be doing in New York? I haven't one good reason to stay here at all." Then she smiled at Sara. "Except for Sara, of course."

"Well, don't pay any attention to me," Sara said petulantly. "I can always go back to Charleston."

"Or you can come out west too!" Maeve cried. "Why not? You can see your mother just as easily from there as you do from here. Or almost as easily. It just means flying two or three extra hours. And your father can come out and visit you whenever he feels like it. Will you come too?"

Sara clapped her hands. "I thought you'd never ask!"

"Golly! Now I'll have a husband, a baby, and my two best friends in the world with me. Could anybody ask for more?"

"Well," Sara said. "How about a twenty-year-old stepson?"

5.

Gradually, the exodus took place. Chrissy and Max and Sasha went first and the Kozlos bought a house on North Rexford in Beverly Hills. Then, Ali was transferred to the home Harry had found near Palm Springs and Chrissy went to visit her there in a chauffeured limousine, since Max did not think it was proper or healthy for a woman "with child" to drive about by herself. Sasha, presented with a bright red Ferrari, enrolled at the UCLA campus in Westwood and almost immediately became the big man on campus. Big, blond, athletically endowed, and with a pleasant, sunny nature, he was liked by everyone— men, coeds, coaches. Max, unable to drive a car himself and possessed of a temperament unwilling to cope with "this ridiculous traffic of madmen," was driven to the studio in a black Cadillac by a chauffeur dressed in the khaki-colored uniform that Max had personally selected. Chrissy, caught in the middle of a fairy-tale existence, devoted herself to being "with child," making a home for Max and Sasha, sunning herself by the pool while reading the manuals on child rearing, being an interested and loving stepmother, and preparing the huge Hungarian meals Max so relished. She had a studio set up for herself but she never seemed to find the time to paint, especially once she started taking lessons in natural childbirth. She had been thinking of writing a book on designs for the home while awaiting the birth of her baby, but she also put that idea away for the time being. Sometimes her role as cook reminded her of the early days of her marriage to Guy. But, of course, *now* she was going to have a baby!

Maeve made the move next. In January she purchased a house in Beverly Hills, even though she spent most of her time at Harry's house in the hills of Bel Air. There, they were able to play tennis and swim in the Roman pool, as Harry increasingly had more time to spare. Maeve worried that Harry, great as his reputation as a moviemaker was, was nevertheless being blacklisted. Harry tried to reassure her—that it was just that fewer movies were being made in the year 1954. Television had made such vast inroads into the movie audience. People were just more interested, at the moment, in watching Milton Berle or Jackie Gleason for free. "I can't complain," he told Maeve. "I've never been happier. Now I have more time to write, which I've always wanted, and time to spend with you. The best part of the day for me is when we sit together in the study, both of us writing. When I look up and see you across from me, wrinkling up your nose the way you do when you're immersed in your work, my heart sings."

Harry bought her a desk that was the twin of his own. "What I really want to buy are those towels that say 'His' and 'Hers,'" he told her. "That's when it's really kosher."

She would go along when Harry entertained at the different hospitals and homes where his songs and dances and little skits always brought a smile to appreciative faces. And as Harry had promised, every three weeks or so they drove down to the home where Ali was. She was talking more, and, when Maeve read to her from the little children's books, she seemed to respond, to follow the story with interest. Still, when it was time to go, it was painful for Maeve not to grab Ali and take her home.

Before Sara left for the Coast, she and her father discussed what would be done with the New York house. It was Maurice Gold who suggested the house become the Museum of Jewish History. The idea pleased Sara inordinately, but she wanted the name to be the Gold Museum of Jewish History and insisted that she and her father share the cost of founding the museum. "And I think Mother would like to be a one-third founder too. And, Papa, I think it would be wonderful if you took a *personal* interest in the museum. Would you oversee everything yourself? The reconstruction of the building? The acquisitions? After all, who's a better executive than my father?" She kissed him. "Any man who could found a great fortune the way you did all by yourself, Papa, can certainly found a little old museum better than anybody else."

Sara wanted him to be busy, to take a real interest in something again. As for Bettina, once she, Sara, was settled in California, she would take her mother to live with her. She had promised her mother this years ago and she intended to keep that promise.

"I'll move in with you," Sara told Maeve, "until I find the house that I really can't live without."

Maeve readily agreed. She knew that Sara didn't like to live alone. And she herself barely used her house.

"But what will you do?" Maeve asked her.

"What do you mean—what will I do? I'll live! Just like everyone else."

"I meant, some kind of work. Maybe acting. Harry still has friends and influence. I'm sure he could make a connection for you. You know, Sara, you'd really make a wonderful producer. It's one of your natural talents."

"Darling Maeve, I know you mean well. But everybody's always after me to do something and I really don't want to. All I want to do, for a while at least, is take the sun, go out to lunch a lot, and shop. And go to a few parties. You and Chrissy aren't the only people I know here, you know. There are oodles of people from New York. Tina Rodman. Willy Ross—he's doing wonderfully, you know. Grace Kelly, of course. Lane Harris. Peggy Astor . . . we went to dancing school together. Oh, mercy, I never told you! Guess who I heard is here and married to some big executive at some studio or other?"

"Tell me."

"Guess."

"Is she from Chalmer's?"

"Yes."

"Is she married to Brad Cranford?"

"Oh, for goodness' sake, you *are* behind the times. You're thinking of DeeDee Dineen. She's divorced from Brad Cranford. She married a count. Automobile money. She's living in Milan."

"Is our mystery woman pretty?"

"No."

"Is she thin?"

"No."

368

Maeve laughed. "Does she tell terrible jokes?"

"Oh you!" Sara gave Maeve a push. "How did you guess? Did you *know* Ginny Furbush was here in Hollywood?"

"No, I didn't know. Ginny's name just popped into my head when you said she wasn't thin and wasn't pretty."

"Guess what her husband's name is!"

"I can't possibly guess *that*. Tell me!"

"Hold on to your sides so they don't split! Finkelstein!"

"Really? Ginny Furbush?"

6.

Maeve sat in Chrissy's country kitchen nibbling cookies while Chrissy prepared Chicken Paprika, a particular favorite of Max's. The maid had come in to announce Sara's arrival but Sara had followed her in.

"It's the first time I've heard of that the maid has to go into the kitchen to announce a guest's arrival to the lady of the house."

"Tsk . . . tsk. What a sheltered life you've led," Chrissy cheerfully answered.

"Oh my, the happy little hausfrau." Sara shrugged off her jacket and sat down at the kitchen table.

"Have a cookie, Cookie," Maeve said, "and get off Chrissy's back."

"First guess who I had lunch with today and then guess who I ran into."

"First guess. Elizabeth Taylor," Maeve ventured.

"No. But she almost looked like her."

"We give up. Tell!"

"Ginny Furbush Finkelstein!"

"And she almost looked like Elizabeth Taylor?"

"Yes, believe it! She's lost about fifty pounds and she's as slim and svelte as—well, *not* Chrissy, for sure. And she's had her nose done *and* her chin. And her hair's dyed blue black. And she has this terrific tan— she plays tennis every day! *She* doesn't look like somebody's cook!"

"Maeve! Help! She's picking on me again!"

"Really, Sara! You are unfair. Chrissy *is* seven months pregnant. Do you really expect her to look like Elizabeth Taylor?"

"No, but I do expect her to look like Chrissy Marlowe who just happens to be seven months pregnant. Look at that maternity dress! It looks like a size twenty-two-and-a-half somebody's grandmother left behind. And there are such *darling* maternity clothes in the shops!"

"Have some cheese and crackers, Sara," Chrissy said complacently, putting a plate in front of her. "It's Szekely cheese. It's Hungarian. I buy it in a wonderful little cheese store in Santa Monica. Max adores it from the old days. Or would you rather have palacsinta? I made them this morning."

Sara shoved the plate away. "I've eaten lunch, thank you. You see what I mean?" Sara appealed to Maeve. "That's all she talks about. That's all she does is clean house and cook the nice, big, heavy meals and take care of those two big lummoxes while they hardly even speak to her at all. After all, she's only a girl-child. A girl-child is not supposed to have a brain in her head. All she's supposed to know is *Kirche, Kinder, Kuche!* . . ." Sara did an imitation of her concept of a fat burghermaster, blowing out her cheeks and making a big stomach.

Maeve tried not to laugh. "Those are German words, Sara, not Hungarian. And it was Hitler who's famous for using them."

"You did say that Kozlo lived in Germany for a long time, didn't you, Chrissy?" Sara asked pointedly.

"Yes, but he wasn't one of Hitler's people, Sara," Chrissy said seriously. "He was a Hungarian living in Germany and he had to run from the Nazis. Besides, did you ever see anyone so sweet and loving to a wife?" Chrissy protested defensively.

"Yes, and Hitler loved children and dogs," Sara muttered in an aside to Maeve, who pushed her arm playfully and shook her head.

"Max treats you like one of his *kinder*. He treats his son more like an adult than he does you. To Max, you're a mindless child who has to be told what to do and then sent to bed with a fond smack on the behind. Even that name he calls you—*schatzi*—that means toy. A toy isn't a woman!"

Chrissy giggled. "It means sweetheart—not toy."

Sara just snorted but Maeve was glad to see that Chrissy wasn't at all offended; she wasn't even upset by Sara's words.

Chrissy said kindly, "Sara, someday you'll find the pleasure of being taken care of, having a man that worries if you're dressed warmly, if you've eaten enough, or if you're coming down with a cold—"

"When that time comes, I'll hire myself a nanny to take care of me, but I'll get a man to screw me!"

Chrissy only laughed. "You'll find out."

"Wait a minute," Maeve said. "Sara, you never told us who it was you ran into while you were having lunch with glamorous Ginny Furbush Finkelstein."

Sara blinked, for a second trying to recall. "Oh, it was Rick Green! He's writing for the movies and was he ever thrilled to see me! He was as sweet as could be. Ginny thought he was divinely good-looking. As a matter of fact, she invited him right then and there to the dinner party she's giving for *us*, all three of us. Max and Harry are included, of course. She's dying to see the two of you. It's a week from today. Tell me, Chrissy darling, do you think Maxey-Waxey will let baby stay out after nine? And do you have anything decent to wear?"

"Wasn't it a super party?" Sara asked Maeve the day after the party, still exhilarated.

"Personally, I was disappointed. Ginny didn't recite one dirty limerick."

"No. I think she *lives* those limericks these days instead of reciting them."

"What do you mean?"

"Just that our Ginny lives a very fast life—the three S's."

"What are the three S's?"

"Dear Maeve, still so innocent. It's refreshing. Sucking, switching, and Satanism."

"I guess I know what sucking is—"

"Yea, team! Rick says she's known for giving the best head in town."

"Rick!" Maeve exploded, her tone reflecting how much credence she gave Rick Green's pronouncements. "And as for switching—I get the general idea. But what does Satanism mean?"

"It means she belongs to one of those cults that worship the devil!"

Maeve looked horrified for a second, but then waved her hand in disgust. "Honestly, Sara, if you can believe a word Rick Green says, you haven't learned a thing."

Sara laughed. "He was just being amusing. But he is a reformed character. He swears he hasn't had a drop to drink since we were divorced. And he *is* successful, so I guess he is keeping his nose to the grindstone and behaving himself."

"I still don't understand why you had to spend the whole evening talking with him. Especially with Willy Ross there. I could see little hearts coming out of Willy and traveling across the room straight to you. That man is still carrying a torch for you, Sara."

Sara giggled. "That's what I love about you, Maeve. You're still an old-fashioned girl. Carrying a torch! That's such an archaic expression. The way to phrase it these days is he still digs me."

"Divine! So why don't you let him *shovel* you?"

"*Very good*, Maeve. As a matter of fact I'm going to—a little anyway. I have dates with both Rick and Willy. Willy *is* a lovely man. I've always adored him."

"So why are you wasting time with Rick? You've already been burned by him."

Sara looked serious for a moment. "Because he's trying so hard to be nice and he has reformed. And I'm thinking of Mama and Daddy. How she forgave him and how that was such a wonderful, noble thing for her to do."

"Maybe Rick isn't worth forgiving. And your father was."

"Oh, Maeve! That doesn't sound like you at all. I would hate to think you were becoming hard, uncharitable."

"Maybe I'm just getting wiser. And I would hope the same for you."

"I'm not marrying Rick again, for God's sake! I'm just seeing him, for old time's sake. And I intend to see Willy, too."

"All right, Sara. Just be careful, please. And for God's sake, stay away from Ginny Finkelstein, will you?"

Sara glanced at Maeve oddly. "What are you afraid of? That I'll get mixed up with Satanism? Golly, Maeve! I've already been *married* to the devil!"

7.

"Marlena is arriving tonight," Sara told Chrissy who was sitting up in her hospital bed. Sara was going through all of Chrissy's congratulatory cards and telegrams. "She'll be here to see you tomorrow."

"You mean she's flying in just to see me?"

"What do you think? It's not every day our Chrissy Marlowe gives birth to twins, you ninny!"

"Chrissy Marlowe *Kozlo*," Chrissy reminded Sara. "Who's taking care of Marlena's children?"

"Aunt Martha and Mama are minding the store. It's nice for them and it's good for Marlena to have a little break, too. Mmmm." Sara sniffed at an arrangement of camellias. "Who sent these? They remind me of Charleston."

"Willy Ross. He sent them to me, but I guess he was thinking of you."

"He is a doll, isn't he?"

"Have you been seeing much of him? As much as you've been seeing Rick?"

"More by far, if you must know. But he's out of town now. On location in Italy."

"Do you miss him?"

"Of course, I miss him. He calls me every day."

"From Italy?"

"No, from next door. Of course from Italy, silly."

"So he had to order my flowers from Italy. How really thoughtful. Are you going to marry him, Sara?"

"How do I know? I think so. It's much too soon to think about that.

It's only been a few months. I'm not going to make any more flying leaps into the soup. I did that twice and you can see what happened."

"Are you in love with him, Sara?"

"Of course, I am. I've always loved Willy. Somewhere in back of my head. Do you know why? Because he loves me *so much,* for one. But mostly because he loves me just as I am. He appreciates what I am. He doesn't want to change me and he's not always at me to do things. He just wants to let me be Sara."

"I just want you to be Sara too." Chrissy took her hand. "And I want you to be as happy as I am."

"Are you, Chrissy, are you really?"

"For heaven's sake, Sara, what do you think? I just gave birth to the two fattest, sweetest little girls in all creation!"

"I meant the rest of it. Max. Keeping house. Having *all of you* tied up in it. And— I know I shouldn't ask."

"Go ahead, Sara. Ask! Nothing's ever stopped you before and we just agreed that you shouldn't change. All right. You don't have to ask, I'll tell you. No, the sex isn't great. But it never was for me anyhow. There was just a lot more of it. And of a more exotic nature, let's say. And do I miss it? Sometimes. Maybe if I had gotten more pleasure out of it in the first place, I would miss it more. Sometimes it's just the excitement I miss, the expectation. I used to think: this time it might be different. This time it might take me to the stars. But in the end, it wouldn't and I always knew beforehand, really, that it wouldn't. So I value what I do have! Somebody who cares for me, even if he thinks of me more as a daughter than a woman! Don't forget—being somebody's daughter is a big deal to me too!"

Sara blinked back tears. "And now you've got two little old darling daughters of your own."

Chrissy kissed Sara's cheek. "Not to mention my darling sisters."

"Will you stop making me piss tears, Chrissy Marlowe . . . Kozlo?"

"All this talk is fine and good but have you seen the babies? Max was here this morning and all he did was stare through the glass at the nursery window. Then he came in and said, 'Schatzi, I thank you. You've done a grand job!' "

They both laughed holding tightly to each other's hand.

"All right! I'll let you take a peek at them, Sara, but you have to be very quiet. I just got them to sleep."

They tiptoed into the nursery and Sara looked at the rosy two, sleeping side by side in matching cribs decorated with nursery-rhyme figures.

"Oh, mercy me, they're getting bigger every day. And rosier," Sara whispered.

"Sh!" Chrissy cautioned, and they tiptoed out.

"They're getting more beautiful every day and I wish I could say the same for you, Chrissy. You still haven't lost all the weight you gained."

"I *am* nursing, Sara. It's hard to lose weight when you're nursing. I have to drink two quarts of milk a day in order to feed them both, don't I?"

"It's too much to nurse two of them. Why can't you put them on bottles like everybody else does these days?"

"Oh, I wouldn't! I love to nurse them, Sara. You can't imagine the joy of having them suckle at my breast, giving them sustenance. It's a divine experience. You'll see when you have your own. Besides, Max would think it was terrible if I didn't nurse them. He loves to watch them at my breast—drinking the *mutter's* milk."

"Charming, I'm sure," Sara said, having made her mind up not to badger Chrissy about Max any more. "Have you been doing the exercises the doctor gave you?"

Chrissy grimaced. "I hate them. And it's hard to find the time. Between nursing and caring for the babies, I hardly even do any of the cooking myself anymore."

"Would you mind telling me what the nurse you hired is supposed to be doing?"

"Well, she's downstairs in the laundry room right now washing the diapers by hand."

"Who washes diapers by hand these days? What's diaper service for?"

"Oh, both Max and Greta—that's the baby nurse—are against diaper service. They say you can't tell who had the diapers before you. And Greta says that with diapers, it's all in the rinsing. They have to be rinsed eight times to make sure all the ammonia and the soap are out."

"Oh, my goodness gracious, I should think so. So who's doing the cooking? I thought the cook quit."

"Max hired another one. She's Hungarian. But Max is not satisfied with her. He says her seasoning hand is off. So we're both sort of doing the cooking. But I don't think she's going to last."

"Oh my Lord! You have to pull yourself together and start taking care of yourself. If you won't do your exercises at home, you'll just have to go to a gym. You can come to Marovski's with me. She's really marvelous. She'll get that fat off you."

"I will, Sara, in a few weeks. I promise. As soon as I get everything running smoothly here."

"How about that overgrown stud you call your stepson? Can't he help out? Can't he at least make a hamburger?"

"Sasha. He's only a boy."

"Some boy! And you just have to find the time to have your hair done. Look at you! Braids! What are you? Heidi in Wonderland?"

"Oh, I'm sorry Maeve isn't here to hear you call me Heidi in Wonderland! She would go out of her mind. It's Alice in Wonderland. Heidi was in the Alps. When is Maeve coming back?"

"I'm not sure. Ever since she won the National Book Award, she hasn't been home more than two days in a row. She's really become a nut for publicity. She must have been on the radio at least twenty times. And the television talk shows! I don't know what she's thinking of. She's always shunned the limelight because of . . . you know. Get me a scissors!" she commanded Chrissy. "I'm going to give you a trim right now and then we're going to shampoo your hair and I'll set it myself. Do you have any rollers? If not, we'll raid the fridge and empty out all the frozen orange juice cans and use them!"

8.

Every time Maeve was interviewed on the radio, she wondered if he was listening. Every time she was on television, she wondered if he was watching with a mad jealousy. Her feelings, as usual, were ambivalent. On one hand, she still feared him because of Ali and Harry; on the other, she wanted him to realize her triumph. That's the reason she was writing, wasn't it? So that he would know the pain, the black despair of being the victim of her vengeance for once.

Where was he? What was he doing? Walking some moor, declaiming in verse mindlessly? Had the debacle of his most recent book finished his writing for good? Or was he holed up somewhere—Truro . . . Boston . . . Aran—writing his magnum opus, taking his time, conserving his literary strength, making sure this time to write *the* masterwork of the century to assure him a place in literature that she could not usurp? Or was he busy planning some new act of retribution against her—a magnum opus of revenge?

She had no choice but to go on living her life as best she could, loving those for whom she cared to the limit of her frail human capability.

9.

They were to have held their annual reunion at the Polo Lounge, but at the last minute Chrissy called—the baby nurse had walked out in a snit that morning at what she deemed Chrissy's interference with the twins. So they would lunch at her house instead. "Anyway," Chrissy said, "I've just redone the dining room and I want you two to see it."

Maeve and Sara were speechless. Heretofore, Chrissy had always leaned toward the modern in interior design but now her dining room was a fantasy of lacy grillwork and filigree festooned with cascades of flowered chintz everywhere—chairs, draperies—even the chandelier wore a bonnet of pink roses and the table was draped to the floor with a cloth decorated with great yellow tulips. Chrissy wore a dirndl skirt to match.

"Extraordinary!" Maeve said.

"I'm overwhelmed!" Sara enthused. "And relieved to see that your artistic brain hasn't been completely chloroformed by the reek of Hungarian goulash."

Chrissy giggled. "That's what we're having for lunch."

"I'm afraid we'll soil that gorgeous tablecloth," Maeve said.

"Oh, I have four others—all in different designs."

"And you designed everything yourself?"

"Of course. It was ever so much fun. Harold Jurgens and his wife were here the other night for dinner. Harold works with Max, and his wife, Leonia, does interior decorating. She's worked on some of the splashiest homes in town and has designed the interiors of a lot of the restaurants. She asked if I would be interested in working with her, designing materials and things . . . she *loved* the chandelier bonnet!"

"So, are you going to?"

Chrissy laughed briefly. "Oh, no . . . no. Max thought the idea was preposterous. He told Leonia I had no time to *play*."

Maeve flashed a warning look at Sara. "When do we get a look at the twins?" she asked quickly, before Sara could say anything.

"After lunch. They should be up and around then."

"And how is Muscles?" Sara asked, referring to Sasha. "We haven't seen him in a while."

"Oh, he's hardly here. You know how boys are. He sleeps late and then he's off. He's on the track team and he's a big ladies' man." Chrissy laughed. "I suspect he's as much an athlete in bed as he is on the track. The girls are forever calling. And it seems they all have cute names that start with an L. Lolly. Lana. Laney. Lita. It's really hysterical."

"A riot." Sara smirked.

"Let me hold little Christy now," Sara said. "And you can hold Georgianna, Maeve."

"You're terrific, Sara. Hardly anyone can tell them apart."

"Their noses are a tiny bit different."

"Oh, silly! All babies' noses are the same," Chrissy told her.

"Nope! I can see a difference."

"Since when are you such an expert on babies?" Maeve nuzzled little Christy's neck.

"Maybe since I'm going to have one myself," Sara said, not looking at Maeve or Chrissy but bouncing Christy up and down.

"Sara! How long has this been going on?"

"Oh—a couple of months," Sara said seemingly nonchalant, putting Christy down in the playpen.

"Are you and Willy going to marry?"

"No," Sara said flatly. "*Rick* and I are going across the border next week and doing that. We've been waiting for Rick's divorce to go through."

"Oh, Sara! I thought you and Willy were—"

"Rick's the father," Sara said without expression.

"But you and Willy— How do you *know* Rick's the father?"

"Because I figured it out. Willy was in Italy when I conceived."

"Still—" Maeve began.

"Still nothing. I can't do that to Willy. Pass Rick's baby off on him as his own. I've done enough to Willy already. It's my own fault. I wasn't constant—"

"You could tell Willy it's Rick's baby. I'm sure, knowing Willy, he would still want to marry you."

"But he would be hurt. I don't think that would be fair to him. Or to Rick. Rick deserves another chance. The chance to be a father to his own baby, doesn't he, for God's sake? And the baby. Doesn't it deserve to have its real father?"

"I know this sounds terrible, Sara," Maeve said, "but I don't think you should marry Rick just because he's the father. It's more important to marry the *right* man. And if you can't go to Willy with Rick's baby, then I think you should have an abortion, marry Willy, and start all over again. It's only a fetus now—it's not a *real* baby."

"Some Catholic you are, Maeve O'Connor! They'll ex-communicate you for sure if you go around talking this way. No, I lost one baby to abortion—"

She smiled sadly at the looks of surprise on Chrissy's and Maeve's faces.

"Yes, I know about the abortion at the Clinique. I snitched a look at the records when Dr. Lutece left the room once. I'm glad that it happened—I mean, that they performed the abortion then. But I can't lose another baby that way."

So that's the way it is, Maeve thought, and that's the way it will have to be. "I'll go with you to Mexico to stand up for you, if you'd like," she offered.

"No, thanks. It's really not necessary."

10.

Sara and Rick stayed at Maeve's house, and Maeve moved in with Harry, this time—bag and baggage.

"It's a little like musical chairs, isn't it?" Maeve told Harry. "I only hope Sara finds some happiness this time with Rick."

But only a month later, Sara lost the baby. Maeve and Chrissy wondered what would happen to Sara's marriage now that the reason for it was gone.

"I wish she would divorce Rick and marry Willy. She is so depressed! I wonder which feels worse afterward—an abortion or a miscarriage," Chrissy mused.

"Can you compare them? It's not a case of either/or, after all. I don't think they have a machine yet that measures misery."

"How long do you intend to sit around the house feeling sorry for yourself?" Rick demanded. "For God's sake, it's not the end of the world. Fuck it! You're not the first woman in the world to have a mis, you know."

"It's the first time for me."

"Jesus Christ! Are you ever going to pull out of it? This place is like a goddamn morgue! Look, Jerry Dresden is having a big do down at his place in Palm Springs. Let's get the hell out of here and go down. What do you say?"

"I really don't feel like going to a party."

"C'mon. It's bound to be more fun than hanging around here. Jerry always has some good films—"

"You mean some of his filth."

"Boy, aren't we getting high and mighty? And he always has some good stuff—"

"What kind of stuff? Pot? Coke? Or something more exotic?" she asked disdainfully.

"Holy shit, you've turned into a real stiff, you know? You're a real drag."

"Oh, go fuck yourself."

"I don't have to do *that*. There's still plenty of ass around that's not only ready and willing, but panting for it, baby."

"Yeah? Well, you'd better do something about your sexual anorexia first."

"What does that mean? That I can't get it up?"

"It means that you're a loser, anyway you dip it." Sara was really too dispirited to fight. "You just better get out some of that stuff you use, what's it called? That vine you sent away for, Pega Palo. . . ."

"Look, try one of these. It'll make you feel better." Rick held out a few pills in his palm.

"What is it?"

"It'll make you feel better."

"But what is it?"

"Desoxyn. An upper."

"I don't want to be up. I just want to be numb."

"Then try one of these. Soon you'll be feeling no pain."

"What are they?"

"What does it matter? Soon you'll be floating."

Sara almost put out her hand to take the pills. It would be so lovely not to feel, just to float in space. But she looked at Rick's face. He reminded her right then of somebody else that she didn't want to think about. Why was he pushing so hard? Did he want her hooked to keep him company?

She pushed his hand away.

"So you swore off liquor, did you? You know, you're a real stand-up chickenshit guy."

He threw the handful of pills in her face. She laughed, and he got down on his hands and knees to retrieve them.

"Sara, it's not your fault you had a miscarriage. Why do you feel responsible?" Maeve asked reasonably.

"I just feel like a failure."

"Why don't you have your mother come out for a visit? A mother is a comforting thing, I've been told," Chrissy said.

"No. Not now. I don't want Mama to come into our house and see what's going on."

"That bad?" Maeve asked.

Sara shrugged. "You know, after my father and I became friends and Mama was friends with him too, I said something to Papa about him and Mama getting together again. I know it was kind of naive of me, even childish, but I was feeling pretty sentimental at the time. Papa smiled sort of sadly and said, 'It's *fafallen, Sara.*' And I asked him what that meant and he said *fafallen* was a Yiddish word. It meant it was too late—a lost cause. Well, that's what Rick's and my marriage was— *fafallen* right from the start. Like my baby."

"Well, then, end it," Chrissy said.

"And admit to another failure? And how about the money? He'd try to grab some of my money in a settlement—this is California. It would almost be worth it to get rid of him, but I can't give him the satisfaction. And I'm not up to a fight for it now. Later on. . ."

"Look, Sara, you have to do something. You have to get out of the house. I'm going to tell Harry to get you a job, anything."

"How about scrubbing the floors at MGM?" Sara laughed morosely.

"Forget it," Chrissy said. "You couldn't even do a good job of it."

After they left Sara, Chrissy said to Maeve in a burst of inspiration, "Don't ask Harry to help Sara get something. Let's ask Willy. I hear he's producing his own pictures these days. He's bound to give her something to do."

"You are a little devil, aren't you? I don't know, though. Maybe it's too much to ask. Hasn't Willy suffered enough? And maybe he's just given up on Sara."

"Willy given up on Sara? Never. I'll bet he'll just sort of drawl in that funny way of his and recite that ditty he once made up to tease her:

> Better Sara late than never,
> Better Sara than someone clever,
> If not Sara, then I'll rot,
> S.G., how about we tie the knot?

Maeve hugged Chrissy. "Okay, we'll try. I only hope Willy's still singing the same old tune."

11.

"What are you so upset about, Maeve darling? It's not so terrible for me to have written this screenplay under a pseudonym. More distinguished writers than I have used a nom de plume through the centuries."

"Not for this reason. Not because their own names weren't good enough for those bastards. Well, your real name is too good for you to hide behind an assumed one. I won't let you do it, Harry!"

"I want to do it, Maeve. I have to do it! I have to work. I have to see my work produced. And if Willy is willing to produce it and act in it, then I'm grateful to him. We're both basically clowns and we understand each other's style. The only difference is, he's about a foot taller and leans toward the ironic while my thing is pathos. But we have a common meeting ground—neither of us can stand Harry Cohn."

Maeve gazed at him somberly.

"Laugh, sweetheart, that was a joke."

"I don't feel like laughing, Harry. I'm surprised at Willy, that he would let you demean yourself by putting a false name on the screenplay."

"He didn't ask me to do that, Maeve. It's I who insist on it. I refuse to have Willy's picture sabotaged by my participation, and that's all there is to it. Suppose, for instance, that Willy was nominated for the Oscar, either for his performance, or for producing the best picture of the year, and nobody would vote for him because the production was tainted by the Hartman name. That would be a hell of a thing, wouldn't it? And what about Sara? She's going to be Willy's executive producer on this one."

Maeve had no answer to that. But she had been thinking about another answer for some time.

"Harry, why don't we just go to Europe? You could work there—France, Italy, even England. This thing has to blow over sometime."

Harry smiled wistfully. "Remember what happened to Chaplin when he left the country? He wasn't a citizen either, and they wouldn't let him back in—for political reasons and some kind of trumped-up charges of moral turpitude. They could say I'm guilty of moral turpitude too. While we're not commiting adultery, technically, we are living in a state of fornication. And they certainly could set me up on the political charges. I might not give a damn for myself—my son's living in

France—but I couldn't take the chance because of you. Your friends are here. And Ali."

Ali! She was almost fifteen. No longer a little girl, no longer a child. She had about given up on ever having her daughter live with her. But leave her behind for good? No, she couldn't do that!

"So, do I have your blessing on this or not? How about Horace Schumacher as my pseudonym? Do you like that?"

"Blessings on thee, Horace Schumacher."

12.

"Sara, I'm a patient man. But even my patience is wearing thin. It talks to me, it says: 'Willy, when, *when?*' "

"I'm not going to let that bastard have a cent of my money, Willy."

"So let him have a few cents of my money."

"No. Nobody's money. Don't worry, Willy. I know him. He'll make a false move and then I'll boot his ass out so far—"

"My patience says, 'Hurry, hurry, Sara. Willy's getting older by the minute. And you, Sara, are also getting long in the tooth.' "

"Your patience has some nerve!"

———————

Sara worked long hours. She wasn't too crazy about going home at night to Rick who waited up for her to taunt her about Willy, about her ability as a producer, anything he could think of. Besides, she had so much to do—she oversaw everything on the picture, the costumes, the cast, the accounting, whatever. When Willy was out of town doing location work, she made sure to stay at the studio late.

Leaving one night around nine, Sara saw an extra, one of the "street scene" players, hanging around outside the studio gates. She stopped her car. "Do you need a ride?" she asked the girl.

"Neh. Have no place to go."

Sara looked at her compassionately. She had had that feeling herself sometimes. "How come?"

"This was my first day's work in a couple of months. I got kicked out of my room last week. Lucky they needed people that looked beat today."

She *was* messy, Sara acknowledged. Auburn hair tied back haphazardly, jeans, a striped polo, and thong sandals on feet that were none too clean. Sara guessed that the girl was in her early twenties.

"What's your name?"

"Clarissa."

"Well, come on home with me, Clarissa. We'll have dinner and you can spend the night."

"Look, Clarissa, there's no reason you can't stay here in this house until you get on your feet. There's plenty of room here and, hell, why not?"

"How about your husband? He'll have a shit hemorrhage!"

"Between you and me, Clarissa, I hope he does!"

They laughed until Sara gasped for breath.

Rick asked Sara what the fuck was she doing—setting up a camp for displaced persons? Sara told him that if he didn't like it he could get the fuck out. He responded with, "You're too eager."

Sara found a job for Clarissa as a script girl and bought her some clothes, and Clarissa started baking pies and cakes in her spare time. "Never had a kitchen like this before. Never even seen one." She asked if she could convert the service bathroom off the kitchen into a darkroom. "Always wanted to get into photography," she said.

Sara said, "Sure."

Clarissa looked at Sara quizzically. "How come you're being so nice to me? I didn't do anything in particular to deserve it."

"You're a human being, aren't you?" Sara asked. "And I've never done anything particularly nice for anybody before. Besides, I don't like staying in this house alone."

"But you're not alone? You've got a husband."

"That's what I said—alone."

They laughed.

"You sure are funny," Clarissa said. "Is it because you're rich?"

"You mean peculiar funny?"

Clarissa nodded.

"Maybe," Sara said. "Maybe it's because I'm rich."

"Well, you're still being nice. I hope you don't get bitten."

"Now what does that mean?"

"You know—people do *bite* the hand that feeds them."

"Are you going to bite me?"

"Maybe. Who knows?" Clarissa shrugged.

Sara laughed. "Clarissa, I think you're the one who's peculiar funny."

Willy said, "Nice home life you people got there. Do you think Rick would mind if I moved in?" But he added, "I understand, Sara. And it's a *mitzvah,* a good deed, that you're doing."

But Willy was wrong. Whatever she was doing, she was doing it for herself.

In the fall, the house across the street changed hands. Sara saw the old occupants, the Funts, move out. She knew them only by name but someone on the block told her they were retired and were moving into a high-rise near the beach. Idly, Sara wondered who would be moving in.

Then one day—it was twilight—Sara got out of her car and was going into the house, when she saw draperies being drawn across an upstairs window and she caught a flash of a man dressed in black—unusual for California—before the draperies pulled shut obscuring him from view. Oh, my God, could it be? Her whole body started to shake and she ran into the house.

Should she call Maeve? She wasn't sure. She couldn't scare the hell out of Maeve if she weren't sure. Maeve would be so scared. How could she do that to Maeve if she weren't positive? No. She would watch the house herself. She wouldn't leave her own house until she knew for sure.

Clarissa! She would ask Clarissa if she had seen anything . . . anybody . . . in the house across the street. She ran up the stairs. Then she knocked once on Clarissa's door and without waiting for an answer, burst in.

Clarissa, auburn hair streaming down her back, stood, legs spread apart, on the bed, her naked body tanned reddish brown except for the white parts that had been spared from the sun by a two-piece bathing suit. Spread-eagled, sweating and crying low, was Rick, hands and feet tied to the bedposts. Clarissa held a leather belt.

Seeing Sara, Clarissa was only a little distressed. "Stay loose," she advised Sara.

Sara dismissed the man across the street from her mind. *If this can be real, then the other must be the dream . . . the nightmare.*

Feeling a little weak, she sat down in a chair. "Maybe I should come back later," she said, "when the action gets a little hotter."

"Excuse me," Clarissa said. "I think I'll go get dressed," and she disappeared into the bathroom.

"Two marriages," Sara said, shaking her head, looking at the still-sweating Rick who was trying to tear loose from his ties. "And I had no idea what it took to give you an erection."

Rick broke loose. "Bitch!" he spat.

Sara laughed. "Me? What did I do?" Then, "It's what *you're* going to do that's relevant. You're going to go down to Mexico with me to

384

facilitate things, to make sure that everything's in order for my quickie divorce, like the gentleman you are."

"The fuck I am!"

"You don't really want me to take this into court here, do you? You'll be laughed right out of town when this story gets around."

Rick pulled on his pants. "Who's going to believe you? Everybody knows you're a fucking crazy woman. Do you actually think nobody knows what you were doing in that clinic in Switzerland so long?"

For a moment Sara was stopped cold.

"She's got me as a witness," Clarissa said, coming out of the bathroom.

"And who'll believe *you*, a crazy freak-out. . . . They'll know *you* got paid off."

"Uh-uh." Clarissa smiled. "I was experimenting with a self-timer. You know, how you take a picture of yourself. Last time, when we . . . you know . . . I had it hidden. I got us down cold in black and white."

"Sorry, Sara," Clarissa said.

"It's O.K., Clarissa. But why did you do it?"

Clarissa shrugged. "For kicks . . . I guess. And under the circumstances, I didn't think you'd care."

"I don't. And it turned out very well for me, actually. But, just out of curiosity, weren't you at all concerned that I might walk in on you?"

Clarissa shrugged again. "I thought you were working late."

"You won't mind if I don't invite you to my wedding," Sara said.

"Hell, no! I understand perfectly."

"I'm terribly fond of you, Clarissa, but I think it would be better if you got your own apartment. I'm going to write you a small check—just to get you set up—"

"Look, Sara, you don't have to do that. You don't owe me anything. It's the other way around. And you don't have to pay me off for any pictures—there *aren't* any."

"I know *that*," Sara said. "That did sound a bit complicated . . . that self-timer thing . . . for a photography novice. . . ."

Sara started to laugh and Clarissa joined in.

"You're okay, Sara, for a rich girl."

It was funny how things worked out sometimes, Sara thought reflectively. If she hadn't taken pity on Clarissa and asked her to stay in her house . . . and if she hadn't imagined a terrible ghost in the house across the street and rushed up the stairs to question Clarissa . . . why, she wouldn't be getting her divorce so easily and she wouldn't be marrying Willy sooner than she thought possible. . . .

13.

I flew in for Sara's wedding to Willy. It was Christmas and Peter was able to come with me. We took Joshua and Adam with us and left baby Petey at home with Mother. Aunt Bettina flew out from Charleston. Maeve and Harry made the wedding on the grounds of Harry's beautiful estate, and it was the usual sunny day in Southern California, and the champagne we drank came from the vineyards to the north. Maeve believed in drinking the local product.

Sara wore white and defied *anyone* to say she wasn't as pure as the driven snow. Maeve, maid of honor, wore pink, and Chrissy, matron of honor, yellow, and a few of the guests made the usual jokes about the maid of honor being always a bridesmaid and never a bride. My sons were the ringbearers for the double-ring ceremony and I thought they looked adorable. The twins, Christy and Georgianna, looking like little flowers themselves, were the flower girls and, toddling along, they dropped their baskets of rose petals and ran to cling to their mother's skirt, while everyone laughed with delight. Chrissy's stepson, Sasha, had been pressed into service as an usher, but he soon disappeared into the house with a young girl guest who was barely sixteen, and everyone thought that was pretty amusing.

With tears shining in her eyes, the bride took her father's arm and that of her mother and walked to the *huppah,* the wedding canopy, where the groom waited for her with his best man, Harry Hartman. Willy wept openly, not being the sort of man who held back his emotions. When the rabbi pronounced them man and wife, the groom smashed the wine glass under his foot with ferocious fervor, then consulted his watch before kissing the bride.

"Well, let's see," Willy said. "It's only been nine years, three months, two days, five minutes and three seconds that I've waited for this moment." After he kissed Sara he announced, "It was worth waiting for."

After everyone finished toasting the newlyweds, it was I who reminded my friends that, as this was Christmas 1955 and we had actually made our debut in Christmas of 1945 (although considered the 1946 season), it *was* our tenth anniversary and we might as well take advantage of us all being together and drink to that!

Chrissy never did mention the man she had seen parked in a black Continental at the bottom of the road winding up to the Hartman house. She had been giving the twins' curls a last minute touchup with her brush in the car as Sasha, who was driving, whipped around the curve and up the road, and she had just caught a fleeting glance of a profile that was naggingly familiar. She had asked Max if he had noticed the man in the black car, but Max had been deep in thought and had not even answered her. She had planned on asking someone at the wedding if they had seen the man and if they knew who he was—it was so annoying to almost match a name with a face and then just miss the connection. But in the excitement, she forgot all about him. And it wasn't until she was home again that she realized whom the man had reminded her of and she was frightened. So she spoke of him again to Max and told him whom he reminded her of, but Max had drunk too much champagne, and he only wanted to get to bed. "What are you going on about, Christina? Such nonsense you talk!"

She wanted to discuss it with *somebody* but she could hardly call Sara, even if she had known where the couple was spending the night. And it was ridiculous to upset Maeve because of a quick glimpse of a profile that could have belonged to anybody. But, just the same, she would skip her trip to see Ali this week, and she would tell Harry to think up some reason he and Maeve shouldn't go there either.

Sara and Willy stayed in Willy's house in Stone Canyon and Maeve sold the house on North Palm Drive. Then Willy presented Sara with a deed. "A wedding present."

"You already gave me a wedding present—those beautiful pearls." She looked at the deed. "This is for a parcel of land, isn't it?" She studied the deed. "Malibu?"

"Right. Glad you could figure that out—I was worried there for a minute."

"What are we going to do with this?"

"You usually build on land."

"What are we going to build?"

"Anything you like. If you want an ice-skating rink, that's what we'll build."

"Oh, Willy! What I would like is a Southern mansion with pillars and gardens—"

"Then that's what we'll build. How about reproducing Tara, Scarlett? Call it Tara At the Beach."

"Oh, Willy! Can we? But call it Charleston Gardens?"

Willy screwed up his eyes. "Frankly, Sara, I don't give a damn!" and he sounded just like Clark Gable.

"Do you think it's possible to grow flowers—roses, camellias, jasmine —at the beach?"

"If necessary, we'll go to Charleston and bring back a ton of the red clay of Georgia. But the house and the land are only part of the wedding present. You get whatever else you want to go along with the house."

"I think I would like to stop working. Do you mind?"

He looked astonished. "Of course I don't mind."

"I want to build the house, work in the garden, and start making babies right away, and when Charleston Gardens is finished, I want my Mama to come live with us. Is that all right?"

"You're the princess. My only function is to serve."

"Oh, Willy!"

"Anything else, Your Royal Highness?"

"Yes. I want us to live happily ever after."

"Absolutely, Your Royal Highness. Your every wish is my command."

"Willy, I'm worried. I feel that I don't deserve to be this happy."

"Don't worry, Sara. It's only your Jewish guilt. It goes with the territory."

14.

"Harry, that was my agent on the phone. She says it's only a rumor but she's heard talk that they're considering *me* for the Pulitzer!"

"Maeve, at your age that's really incredible! But I'm really not surprised. *Heaven's Redress* was a beautiful, beautiful book."

"Well, I haven't won it yet. I almost hope I won't."

Harry smiled gently. "That's not a nice thing to say. It shows an unbecoming lack of gratitude to the gods."

"It's the gods I'm worried about, Harry. They're known to become awfully jealous. And then something terrible can happen."

"Maeve, we've already paid our dues. Only good things will happen now."

Maeve wished she could believe.

15.

Max came home and announced, "I've resigned from the studio."

"But why?" Chrissy asked. "I thought you were so happy there."

"Ach! Happy! Happiness is for children!"

Chrissy followed him into his music room. "But why did you resign?"

Max didn't answer right away. He was already seated at his grand piano and he picked at the keys tentatively. Then he sounded a few loud, dirgeful notes.

"I must do something more meaningful with my life than write music for stupid movies. I must compose music that will live forever."

The next morning, Max left the house early and didn't come home until late in the day. When he did come home, Chrissy asked, "Where were you, Max? If you didn't go to the studio—"

"Questions! Questions! Always questions! Just have the maid serve the dinner."

"Lily quit."

"Then have the cook serve the dinner."

"She left early today. She had to visit her mother."

"Then *you* serve the dinner. Is it too much to expect you to run the house? Why can't you hold on to servants?"

"Lily said Sasha made improper advances—"

Max looked at her strangely. "Women! They are always saying these things. First they invite the advances and then they scream. It's all in their heads."

Again, the next day, Max left early and came home late. Again Chrissy asked him where he had been.

"I will tell you when I am ready. Did you hire a new maid?"

"Not yet, Max. I didn't have a chance—"

"Why? What were you doing?"

"I was over at Sara's. She wanted to consult with me about the house they're building."

"What did she want to consult with you about? Are you an architect and I don't know about it?" he asked with sarcasm.

He saw the look on her face and tried to smile. "I was only joking, Schatzi. Why does she have to consult with you?"

"*She* values my opinion on artistic matters. She wanted my ideas on certain designs."

"You are too busy with your own house. I won't have the girls neglected."

"How can you say such a thing, Max? Have I ever neglected the twins?"

"Of course not," he said a little guiltily. "But you might get carried away and forget."

"Forget my daughters?"

"Enough of this discussion! Can we eat tonight or did you forget the dinner?"

"Max, for weeks now you've been gone for twelve . . . fourteen hours at a time and you don't tell me where you've been or what you've been doing."

"I am working on an opera, if you must know. *The* opera of the century. For a century there hasn't been an original great opera. Did you know that? Ach! What do you know about music?"

"What is the opera about?"

"It is a Greek tragedy."

"But who is doing the libretto?"

He glared at her suspiciously. "A great writer who is doing me the honor of working with me. Someone who accords me more respect than I am given in my own house."

Chrissy was bewildered. Since when had she not given Max his due respect? "But I have always respected you, Max."

"Then don't ask so many questions. *I* am not a child."

"And neither am I. You may be as mysterious as you like, but I should know where you are. Suppose there is an emergency? With the twins, or something. I have to be able to reach you."

"Very well. I will give you the telephone number. But you are not to disturb me with any of your nonsense. It is to be used only in a true emergency. Where is Sasha?"

"I don't have the faintest idea. You know Sasha. He doesn't say where he is or where he's going. He's probably jumping into some pretty young thing this very minute. . . ." And, personally, she didn't blame him. It was probably a hell of a lot more fun than she was having.

"It's not becoming for the mother of daughters to talk like that."

"Oh, fuckers!" She hadn't said that in years.

She thought Max would choke.

"This is all that Sara's doing."

"What does that mean?"

"Sara is a loose woman."

"Sara? Sara is no more loose than I am."

"That is exactly what worries me."

Chrissy stared at him unbelievingly then left the table and slammed into her bedroom. She looked into the full-length mirror. Sara was right.

She *was* overweight and dowdy. Tomorrow she would go on a diet, start at Marovski's gymnasium, swim every day, go to the hairdresser's, and buy a whole new wardrobe. No, she would wait until she lost at least ten pounds for *that*.

"Why are you so thin all of a sudden?" Max asked querulously.

"Because I've taken a lover!" she said. "What do you think?"

Max turned bright red. She thought he was going to have a stroke.

"I'm not *so* thin. I was overweight so I went on a diet."

"And that outfit you're wearing. Do you think a woman with children should wear such an outfit?"

"This?" She pulled at her halter. "Every woman up to the age of eighty wears a halter in Southern California."

"You want the men to look at you!"

"You're getting tiresome, Max."

"It's that Sara. She's a bad influence."

"Don't you dare say a word against Sara."

"And your friend Maeve. Living with a man in sin. A Communist! All those Communists are the same. They believe in free love!"

"Who's been talking to you? What's got into you? Sara and Willy, Maeve and Harry—they're our friends."

"Your friends. Are you sure they can be trusted to keep your secrets?"

"What secrets? What's happened to you?"

"Don't ask me what's *happened to me!* I know all about that trick. It's what's happening to you that I'm talking about. Dressing like a whore! Going to bars, picking up men!"

"You're crazy!"

"Crazy like a fox! I *know* you were at the bar at the Beverly Wilshire! You were seen!"

"Seen by whom? Are you having me followed, you crazy old man?" *Oh, my God, what have I said?*

She apologized immediately. "You've upset me so, making these accusations. . . . I did have lunch at the Wilshire with Sara and Maeve. On the way out we saw Brian Donovan whom we all know and like, at the bar, and we stopped for a minute to chat. I want to know who saw me, who told you. . . ."

"I don't have to tell you anything. It is you who have committed the acts of shame."

"Max, I warn you! You are going too far!"

Has he already gone too far? she wondered. She really was getting fed up! What had happened to Max? He had always been a little difficult but he was getting impossible! Was he getting senile? Was he having a nervous breakdown? And he *was* drinking. Why did everyone drink so much? In a few months' time Max had deteriorated into—she didn't know what. She would really like to know what was going on with him.

Who was this mysterious person he was working with? Why the deep, deep secret? And why was Max obviously drinking when he was supposed to be working? *Mysterious person?* Could it be? . . . No, she was getting paranoid. What would he want with old Max? Maybe this mysterious stranger was simply a figment of Max's imagination? If she could only talk Max into going to a psychiatrist. But no, that was impossible, too. Max would only scorn her—ask her what did a fool like her know about anything? No, all she could do was let Max run his course. But she hoped it wouldn't take too long for whatever it was to work itself out of his system. She was running out of patience, and Max—he was running out of time.

Chrissy and Sara sat by Chrissy's pool. Chrissy lit a cigarette. She had recently resumed smoking, after having stopped when she first became pregnant. Max had insisted at that time.

"You're smoking again, Chrissy?"

"Yes. . . ."

"Why?"

"What kind of a question is that? I'm smoking because I want to—"

"And your nerves are very bad."

"Tell me something I don't know. I'm worried about Max. He's acting like a crazy person. He's jealous . . . he accuses me of making up to other men . . . he's mysterious . . . he's become unkempt . . . and he's drinking . . . heavily. . . ."

"How long has this been going on?"

"I don't know . . . six . . . seven months. . . ."

"You're not thinking of—"

"A divorce? I hope to God it doesn't come to that. The girls—" She sighed heavily.

"Look," Sara said. "You have to get away a little bit. Why don't you pack up the girls and come stay at the beach with us for a week or two? Maybe Max will come to his senses while you're gone. It is summer and you remember what I always said about being in town for the summer?"

Chrissy laughed but it was not a merry laugh.

"I can't. I really do think Max is having some kind of a breakdown and I *have* to be here. When is your own house going to be ready?" she asked to change the subject.

"You *know* builders! If I weren't renting next door to keep an eye on them it would be two years from now."

"It's only been a few months, hasn't it, that they're working on it?" Chrissy asked, not really thinking about what she was saying.

"Four . . . to be exact." Sara got up. "I'll be running along. Please,

392

Chrissy, take care of yourself. And if you need me, holler! And see if you won't change your mind about coming out."

"I will. You don't mind seeing yourself out? I think I'll just sit here a while longer."

Sara frowned. She would ask Willy if he could think of something to do about Max. Maybe the old coot should be institutionalized? Of course, she was being uncharitable but she never did like him. She never thought Chrissy should have married him. Of course he was jealous of Chrissy. Older men were always jealous when they had young wives. She didn't like the look of Chrissy sitting there by her lonesome by the pool. She wished Maeve was in town. She would have to talk this whole thing over with her.

Chrissy was still sitting at the pool when the girls' nursemaid approached her. "The girls are asleep, Mrs. Kozlo. Will it be all right if I leave now? I have an appointment for eight."

"Go ahead, Agnes."

She debated whether to eat without waiting for Max or take a dip. She wasn't hungry anyway. She liked to swim this time of day, when it was all golden, just before the sun disappeared.

She was in the pool when she heard Sasha brake his car in the driveway. Although the pool was in back of the house, the screech of the Ferrari's tires was clearly audible—Sasha must have stopped on a dime, pulling in at eighty miles per hour.

He came running to the pool's edge.

"Are we eating soon?"

"Are *you* eating at home tonight?"

He grinned. "I thought I'd give you and Dad a break."

"Lucky us. Your father isn't home yet."

"Dad's never home much anymore. What's going on?"

"Working hard, I guess."

"As long as we're not eating yet, I think I'll have a swim too."

He pulled off his shirt, unbuckled his belt and started to pull down his zipper.

"How about a suit?" Chrissy asked.

"Wearing it," he laughed. "Scared you?" He dropped his jeans. He was wearing a miniscule pair of trunks. "Just came from the beach," and he dove into the water from the side of the pool and came up from behind her, tackling her legs, pulling all of her beneath the water. She wrestled with him and, accidentally, his hands cupped her breasts, surprising them both.

"Hey, take it easy, Tarzan!" she sputtered. "You almost drowned me." She climbed out.

"Aren't you going to swim anymore?"

393

"I'm going to dry off. You can give me a diving exhibition."

She lay down on the chaise and toweled her hair, watching as he poised on the diving board. God, what a physique! The phrase, she believed, was Greek god. No wonder the girls laid down in droves for him.

He emerged from the water. "How was that?" he asked, like a small boy.

"Terrific!" she called out, smiling affectionately at him. She leaned back, picked up the glass of wine from the table beside her. Sipping, she watched as he perched on the board again—the beautiful animal, tanned, wetly gleaming, the setting sun turning him an incredible gold.

"Is that how you tempt my son into cuckolding his father?"

She swiveled her head around.

Max stood there, tired and old-looking, his white hair sticking out in wild tufts in all directions, dressed in a dark suit and a white crumpled shirt. He was an anachronism in the yellow California late afternoon.

Chrissy felt as weary as Max appeared. "What the hell are you talking about?" she asked without heat.

"The daughters lie asleep while the wanton mother displays her body lasciviously to an innocent boy in his prime . . . like Eve offering the apple to Adam."

"This is your ordinary two-piece bathing suit, the likes of which is seen by thousands every day at the beach—hardly a wanton display," she said dispassionately. "As for innocent Sasha, I dare say he's seen hundreds of women in their birthday suits, and always looking down."

"Hold your tongue! I've been standing behind the shrubbery for minutes now—don't tell me any more of your lies. And this is not the first time I see how you live only to tantalize him—"

"Don't say anything more, Max. You've already said far too much."

She watched him loosen his tie as if unable to breathe.

"Hi, Dad!" Sasha came over uncertainly, not sure if he should intrude.

"Go inside! Cover your eyes!"

Sasha looked at Chrissy questioningly.

"Why don't you go get your dinner, Sasha? Everything's ready on the stove."

Sasha went into the house slowly, turning around to take another look at his father and stepmother.

"Take a swim, Max," Chrissy said. "Before you lose the light. It's been a hot day and it will be dark soon," she said forlornly.

"What kind of a woman seduces a boy into betraying his father?" he asked, shaking his head, staring into the water.

She wanted to ask him where he had gotten such ideas. Who had put those ideas into his head? But it was too late for questions, too late for answers. She started for the house, mounted the stairs, stopped suddenly. Someone was feeding him these ideas, encouraging him to drink, to make these accusations against her. . . . *The Greek tragedy* . . .

the libretto . . . the mysterious stranger. Someone was trying to destroy Max, to destroy her marriage . . . to destroy her home, and there was only one person that could be. *God, I've been a fool, denying what a blind person could see, what an idiot could figure out . . . that time . . . Sara's wedding . . . the man in the Continental.*

She took off her wet suit, put on a robe.

Was she just being hysterical? Melodramatic? Letting her imagination go wild? Was she so distraught herself, she was writing a scenario that didn't exist? No, she didn't think so.

She found the telephone number that Max had given her, the number at which he could be reached in case of an absolute emergency. She dialed and held her breath. The phone rang five, six times and then the operator's voice: "The number you have called is not in operation. . . ."

Had the number *ever* been in operation? Had it been a phony number all along? Now what? she asked herself. What is my next move? She *was* convinced that she had not been dreaming this nightmare. But was *he* trying to destroy Max just to destroy her marriage? Touch her life with his evil hand as he had Sara's—just to get even with Maeve? Or was it more than that this time? Was her broken marriage just a by-product of his plan to find Ali?

She herself had told Max a long time ago about Maeve's father and what he was all about, that he was the father of Maeve's daughter. Would Max, under those circumstances, have told him where Ali was? *Had he discovered Ali's whereabouts from Max?* That was the crucial question. With a feeling of dread, Chrissy went downstairs to find out the answer. But in her heart she already knew. Max, in his present condition, had been an easy target for Padraic.

Max was in the music room drinking from a silver flask.

"I wouldn't drink any more, Max."

He ignored her.

"Did you tell him where Ali was?"

He didn't answer her.

"Everything he told you was lies. I told you what he was before—why didn't you believe *me?*" Chrissy asked quietly.

He looked at her with contempt. "Those silly stories you told me about Maeve and her baby and her father? That ridiculous story about Sara the harlot? What kind of a fool do you take me for? The hysterical stories of a warped child's mind? Of course I didn't believe you." He laughed bitterly, took another drink from his flask. "But you weren't really a child, were you? You are Circe, a destroyer of men. You have destroyed me with your whorish ways. I cannot even work. He is no longer even interested in working with me. My opera . . . my Greek tragedy . . . will never be finished now. . . ." He wept.

"Max, *did* you tell him where Ali was?"

But he wept and didn't answer her.

Chrissy went into the kitchen to send Sasha to his father. Oh, yes, this Greek tragedy was finished.

Sasha sat at the kitchen table eating quickly. Chrissy guessed that he wanted to finish and leave the house—to go where there was music and easy laughter.

"What's wrong with Dad, Chrissy?"

"He's not well, Sasha. He's—" She started to cry.

"Don't cry, Chrissy. It'll be all right."

"No, Sasha," she said. "It won't. Not for us."

He got up from the table and came over to her. "Please don't cry, Chrissy."

He put his arms around her, to comfort her. She closed her eyes. The strong, young arms felt good. His body pressed against her, that strong, young body, those long, taut, muscular thighs. Her breasts were crushed against his chest and her body wanted to lean into him, press, crush back, to surrender to the urgency it felt. She had forgotten that she was young —her body had almost forgotten that it could respond, feel, that it wanted to be caressed, loved, crushed, felt of, made love to with strength, vigor and passion. The body had almost forgotten, but then the body remembered, her loins and her breasts remembered.

Sasha, all-natural animal, all reflexes, hardened. His hips moved against her and his hands untied her robe and now it was her bare flesh against his, except for the still-damp bathing trunks. Her nipples erected at the flick of his tongue. Her fingers traveled down his back, her hands pressed him against her harder. His mouth came up from her breasts and found her mouth, his tongue fought to make entrance. Oh, her mouth remembered too!

Then her head remembered. She couldn't do this to the golden Sasha. She pushed him back, away from her and, sobbing, she sunk to her knees. He misunderstood her and, pulling down his trunks, thrust himself at her.

"No," she cried out. "No! Go to your father, Sasha, and comfort him! He needs you!"

Sasha, confused, pulled up his trunks and ran from the room.

Chrissy retied her robe. *He* had not won out completely. Yes, Max had betrayed them all. But at least she had not betrayed herself and Sasha had not betrayed his father.

She went back up the stairs. Tomorrow she would take Christy and Georgianna and move in with Maeve and Harry. . . . Tomorrow she would have to tell Maeve that her father was back and that Max may have revealed Ali's whereabouts. . . . Let her sleep tonight a peaceful sleep—her last for who knew how long. . . .

Oh, my God! Max probably didn't even know whether he had revealed where Ali was or not . . . he was so befuddled and Padraic was so clever. *But Max had said that Padraic was no longer interested in working with him!* That meant Padraic had *already* got what he wanted!

"Hello?" Harry answered.
"Harry! Is Maeve there?"
"Chrissy? Maeve's out of town. In New York."
"Harry! Oh Harry, he's back and he knows where Ali is!"

16.

Harry hung up the phone. "He just bullied his way into the home and grabbed her. But the agency I've hired has already located him. He has her in a shack near La Paz at the tip of Baja California," Harry said. "They've been spotted from a copter. I'm flying down to San Diego where I'm meeting two members of the team. They've got a chartered plane to take us down into the interior. There's some kind of a rough landing strip there. Then we switch to the helicopter. In the meantime, the team is watching them from some kind of a pick-up truck nearby."

"Oh, Harry! It sounds terribly scary," Sara said. "And dangerous!"
Willy patted Sara's shoulder.
Chrissy wrung her hands. "Ali must be terrified!"
"I'm leaving immediately. What I want you three to do is stay here and wait for Maeve. If we're lucky, I'll have Ali back before Maeve's home from New York. And if she calls, try not to give anything away."
"Harry, you should be here when Maeve comes back—just in case we don't have Ali back by then . . . yet." She said a silent prayer. Please, God!
"I have to go with them to get her. Ali knows me," he said quietly. "I don't want her frightened any more than she must be already."
"I'll go," Chrissy said. "She knows *me*. We're friends. And you can stay here and wait for Maeve."
"No. *I* have to do this myself . . . for Maeve."
"Let me go with you, Harry," Willy offered. "It sounds like you're going to need all the help you can get."
"I'd appreciate it if you stayed here with Sara and Chrissy and waited for Maeve too, Willy. They'll need you. And I have plenty of help. I've got six armed men from the agency and we've got the Mexican police, too."
"Oh, dear God! What have I done?" Chrissy cried.

397

Sara rushed to her. "It's not your fault, Chrissy. When Maeve was with me at the clinic and I begged her pardon for not believing her, she said: 'There is no question of forgiveness. We are all victims.' "

Maeve called a few hours later and Chrissy answered. If Maeve grew suspicious, Chrissy, at least, had a valid reason to be at the house.

"Where is Harry?" Maeve asked.

"Oh, at a story conference with Willy."

"Oh? And what are you doing at my house, Chrissy? Did you take pity on poor Harry and come over to do some cooking?" Maeve joked.

"I've left Max, Chrissy. I've moved in on you and Harry with the twins for the time being. I even brought Agnes along with us."

"Oh, Chrissy dear, I'm so sorry. What happened?"

"I'll tell you about it when you come home."

"I feel dreadful that I'm not there. You must be terribly upset. You *sound* awful."

"No, I'm O.K. Really, cross my heart. And Harry and Sara and Willy are very comforting. Sara is already planning my next wedding."

Maeve chuckled. "All right, Chrissy dear. I'll see you soon. Tell Harry I'll be home tomorrow night, and kiss the twins for me."

"Do you think she guessed anything?" Sara asked, biting long silver fingernails.

"No. But what will happen if Harry isn't able to . . . if he doesn't . . . bring Ali back?" Chrissy's fingers clawed through her hair.

Sara agonized. "I don't know. It will probably be the end of Maeve. . . ."

Chrissy moaned.

"Come on, you two crêpe hangers," Willy said. "Let's have a little positive thinking around here."

"Let's sit outside on the terrace and watch the twins play," Sara said. "It's better than just waiting by the phone."

"It's all my fault," Chrissy said again. "I should have known. I should have guessed when Max started acting crazy. When he said he was working with an important writer and wouldn't tell me who. And the day you two got married—I *thought* I saw someone who reminded me of *him*."

"Then it's my fault too. I thought I saw him in the house across the street on North Palm Drive, but I dismissed the whole thing from my mind," Sara said.

"But, Sara, maybe I *did* know all along it was he. Maybe subconsciously I knew it and I let it all happen—let him destroy my marriage because I wanted it destroyed. Maybe I just wanted *out* and I let him do my dirty work, in which case I'm guilty as sin."

"Goodness gracious, Chrissy Marlowe, don't we have enough to worry about without your subconscious getting in on the act?"

"There's still one question that bothers me—he tried to destroy you, Sara, to get back at Maeve. But does he want Ali to destroy her too, or does he want Ali for himself?"

The two women stared at each other.

"Please, ladies, remember—" Willy said. "The good thoughts. . . ."

Maeve came home before Harry. Sara and Chrissy made a stab at lying to her, but in the end, Willy took her aside and told her everything.

"Ali!" Maeve screamed, then cried, "Harry!" and sank to the floor in a faint.

When she came to, stretched out on the couch in her living room, she begged Chrissy to tell her all the details. Bleakly dry-eyed, she listened. When Chrissy was through she wondered what roles her father had earmarked for Harry her lover and Ali her daughter. Then she thought of something she had never really considered before—her daughter was her sister too. . . .

Two cars, one black, the other white, pulled up in the circular driveway in front of the house. Four men from the agency Harry had employed jumped out of the white car and a U.S. marshal out of the other. Willy, watching from the window, ran into the front hall and flung open the door. Maeve followed like some wounded bird. "Is it they, Willy?"

"Miss O'Connor?" the marshal asked.

"Yes?" Maeve whispered.

"We've brought your daughter home, Ma'am."

Another marshal backed out of the black car, assisting the slim, frightened girl.

"Ali! Oh, Ali! Thank God, thank God!"

The girl ran into Maeve's arms. "Maeve . . . Maeve. . . ."

Maeve kissed her daughter repeatedly while the four agency men and the two marshals watched from the doorway, and Chrissy, Sara, and Willy, from inside the house. Then Maeve looked up at the marshal. "Harry?" She turned to Willy, Chrissy, and Sara. "Harry!" she screamed. "Where is Harry?"

Chrissy came over, took Ali by the hand and led her to the stairway, murmuring endearments. "Harry . . ." Ali said to Chrissy and smiled.

Sara and Willy ran to Maeve's side. "Marshal?" Willy inquired.

"Tell me," Maeve implored. "Please. Where's Harry? Was he hurt?"

"No, Ma'am. Mr. Hartman's in Tijuana. He was stopped by Immigration, Ma'am. We were just called in to accompany your daughter here. Sorry about Mr. Hartman, Ma'am. I've always been a fan of his." The marshals left but the agency men stayed.

Maeve collapsed against Willy who held her up, half-carried her into the living room and seated her on the sofa. "Sara, bring the gentlemen inside. Sit, gentlemen, please."

Maeve looked at them, her eyes pleading.

One of the men cleared his throat. "We were in the chartered plane preparing to go on to San Diego, but Immigration had us brought down before we made the border. Mr. Hartman—" he paused, searching for the right words, "was denied re-entry into the country as an undesirable alien. I'm sorry, Miss O'Connor . . . but at least we got the girl—"

"Yes . . . thank you . . . I'm grateful for that. Willy?"

"Sara, get the gentlemen a drink. Maeve, I'm going into the library to make some calls. You just relax and we'll get this whole thing straightened out. Okay?"

"Yes, Willy. Thank you." She turned back to the agency men. "Please, if you don't mind . . . tell me what happened in Baja?"

". . . It was easier than we thought it would be. Pardon me, Ma'am, but we didn't know what the hell to expect. We were afraid if we rushed the house, he might harm the girl, so we just kept it under surveillance, waiting to see if he would come out of the house, away from the girl. Finally he did. And then we watched for a few minutes. He walked up to the top of this hill that overlooked the harbor and it looked like he was talking to himself. We don't even know if he saw us or what—it was like he forgot about the girl and the shack. He was waving his arms and shouting. We just ran in and got her out. She looked scared but when she saw Mr. Hartman she smiled like the sun had come out and ran to him and he just picked her up and carried her out and we ran for the copter, but we didn't even have to. That guy . . . excuse me, Miss O'Connor . . . your father . . . it was like he never even knew we were there. . . ."

"I want a couple of you to go back to Mexico with me," Maeve said to the men from the investigative agency.

"But why, Maeve?' Sara asked. "It's not necessary. Willy and I will go with you."

"No. I mean, yes. I *want* you and Willy to come to Tijuana with me. But I need one or two of these men to come with me too."

"Why, Maeve, why?" Sara's voice rose. "What are you thinking of?"

"Please, Maeve, I beg you," Harry implored. "Don't do this. You have Ali with you and now that she is no longer a secret, she can live with you . . . us. We'll get security . . . he'll never be able to come near her again. I don't want you to see him—"

400

"Harry's right," Sara said. "Why must you see him? Willy, you tell her we're right."

"I can't," Willy said.

"Willy!" Sara said angrily. "What are you saying? That Maeve should face him? That's terrible!"

"Sometimes people have to do the very things that hold the most terror for them so that they can live free."

"Then I will go with you," Harry said.

"No." Maeve touched his hand, his face. "You've already gone to hell for me. I must talk with him alone. Just he and I. I'll be perfectly safe. He won't harm me—I'm sure of it. And the two detectives are going with me. They're going to keep an eye on me from just a short distance away."

"No!" Harry cried.

"Yes, Harry. I must."

17.

They saw him up on the hill as soon as they alighted from the helicopter.

"Wait here," Maeve commanded them. "If I need you, I'll call you. I have that transmitter you gave me right in my shoulder bag." *Along with something else. . . .*

She had to do this for Ali. Otherwise, Ali would never be truly safe again. Aunt Maggie had tried to do it for *her,* and had failed. But even Aunt Maggie knew what had to be done. They had all waited too long . . . and so much had happened. Sara. Chrissy. Even Harry had been drawn into this evil web. Now, he might never be allowed to reenter the country. No, too long . . . It was enough, truly enough. Any just god would agree that it was enough. . . .

Walking up the hill, Maeve understood why he had been drawn here. Here, hard by the mountains of Baja, lay a rock-strewn countryside, a wilderness of spiky cactus and squawking, vivid parrots. As she made her way over the rocks, she kept her gaze on his black form. He was wearing his cape even though it was hot and steamy, so humid that it was difficult to breathe.

In Aran she had been angry, so full of wrath and vengeance, but still afraid. Now she was not afraid and no longer angry. She was determined. But sick with sadness over what had to be done.

Now, coming closer, she saw that his crown of black curls was garlanded with wild flowers.

" 'Blow, winds, and crack your cheeks! Rage! Blow!' "

He thinks he's King Lear!

She approached him.

" 'Do not laugh at me; For, as I am a man, I think this lady to be my child Cordelia.' "

Maeve responded in kind: " 'And so I am, I am.' "

Oh, were it only possible that she could play Cordelia to his Lear—if she could only find him thus—mad—and make him well, as Shakespeare had written it. But this was beyond her God-given abilities. It could not be. She cried because she could not really play Cordelia.

" 'Be your tears wet? Yes, faith. I pray, weep not:

" 'If you have poison for me, Cordelia, I will drink it . . .' " He smiled and then said, "And if you don't, no matter, I have my own." Then he continued: " 'I know you do not love me; for your sisters . . .' " He stopped as if trying to remember the lines. "No, not Regan and Goneril. Maeve and Ali. Are they not the names of my other daughters, the other daughters of Lear—*they* have wronged me. But you, Cordelia, I think you have no cause to despise me—"

She stuck to the original lines. " 'No cause, no cause,' " Maeve wept.

"For you, Cordelia, I will drink the poison. I have obtained some . . . or have I said that?" He looked confused.

"No!" Maeve cried out. "No! . . ." She shook her head in despair. She had come here to commit a deed, yet she could not bear to do it . . . no, she could not . . . and by the same token, she could not allow him to do it for her.

"Oh, Father, what are we to do?" she cried.

"We must do what has to be done, my daughter, my love."

She looked at him. For a moment he sounded like he had when they lived in Truro . . . in the good times. Had he finally gone over the line completely as his mother had, taken refuge in literature in his madness? Or was he only pretending? . . .

"But why, Father, why?"

"It is appropriate. I have seen the light, let us say, a moment of clarity. . . ." He laughed, then sobered. "I have seen her . . . that which I have wrought and I am mad with despair." He shook his head. "There is nothing left . . . everything is gone."

He looked deeply into her eyes and his eyes were bluer than she had ever seen them. "Be generous, because I have loved you, and give me this moment."

He held out his hand. She could not deny him.

"Come, Cordelia, in the hovel below I have some nectar of the gods. We will drink a toast to each other. And then I will drink . . . of something else. . . . Please!"

She took his hand and together they descended to the house below the hill.

Padraic bowed. "Enter, fair lady."

Maeve sat down at the rough-hewn table and Padraic set two glasses on the table, and beside them a clay gourd and a small glass bottle.

" '. . . This prison where I live unto the world.' "

He poured two drinks from the clay gourd and handed her one.

"We will drink to each other." He lifted his glass. " 'Sweet partner, I must not yet forsake you.' " He drank. " 'I will lie with thee tonight.' " *And now he is Romeo.* She tried not to cry.

She drank and wiped away the tears.

Then he lifted the small glass bottle.

"Oh, no!" she cried out. "I cannot bear it!"

"And I . . . I cannot bear to live!"

"Wait!" She kissed him.

" 'Thus with a kiss I die.' "

He drank and Maeve sat there and watched him.

"It is a far, far better thing that I do . . . than I have ever done. . . ." And he laughed and held out his hand to her once more.

She gripped it tightly and thus they sat until it was nearly dark outside. Finally, she closed the lids on his eyes and kissed him again.

Walking away from the house, Maeve looked up and saw the first star of the night.

HOLLYWOOD 1966

1.

"Have I got good news for you, Princess!" Willy came into the den and kissed Sara who was curled up on the leather couch, watching television.

"Sh!" Sara put a finger to her lips. "It's Chrissy . . . on the Carson show."

Willy sat down next to Sara, unfolding his length gradually, putting his arm around her, nuzzling her neck.

"Doesn't she look marvelous? She's wearing her hair the very same way she wore it at our debut, the bangs and the blunt cut with the ends turned up."

"And that smile!" Willy said. "That great, big, wide smile. On TV, that smile is worth a million bucks."

The show went to a commercial and Willy asked, "What's she hustling this time? Besides that dynamite smile."

"Her latest project—a book called *Designs for Country Living*. Darn! How I wish she'd come back here to live. I miss her so! It's really mean. Chrissy in New York, Maeve in Mexico, and Marlena in New Jersey."

"At least you do get to see them a few times a year, sweetie."

"Oh—they're back. Let's listen."

". . . I think the proper prescription for a divine life is a busy life, Johnny, full of work, children, and the *right* husband." Chrissy gave a little laugh and Johnny raised his eyebrows and the studio audience laughed. "I'm up at five working, so that by the time I sit down for breakfast with Leland and the children, I've already gotten in at least two hours of work. Then Leland goes off and Christy and Georgie, they're twelve, go off to school and Sara Maeve and I play together. . . ."

Then Johnny asked how old Sara Maeve was, and Chrissy answered, "Oh, she's four. But I don't believe in nursery school. I try to keep them home with me as long as possible. That's why I wouldn't send Christy and Georgie away to boarding school. Weekends we try to get up to our farm in Connecticut where we keep five dogs, two cats, and a horse."

Johnny said something Sara did not catch. "What did he say?" she asked Willy.

"Something about that's quite a menagerie, and I must say I agree."

"Golly, yes," Chrissy said. "And sometimes my stepson, Sasha Kozlo, comes down with his wife, Molly, and their two little boys. Then, we really have a full house—a madhouse, really." Chrissy laughed. "It really takes a lot of organization. That's what my book, *Designs for Country Living*, is all about. It tells how to furnish a country house, there are special recipes for those long weekends, how to make a guest more comfortable. . . . And of course, there's my collection of special designs for the country—my ginghams and florals. There's even a special chapter on the country nursery—"

Johnny made one of his sly, naughty-boy leers, and asked if Chrissy was trying to tell their audience something.

"Well, the design for the nursery *is* a copy of the one I just installed at Prescott Farms—" She giggled. "I *am* expecting late fall."

Then Johnny told the audience that they had heard another first on the "Tonight Show" and thanked Chrissy for visiting with them and for letting everyone in on her big secret. Then he held up her book to the camera and told Chrissy he had really enjoyed reading it.

Chrissy leaned over, kissed Johnny on the cheek. "*Sure* you did!" she said charmingly. "Golly, it's been fun!" And she flounced off in a ruffled, long-skirted gingham gown.

"Oh, my goodness, what a girl!" Sara exulted. "Leave it to Chrissy Marlowe to announce on national television that she's pregnant at the age of thirty-eight."

"I love the way you girls refer to each other by your maiden names. Her name is Chrissy Prescott . . . remember? And yours is Ross. Remember me—old Willy Ross?"

"Yes, I remember *you,* you silly. I was thinking of Chrissy—the old Chrissy. This Chrissy makes my head whirl—busy making money, babies, art, books; happy, successful—it's not the same girl the newspapers used to call the 'poor little rich girl.' Actually, we were all poor little rich girls, you know," she told Willy wistfully.

"That's funny. I didn't know that. When I met the three of you, I never thought of any one of you in that way. God, I was dazzled! I thought the three of you were royal princesses—America's own—shiny, glorious, regal!"

"And now," Sara pouted, "you're not so dazzled anymore?"

"Who says?" He switched off the set. "Come to bed, Princess. To the royal couch."

They walked upstairs, arm-in-arm.

"I have to check on little Billy."

"Good. We'll check him together."

When they came out of their son's room and carefully closed the door, Sara remembered that Willy had never told her his good news.

"Oh, that!" Willy snapped his fingers. "Nothing at all. Only that the

State Department is officially inviting Harry Hartman back into the country."

"Oh, Willy! Thank you!"

"What are you thanking me for? I'm not the State Department."

"No, thank God. But you *were* the chief instigator, pulling all kinds of strings. I just hope they accept and come back. To have Maeve nearby would be heaven."

"Well, we'll try to talk them into it when they're here. They *are* coming to accept the special award the Academy is presenting to Harry, aren't they?"

"This is ridiculous, Sara. We can't invite the whole world to the Oscars. I don't know if it's nice for me to try and get more than one table. We're not playing Monopoly—I'm not the only nominee, you know."

"You're the only nominee in your category who's going to win this year!"

"Sara, Sara, there you go again! I've been nominated four times in the past and four times I haven't won. What makes you think this year will be different? Everybody says comedic roles do not win Oscars and I have to believe them."

"This year will be different," Sara said. "This year is your year and Harry's year. It'll go down in motion-picture history—Willy Ross and Harry Hartman, the big winners."

"Harry was always a winner."

"So was . . . is . . . Willy Ross."

"Okay, Princess. For that statement alone, you can invite anybody you goddamn please. I'll buy out the room. No one else will be able to get a ticket. The audience will be made up entirely of Sara Gold Ross and friends. They won't even be able to let the other nominees in. What's the count?"

"You, me, Billy."

"Do they let four-year-olds in?"

"They'd better, or they'll hear from me. Then, there's Mama and Charles."

"Will they be back from their honeymoon?"

"Maybe not," Sara giggled. "When a lady marries a former matinee idol, I imagine the honeymoon takes forever. But we'll count on them anyway. We can always give the tickets away. And Daddy . . . he's flying in."

"All right for Daddy! But you have to promise me one thing, Sara. No matchmaking this time."

"Don't be a little old asshole, Willy. Of course I don't promise."

Willy rolled his eyes. "For a guy who's always a winner, I get called the prettiest names. Next?"

"Chrissy, of course. But I have to find out if Leland is coming. Who would think Chrissy would end up with a lawyer, of all things. Who would have thought it would last all these years? God must have sent him to Chrissy when she needed him most—when Max tried to take Georgie and Christy away from her, that son of a bitch."

"Sara," Willy reproached her. "You know it's not nice to speak ill of the dead. Besides, Max was a sick man. And God didn't send Leland to Chrissy—you did."

"Maybe so. Then I guess I have only myself to blame that Chrissy lives in New York. Do you think we could ever persuade Leland and Chrissy to switch their base of operations?"

"I seriously doubt that, Sara sweetheart. He and Chrissy are almost professional New Yorkers."

Sara sighed. "I suppose you're right. They're always in the New York columns—first nights, sponsors of charity balls, gallery openings. . . . Did I tell you they went to Truman's party in matching military motif costumes?"

"*I've* been thinking of matching your makeup myself. I'm going to spread that dead-white foundation stuff of yours all over my face and paint my lips to match yours. I bet we'll make the *Hollywood Reporter*'s gossip column. They'll refer to it as the Ross signature makeup."

"I knew it. I told you. You're a winner, Willy Ross. One way or another."

2.

There were many mini-skirted evening dresses, see-through and sequined, in the Academy Awards audience, as well as black satin cowgirl outfits replete with leather boots. But Maeve, Sara, and Chrissy wore white ballgowns so that Willy was prompted to ask, "Are you sure you're not making your debut tonight?"

"I know a special occasion when I see one," Sara had said when she chose her gown and imposed her choice on Maeve. Maeve and Harry, along with Ali, were staying with Sara and Willy at Malibu. Sara, distressed that Harry did not look really well and Maeve appeared very tired, had spent every available minute trying to persuade them to accept the government's invitation to stay in the United States and pick up their lives where they had left off ten years before.

"Sara darling, I know how much you want us to stay and I know that Willy has been lobbying on Harry's behalf and that the political climate has changed in Hollywood. But we've changed too—we have other commitments now. The work we've been doing with the really underpriviliged children of Mexico—the schools we've started and the orphanage. And Ali! She's a woman now and she's been such a help with the children. She can't teach and she can't do administrative work but she knows how to love and play and transmit warmth and caring. Sara, her life hasn't been empty and worthless in Mexico—it's been meaningful and full of love. . . ."

"Why can't you do the same thing here in L.A.? God knows, there are plenty of kids here that could use help."

"And plenty of people available to help them. We're needed there. We're committed, Sara. We're deeply involved. Oh, come on, Sara. Mexico isn't all that far away."

Finally, even Sara had to give up.

Chrissy and Leland had arrived only a few hours before the ceremony. "Leland's running for councilman so you can imagine our schedule! But I wouldn't have missed this night for all the world. Harry being honored . . . Willy getting top-dog prize—"

"Not yet he hasn't," Sara said. "Just keep your fingers crossed."

"Fingers? Fuckers! And all this time I thought it was supposed to be my legs—"

Sara punched her lightly on the arm. "It's too late for that, Miss Preggie. Speaking of Perpetually Pregnant, what did Marlena say when you spoke to her last?"

"She wasn't doing much talking. She did say if it had only been one of the kids who had the measles, she would have still come. But seeing as it was she herself with the red spots, she just gave in and collapsed."

Sara giggled. "Wouldn't it have been funny if she *had* come and broken out with the red spots right at the Awards?"

"Hilarious!"

"Her Royal Highness of Monaco is going to make the special award to Harry," Sara told the others. "I haven't seen Grace since her wedding. She's as pretty as ever even if she has gained a few pounds."

"Now, now," Willy cautioned Sara gently.

"I'm not going to say one adverse thing, so you can relax, Best Actor." Then, "Willy is always afraid I might say something that will not reflect well upon me—he wants me to sound *ever* like the perfect, gracious lady."

"Which is what you are, Princess." Willy patted Sara's hand.

"Sh! The speeches about Harry are starting—"

Finally, Grace Rainier introduced Harry. ". . . It is my pleasure to present the Academy's special award for distinguished service to the art and science of American moviemaking to—Harry Hartman."

There was a thunderous applause and Harry walked on.

His voice was hoarse with emotion. "I thank all the people of America. I have never stopped loving you. I thank all my friends who have not forgotten me. Although I have not made films for many years now, my life has not been empty. It has been as full as any man's life can be, full of work and caring and love. For this, I thank my daughter, Ali, and my wife, Maeve, who has enough heart for all of us." His voice cracked. "It's she who has taught me one of the greatest attitudes of love—forgiveness—even for those who might have thought ill of me. There is nothing that is going to save this world but love, my friends. All of you, for God's sake, love one another!"

"Oh, jeepers creepers, what a fucking corny speech!" Chrissy muttered, crying copiously. "Did you write it, Maeve?"

"Me?" Maeve hugged Ali. "What would I know about love?"

Princess Grace stayed on to make the Best Actor award. She read the list of nominations then asked for the envelope with the name of the winner.

"She doesn't know that if she doesn't read the right name now, she's a goner—we're all going to put a hex on her," Sara whispered.

"The winner is—Willy Ross!"

Willy stood up awkwardly. He kissed his son and then his wife and then a very lovely-looking older woman, Bettina Renault. Pointing at her, he said loudly, "My mother-in-law! Would you believe it? Actor kisses mother-in-law?"

He lumbered up onto the stage and kissed the presenter. "Everybody told me not to expect to win this prize. They told me funny men don't win prizes. Well, this one has. So, instead of thanking my director, my crew, my fellow actors and the whole goddamn bunch of great guys that helped me win this award, I want to thank the lady who made me feel funny *inside*. With all apologies to an old friend, the very lovely Princess of Monaco, I want to thank a very real, beautiful American princess, Sara Gold Ross."

"Oh, poo!" Sara said.

Epilogue

NEW YORK 1976

We've been having cocktails for over an hour and not a bite to eat, and the waiter hovers. Finally, Sara sighs, "Very well. I suppose we do have to eat something." She consults the menu for all of us.

"Are we all eating today?" she asks. "Maybe Chrissy had better not, what with all the liquor she has consumed." Sara sucks in her cheeks, trying not to laugh. Chrissy gives Sara's elbow a pinch which Sara ignores. "Roughly counting, I would say Chrissy had at least two thousand calories already," Sara says.

"Oh, you bitch!" Chrissy laughs.

"All right, Chrissy—get fat! What do we care? And then, when you're on television in your swimsuit with your fat buttocks revealed for all the world to see, we'll all just sit back and laugh. We'll laugh ourselves sick!"

"C'mon, Sara," Chrissy says with exasperation. "Will you cut the bull and let us see the menu too? God! Who else but you would tell the waiter one menu would do for all of us?"

"There is no need for a lot of fuss and feathers. We'll all have the lobster salad and asparagus vinaigrette and, of course, champagne."

Sara gives the order to the waiter and hands him back the menu.

"One of these days, Sara Gold Ross, pow!"

Sara giggles. "I always said you had a taste for violence, Chrissy. You *were* always threatening to beat up your poor Aunt Gwen. Incidentally, how is the old girl getting along?"

"Still going strong. When you have a will of iron, which Aunt Gwen has, and lots of the old scratch, and old Gwen certainly has that, you last forever. How is your Dad by the way?"

Sara beams. "That's my news for the day."

We all had been so busy laughing and just fooling around nobody had yet given their latest news, so now we all center our attention on Sara.

411

"Papa's at last agreed to come live with us! I can't tell you how happy that makes me. He is eighty-three, after all. And I hated thinking of him living alone. But that doesn't mean we don't have plenty of room for you too, Maeve. You and Ali. We have a room with your name written on it."

"That's sweet of you, Sara, but—"

"But she's coming to live with me," Chrissy says. "Until she's ready to get her own place, anyhow. I need you, Maeve!"

Maeve smiles wryly. "You need *me*, Chrissy? It seems to me you're doing just fine."

"No, really. I need help. I've just bought a gallery and I've started a perfume business. I—"

The waiter serves the food and we wait impatiently for him to be done.

"A gallery *and* a perfume business?" I ask, amazed. "In addition to your bathing suits? What's with you? Are you becoming a business tycoon?"

"Some business tycoon," Chrissy says with heavy irony. "All I'm trying to do is recoup a little of my Marlowe fortune. The truth is, I was almost broke!"

We all stare at her incredulously.

"How did that happen?" Sara asks, in a state of shock.

"It was easier than you suppose," Chrissy says, laughing ruefully. "First of all, I *never* had the fortune you two had," she says to Sara and Maeve. "I mean, I had all the publicity, but it was never as much as—well, anyway . . . First there was my marriage to Guy. My money supported that marriage and, then, when I was married to Max—he never made anywhere near the money we spent. I suppose you might say I was guilty of the WASP cardinal sin—spending principal instead of just income. And with Leland, we were so divinely happy—we never gave a thought to money. We just spent it like there was no tomorrow because we just lived for the day. . . ." Her voice trails off and she bites her lip. "But it *was* heaven so I have no regrets, only gratitude. But after Leland died, there were so many political debts to pay off, not to mention the medical bills. Cancer's not only a fucking killer . . ." She pauses a minute, trying to find her voice again . . . "but a bitch on money. I dragged poor Leland all over the world, as you know—looking for the miracle that didn't exist. And when the air cleared, there wasn't much left. I still had the farm in Connecticut and the place in Palm Beach besides the apartment in New York to keep up. I know I should never have tried to hold on to everything. But I didn't want *everything* to change for the children. The twins had to have their college and debut . . . of course, I still have to do the same for Sara Maeve and Marlajane. . . ."

"A debut in this day and age," Sara mutters. "What are you thinking of?"

"You have to admit, Sara, that the twins' debut *was* fun for all of us, going back down sentimental alley."

"Yes . . ." Sara smiles. "It *was* fun."

"Well, that's all beside the point now. And of course, Sasha had some trouble that I had to help him with—the money just went. One day I woke up and the lawyers said, 'Chrissy Marlowe Prescott, you blew it!' "

"Goddamn it, Chrissy, if you needed money why the hell didn't you say so?" Sara is so angry there are tears in her eyes.

"Yes!" Maeve says. "What's money for if not to help? Really, Sara! What are friends for? I'm very disappointed that you didn't feel you could come to me."

"You're not getting the point. I was almost broke, so I took the last of my money and started a gallery and the perfume business. And I do get money from all my designer home fashions and the designs for the home books. And now I've signed the swimsuit contract—one million dollars for five years! Don't you see? I'm building my *own* fortune! I'm a real Marlowe, after all!"

Finally, we all do get Chrissy's point and we are really excited for her. Maeve jumps up and kisses her and Sara applauds so loudly everyone turns to look at us.

"You really are terrific, Chrissy," I say. "You make my news seem really *insignificant.*" But I guess I really don't mean that.

"What *is* your news, Marlena?" Sara asks me. "You were supposed to tell us about an hour ago. You can't possibly be having another baby and you're already a grandma. What is it?"

"I didn't want anybody to know until I was through—I went back law school and now I've not only graduated but I've passed the bar!"

"Oh, gloriosky! I *am* proud of you, Cuz!"

"Oh, yes," Maeve says. "What a thing to keep to yourself all this time!"

"I am proud to know you, Marlena," Chrissy says. "And what's more—I'm going to be your very first client. God knows I need help! That's why I insist Maeve come stay with me and help me. You can run the gallery, Maeve—"

"I must say," Sara says, "that is the most asinine thinking I have ever heard. . . . Maeve, who's won all kinds of literary awards, is supposed to help you with your money-making machine? I want her to come to Malibu. There, Maeve, you can write if you feel like it, or just bake in the sun and relax if you don't."

"And I don't have to say it, Maeve—you *know* you can always stay with Peter and me whenever—"

"No, you don't have to say it." Maeve put her hand on mine. "You're all being darling, supportive and wonderful, as always. But I *do* have plans—" Maeve says.

We all lean forward expectantly. This is what we all have been especially waiting to hear.

"Before Harry died, we were working with an agency in Vietnam. Harry had been sick for years with a heart condition but we had no idea he would— We had planned on bringing a group of Vietnamese orphans to this country—Harry was especially concerned about the orphans who were interracial. Now that Harry is gone, I intend to go on with this project. But instead of working with them in California, I'm going to go on with the work in the Boston area. Ali and I are going home . . . at last. We're going to live in Louisburg Square, the house that my grandmother Margaret left to my father. It's mine now and I think that's where we belong, Ali and I. Everything keeps changing yet everything stays the same. No matter what, I'm still an Abbott and an O'Connor and so is my daughter. I can't explain it but there's a rightness to it, somehow. My ghosts are gone and, who knows, maybe in Louisburg Square I'll write my magnum opus and win the Nobel!" She laughs.

Sara puts her hand over Maeve's and then Chrissy lays hers over Sara's and I lay mine on Chrissy's.

"Fuckers!" Chrissy says. "I dare anyone to call us the poor little rich girls now!"

Sara calls for toasts.

Chrissy raises her glass. "I'll drink to Maeve and her Vietnam orphans and her future Nobel Prize."

"And I'll drink to Marlena and her law degree," Maeve says.

"I have to drink to Uncle Maurice going to live with Sara and her happy family. To their good health!"

"L'chaim!" Sara drinks from her champagne glass. "And I'm drinking to Chrissy and her classy-assy bathing suits! And I just had the most marvelous idea! Chrissy, what do you say we do a little matchmaking? My papa and your Aunt Gwen? What a team!"

Chrissy roars and Maeve and I giggle as Sara calls the waiter over to bring us another bottle of champagne.